**PHOENIX CENTER, THIS IS AIR FORCE 56.**

The voice was that of the pilot of one of the two F-16 fighters that had been dispatched from David Monthan Air Force Base near Tucson, Arizona. They had positioned their fighters on each side of the stricken airliner. The west coast of the Mexican mainland was almost directly below as the two pilots peered through the windows of the red and blue airliner, hoping for some sign of life.

"Go ahead, Fifty-six."

"Nothing seems to be moving inside the cabin. The passengers are wearing oxygen masks, but no one appears to be breathing. I want a closer look at the pilots. Stand by."

"Roger."

"I'm back up front now. I can see the pilots clearly. They're both wearing oxygen masks."

There was a short, delay, then . . .

"They don't appear to be breathing, either."

## ACTION ADVENTURE

SILENT WARRIORS (1675, $3.95)
by Richard P. Henrick
*The Red Star*, Russia's newest, most technologically advanced submarine, outclasses anything in the U.S. fleet. But when the captain opens his sealed orders 24 hours early, he's staggered to read that he's to spearhead a massive nuclear first strike against the Americans!

THE PHOENIX ODYSSEY (1789, $3.95)
by Richard P. Henrick
All communications to the USS *Phoenix* suddenly and mysteriously vanish. Even the urgent message from the president cancelling the War Alert is not received. In six short hours the *Phoenix* will unleash its nuclear arsenal against the Russian mainland.

COUNTERFORCE (2013, $3.95)
Richard P. Henrick
In the silent deep, the chase is on to save a world from destruction. A single Russian Sub moves on a silent and sinister course for American shores. The men aboard the U.S.S. *Triton* must search for and destroy the Soviet killer Sub as an unsuspecting world races for the apocalypse.

EAGLE DOWN (1644, $3.75)
by William Mason
To western eyes, the Russian Bear appears to be in hibernation—but half a world away, a plot is unfolding that will unleash its awesome, deadly power. When the Russian Bear rises up, God help the Eagle.

DAGGER (1399, $3.50)
by William Mason
The President needs his help, but the CIA wants him dead. And for Dagger—war hero, survival expert, ladies man and mercenary extraordinaire—it will be a game played for keeps.

*Available wherever paperbacks are sold, or order direct from the Publisher. Send cover price plus 50¢ per copy for mailing and handling to Zebra Books, Dept. 2378, 475 Park Avenue South, New York, N.Y. 10016. Residents of New York, New Jersey and Pennsylvania must include sales tax. DO NOT SEND CASH.*

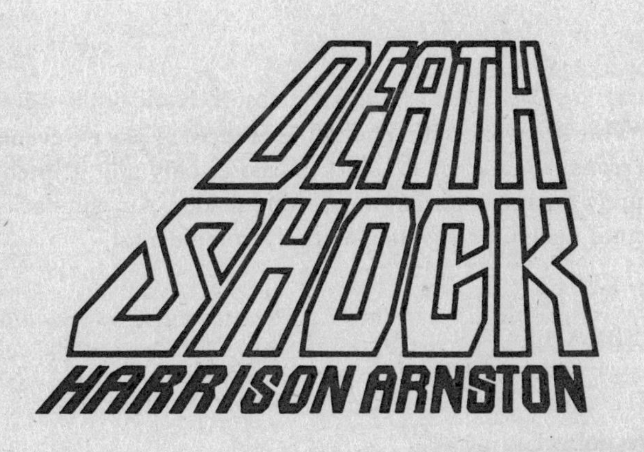

ZEBRA BOOKS
KENSINGTON PUBLISHING CORP.

This is a work of fiction. All references to places, events or persons is made for dramatic purposes only and is intended purely for the entertainment of the reader. Any similarity to actual people or events is entirely coincidental.

ZEBRA BOOKS

are published by

Kensington Publishing Corp.
475 Park Avenue South
New York, NY 10016



First printing: June, 1988

Printed in the United States of America

*For: Terry*
*Who taught me how to love again.*

*Special thanks to Robert Duato, pilot extraordinaire.*

# PART ONE

# Chapter One

"Los Angles Center, PacRim Two-three-four."

The air traffic controller handling westbound departures from his position in the Palmdale, California air traffic control center, pressed the small button on his headset cord and acknowledged the call from the Lockheed 1011 now one hour and ten minutes from LAX. "PacRim Two-three-four, Center . . . Go ahead."

The voice of the captain, or perhaps it might have been the first officer at that point, the controller wasn't sure, seemed strained. Unlike the calm, assured, almost bored voices controllers were accustomed to hearing.

"Center, PacRim Two-three-four . . . We are declaring an emergency and request an immediate vector back to Los Angeles."

Those words triggered a quick response from the controller. He scanned the radar screen in front of him as his hand pushed another button on the console, which would bring a supervisor on the double. "PacRim Two-three-four, Los Angeles Center. Turn right to a new heading of zero, seven, niner. Descend and maintain flight level three, three, zero. Advise the nature of your emergency."

The words were hardly out of his mouth before supervisor Paul Graham was at his side, plugging his own headset into a jack, listening to the conversation between the aircraft and the controller. The voice of the pilot seemed uncertain, afraid.

"Center, PacRim Two-three-four . . . We have some sort of . . . illness on board . . . don't understand it . . . the crew, the passengers . . . everybody . . . terrible cramps . . . nausea . . . diarrhea . . . it's . . . crazy."

Paul Graham felt a chill as he listened to the voice of the pilot. That one word, "everybody" was the key. It automatically ruled out food poisoning, because the three members of the flight crew never ate the same thing. The supervisor's mind raced as bits of information fell into slots in his memory. PacRim 234 was on a flight from Los Angeles to Honolulu. It had left on time, at 1240, with 245 passengers and a crew of 14.

He glanced at his watch and did a quick calculation. The flight was about four hundred and fifty miles from LAX. He tapped the controller on the shoulder and pressed the button on his headset, struggling to keep his voice calm. "PacRim Two-three-four, Los Angeles Center. Have you polled your passengers to determine if there are any medical people on board?"

"Center, Two-three-four. Affirmative. No doctors. Look . . . this all started less than fifteen minutes ago. The food hasn't even been . . . served yet. My flight engineer is cramping so bad he can't sit up straight. The first officer is in terrible pain. Get a doctor on the radio! I don't know how long . . . I can even talk to you!"

Graham's gaze was riveted to the screen in front of him. He watched the little mark with the symbol "PR234" beside it and observed that the plane was following instructions, making a long, gradual turn. He turned to the traffic controller and almost yelled at him. "Follow the drill. Keep talking to him. Clear the other traffic and vector him into El Toro. I'll do the rest."

The controller nodded and resumed talking to the stricken pilot, while Graham removed the headset from his bald skull and grabbed the telephone. He punched two buttons and waited impatiently. It was answered on the second ring. "Operations, Green . . ."

"Sam, Paul Graham. We have an emergency. PacRim Two-three-four is headed back to the coast. I need a doctor on this line immediately. Extension eighty-five. Contact El Toro and advise them that we have an emergency landing of a commercial aircraft within one hour. Advise the Coast Guard as well."

"Roger, Paul . . . what's the problem?"

"The pilot reports the entire crew and all souls on board are sick as hell. It's like food poisoning, but it isn't. It's worse. Much worse. Sam, we don't have a lot of time."

Graham hung up the telephone and put the headset back on. The controller was clearing the path for the TriStar and advising all other aircraft on his frequency to change to another. A different controller would take over the duties of normal departure traffic. This one would stick with PacRim 234. The pilot was still talking, his voice reflecting obvious, undisguised fear, as well as the physical pain being experienced. Paul Graham's mind was still racing as he listened to the controller give the pilot still another heading, one that would take him out of the regular air lane. Another course correction would be made in about two minutes.

He'd ordered the landing site changed from LAX to El Toro for several reasons. Los Angeles International Airport, which almost everyone in the business referred to by its designation, LAX, was an airport that operated four east-to-west runways. Because of noise-abatement laws and the almost ever-present ocean breezes, planes took off and landed in a westerly direction. Several times during the year, the winds would shift and come howling in from the desert, forcing a reversal of the procedure. On those occasions where take-offs and landings were necessarily west-to-east, screams of protest were invariably heard from various citizen's groups and politicians. The noise of an airliner taking off was several times greater than the noise of one landing, and because of the anticipated furor, borderline situations, where the winds were steady at ten knots, the maximum allowable tail-wind for landings, the east-to-west pattern was maintained.

If it weren't for the winds today, he could have PacRim 234 come directly in and land west-to-east. Regular in-bound traffic could be diverted to Ontario or Long Beach, as they were when the morning fog rolled in at certain times of the year. Departures could be delayed until 234 was safely down. But as all of this passed through his mind, Paul Graham made one of the instant judgments that he was trained to make.

First, he assumed that there wouldn't be time for PacRim 234 to make the normal approach, flying over the city, doing a 180 degree turn and letting down for an east-to-west landing. So, if anything, it had to be a straight-in approach. But today, a straight-in approach was out of the question. The winds were running at 20 knots, coming from the west, making a west-to-east landing dangerous for even a healthy pilot. In this case, it would be disastrous.

Second, El Toro was a military airport some 40 miles southeast of LAX. It had a long runway that might allow for a straight-in approach, because the winds were usually less forceful, and, should there be a crash, the loss of life on the ground could be considerably less.

Crash . . . They never called it a crash. They always called it an accident. Graham wondered why the word even entered his mind. After all of the years of training, it shouldn't have.

Third. In the event there was an accident, security would be much more manageable at a military base than a busy place like Los Angeles International Airport. For some reason, Paul Graham was convinced that PacRim 234 was going to crash.

Shirlee Simms had been listening to the scanner on her desk with half an ear as she entered copy into her word processor. When she heard the word, "emergency," both ears and both eyes were focused on the small radio. She watched the little lights flashing as the radio scanned the various frequencies being monitored until she heard the strained voice of the man who'd used the word. She pushed a button and froze the frequency at 125.4 megahertz.

Within two minutes, she was fully aware of the problem. An airplane was heading for El Toro with a very sick crew. It might not make it.

She grabbed the roller file on her desk and searched for the number of PacRim Airlines, found it and dialed the number.

A cheerful voice answered, "Good afternoon, Pacific Rim Airlines."

"Good afternoon, this is Shirlee Simms of Channel Three News. I'd like to speak to your public relations director, please."

The cheerful voice said, "That would be Donald James. One moment please."

In a moment, the pleasant voice of the p.r. man came on. "Mizz Simms, this is an unexpected pleasure. What can I do for you?"

His casual manner told Shirlee what she wanted to know.

He didn't know!

For a moment she considered telling him, then discarded the idea and decided on an indirect approach. She pushed a button which activated a tape recorder. "Mr. James, I'm recording this conversation. Is that all right with you?"

There was little hesitation. "No. At least not right this moment. Tell me what you have on your mind and then I'll decide. Okay?"

She shut off the tape recorder. "Mr. James, we're doing a piece on some of the smaller, struggling airlines. It's no secret that Pacific Rim has been looking for financial help. Before I put this thing to bed, I just wanted to touch base and make sure I've got my facts straight. For example, your flight number . . . Two-three-four. Word is that Flight Two-three-four usually leaves here less than half-full, which means it loses money every time out. Why would you keep that route if it constantly loses money?"

The voice suddenly seemed less friendly. "Where in heaven's name did you get that? From one of our competitors? It couldn't be further from the truth. Flight Two-three-four has been running at better than ninety percent for the last three months! Everybody in the business knows that! If it wasn't for that particular flight, the viability of this airline would be in serious doubt."

Shirlee Simms smiled as she took down what was being said in shorthand. "I'm sorry, Mr. James. Perhaps my notes are mixed up. Give me some more details, if you would. I'm glad I decided to check it out with you."

"So am I. We have enough trouble as it is." He sighed and then, swinging into his salesman's voice, started to give her what she was after. "Flight Two-three-four is our champagne flight to Honolulu. We offer lowest fares to the Hawaiian Islands while at the same time offering better seating than our competition. Our two Lockheed ten-elevens seat a maximum of three hundred ten passengers because of the wider, more comfortable seats. We provide food which has been rated as equal to the best in the industry. And, our on-time rating is second to none."

Shirlee chuckled over the phone. "Well, somebody sure steered me down the wrong alley. I'm sorry."

"Who was it?"

"You know I can't say, but I'll tell you this; there won't be a next time. Today, for instance. How many passengers are you carrying today? And how many crew members?"

There was a hesitation. The man was getting suspicious. "Mizz Simms, just what kind of piece are you doing? I mean exactly?"

She chuckled again. "It's sort of a comparison thing. We're taking the total number of flights to Hawaii on a given day like today, breaking down the number of passengers on each flight and charting the share of the market each airline has. Then, we're interviewing passengers to determine why they take each particular airline."

It was the wrong thing to say. His suspicions were aroused even further. His voice was cold and hard as he said, "Mizz Simms, give me your number. I'll call you back."

She had to continue with the charade. "Sure. But, my deadline is about fifteen minutes from now. My number is six five seven dash eight seven seven three, extension two five four.

"I'll call you."

The line went dead.

Shirlee listened to the radio as she wrote copy on a yellow pad furiously. There was a doctor talking to the pilot.

". . .your symptoms."

The pilot was answering, but his voice was halting, weak. "Terrible cramps. I've never been so sick. The cramps just double me over . ."

"Are you on oxygen?"

". . .Yes. Ever since this started."

"Are there lots of cola drinks on board?"

". . . Don't know. Couldn't reach them anyway . . . can't move. Jesus!"

"Captain Walters! Drink as much liquid as you can, as fast as you can. Cola might help with the nausea."

There was silence.

"Captain Walters!"

Another voice could be heard.

"PacRim Two-three-four. Los Angeles Center. Acknowledge . . "

Silence.

Shirlee waited for a moment and then rushed into the next office, that of news director Bill Parkins, handing him the yellow legal pad without a word.

He was in the middle of a conversation with another reporter and seemed annoyed. "Shirlee! If you don't mind!"

Her eyes were burning with intensity. "Read it!"

His gaze went from her face to the yellow pad. As he read it, his eyes seemed to grow larger and he leaned forward in his chair, his body tensing perceptibly. "Are you sure?"

"Positive!"

"Holy shit! Go with it! I'll alert the network."

She grabbed the yellow pad and ran into a nearby studio, positioning herself behind the desk. As the crew turned on the equipment, she pulled out a compact from her purse and hastily applied makeup. It wasn't the best, but it would have to do. Quickly, she brushed her hair as one of the large cameras in the studio focused on a graphic that showed the station logo. In a few moments she heard the voice of one of the directors in her earpiece.

"Okay, Bill, you do the break and then we go to Shirlee. Six seconds . . . five . . . four . . . three . . . two . . . She heard the voice of Bill Parkins as he intoned, "We interrupt this program for a special bulletin from UBC News."

Shirlee looked into the camera facing her and watched the red light flick on. She started to speak, glancing at her notes.

"This is Shirlee Simms, UBC News, Los Angeles. UBC News has learned that a Pacific Rim Airlines Lockheed ten-eleven, with possibly as many as three hundred twenty-five passengers and crew on board, is heading back to California after aborting a regularly-scheduled flight to Hawaii. According to informed sources, the crew and passengers on board Pacific Rim Airlines Flight Two-three-four had been stricken with a serious illness. At this time, the aircraft is being directed toward an emergency landing at El Toro Marine Air Base, which is located south of Los Angeles. At the moment, radio contact with the aircraft has been lost. UBC News will interrupt normal programming again, as soon as further details are known. Repeating the bulletin, UBC News has learned . . ."

# Chapter Two

There were four of them, seated at a small round table in the office of Baxter Williams, the beleaguered president of Pacific Rim Airlines.

For weeks now, the press had been after Baxter Williams, hounding him unmercifully, he felt, as he made the rounds trying to raise money for his fledgling airline. Speculation had run rampant, driving the value of the stock down, at a time when it needed stability. Twice, he had been close to getting the money he so desperately needed, and both times, the deals had gone sour in a sea of printed rumor and gossip.

There were unfounded reports that the FAA was about to pounce on the airline for alleged maintenance infractions. Not true. The FAA had given both aircraft a clean bill of health. There was a report, denied, that the crews were being overworked, that one of the pilots had quit because of the constant pressure to spend more than the allowed number of hours in the air. Again, not true. In fact, he'd been fired for failing his semi-annual physical. Minute traces of marijuana had been detected in two separate drug tests, the first a full screen and the second a specific. The traces were minute and despite the fact that there was a possible margin for error, the pilot had been cashiered. He'd run to the press screaming he'd been set up for complaining.

The pilot's log had been made public, which proved that his flying time had been well within limits, but that failed to dim the flames.

And now this.

The final blow.

No matter what happened, Baxter Williams knew that his airline was finished.

Somebody had set out to do him in . . . and they'd succeeded. His face reflected the rage that still burned within him, even after he'd made an intemperate outburst less than five minutes ago. He'd ranted and raved about his enemies, the banks, the investment brokers, the FAA and especially the media. They'd all had a hand in ruining him.

Donald James was staring at him, undisguised revulsion clearly visible in his eyes.

Screw him, thought Williams. So, I'm feeling sorry for myself. I have a right. It was my damned airline, not his.

Walter Perkins, the attorney for the airline, was busy on one of the three telephones that adorned the small table. The fourth person in the room was chief pilot Frank Albert, listening carefully on another telephone. His face was ashen as he nodded wordlessly from time to time. The handsome features of his face were distorted by the pain of knowing that a terrible tragedy was being played out.

There was a soft rap on the door, then a young woman entered the room and handed a piece of yellow paper to Williams. He glanced at it and then give it his full attention. After digesting its contents, he handed the single piece of paper to Donald James.

The public relations man picked up the third phone

and dialed a number. His voice was soft and filled with sadness. "Tommy. Donald James. I have that information for you now."

Baxter Williams watched the three men. They were all talking on different telephones dealing with different aspects of the same problem. For what? It wasn't going to change anything. There was nothing anyone could do. One of their airplanes was flying on automatic pilot at a height of thirty-three thousand feet. It was heading east on a heading of zero, nine, nine degrees. It had been unable to make a course correction and now, based on the present speed, course and winds, it was going to continue to fly east, passing some 400 miles south of Los Angeles, continue almost due east, until it finally crossed the east coast of Florida, where it would run out of fuel and fall into the Atlantic Ocean.

Two hundred and fifty-nine people would be dead. And the media would say it was all Baxter Williams's fault. The truth, whatever it was, would never be known.

They'd spent millions bringing the remains of the shuttle "Challenger" to the surface. They might or might not do the same with his airplane.

And according to the figures, Flight 234 was going to impact in just about the same spot.

Of course, no one knew the exact throttle settings, or the wind changes that might make a difference. A difference of perhaps 500 miles. But one thing was certain. The sophisticated electronics on board the 1011 were such that nothing would alter its course. Like some gigantic lemming in the sky, it would continue its path over the cliff to destruction. And there was nothing anyone could do.

The lobster bisque he'd had for lunch announced its intention to depart his stomach without warning. Baxter Williams lurched to his private bathroom, leaned over the toilet bowl and was very ill. At that instant in time, he wished with all his heart that he was on board Flight 234.

"Phoenix Center, this is Air Force Fifty-six."

The voice was that of the pilot of one of two F-16 fighters that had been dispatched from David Monthan Air Force Base near Tucson, Arizona.

"Air Force Fifty-six, Center. Go ahead."

"Center, we're in position now. The coast is just coming up. So far, there are no signs of movement inside the aircraft starboard."

"Air Force Fifty-six, we copy."

"Phoenix Center, Air Force Seventy-three. No signs of movement on the port side."

"Roger, we copy."

The two fighters, one on each side of the stricken airliner, had positioned themselves as close as possible to the 1011. The pilots had made visual contact with the plane about halfway across the Gulf of California. The west coast of the Mexican mainland was almost directly below as the two pilots peered carefully through the windows of the red and blue commercial airliner, hoping for some sign of life. There was none. Neither in the passenger sections nor the cockpit. Both the pilot and the first officer of the airliner were slumped in their seats, clearly unconscious, their oxygen masks still in place.

"Air Force Fifty-six, Center."

"Go ahead."

"Try radio contact again, please."

"Roger."

The pilot of one of the fighters pushed some buttons, adjusting his radio to 125.4 megahertz.

"PacRim Two-three-four, do you read?"

There was no answer. The pilot tried again without success.

"Phoenix Center, this is Air Force Fifty-six."

"Go ahead, Fifty-six."

"I have no response. The two pilots have been observed in their seats. There is no movement. Both pilots are wearing oxygen masks, as are many of the passengers. Nothing appears to be moving inside the cabin. As best I can tell, the passengers do not appear to be breathing. I want a closer look at the pilots. As for the outside, I see no signs of external damage. The aircraft is heading zero, niner, niner at mach point eight one."

"Roger."

"I'm back up front now. I can see the first officer clearly. Stand by."

"Roger."

There was a short delay and then . . .

"Center, Air Force Fifty-six."

"Go ahead."

"They don't appear to be breathing, Center. Air Force Fifty-six standing by."

"Air Force Fifty-six. Please stay with the aircraft until you are joined by additional Air Force traffic."

"Roger. Air Force Fifty-six standing by."

Dan Wiseman looked at his watch. It was 6:10 in the

evening. Darkness had already come to Washington and it was snowing. Traffic would be almost impossible. Every time it snowed in Washington, the world seemed to come to an end.

When he'd been promoted to the position of assistant director a year ago, he'd been excited about coming to this nerve center of power, while at the same time aware of how much he'd miss California. But California held many bitter memories as well.

His sixteen year marriage had disintegrated for no reason that he could understand. When he was a young agent, it never seemed to bother Bernice; the long hours, the time away from home, sometimes for weeks on end.

But in California, she seemed to think that a resident agent in charge was an executive who was no longer required to be in the field. As a man who could dictate his own schedule, coming and going as he pleased. It wasn't true and he'd tried patiently to explain it to her. Without success.

A marriage that had worked foundered on the rocks of some strange misunderstanding. Bernice had changed; turned from being a supportive, loving, giving woman into a screeching shrew. He couldn't understand it. He'd tried to talk to her about it and she'd just gotten more angry. He'd suggested they seek outside counseling but she'd refused. Instead, she turned to a lawyer.

Dan didn't stand in her way, but he never really understood it.

The appointment to Washington had taken him away from those memories, at least physically. It had helped. He plunged into his new responsibilities with a vengeance and that also helped. Now, he found himself thinking less and less about Bernice, although he ached for the sound of the voices of the children every single day.

He picked up the photograph of himself with the two of them and stared at it. Even though the picture had been taken less than two years ago, it seemed like decades.

Three smiling faces. His own, a man looking less than his then forty years, the sandy hair clipped short, military style, the rugged good looks that had made him such a big man on campus still there, fresh, the blue eyes almost leaping from the photo. Danny, 16 then, grinning broadly, the unkempt black hair down around his shoulders, the faded blue jeans and the T-shirt that proclaimed his allegiance to a rock group known as "Twisted Sister." The hair was Danny's little joke. It was really a wig which he wore every time he was out on "parole" as he put it. And he'd insisted that the family photograph show him wearing it, because, in his words, the wig revealed the "real" Danny Wiseman.

Now out of private school and attending UCLA, Danny no longer needed the wig. He could, if he wanted, wear his hair down to his knees. The strange thing was that he continued to wear his hair short, like his father.

Dawn, even at 14, displaying a portent of things to come. She'd break a lot of hearts before she even reached 17, Dan thought. Her eyes were filled with warmth and affection and a maturity far beyond her chronological age.

Every three months, Dan would see the children and he never ceased to be amazed at the depth of their feelings and the workings of their minds. They were great kids, both of them, and Bernice had had the wisdom not to poison their minds against him. They seemed to have accepted the divorce with equanimity, thank God.

The intercom chirped.

"Mr. Wiseman. The director would like to see you, please."

He put the framed photograph back on the desk and barked at the intercom. "On my way!"

The walk was a short one. Edward Spencer, director of the FBI, was standing in the center of his large office, along with two other men, both of whom Dan recognized, and all three were staring at a television set. The director hardly moved as Dan entered the room. He pointed to the television set and asked, "Have you been following this?"

Dan glanced at the television set. "Following what?"

The director sighed and shut off the television set. Instead of answering, he introduced Dan to the two men as though it were for the first time.

The smaller of the two was Mickey Serson, the president's senior advisor and long-time personal friend. The other man was CIA deputy director Willard Long. Their presence in the room was a tip-off that something serious was afoot. The director walked to the window and looked out at the snowstorm that seemed to be growing in intensity. Without turning around, he said, "Dan, a commercial airliner with two-hundred-fifty-nine people on board is heading toward Florida. It's flying on autopilot and everyone on board is unconscious . . . perhaps dead. In about three and a half hours, the thing will run out of fuel and crash."

The director turned to face a shocked Dan Wiseman. The FBI head thrust his hands in his pockets and sighed deeply.

Mickey Serson picked it up from there. "There were a few minutes of radio conversation between the plane and the ground before contact was lost. We sent up some Air Force fighters to have a look and the initial reports indicate that there is no movement inside the aircraft. None at all. Before we lost contact, the pilot complained of severe abdominal pain, with accompanying nausea and diarrhea. Apparently, everyone on board was afflicted."

Dan asked, "What in the world could have caused such a thing?"

Edward Spencer, his hands still in his pockets, paced the floor as he answered the question. "We're not sure yet, but I've talked to the CDC in Atlanta and they are of the opinion that whatever it is, we can rule out such things as cargo spillage, normal viral infections and the like. This happened so fast it has to be something special. Until we know differently, we're taking the position that it's some sort of terrorist attack involving the use of biological weaponry."

The words sent a chill down Dan's spine.

The FBI had prided itself on its ability to prevent scores of planned terrorist attacks from ever taking place on American soil. The possibilities of such attacks were always in the forefront of the bureau's thinking and considerable resources were used to make sure it never happened. There was the constant fear that some day it might, and that the first successful one would be a signal to the many groups inside the country who had an axe to grind.

But even then, an attack was expected to come in the form of a bomb or other visible weapon. The potential of biological weapons being used was given a low level of probability.

Dan's attention swung from the director to Willard Long. The tall, dark-haired deputy director removed the pipe from his mouth and said, "As I've just explained to Director Spencer, we have no information that would lead us to believe that the known terrorist groups have been able to acquire such weapons. So we can't be of much help. We'll alert our people, however. Something might turn up."

Spencer stopped pacing and stood in front of his desk. "Dan, we've been assigned jurisdiction in this case. I want you on your way to Florida within the hour. You are to take full charge of the entire matter. All inquiries are to be directed toward you. You, in turn, will report to me. Word is going out now to the National Transportation Safety Board, the airline, the air traffic controllers, the insurance company and every other interested party, that this is classified until further notice. All statements are to be cleared through my office.

"I don't know what the hell we're dealing with here, and until I do, I want the lid on tight. I'll funnel everything I get to you en route. I suggest Orlando as a destination. You and the airliner should get there at about the same time. Use the bureau's Lear. Take Doctor Evans and Gil Parker with you. The doctor will be in charge of the medical examinations with the help of two specialists from Atlanta. Gil will keep the press off your back. All Florida offices will be alerted to provide full assistance.

"This is to be treated as a top secret investigation at this point. Nothing is to be released to the press that hasn't been cleared. That's imperative."

Dan Wiseman couldn't believe what he was hearing. It seemed like some sort of strange, impossible nightmare.

His brow wrinkled as he thought out loud. "You said this is being viewed as a possible terrorist act involving biological weapons. Exactly what kind of weapons?"

The director answered, "We just don't know. Something made everyone so sick they all passed out within minutes. Atlanta says that the symptoms are similar to salmonella, except for the speed and intensity of the attacks. No virus or bacteria works that quickly. They rule out toxic gases that might have been created by some exotic illegal chemical brought on board or shipped as cargo. The symptoms, according to the doctors in Atlanta, would be more related to difficulty in breathing, at least in the initial stages. Whatever hit those people on that airplane went directly to the stomach and intestines, which normally suggests something was ingested. But the odds that all of the passengers and all of the crew ingested the same thing at the same time are so remote as to be out of the question.

"Unless, of course, it was designed that way, which brings me back to the biological weapons angle."

Dan shook his head. "But you said Atlanta was sure that no virus or bacteria could work that fast."

"That's right. The ones we know about."

Dan glanced again at Mickey Serson. "Mr. Serson, do we have anything in our own arsenal that causes these symptoms?"

It was a direct question about a subject that was not often discussed. Serson ran a hand through his hair and let his gaze fall to the floor. "We're talking with the Pentagon about that now. As you can appreciate, the extent and nature of our biological weapons program is a highly-classified secret. But the president wants you to know that you'll receive complete cooperation. If there's any connection, you'll be advised."

It wasn't much of an answer.

Wiseman had the feeling that the president's man knew much more than he was prepared to reveal. He let it go for the moment and addressed another problem. "Florida is a rather narrow peninsula. If the plane falls into the Gulf or the ocean, it's possible that we may never know what caused this."

The room grew quiet for a moment and then Serson said, "The president feels that's unacceptable. According to estimates given by the airline, the plane will run out of fuel after it passes the east coast of Florida. We've got a steady stream of military aircraft flying chase, keeping an eye on things, but it really looks bad. Before a final decision is made, some Air Force fighters with special equipment will be sent up from the Cape. The jets will be equipped with heat sensors that can measure the temperature of the bodies of those on board. It might not be conclusive, because the illness itself can lower body temperature, but it might give us a better idea. Right at this moment, we have a visual report from the Air Force chase planes that nobody is breathing.

"There'll be more tests before any decision is made, believe me. But the president is prepared to shoot the thing down if that proves necessary. We simply can't let it crash into the ocean. We have to know what caused this."

The words hit Dan like a sledgehammer. Serson continued. "Once the plane hits the ground, the impact area will have to be sealed off immediately. There's a very real danger of contamination. We have a special Army unit being activated now. They'll be in Florida in time. You'll be fully briefed en route. There really isn't any other choice."

Dan stared at the man. He was talking about shooting down a civilian airliner with 259 passengers on board. Impossible! This simply could not be happening!

But it was.

And at that moment, Dan Wiseman gave thanks to a God he believed in. He gave thanks that it was not he who had to make that kind of decision. That kind of decision could ruin a man's life forever, no matter what the rationale, no matter what the ultimate good.

Wiseman turned away from Serson and spoke rapidly to the director. "Where did the flight originate?"

"Los Angeles. I've already advised Al Disario. He'll have a team checking out that end." The director pointed to the window and said, "I'd suggest you get moving before the highway becomes impossible. Take an escort. You'll need it."

Wiseman had a few other questions, but they would have to wait. The director was right. If he waited much longer, he'd never get to the airport in time to make it to Florida before the plane was due. Dan went back to his office, put on his overcoat, grabbed his briefcase and left.

And just south of Houston, Texas, at a height of thirty-three thousand feet, two F-14s from the Naval Air Station at Corpus Christi drew close to the PacRim 1011. Each F-14 contained two airmen, with the man in the second seat of each aircraft taking all manner of photographs. Regular, telephoto shots, color and infra-red. Sides, top and bottom. Every inch of the aircraft was photographed, even as the sun, moving away from them quickly now, faded in the west.

And a nation of television viewers, alerted to the impending disaster, positioned themselves in front of their sets, mesmerized by the unfolding drama. Some casually eating dinner, or drinking cocktails, others empathizing with the victims, in the air and on the ground. Some weeping softly, while others felt a sort of vicarious excitement.

In Las Vegas, a man approached one of the windows of a sports book and asked if they were giving odds on whether the plane would hit the ground or the water. The man standing behind him became infuriated and punched him in the face. Both were arrested.

And in San Francisco, lawyer George Barnes was frantically assembling his troops.

And in Hartford, Connecticut, insurance adjuster William Powers was assembling *his* troops.

And Pacific Rim Flight 234 continued peacefully toward the east.

# Chapter Three

Elizabeth Martin felt her knees starting to ache. It was a familiar signal from her body that she'd spent enough time in the garden, tending her precious flowers. She tried to spend a few hours every day in the garden, weeding, fertilizing, nurturing, beaming with pride at the full spectrum of colors that almost covered the backyard of her Costa Mesa home and filled the air with a pleasant combination of fragrances.

It was becoming a ritual. A daily ritual that replaced some of the loneliness, the emptiness she felt. Ever since Mark had taken that new job, he'd been on the road. Already, it was the end of January and she could count the nights he'd been home on the fingers of one hand.

She stood up and stretched her body, carefully and slowly. She shouldn't complain, she thought. When Mark's former employer had closed up shop forever, things had looked bleak. The mortgage on the California home in the Mesa Verde tract was a killer and the money her father had lent them would carry them for less than four months. She didn't want to ask for more. The bad news had come just three weeks before Thanksgiving and they'd suffered through the worst Turkey Day in their eleven-year marriage.

But the good news had come more quickly than they had expected. Mark had been hired by one of his former competitors early in December. The pay was even better than before and the firm was solid, growing, but he'd be on the road again. Always on the road. As western sales manager, he'd travel fourteen states constantly, working with the company salesmen to drum up business. He'd be home most weekends, but there were times when it wasn't worth it as far as the company was concerned, and he'd be expected to spend the weekend in a motel when working Washington or Montana.

Right off, he'd been away for two weeks of training in Denver. He'd called her every night and they'd talked for almost an hour each time. It was an extravagance they couldn't really afford, but they told each other it would be their Christmas present. Between Christmas and New Year's he'd been at the Newport Beach office and then, the first Sunday night after New Year's, he'd boarded a plane for his first trip. She saw him twelve days later.

The telephone bill was staggering.

The old job had been wonderful. He'd spend all but three or four days a month at his desk. Home almost every night by six, his smile lighting up the house, his warmth making her feel safe and secure.

She shrugged. Be thankful, she thought. It won't always be like this. It could be worse. Much worse.

"Liz?"

The voice was that of Janet Talbot, her neighbor and friend. At the moment, the woman had her back to Elizabeth as she carefully closed the side gate behind her.

"Hi, Janet. I guess it must be after five. How'd it go today?"

The slender woman had a look of consternation on

her face as she walked slowly toward Elizabeth. "Oh, it's okay. If the boss wan't such a nerd, it'd be a lot better. I like the work but God! He's such a pompous ass."

Elizabeth's head rolled back as the laughter tumbled out. Janet was such a character! She was only thirty-five, the same age as Elizabeth, but she looked much younger. Long, blond hair, sparkling blue eyes, exquisite skin. A true American beauty.

And totally unaware of the effect she had on men. Her pleasant personality and easy-going manner caused her no end of trouble. Many men thought signals were being sent, when in fact, they weren't. It caused a lot of confusion.

Elizabeth noticed that Janet wasn't smiling. She hadn't smiled since she'd entered the backyard. She was standing there, wringing her hands, obviously troubled about something. Elizabeth reached out and took one of Janet's hands in her own. It felt cold.

"Janet, what is it? Did something happen today?"

Their eyes met and Elizabeth could see the concern in the blue eyes. Something was wrong. Very wrong.

The woman turned away from her. her voice was filled with dread. "Liz, I'm your friend. . . . I don't know." She stopped speaking.

Elizabeth reached for her arm and pulled her back so that they were face to face. "What *is* it? For cryin' out loud, we're friends! You can tell me."

Janet stared at the ground. Then her hands flew to her face as the tears came. "Liz, didn't you say that Mark left this morning for Hawaii?"

Elizabeth Martin felt her heart stop still. The air seemed to have been sucked out of her lungs . . . and then, her heart started beating again, unmercifully.

Pounding wildly inside her.

"What's happened?" The voice was almost a croak.

The words came gushing out now, a torrent of concern. "Oh Liz! I'm so scared! A plane on its way to Hawaii is in trouble. They said which airline. Pacific Rim. Flight Two-three-four. Was Mark . . . ?"

Elizabeth searched her memory. "I don't know. I don't know! He never told me what flight he was taking! Oh my God!"

She pulled off her gardening gloves and threw them to the ground. Then she ran inside the house and grabbed the telephone. Janet was right behind her, unconsciously chewing at one of her carefully manicured nails.

"Burkhart Industries."

The voice was not that of the receptionist, but rather a man.

"This is Elizabeth Martin. I need to talk to my husband's secretary."

"I'm sorry Mrs. Martin. This is security. The place is closed. Everyone's gone home."

Of course.

"Well, can you give me her home number? Please! This is urgent!"

"I'm sorry Mrs. Martin, we're not allowed to do that over the telephone. Company policy."

Elizabeth started to scream into the telephone but stopped. Through the kitchen window she could see the very woman she was trying to track down. Patty Heran, the secretary whom Mark shared with three other executives of the firm, was walking up the front pathway and the look on her face told Elizabeth Martin the worst. She hung up the phone and slumped heavily into a chair.

Janet answered the door. Patty was crying and Janet was crying and they were telling Elizabeth that the plane was still in the air. That it was on television and there was still a chance.

And Elizabeth Martin stared at the wall.

Her voice was a whisper. "He's on it? There's no mistake?"

Patty nodded, the tears rolling down her cheeks and falling onto her blouse. "I made the reservations for him. Oh, Mrs. Martin! I'm so sorry!"

Janet walked to the small television set on the kitchen counter and switched it on. The screen filled with the image of a woman interviewing a man, and they were talking about the airliner. The three women watched in silence.

". . . possible?"

"It's quite possible. Based on the information given to me so far, you can rule out any normal thing such as food poisoning or some ordinary infectious disease. My guess it that it's a toxic gas of some sort. Since the press are being closed out at this time, we don't have access to the communications between the plane and the ground, if any. But, it could be that the gas, or whatever it is that caused the problem, is *not* fatal, that consciousness could return at any moment.

"We still have a few hours before the fuel supply runs out. If consciousness returns at any time before then, the plane could be landed at any number of airports, either civilian or military."

The blond newswoman turned away from the man she was interviewing and faced the camera.

"If you've just joined us, we've been talking with Doctor Lyman Jordan, a virologist, who has been discussing with Channel Three News the various possibilities concerning the strange events unfolding in the skies above us today. To recap, Pacific Rim Airlines Flight Two-three-four, on a flight . . ."

Janet turned the volume down and placed her hand on Elizabeth's shoulder. "Liz, it's not over yet. Hang in there, honey."

Elizabeth Martin smiled weakly. She didn't answer. She wanted to hope. She wanted more than anything in the world to hope.

She was afraid to hope.

It was so unfair, Elizabeth thought. So incredibly unfair! She had to sit there, waiting and wondering, not knowing until . . . whether or not her husband was alive or dead . . . whether or not the plane would land or crash . . . it was impossible!

It had to be a nightmare. Nothing this cruel could be real.

Donald James stood in front of a forest of hastily set up microphones and a score of bright lights and faced the press.

"My name is Donald James and I am the director of public relations for Pacific Rim Airlines. I have a short statement that I will read.

"Pacific Rim Airlines Flight Two-three-four has encountered some difficulties in the air. We are unsure as to the exact nature of the problem and every effort is being made to correct the difficulty.

"The Federal Bureau of Investigation has taken charge of the investigation into this matter and has instructed Pacific Rim Airlines not to discuss the matter with the media or anyone else. All inquiries are to be directed to the FBI.

"That is all I have at this time."

He turned and headed back into the building, ignoring the screams and shouts of the reporters demanding answers to questions. He walked down the short hallway and re-entered the conference room, where a red-faced Baxter Williams was arguing with one of the FBI men who'd arrived less than a half hour ago.

Williams, his face contorted with anger, said, "Look, you tin-pot bureaucrat, it's *my* airplane. I have a right to listen to the radio traffic. I can understand why you've scrambled the communications so that the press can't listen in, but I demand to hear what's going on!"

The FBI man, his dark suit in stark contrast to the wildly flamboyant sports jacket the airline executive still wore, kept his temper in check and his voice even, controlled.

"Mr. Williams," he said, "as I've tried to explain to you, I have nothing to do with that. I am here simply to advise you of the nature of the investigation at this point. You don't seem to understand the seriousness of the problem."

Williams was screaming now. "Seriousness? What the fuck do you know about seriousness? I'm outta business no matter what happens now! Every nickel I ever . . ."

*"Shut up!"*

The voice was that of Donald James. His hands were formed into fists, the arms rigid at his sides. His dark eyes blazed with an anger he'd never known before. At six foot, four, he seemed to tower above the diminutive Williams. The public relations man had wanted to tell his boss what he thought of him for months, but he had a job to protect. Now, it didn't matter.

His voice was a growl, the expression of a man close to the edge of control, about to go over that edge.

"You sniveling self-absorbed wimp! There are two hundred fifty nine people either dead or about to die. Two hundred fifty nine families that will have to live with the loss, not to mention the people outside the families who will suffer, and you're worried about your precious airline."

The rage was building now. "You don't have an airline. You never had an airline! You managed to scrounge enough money to lease two airplanes from another airline, and managed to pull together a bunch of previously-unemployed airline workers. Two planes! Big deal!

"The death of Pacific Rim Airlines is a tiny, insignificant thing compared to the tragedy of two hundred fifty nine lost lives. Most of the money you'll lose belonged to other people. Such is not the case with those two hundred fifty nine souls on board. They're the ones who lose everything. All you lose is money.

"So stop your bleating. Just sit down and shut up and let the people who have to deal with this do their jobs. Stay the hell out of everyone's way."

The FBI man had a wide grin on his face. Williams, on the other hand, looked like he was about to blow a blood vessel. "You can't talk to me like that! You're fired! Right now! Get the hell out . . ."

It was then that Donald James reached out with a looping right fist that caught the bald man flush on the chin. Williams jerked back against the wall as though yanked by some invisible hand, blinked once, moaned, closed his eyes, and slid slowly to the floor.

The FBI man moved quickly to Williams's side, picked up an arm and checked for a pulse. He turned and spoke to James. "He'll live, but you hit him pretty hard, fella. Better get the paramedics in here."

Donald James was shaking with anger. He picked up the telephone and called the paramedics. While they waited, the FBI man used a tissue to wipe some blood away from the lips of Williams. As he did so, he said, "Okay . . . back to the problem. The passenger list is to be printed and given to me, then the program dumped. We don't want anyone getting their hands on that list. Understand?"

James shook his head. "No. I can't do that. If you want to do it, that's up to you. But for us, it's a straight violation. Dumping a program can get me put away. I don't need that."

The FBI man grimaced, the frustration plainly visible. "Look, these instructions come direct from Washington. Don't you understand how important this is? We need to check out every passenger on that airplane and we need to do it before the press and the insurance companies and the ambulance chasers are swarming all over the families. I can get a court order, but that takes time. I don't have the time."

James stood his ground. "I don't care. That . . . you'll have to do it yourself. The computer room is down the hall. The operator will show you how it's done, but I won't order her to do it. You can tell her I said it's up to her."

The FBI man sighed. "Fair enough," he said. Then he left the room, leaving Donald James with the still-unconscious Baxter Williams, a dark bruise now forming on his cheek. Somehow, the sight of the injury made

Donald feel better.

In the pilots' ops room at MacDill Air Force Base in Florida, Col. Roger Basehart was briefing two F-16A pilots on a quickly-ordered mission. The expression on his face was grim.

This, he thought, is not what these men were trained for. This mission was an abomination. His protests had been heated and in the end, he'd been given permission to seek volunteers. He wouldn't have to assign the mission arbitrarily. Just as long as they were in the air within 25 minutes. Even as he got ready to discuss the mission with the two young men sitting patiently in their seats, the aircraft were being prepared and armed.

The two men he'd picked to interview first were, in his opinion, the most likely volunteers. He prayed his judgment was right.

"Gentlemen," he began, "we are stuck with a situation that requires . . . Well, let me just lay it out for you."

He took a deep breath and went to the blackboard. He drew a rough outline of the Gulf of Mexico with the chalk and placed an X at a point almost midway between Houston and Tampa. Then he turned and leaned against a desk.

"That mark represents the present position of a commercial airliner headed this way. We've been advised that the plane might have been attacked by a terrorist using biological weaponry. Preliminary indications are that all of the crew and passengers are dead. The aircraft is on autopilot and unrecoverable."

The two pilots looked at each other and then cursed. One of the pilots, Capt. Richard Parker, asked, "How do they know all of this?"

Colonel Basehart shook his head. "They don't know. In fact, they don't know that it is a terrorist attack at all. Based on the limited information I have at the moment, I suspect they're simply using the process of elimination. There was some radio traffic between the pilot and the ground but it was inconclusive. All they know is that something disabled everyone on board in a hurry.

"There've been some visual contacts made since this began and the report is that nobody is breathing. There'll be a final check before your mission is carried out."

The other pilot, Capt. Don Whelan, had a question. His face reflected his concern. "Just what is our mission, sir?"

Basehart looked at Whelan and then Parker. Then his head turned and he looked at the blackboard again. "If the passengers are all dead, we have to shoot the plane down. We can't take the chance that the thing will simply run out of fuel and fall into the ocean for two reasons.

"One, we need to know what happened up there. In order to do that, we have to recover the aircraft. That's a lot easier to do if it impacts on the ground. Two, there's a possibility that whatever was used to kill the passengers and crew is highly dangerous. It may need to be isolated and decontaminated.

"There's a special biological weapons decontamination team coming in from New Orleans. They'll take care of that part of it. At this moment, two F-16s are already in the air and will rendezvous in about ten minutes. They have some special equipment that will take heat readings of the passengers and crew through the windows. Washington says they'll be able to confirm that the passengers are dead before you actually carry out your mission."

Captain Parker asked, "What if some of them are alive?"

Basehart didn't hesitate. "We'll deal with that if it becomes a reality. Right now, we'll proceed as though everyone is dead."

Colonel Basehard grunted, then continued. "I know. I know. It sucks. That's why I've asked for volunteers. The intercept will have to take place at a position that should allow the plane to crash in a relatively open area. We'll have the coordinates for you once you're in the air."

He paused and ran a hand through his short hair. He had difficulty meeting the stares of the two pilots.

Captain Whelan spoke out, to no one in particular, more thinking out loud than anything else. "So this whole thing depends on the readings of some high-tech instrument and the correct analysis of those readings? Shit, Colonel, I can't buy that."

Colonel Basehart looked puzzled. "What do you mean, Captain?"

Captain Whelan seemed angry. "I'll be happy to tell you, sir. I flew a lot of reconnaissance missions before I switched to tactical. Those F-16s will take the readings on film which has to be developed on the ground and analyzed by computer. The computer reads the differences in the color tones and gives differences based on a standard. We're talking hours here, not minutes. There's no way they can tell whether or not those people are alive.

"So this whole thing is bullshit. You can bet we're gonna be told that they're all dead, and the crap about the temperature readings is just Washington's way of trying to assauge whatever guilt feelings they think we might have. Is this mission really voluntary?"

The colonel nodded.

"Then," Captain Whelan said, "I'd just as soon pass, sir."

Captain Parker grabbed the arm of his agitated friend and said, "Hold on a minute. Colonel, let's back up a bit. You said that they think it was a terrorist attack but they aren't sure. Can you be a little more specific?"

Colonel Basehart shook his head. "It's difficult. But this mission was ordered by the president personally. It's classified top secret for obvious reasons. But the operational orders have come through placing the responsibility directly with him. I'd say if the commander-in-chief is prepared to stick his neck out that far, there must be something to go on. Like I said, they used the process of elimination. There was some radio chatter between the plane and the ground before communications were lost. The pilot described his symptoms and those of the other passengers and crew. They were identical and immediate.

"Some Pentagon doctors concluded that there was nothing, outside of biological weaponry, that could have created such symptoms. We'll never know unless we recover that airplane. That's what makes this so damned important.

"As for the high-tech temperature probe, it's something new that's been developed in the two years you've been away from recon, Captain. I can tell you this: they aren't lying to us about that. Some infra-red shots were taken and they're being processed now. We'll have that data before the mission begins."

There was silence in the room, save for the sound of three men breathing hard. Then, Captain Whelan asked, "How is this to be done?"

Colonel Basehart answered, "Cannon. I want you to position yourself as close to the engines as possible, and knock out number one and number two. It's a one thousand eleven. Leave number three alone. They've done simulated spins with the number three engine still running and they think they can roughly predict the impact area. If you shoot out all three, there's no knowing what will happen. As for the Sidewinders, they could do so much damage the plane might come apart in the air, sending the wreckage over too wide an area.

"However, you will be carrying two Sidewinders each. Just in case. Your cannons carry five hundred rounds and that should be more than adequate. But we don't have second chances here. Sidewinders are a last resort. You'll fly one up the number two engine if you have to. That'll blow off the tail for sure. Perhaps the rest of the thing will stay in place.

"In using the cannons, you have to be careful. Especially with the number one engine. Aim low and bring it up slowly. That way you'll avoid hitting the fuel tanks."

Again, there was silence in the room. Colonel Basehart lit a cigarette and noticed a slight trembling in his hand. "Look, I know it's a bitch."

Captain Whelan stood up. "Okay."

Captain Parker asked, "Anything else, sir?"

Basehart shook his head. "No. Takeoff in ten minutes. You'll have the coordinates as soon as you reach altitude. Good luck."

The two pilots turned and headed out of the room. They hardly heard the colonel as he said, "I appreciate it."

Frank Tercel sat and stirred his highball as he waited at Santa Monica Airport for George Barnes to arrive in his private jet. Tercel glanced at the briefcase sitting on the barstool beside him and smiled.

It had taken a thousand dollars, but it was worth it. As soon as he'd received the call from San Francisco, he'd rushed out to the headquarters of Pacific Rim Airlines and managed to snow his way into the computer room, using false identification that made it appear that he was an insurance investigator.

He'd talked to the dark-haired vixen who normally looked after reservations, but now seemed to be in shock. He'd asked her for a print-out of the passenger list for Flight 234 and she'd said she couldn't do it unless Mr. Williams gave his okay.

Tercel had known that time was running short, so he pulled up a chair and had a heart-to-heart with the woman.

"Look honey," he'd said, "I don't know whether or not you realize this, but your airline is outta business and you're out of a job."

She looked at him as though he knew what he was talking about. It was no secret that the airline had been in trouble for some weeks now, and even an idiot would know that this disaster would be the final straw.

"I work for the insurance company that stands to lose its ass over this thing. Now you and I both know that Mr. Williams is a jerk. He ain't about to cooperate with nobody. I need that list and I need it now. Tomorrow, you'll be lookin' for a job. Why not make it easy on yourself and give me the list? I'll give you one thousand bucks. I've got it right here . . . in cash. It'll tide you over until you get a new job.

"You know the list will be released in a few hours anyway, so what's the big deal?"

She'd looked at him with wide eyes, chewed on her lower lip for a while and then made him a print-out. Not a moment too soon. As he was walking down the hall and out of the building, he saw a guy who could only be a fed coming in.

So he had the list. And in fifteen minutes, George Barnes would arrive. Barnes was one of the most famous ambulance chasers in the business. A multi-millionaire lawyer who moved fast and hit hard.

And Frank Tercel was one of Barnes's bird-dogs. He'd get a fat fee for every client he managed to sign up. It wasn't exactly kosher, but in the words of George Barnes, if you didn't cheat, you didn't win. He'd already looked at the passenger list. There were over one hundred people on that plane who lived within 100 miles of Los Angeles. If past history was any guide, at least twenty of the bereaved families would want a famous lawyer like George Barnes to represent them in a law suit against the airline.

Actually, the suit would be against the airline's insurance company. Pacific Rim Airlines was broke. But Butler Casualty Insurance was not. Tercel took another sip of his drink. Good times were upon him, he thought.

Good times were upon him.

## Chapter Four

Dan Wiseman sat in one of the rear-facing seats aboard the Lear, across from Doctor Bruce Evans, one of the bureau's doctors, as the young internist ran over his reasons for the assumptions he was now making.

The doctor's thick, brown mustache bobbed as he spoke. "There are over a thousand different salmonella bacteria types, Dan, and none of them act this swiftly. Typhoid fever is actually caused by salmonella, and even then, the incubation period is from three to twenty-five days. One of the most common illnesses, often referred to as the twenty-four-hour flu, is usually a salmonella infection if diarrhea is present. Over a thousand people die in the U.S. every year from the various salmonella infections, and that number is rising.

"The main cause is improper food preparation. Under-cooking, especially turkey. Or leaving food around after it's been cooked. Emergency rooms around the country fill up at Thanksgiving and Christmas. Of course, it can also be caused by food-handlers not observing proper care, such as washing their hands after defecation.

"Food inspectors checking restaurants have found frozen food left out to thaw instead of being refrigerated, and found it loaded with salmonella bacteria. It's a real problem in restaurants, but most infections originate in the home.

"In any case, because of the symptoms as related by the pilot, it looks like a salmonella-type infection, except for the incredibly fast incubation period. And the intensity of the attack."

He toyed with his mustache and then resumed. "Now, another thing is the fact that most salmonella infections have to do with ingestion; something that goes down your throat. Food would be the obvious place to look. Except that the pilot said the food hadn't been served yet, and all airlines have rules prohibiting the cockpit crew from eating the same thing."

He paused and shook his head. "Maybe the cockpit voice recorder will tell us something."

Dan grunted. "You can forget that."

"Why?"

Dan told him something he remembered from a previous investigation. "Well, the cockpit voice recorder uses a tape with a limited time. Usually thirty minutes. After the first thirty minutes, it records over the previous conversations, so all you have is the last thirty minutes of actual flight. In this case, that won't help us at all."

Doctor Evans sighed and continued. "Well, it probably doesn't matter much. As I've said, we can rule out food. We can rule out normal salmonella, and a host of other possibilities.

"We have to assume it's a laboratory-produced bacteria, a 'designer' bug, so-to-speak. According to the scuttlebutt I've heard, the Russians have been spending lots of time and money developing an extensive arsenal of biological and chemical weaponry and we have been trying to keep pace, on a much smaller scale."

Dan looked at his watch. They were an hour away from Orlando.

Biological warfare. Dan knew that the two biggest arsenals of these grotesque weapons were located in Russia and the United States. But there were other countries involved in research. Small countries with limited budgets and big ideas. The new technology of genetic engineering was opening doors to many medical advances. Like anything else, the new knowledge could be used for less worthy purposes. He leaned forward as he said, "Seems to me I read a brief not too long ago about some Russian biological weapons being tested in Afghanistan, but they attacked the nervous system. This is something new, then?"

Evans shrugged. "I don't really know. I've heard rumors, like everyone else. The Pentagon keeps a very tight lid on this kind of thing. But I've heard stories indicating that some pretty heavy-duty genetic engineering experiments were being conducted in Huntsville. They started about three years ago."

The doctor stopped talking and placed his hands at his temples.

"What is it?" Dan asked.

Evans held up his hand. "I'm trying to remember something that might tie in." He paused for a moment and then his face brightened. "Yes . . . yes. Three years ago, the bureau debriefed a Russian defector—name of Baron—no, that's not it—Barakov. Yes, Barakov."

The doctor was getting excited. "This guy had information about some new biological weapons that the Russians were working on. That's when Huntsville got involved."

Three years ago. Dan was in California three years

ago and Edward Spencer, the director, was still a federal judge in Michigan. And President Dalton was a senator from California.

"Are you sure about this?" Dan asked.

Evans nodded. "I'm sure that's his name. I'm sure he had something to say about biological weapons. I don't know what. The Pentagon would have all of the details. So would the bureau. That debriefing would be on file somewhere."

Dan picked up the yellow legal pad beside him and made some notes. Then he asked, "The rumors about Huntsville. Tell me about that."

Evans leaned back in the seat and bit his lower lip. "They're just rumors, you know. That's all."

Dan said, "I understand."

The doctor spoke slowly, as though recalling the information from some memory bank. "The DNA in some existing bacteria is altered and the new bacteria is combined with a property that knocks out the body's natural immune system. Then, through some additional genetic engineering, the combination is strengthened to the point where it's a fast-acting killer. The bacteria is inhaled, enters the blood stream and races through the body. It initally attacks the intestine, causing almost immediate distress, then death."

Dan glanced out the window of the jet and then turned back to the doctor. "If these rumors are true, could this be the thing that caused the problem on that airplane?"

The doctor thought about it for a moment and then said, "Absolutely. The whole project is very hush-hush, so I don't know for sure. But the Pentagon would know. All of it."

They both grew silent for a moment and then Dan said, "Serson said we'd have their full cooperation. That usually means they intend to stonewall. Did you tell this to Spencer?"

Evans shrugged again. "No. As I say, it was just rumor. Besides, I really didn't have the time. He just wanted an opinion on what could have caused the problem on the airplane. I contacted Atlanta and then had them talk directly to him."

Dan wondered to himself. Who would do such a thing? And how the hell would they get their hands on this stuff? Security in Huntsville was tighter than most nuclear missile sites. Could they rule out Huntsville?

Not yet.

And for what end? Why an airplane? Just for the sake of killing? He thought about it some more and then answered his own question. They probably used an airplane because it was a completely closed environment. They could kill everyone on board and not risk an epidemic. As for who? Any number of groups would be eager to take credit for this within the next few days.

And the group truly responsible would make their reasons known. Otherwise, there would have been no purpose whatsoever. These people always had a purpose, however misguided.

Dan sighed and slumped deeper into his seat. "So it starts," he said. "This'll be the first one, Bruce. Over the past few years, we've stopped about two hundred terrorists attacks from ever taking place in this country. This one got past us.

"It has to be a new group. With the help of the NSA, we've been able to keep pretty close tabs on most of the crazies. We've infiltrated most of the big outfits quite successfully. But we never got a whiff of this. Not a whiff! Aside from making us look bad, it scares the hell out of me.

"Whoever they are, they've got money and resources. Lots of both. What does it take to produce something like this, Bruce?"

The doctor picked at his mustache as he answered. "Like you said—money and resources. The technology exists to produce it, along with the knowledge, and that knowledge, although not common, is widespread. A few million dollars worth of equipment combined with the right people could produce this kind of thing in a matter of months."

Dan asked, "Could you?"

"No. I'm an internist. You'd need a lab man. A research type. A microbiologist. It's a growing industry. Genetically altered bacterium are being used to protect strawberries in Florida and potatoes in Idaho. There are thousand of people involved in research all over the world. And like any other group, there are those who can be reached. It's just as easy to produce something evil as it is to produce something that has a worthwhile purpose."

Once again, Wiseman picked up the yellow legal pad on the seat beside him and made some additional notes. In large, bold letters he wrote down the word "Pentagon" and underlined it. Beneath that he wrote "Huntsville" and underlined that as well. Then he circled a word he'd previously noted. It was the Russian defector's name.

He looked up and said to the doctor, "One thing's for sure. The Pentagon is going to have to help us on this thing."

Then he got up from his seat and moved to another

where the radio-telephone was stationed. He dialed some numbers and waited. Then he asked for the director. It took only seconds.

"This is Concord."

Dan was aware that they were using an open radio link. The director was using his code name.

"This is Blue Three. Request following: list of all employees of medical firm last five years. Full workups. Also confirmation on possible connection with patient. Request associate company investigate competitors fully. You copy?"

There was a pause and then the director said, in a voice that sounded somewhat uncertain, "We copy."

Dan continued. "Concord, pull the file on a visitor with visa problems who was interviewed three years ago. A.D. Murphy would remember the case."

Again, there was an acknowledgement.

Dan thought to himself that his request for complete files on all of the employes of the Huntsville biological weapons research unit would cause some sparks to fly. As would his request that the CIA develop a full report on all countries that could have produced something capable of causing the problem on board the airliner. But it had to be done. The question was; would it?

It damn well better be, he thought. He'd been put in charge of this investigation. The director could have picked other assistant directors who had held the position longer. But he'd been picked for a reason. He thought he knew what it was.

Dan Wiseman wasn't interested in the politics that permeated the FBI just like they permeated every other government agency. He was a man who just wanted to get the job done, no matter how many toes he stepped on. It wasn't that he wasn't diplomatic—in fact, he was usually quite capable of handling tricky situations satisfactorily. It was more his dogged persistence in getting to the truth. Of being able to cut through the bull and get to the core of the matter. And since the divorce, he'd been even more so, a facet of his personality that hadn't escaped the attention of the director.

This case was important. There was no time to play games, political or otherwise. Too much was at stake.

Mickey Serson had said there'd be full cooperation. Now was the time for the president's man to prove his word was good for something.

After signing off, Dan returned to his seat across from Doctor Evans. "I just talked to Spencer. I want the full scoop on Huntsville."

The doctor uttered a low whistle. "Good luck, my friend." Then he sighed and looked out the window. "It's really a crock, Daniel. A real crock. The Russians have maybe half a million tons—that's tons—of chemical weapons. Perhaps half again that in biological weapons. There've been meetings to try and ban the stuff, we've signed treaties doing just that, but it goes on and on . . .

"There's enough nuclear weaponry around to kill us all several times over. Everyone knows that. What they don't know is that there's also enough germ warfare material sitting on shelves to kill us all as well. If they don't get us one way, they'll get us another. Great, huh?"

Dan ignored the question. The doctor asked, "You don't think this has anything to do with Huntsville, do you? Not really? What about some group supported by the Russians?"

Dan shook his head. "No. I don't think it involves the Russians at all. I don't think it involves the normal political groups either. This is something tied to something else. Like a message of some sort . . . or a demonstration. Whoever they are, they want to impress us with their power. Make us sweat. And the damn thing is, they're doing it.

"As for Huntsville . . . who knows? We've had a lot of Americans do some terrible things the last few years. People cleared top secret handing information to whoever wants to pay the price. Anything's possible."

He paused and scratched his head. Then he said. "A few years ago, I'd have never said such a thing."

Dan didn't like what he was thinking. He decided to change the subject. "What are our chances of finding out exactly what this thing is? Assuming you have access to the plane."

"Excellent, as long as the plane impacts on the ground. The men from Atlanta are bringing with them equipment that can give us some of the answers within hours, such as whether or not we're dealing with a substance that's still contagious. They'll need to send samples to Atlanta where they have an electron microscope before we'll know exactly what the bug is."

"What about the germs themselves?" Dan asked. "What are the chances that they're still contagious?"

A cloud seemed to come into the eyes of the doctor. "I don't know. Maybe. Maybe not. As long as everybody wears protective clothing, we might be all right. I won't know what we're dealing with until I've had the chance to see the results of the on-site tests." He paused and then said, "However, if it's what I think it is, we might have a problem. We'll take air, soil and water samples around the crash site. That'll tell us."

"And what if the samples come up positive?"

"Then," Doctor Evans replied, his expression never changing, "we can all kiss our asses goodbye."

Dan looked at the young doctor, whose face displayed a strange detachment. "You can't be serious!"

It was then that the face finally changed expression, taking on a starkness, a coldness—almost an angry look. "I was never more serious in my life, Dan. It's possible that someone let the genie out of the bottle. We may never be able to put it back."

There were four F-16s now accompanying the Pacific Rim 1011 as if flew toward the west coast of Florida. Two of the F-16s were making passes at the sides of the airliner, their wing-mounted probes taking readings which could be seen inside the cockpits of the fighters.

The other two F-16s were hanging back about a mile, waiting for the final word.

The radios in all four aircraft had been modified. What was being said was intelligible only to themselves and to a single radio on the ground, located at MacDill Air Force Base.

In the operations rooms, Col. Roger Basehart listened to the radio traffic between the four aircraft.

"Thirty-four, we have less than a minute. You have a final reading yet?"

"Stand by . . . Roger . . . We've triple-checked the numbers. The ambient temperature inside the target is minus sixteen degrees Fahrenheit. Temperature of the pilot is forty-seven degrees Fahrenheit. Temperature of the first officer is forty-four degrees Fahrenheit. They're all dead. Heating system must have failed."

"Roger thirty-four. Many thanks for the help."

"Thirty-four. We're outta here. Good luck guys."

Colonel Basehart let a deep sigh escape his lungs. It seemed as though he'd been holding his breath for hours. The tension drained from his body as though he had pulled the plug on a bathtub full of water.

They were all dead.

There was no question.

The two pilots could shoot the plane down without qualms.

Captains Whelan and Parker were preparing to do just that.

"MacDill, this is Air Force Seventy-seven."

Basehart pushed the button on his headset and answered. "Roger Seventy-seven, MacDill. Commence attack in thirty seconds. Mark."

"Roger MacDill."

The two F-16s moved into position behind and below the airliner. They had already determined how they would carry out the mission. Parker would send a short burst of cannon fire into the number two engine, the tail-mounted one. The failure of that engine would not seriously affect the stability of the plane, at least for a moment.

Then Captain Whelan would, from a position slightly below and behind the port wing, fire a short burst into the number one engine, hanging in a pod below the wing. Tracers would give him a clear line on the direction his shells were taking, allowing him to avoid hitting the wing.

"Remember Rich, as soon as the engine goes, the plane will slow down."

"Roger."

Parker moved into position, and checked the display

on his instrument panel. Time was up.

He squeezed the red button on the control stick and the F-16 shuddered slightly as the M61A-1 cannon, located to the left and slightly behind the cockpit of the fighter, chattered. At the same time, Parker activated the speed brakes on the F-16.

He could see that the shells had hit the mark. He pulled back on the stick and the F-16 rose slightly, allowing pieces of debris to slip below him.

A moment later, the other F-16 opened up, the tracers lighting up the night-time sky. A small adjustment and the cannon on Captain Whelan's F-16 chattered again. This time, the 1011 shuddered and slowed dramatically. Both fighters found themselves now above and ahead of the airliner.

"Jesus!"

"Seventy-seven, MacDill. What's happening?"

"MacDill, Air Force Seventy-seven. We're going around again. The one thousand-eleven is still flying. It's making a slow turn to port and descending. But it's . . . Stand by."

The 1011 seemed to be gliding. The left wing had dipped slightly and the big airliner, two engines destroyed, was making a slow, lazy turn. By now, they were thirty miles east of the west coast of Florida.

"MacDill, Seventy-seven. I think the thing ran out of fuel. Just at the time we took out both engines. It's acting as though all three are out."

"Stand by."

Colonel Basehart's mind was racing. The whole plan was coming apart. The plane was supposed to have gone into an immediate spin. It hadn't. What were the chances that it would run out of fuel at the precise moment . . .

He scanned the radar screen. The position of the two fighters was clearly marked.

"MacDill, Seventy-seven."

"Go ahead."

"MacDill . . . we've almost done a one-eighty here. The . . . okay, it's going into a spin now. Looks like it may impact in Tampa Bay! You want the target destroyed?"

A thousand possibilities raced through the colonel's mind. A Sidewinder missile might miss and hit the ground. Aside from that, any missile hitting the airliner would be proof positive that it had been shot down. Something everyone was attempting to keep secret. If the airliner hit the bay, it would be easy to recover. The thing they had wanted to avoid was losing it in the Atlantic.

The anger rose inside the veteran airman. They hadn't needed to shoot at all! The plane had run out of fuel by itself! Whoever had given them the estimates had screwed up. Another minute. One lousy minute of delay and they would have known the plane was out of fuel.

He barked into the headset. "No! Just monitor."

"Roger."

There was nothing Colonel Basehart could do except listen as the two pilots gave a running description of the last moments of Pacific Air Flight 234. It was spinning now, out of control, the dead bodies of 245 passengers and 14 crew members strapped securely to their seats, oblivious.

Dan Wiseman sat in the Lear, now on the ground at

Orlando International Airport, and listened to the radio-telephone. An FBI agent monitoring the radio traffic between the planes in the air and Colonel Basehart on the ground was passing that information along telephone lines to another agent in Orlando, who, in turn, was using a scrambler radio to pass the data to Dan in the plane.

Also on the ground were three C-130H Hercules aircraft, their cargoes of special protective equipment and troops already off-loaded, placed on trucks and awaiting orders to move. The special team of biological weapons people had arrived from New Orleans a short time ago, having been briefed on board the aircraft for this, their first actual exercise since the formation of the unit in secret, four years earlier. It was deemed inadvisable to let the American people know that a special unit had been formed to counter the effects of a germ warfare attack. There was enough paranoia already.

They were all waiting. Waiting for PacRim Flight 234 to crash somewhere in Florida. Waiting to rush to the scene, check for possible contamination and then react to that disaster as quickly as possible.

The words of Doctor Bruce Evans seemed to haunt Dan as he listened to the relay from MacDill. Bruce had said that if, in fact, the bacteria were still alive, they would all be in serious trouble. The words coming through the radio telephone broke through his morose thoughts.

"Twenty thousand.

"Fifteen thousand.

"Ten thousand.

"They say they've hit some turbulence and the plane has shifted course a bit. They say it's gonna hit the ground."

"Where?"

"Here on the east coast of the peninsula. Jesus Christ! It's heading right for the peninsula! Stand by."

In the air, pilots Parker and Whelan watched in horror as the 1011 neared its impact area on the ground, a spot right in the middle of Pinellas County, one of the most populous counties in the state of Florida. There was nothing they could do.

At 11:13 p.m. Eastern time, the Pacific Rim Airlines Lockheed 1011, having been in the air for seven hours and thirty-three minutes, crashed into the ground.

A few startled people had heard what sounded like a tornado seconds before it hit.

People as far away as a mile were shocked away from their television sets by the sound of the crash. No one knew at that moment that by some miracle, the plane had crashed into one of the few remaining open areas in the county.

In Orlando, men and material were being rushed back onto the Hercules transports that had just been unloaded. The airliner had crashed almost a hundred miles away. They had to get there immediately. It would be quicker to fly.

The Lear of Dan Wiseman was in the air within two minutes. At the same time, fire trucks and police from as far away as Tampa and St. Petersburg rushed toward the smoldering crash site, where heat from hot, jagged metal had started numerous grass fires.

Already, hundreds of curious residents were clambering into cars and trucks, or moving on foot, heading toward the dim light in the sky, wanting to see if this was, indeed, the same plane they'd been hearing about on television all night.

As the Lear climbed for altitude, Dan Wiseman was on the telephone, telling the dispatcher at the other end of the radio to warn the firemen and policemen to keep their distance. They were to stay at least 200 yards away from the crash site unless wearing protective clothing.

He was assured those orders would be followed.

Dan hung up the phone and wondered if Bruce Evans's fears would be realized. Was the genie indeed out of the bottle?

In a few moments they'd know the answer.

## Chapter Five

President Robert Dalton sat behind the massive desk in the Oval Office and eyed his friend and advisor, Mickey Serson. The president was a careful man, who some had accused of being unimaginative. Throughout his political life, he'd been an uncharismatic campaigner who managed to win. During the presidential primaries, to almost everyone's surprise, he'd done extremely well. It seemed the American people were ready for a steady, careful and controlled man after years of sitting on the edge of their seats. His success in the primaries had given him the party's nomination on the first ballot and again, to almost everyone's surprise, he won the presidential election handily.

He was 56, undistinguished in appearance, standing just under six feet tall, fit, but not athletic. His face was rather round with eyes that seemed a touch too close together. The complexion was ruddy and the fulsome head of hair was almost completely gray. The rimless glasses he favored gave him just the appearance of wisdom people wanted to see in him. The glasses, like everything else relating to his appearance, had been chosen by Robert Dalton, who'd flatly refused to listen to a single word from the image-makers throughout his career. His popularity seemed to rise on a graph in direct proportion to the public's awareness of that part of his character.

There was another factor that many had felt led to his becoming president of the United States. In the midst of the long series of primary campaigns, Wilma Dalton, his wife of thirty-one years, had unexpectedly suffered a stroke and died a short two days later. Dalton had pulled out of the campaign, but two months later, at the urging of a group of supporters that included his three grown children, reentered the fray. He was buoyed by an outpouring of sympathy and empathy from all over the country.

He'd been president for little over a year and it was already apparent that the public perception was not always reality, and the wisdom had failed to surface. The honeymoon with the press, while not yet over, was in serious trouble. As he listened to Mickey, he was instantly aware that no matter what happened from here on in, he was now a target for increased criticism.

As he had ordered, the plane had been shot down. So far, very few people were aware of that fact. But the speculation as to what had caused the passengers and crew to become ill was running at a fever pitch.

The words, "terrorist attack" were being used by the media with abandon, without regard for the consequences.

Clearly, that was the most dramatic explanation, but until he knew more, the president could neither confirm nor deny it, while at the same time, he had to be very careful not to appear to be covering up some terribly unpleasant news. The American people were thoroughly weary of being conned.

Mickey Serson was reporting news that was at the same time horrific and good. The plane had crashed in the middle of a heavily-populated area of Florida, but seemed to have avoided killing anyone on the ground. However, the decontamination team was much farther away than expected and was not yet on the scene.

And the director of the FBI, whom the president had asked personally to take charge of the investigation, had requested access to everything concerning the biological weapons research center in Huntsville, Alabama.

The president had pledged his full support to the investigation and already that pledge was about to present problems. Big problems. The Huntsville operation was one of the nation's most closely-guarded secrets. Once the information was in the hands of the FBI, the chance of leaks was increased dramatically. Civilians weren't always cognizant of the reasons behind such things as the need for this kind of research. Not to mention the fact that the Pentagon abhorred the release of secrets to anyone for any reason.

He removed a cigar from the wooden box on the desk and went about the business of preparing it for smoking. He carefully clipped the tip, then ran his tongue over the thick brown wrapper, thoroughly wetting it down. Finally, he used a wooden match to light it.

Mickey Serson watched the ritual and waited impatiently. Dalton always followed the same pattern when he was trying to make a decision and sometimes it was very disconcerting, a fact of which the president was fully aware. Mickey said, "You realize that you'll need to make some sort of statement immediately. Already the media have this thing pegged as a terrorist attack. If nothing else, you'll have to express your condolences to families of the victims."

Dalton looked at him sharply. "I'm aware of that," he

said, a trace of anger in his voice. "But I can't comment on something I don't know. We're all guessing on this thing. It might be something else altogether. I'd look pretty stupid if I said this thing was caused by some terrorist group and it turned out to be leaking hydraulic fluid or something. We're relying totally on the few minutes of conversation with the pilot and the opinions of some doctors in Atlanta. Supposing that wasn't even the pilot on the radio? Or supposing he was frightened and . . ."

Serson sighed. "Look, I know how you feel, but you'll have to face the facts. Nothing else could have happened. It has to be either a terrorist or some crazy looking for insurance money. Maybe a passenger brought something on board and committed suicide as well as wiping out everyone else. You have to tell them something!"

The president stood up and faced Serson, the anger growing in his eyes. "I know I have to tell them something, but what exactly do I tell them? We don't really know what happened and I'm damned well not going to add to the fires of speculation. The goddamn press is always ready to print the worst! The fact is we don't know what happened and until I do know—exactly—I'm going to tell it like it is. I just don't know!"

They glared at each other for a moment and then the president asked, "Who's in charge of Huntsville?"

Serson looked through some notes and said, "A two-star general by the name of Waldo Smith."

Dalton barked, "Get him up here, and tell Tim I want to see him immediately." Tim Belcher was the president's press secretary.

Serson started to say something and then stopped.

The president was rubbing his temples, his face contorted in pain. Serson moved toward the desk and asked softly, "Another one of those headaches?"

Dalton dropped his hands and glared at him again. "No. I'm fine. Just get with it, will you?"

Serson stood still for a moment and then turned on his heel and left the office.

President Dalton looked quickly at his appointment list for the next day. He'd cleared four hours for a meeting with his personal physician in the afternoon. It was billed as a normal, routine physical. It was anything but.

In the crush of media attention the plane crash would receive, he'd be expected to postpone the physical. But he couldn't do that. It had taken too long to set it up. It was an appointment that had to be kept.

In a small, run-down motel room not far from the Los Angeles airport, a red-headed man sat in his T-shirt and shorts on the edge of the bed and watched with fascination as the news was broadcast on the television set in the corner of the room.

". . . has come to an end. From New York, here is Brent Hughes."

"Good evening. The incredible story of the stricken Pacific Rim Airliner that has captured the nation's attention this evening, and indeed, the entire world's attention for that matter, has finally come to an end. A sad and tragic end.

"Just minutes ago, the Lockheed ten eleven, with an unknown number of passengers and crew, apparently exhausted its supply of fuel and crashed in Palm Harbor, Florida, a community located just north of Clearwater. For a report, we go now to our affiliate in Tampa, WPTT and reporter George Miller."

So, the red-headed man thought, the stupid thing had crashed on land. Not good. The men he worked for hadn't told him their entire plan, but he'd known that the plane was supposed to have fallen into the Pacific Ocean where it would never be found.

There was going to be a problem, he thought, about the rest of his money. They'd given half to him before he placed the device on the plane, and the other half was to come once the news of the crash was confirmed.

Well, the hell with the other half of the money. Ten thousand was enough. These people were crazy. And unpredictable. That's why he'd taken a hike from the Holiday Inn and taken a room in this dump. As soon as he'd heard the news that the plane had made a U-turn and was headed back to the States.

He stood up and stretched. He was starting to feel that familiar feeling of depression again. Damn! It kept coming quicker and quicker. At this rate, he'd run out of stuff in about two days.

He pulled open a dresser drawer and removed his shaving kit. Taking a container of talcum powder from the kit, he carefully removed the cap and tapped the edge of the container, allowing some of the white powder to fall to the imitation walnut surface of the desk. He screwed the cap back on and placed the container back in his kit. Then, with his finger, he pushed the powder into a small mound, then separated the mound into two smaller mounds of equal size.

He leaned over the first mound, and holding one side of his nostril closed, inhaled the white powder. He blinked, smiled and repeated the procedure with the other nostril.

Damn! It was good stuff. He could feel the confidence surging through him almost immediately.

Within seconds, he felt that welcome sense of well-being returning. The depression was gone.

Screw it! He had ten thousand bucks in his jeans and enough coke to keep him for two, maybe three days. Tomorrow, he'd leave this dump and head for Vegas. He felt lucky. The last few times he'd been to Vegas they'd cleaned his clock. Not this time. It was time his luck turned. He was on a roll! He watched the TV set again, this time with a smile on his face.

". . . has crashed in an open area just yards from busy Highway Nineteen here in northern Pinellas County. The fires have been put out and the entire area is being cordoned off by what looks like hundreds of police and emergency vehicles. Police are having some difficulty keeping the growing crowd at bay, while they set up a perimeter around the crash site. As our helicopter passes over the site, we can see a number of fire trucks pouring foam over the wreckage. It would appear from this vantage point, that the chances of anyone on the ground being hurt are remote, although that is simply a guess on my part.

"However, I've been over this area many times and I'm sure that this is an open area, although it's surrounded by residences. A miracle, to say the least.

"I've just been advised by our pilot that we've been ordered to leave the area immediately, so we'll land at St. Petersburg Airport and come back here on land. This is Traffic One from WPTT, in Tampa-St. Pete."

"Thank you, Roger. Once again, we have received no

official word from the FBI, but we understand that a news conference will be held within the hour. Maybe we can get some answers then. In the meantime, we have confirmation from several sources that the plane was indeed the Pacific Rim ten-eleven and that it has crashed in Palm Harbor. There are reports . . ."

The red-haired man switched off the television set and put on his clothes. He was restless. He wanted some action. It was early in the evening.

He'd intended to lie low, but now it seemed silly. They didn't know where he was. There was nothing to be afraid of. The hell with it.

He looked at himself in the mirror and grunted with satisfaction. He reached into the shaving kit and pulled out the container of talc and placed it in his pants pocket. Then he grabbed the key to the room and put it in the other pocket.

He reached for the door handle and turned the knob. It was his last act on earth.

There was a man standing in the doorway. A large man with a swarthy complexion and deeply hooded eyes. He had a gun in his hand. And it was pointed right at the red-headed man's chest.

The swarthy man seemed to be grinning as he pulled the trigger on the gun with the long barrel. It popped three times and the red-headed man felt a sudden and severe pain in his chest.

It was impossible! They couldn't have found him!

His face was twisted into an expression of surprise and shock as he looked at the man with the gun in his hand.

Then he fell to the floor.

It was like a dream.

There were two of them. He could hear them talking and laughing as they went through his pockets and took everything. He could hear them taking his stuff from the drawers and placing it into a suitcase.

He could even hear them as they got ready to leave and rolled him over on his back. The man was pointing the gun at his forehead now. The red-headed man wanted to tell him to stop, but he couldn't speak. He could only lie there on the floor on this back and wait for the darkness.

It wasn't long in coming.

The look on Doctor Evans's face told it all. He stared out the window of the Bureau Lear as it turned on final approach to St. Petersburg Airport.

The airport was about twelve miles from the crash site. The FBI had warned the state police department that people must be kept away from the crash at all costs. But they'd expected the site to be somewhere in the middle of Florida, not in a heavily-congested urban center.

From the radio reports that were being monitored on the FBI plane, it was obvious that as many as twenty or thirty people had been within five or ten feet of some of the wreckage. Some had even taken small pieces away as souvenirs. Things were starting to shape up now, but the damage might already have been done.

The look on Doctor Evans's face was of pure horror.

"You scare me, Doctor," Dan said.

Evans turned and played with his mustache again. "I'm sorry. I can't help it. They didn't follow instructions, damn it. People have already been too close.

Damn!

"If only . . ."

"What? If only what?"

"It's the numbers," the doctor answered. "The temperatures. According the the Air Force, the heating system on the airliner went out and the interior of the plane was well below zero. But the bodies were still measuring temperatures above freezing. If they had frozen solid, my guess is that the bacteria would have been killed. There's a possibility that the bacteria is still alive, using the bodies as a host.

"Now that it's on the ground, there's been contact already. We'll have to work very fast. I want you in your protective clothing before we get there. You can change in the truck."

Nothing the doctor had said made Dan feel any better. He was jerked in his seat as the plane landed, hard and fast. In a few minutes the transport planes would be landing, and the troops, already dressed in protective gear, would be taken to the crash site by hurriedly summoned trucks brought over from MacDill.

The man who would be the official FBI spokesman, Gil Parker, was still on the radio link to Washington, preparing the first of what would be many statements to the press.

The Lear fast-taxied to the cargo site of the terminal and came to a stop beside a waiting U.S. Air Force police van, its blue and red lights flashing in the night. Dan, Bruce and Gil moved quickly out of the aircraft and into the van, pulling on the bright orange protective gear as the truck careened through the near-empty streets, heading for the crash site.

Fifteen minutes later, they arrived at the scene.

It was an awesome sight.

The plane had crashed almost in the center of a soccer field in a sports park less than a tenth of a mile from the busiest thoroughfare in Florida, Highway 19. The sports park was surrounded by businesses and homes. One small gust of wind could have nudged the plane toward a crash site that could have killed many on the ground.

The impact had created a crater thirty feet deep that had broken through the tender limestone and brought an underground water supply to life. Because of the softness of the ground, most of the wreckage was confined to the impact area. Some parts had spun off as the plane impacted and the ground around the crater was littered with small pieces of metal. In the crater itself, nothing was recognizable, other than a small part of the tail section. Most of the wreckage was covered by water, on top of which floated countless pieces of flotsam, seat cushions, bits of insulating foam, and mountains of fire-fighting foam that had been poured over the wreck by the firemen.

Spotlights had been erected, powered by portable generators, and the light cast on the foam-covered scene seemed to give it a surrealistic Christmas look.

Some of the police and firemen ringing the area were protected by special clothing, but many were not, even though they'd been given instructions to stay away from the immediate area without such precautionary measures.

Bruce was right. The genie was out of the bottle. If the bacteria that had caused this disaster was still alive, it could never be returned.

The doctor cursed, the oath heard even through the

black neoprene mask he was wearing, and hurried toward the crater, a large black case in his arms. The police had established a perimeter that was roughly 200 yards from the center of the impact area. It wasn't nearly enough. Dan rushed to one of the officers and told him to push it back to 400 yards.

The cop wanted to know who in hell he was, so Dan had to unbuckle part of his protective suit to get at his credentials. He clipped them to the outside of his rubber suit and the cop got on the walkie-talkie.

It was chaos.

Where were the troops! Damn!

Even as he expressed the thought of himself, he could hear the sirens of the trucks as they raced north on Highway 19 toward the scene. Because of the short landing and take-off capabilities of the Hercules, they had landed at a small airport in the middle of Clearwater, some six or seven miles closer.

The sight of all of the new arrivals in special gear had the desired effect. Even the most curious sensed that there was real danger here. The television reporters had said this whole thing had started with a germ of some kind on board the airplane. A germ that could kill. Despite their curiosity, they took the orders to move farther away with little protest.

Dan moved to the edge of the crater and watched as Bruce Evans took soil, air and water samples, then scrambled up the side of the crater and opened his black suitcase.

The doctor, still wearing his protective gear, worked feverishly, mixing various chemicals and preparing slides, which he put under a microscope. He shook his head and put everything back in the suitcase. Dan could feel his heart start to beat wildly inside his chest. He moved closer to Bruce and yelled through his mask.

"What's the problem? Are we in trouble?"

The doctor stood up and started running toward one of the light banks, answering as he ran. "I don't know, not enough light. Dan, we need some divers. I need to get to some of the bodies and they're all underwater. And find those guys from Atlanta!"

Dan nodded and started barking into his walkie-talkie. Bruce put the suitcase down near the bright lights and started putting the slides through the microscope again. Then he slowly removed his mask and helmet.

Dan looked at him, his heart in his mouth. "Well?"

Bruce smiled. "What I have here is nothing. That's a good sign, but I won't really know until I examine one of the bodies."

So far so good. "Okay, Bruce, I'll talk to the Army people. In the meantime, you keep taking samples."

The doctor nodded and Dan looked around to see if he could locate the command trailer. He spotted it, parked on the side of the road leading from the highway, and walked toward it. Two military policemen guarded the single entrance to the small mobile trailer.

Dan asked for Colonel Pritchard, the commander of the special unit. One of the military policemen looked at Dan's credentials and told him to wait. In a moment, he was ushered into the trailer.

Colonel Pritchard sat behind a bare plywood desk, drinking coffee from a foam cup as he spoke into a field telephone. Two other men, both garbed in protective gear, stood near one of the walls. Dan introduced himself. "I'm assistant director Wiseman, FBI. You two wouldn't be from Atlanta, would you?"

One of the men nodded. "Yes. I'm Doctor Collins and this is Doctor Perkins. We're supposed to meet you and . . ."

Dan pointed to the crater. "Look for a doctor named Bruce Evans. He's wearing an orange suit with FBI stenciled on his back. Where's your equipment?"

"In the truck."

"Well, get it and fast."

The two men hurried out the door.

Dan poured himself a cup of coffee as he waited for the Army man to get off the phone. The colonel was a big man, his black hair clipped short, his ruddy complexion flushed from the adrenaline flow, his dark eyes alert and intense as he spoke quickly and decisively on the telephone. He put the telephone back in its case and held out his hand. "Mr. Wiseman, Col. Walter Pritchard. We need to talk."

Dan looked at him in surprise. "What's on your mind, Colonel?"

"My instructions are that I'm under your command. That's unacceptable. You're a cop. This is a dangerous situation involving matters you know nothing about. I haven't had time to discuss this matter properly with my superiors but now that you're here, I'd suggest that you place me in command."

Dan could hardly believe his ears. "Colonel," he said, "we have more important things to worry about. I need some people in protective gear who can get into that water and bring up a body fast. Doctor Evans feels it's imperative that we examine one of the victims as quickly as possible.

"Also, we need to quarantine everyone who's been within thirty feet of the crater. You'll need a hell of a lot more troops than you have now. I don't care where you get them, but I'd like it done immediately."

The colonel stood there and stared at him. "You haven't addressed my suggestion," he said.

Dan turned and reached for the door. "I don't intend to, Colonel. Now let's get moving."

The colonel still wasn't moving. Dan's voice rose in intensity. "Now, Colonel!"

Colonel Pritchard reached for the field telephone.

Donald James stood on a small platform and faced the one hundred and sixty people who had been allowed into the conference room at LAX. Beside him stood FBI special agent Jim Taylor.

The people allowed in the room were those who had proven to the FBI man's satisfaction that they were immediate enough relatives of those on board Pacific Rim Flight 234. Although it was widely known that the plane had crashed, there were official notifications to be given and the long, arduous process of attending to the aftereffects of the tragedy had to be initiated. James approached the microphone, adjusted it slightly and began his remarks.

"Ladies and gentlemen," he said, "my name is Donald James. I have the sad duty to inform you that Pacific Rim Airlines Flight Two-three-four has crashed in Florida and there are no survivors."

The room immediately filled with the sounds of wails and screams. From some, curses were hurled at the public relations man, as though he, representing the airline, was somehow responsible for the deaths of their loved ones. James waited for the din to recede and then continued. "The Federal Bureau of Investigation has taken full charge of this accident and will handle all details pertaining to identification matters. I'd like to introduce Special Agent Jim Taylor, but before I do, I'd just like to say that, on behalf of Pacific Rim Airlines, and myself personally, our deepest sympathies go out to you all."

Even as he said it, he realized how hollow, how redundant the words seemed.

Special Agent Taylor approached the microphone.

"Ladies and gentlemen," he said, "At ten a.m. tomorrow morning, transportation will be available for those wishing to go to Florida. Transportation will be limited to two members of each family. If you are unable to meet the ten o'clock time frame, other transportation will be arranged for you at no cost.

"There are three young ladies located near the far wall, seated at desks. They will assist you in making the necessary arrangements.

"This accident is being investigated and no comments are being made at this time. You will probably be contacted by many people in the days ahead. Lawyers, reporters and others. The FBI requests that you refrain from speaking to any of them at this time. As soon as more information is available, you will be contacted. We've set up a hotline and the young ladies will give you that number and instructions as to accessing. That access will be limited to immediate relatives only.

"Should you have any questions, we urge you to call the hotline. Please pay no attention to what you may read in the newspapers and see on television. Much of that information may be erroneous. For the straight facts, contact us.

"That is all I have at this time."

The audience shouted questions that were being ignored. James felt compelled to speak to them again. He stepped back in front of the microphone. "I realize that you have many questions and I understand your frustration. Please try to understand that because this was not a . . . normal accident, there are many things to be considered.

"The FBI is working very hard, I can assure you. Please try to be as patient as possible."

It didn't help much. There was so much they all wanted to know.

The key question in most minds was why? Why their loved ones? Why them?

Why indeed, thought Donald James, as he left the room, the sound of the wails and screams filling his ears.

At almost the same time, some 2500 miles from Los Angeles, a grim-faced Gil Parker stepped in front of a bank of microphones and battery of television cameras in a press area set up outside the 400 yard perimeter of the crash site to give the first official comments on the accident.

"My name is Gilbert Parker and I will be acting as the official spokesman for the Federal Bureau of Investigation throughout this investigation.

"For your information, all releases will be handled through this office, as the FBI has assumed complete jurisdiction in this matter.

"At eleven thirteen p.m. this evening, a Lockheed ten-eleven aircraft, leased to and operated by Pacific Rim Airlines, crashed in Palm Harbor, Florida after the passengers and crew became stricken with an illness that has not yet been determined.

"The list of passengers and crew will be released at noon tomorrow, as soon as all next-of-kin have been notified, and preliminary investigations begun.

"I can tell you that the aircraft held two hundred forty-four passengers and a crew of fifteen. I can also tell you that we are certain that all of the passengers and crew were dead before the aircraft ran out of fuel and crashed."

There were shouts from the reporters. Parker held up his hand for silence and it was some time in coming.

"Specially equipped fighter planes were able to take a variety of readings inside the aircraft before it ran out of fuel and those readings confirmed that the passengers were indeed dead.

"We believe that the passengers and crew were killed by a toxic chemical as yet unidentified. A complete investigation has already begun and details will be released as they become known. Until that time, we urge you to refrain from making unsubstantiated statements that could hinder the investigation and possibly cause unnecessary anxiety. At this time, we don't know if the chemical was released accidentally or deliberately.

"The president has ordered that all law enforcement agencies as well as state and federal agencies, cooperate with the FBI in finding out exactly what happened. As I have already stated, that investigation has already begun. Aside from one health warning, that's all I have at this time except to say that the president will be addressing the nation in—" he stopped and looked at his watch—"about six minutes."

More shouting. Parker waited patiently, refusing to

be drawn into a question and answer session. Then he continued. "Because of the peculiar nature of Florida's sub-soil structure, the aquifer is very close to the surface of the ground in many areas. The impact of the crash appears to have caused a breach in the limestone upper crust and the plane has penetrated the aquifer. Initial tests have not revealed any contamination of the water supply, but until further tests are completed, we have issued a directive that condemns the entire water supply for Pinellas and Pasco Counties. All local government bodies are ordered to make immediate plans to shut off water supplies and set up alternative systems.

"At the same time, we have issued a directive that orders all people who have come in contact with the wreckage or anything in the immediate area, to report to a special medical area that is being set up at this time, located in the northwest corner of this field, for tests to determine if they have been exposed to any toxic chemicals. This is a precautionary measure.

"The Army Corps of Engineers will be arriving within the hour to assist in the removal of the wreckage from the crater which has been created. Until the entire wreckage has been removed, the bodies of the victims recovered and examined, we will have to insist that the area now roped off be considered an absolute off-limits area, not to be entered by unauthorized persons and then only with protective clothing. Because the impact crater has penetrated the aquifer, we have no estimate at this time how long the recovery process will take.

"As for the actual events leading up to the crash, I can tell you what we know so far. The aircraft was en route to Hawaii from Los Angeles and had been in the air about an hour when the pilot complained of feeling ill. Within ten minutes, it was evident that all of the passengers and all of the crew were suffering from the same illness.

"Attempts were made to bring the aircraft safely back to Los Angeles . . . actually a military base close by, but the entire crew lost consciousness before this could be achieved. The aircraft continued east, on automatic pilot, until it ran out of fuel and crashed.

"As I have stated, we are convinced that a toxic chemical was released on board the aircraft, causing the deaths of all passengers and crew. At this time, we don't know what the chemical was, or how it might have been released. That's all for now."

The reporters were screaming hundreds of questions at the man as he turned and left the press area without answering one of them.

# Chapter Six

Helen Porter, a senior investigator with LAX security, had completed typing up the interviews she had held with the maintenance people who had serviced Pacific Rim's Flight 234 before departure.

She'd begun to conduct the interviews as soon as she'd heard the initial reports of the airplane's difficulties in the air. First, she'd talked to the mechanics who'd refueled and ground-checked the plane, then she'd moved to the food service people and finally the staff who'd spruced up the interior, cleaning ashtrays and toilets with practiced efficiency. She knew her work would be repeated by the FBI. In fact, they were probably interviewing the same people she had already. But she wanted to know for her own sake. Someone had breached LAX security. It made her look bad. She didn't like looking bad.

Once she'd been a cop, but that seemed a long time ago. Now, at age 33, she was employed by the airport authority and took her job seriously.

Instinct told her that someone had done something to that airplane and she wanted to know what it was. It was as though they had attacked her personally.

She was an attractive woman, with dark hair and eyes, a straight nose and full lips. Her five foot, seven inch frame held a body that was lithe and tanned, with proportions that caused many a head to turn in blonde-mad California.

She glanced through the reports and stuffed them in her briefcase. Five of the interviews had revealed something that caught her attention and she wanted to check it out with the airline before she turned copies of her files over to the FBI. She looked at her copy of the personnel directory and noted that the p.r. man for Pacific Rim was a man named Donald James.

She left her office and got into her car, started it and headed for the offices of Pacific Rim Airlines. As she approached, she noticed the platoon of reporters standing outside, still trying to get some information. She parked the car, clipped her badge to the front of her blouse, and strode toward the front door of the building. The uniformed policeman let her through.

The inside of the building was also crowded with people. Policeman, both uniformed and plainclothes, milled about as other men and women looked over computer print-outs and other data. A man in a dark blue suit with hard eyes and short hair looked up and approached her. He glanced at her badge and asked, "Lookin' for someone?"

Helen looked at his own badge. It said FBI.

"I'm looking for Donald James. Is he around?"

The hard-eyed agent grunted. "No. Right now he's looking after some of the families of the victims. If you've got some information, I'll be glad to take it."

Helen Porter hesitated. She wanted to be sure of her facts before she talked to the FBI. The agent, perhaps sensing her feelings, forced a grin to his lips and stuck out his hand. "Al Disario, Ms. Porter. I could use your help."

She took the hand and shook it. "Well," she said, "I wanted to check it out before I talked to you people, but—"

"What is it?"

"I talked to the mechanics and everyone else who was near that plane before it took off. Nothing out of the ordinary there. They've all been with InterState for years."

Pacific Rim Airlines employed no mechanics of their own. Instead, they contracted with InterState Airlines to maintain and service their two 1011s, now reduced to one.

Helen continued. "I've checked out the records of everyone who worked on the plane from the moment it arrived from Hawaii last night—well, the night before. You know what I mean.

"Nobody remembers seeing anyone near the plane who shouldn't have been. The records of everyone seem clean. The baggage handlers check out, food handlers—all regular people.

"Except for one.

"Five of these people reported seeing an FAA inspector in and around the plane."

"An FAA inspector?"

"Yes. Some of the mechanics remember an FAA guy checking something in the nose of the airplane. That's where the radar dish and the heating controls are located. He spent about five minutes up front and then went into the plane where he stayed for about fifteen minutes.

"Normally, FAA inspectors are accompanied by someone on the maintenance crew. This guy worked alone. I've talked to two of our own people who observed him and they checked his credentials, which were in order. The thing is, he never gave a copy of his report to anyone on the maintenance crew and that's really strange. I think it might tie in."

"There's only one way to find out," Disario said. He moved quickly to one of the inner offices, consulted a small pocket telephone directory and dialed a number. As he waited for an answer he cupped a hand over the mouthpiece and said to Helen, "Don't leave yet."

She nodded.

He was on the phone for ten minutes during which time Helen Porter consumed two cigarettes. When he was finished, he had a grim look on his face.

"I want to talk to this Williams character." He pointed to the files in her hands. "Are those the interviews you conducted?"

She nodded.

"Good." He turned to one of the other agents and called him over. "Jim, this is Helen Porter, LAX security. She's been doing a little of our work for us. Sit down with her and take her statement, then go over the interviews she's conducted. I'll be back in a few minutes after I see Baxter Williams."

He started to leave and stopped. "Ms. Porter, I really appreciate the help. Nice work."

"Thanks."

Then he turned and left the office.

Elizabeth Martin sat in the chaise lounge chair on the back patio, her body wrapped in a blanket to ward off the cool night air, and stared vacantly at her precious flowers, their colors muted in the moonlight. Beside her, Janet Talbot, her neighbor and friend, also wrapped in a blanket, sat quietly, holding the hand of her friend.

It had been two hours since the doctor had come and administered a sedative, an hour since Elizabeth had finally stopped crying and took to sitting in the outside darkness, as though the house itself was some sort of prison.

Janet had been on the telephone and talked to Elizabeth's parents, who were making arrangements to come to Costa Mesa and be with her during the time of their daughter's grief. And now she sat beside her friend and sipped some white wine as she tried to find a way to ease the pain so evident in the face of the completely devastated woman.

It was impossible. The crying had stopped, but the shattered soul of Elizabeth was laid bare for all to see, alone, as every shattered soul is alone, except for those rare individuals who have made some connection with a force that can reach out and provide solace at such a time.

When they had first learned of the problem with the airplane, they had stayed at home, watching television, hopes rising and falling on the words of assorted experts who predicted either successful landing or doom. It had been the cruelest of times, persisting until the final announcement that the plane had, indeed, crashed.

During those horrible few hours before the actual crash, telephone calls to the airline and the FBI had elicited no information other than the instruction that Mrs. Martin should come to LAX where a special room had been set up for relatives of those on the aircraft. She was to bring proper identification. When Janet had broached the subject, Liz had refused, saying, "No, there's no need. The plane won't land there even if there was a chance. No . . . I'll stay here. If Mark survives, he'll want me here so he can call."

So they had stayed, and the news of the crash seemed almost anti-climactic when it came.

A man had called from the airline, confirming the news that the plane had crashed and that Mark's name was on the passenger list. He had told Janet that Liz would be flown to Tampa at the airline's expense to make proper identification of the body. A plane would be available at ten in the morning and if that was inconvenient, she was to call a special number to make other arrangements. He gave his name as Donald James and said how sorry he was.

Janet had immediately phoned her doctor, who had come and attended to the distraught Elizabeth.

And now, they sat silently in the darkness, holding hands, not talking, just sharing a pain that seemed unbearable.

The thoughts were too horrible to be expressed. In the morning, Elizabeth was expected to fly across the country to view the shattered remains of her husband, if in fact his body had even been recovered. It was an action she would refuse to carry out. She wanted to remember him whole. The ready smile, the tender touch, the earnest look in his eyes when he confronted a particularly vexing problem.

She knew he was dead. She could feel it in her heart. A coldness that had gripped her earlier in the day was confirmation enough for her. There was no need to be put through the agony of identifying a body that no longer represented her husband. No need.

He was gone and that was all that really counted. She'd stay here in California and grieve her loss. Surrounded by memories and friends and family that renewed her spirit. Surrounded by tiny fragments of their life together. The smell of his aftershave on the still-unwashed towel, the smell of his hair in the brush, the sound of his voice on the telephone answering machine.

She'd watch the video tape they'd done when they went to Yosemite, where he'd put the camera on a tripod and the two of them had carried on like school children, hamming it up outrageously.

Those were to be her final memories of Mark. Not some mangled mess of unidentifiable flesh.

She wouldn't do it.

There was no way she would do it. They couldn't make her do it.

In one of the penthouse suites at the Los Angeles Marriott on Century Boulevard, George Barnes, his gray hair askew, his jacket off, exposing the red suspenders he favored, took the cigar out of his mouth and spoke to the five men and one woman in the room. His manner was brusque, as usual, and he dispensed with the small talk, as well as the charm. Charm he reserved for clients and juries.

"All right," he said, "you have the breakdown." He looked at his watch. "It's now one forty five in the morning. I want you all at your first call by eight. You know the procedure, so I won't bore you with the details. Just remember, we have until noon to make hay here. As soon as the passenger list is officially released, every ambulance chaser in the country will be on this like white on rice. So we have a head start, thanks to Frank, and we better damn well take advantage of it.

"You've all worked with me in the past, so you know how I operate. I'm good for it and even though you may have to wait for the bulk of your pay, you know you'll get it. But, as in the past, I'll pay five thousand for every client you sign up, and you'll get two percent of any settlement or judgment actually received.

"You could end up millionaires if you work hard and fast. This one really stinks. My gut instinct tells me that they'll want this one settled quickly just to keep the press off their backs. Obviously, somebody killed all of those people and may, I say may, never be caught. No matter. There are plenty of people to share part of the blame. The airline, LAX, Lockheed—whatever. Everybody will be in the spotlight. The heat will be terrible and I intend to keep it turned up full."

He paused and took another drag from the fat cigar. "Okay, let's get with it. I'll stay here. I'll have at least three lines available, with experienced secretaries to man them. I want to hear those phones ring tomorrow. Now, get lost."

The six "bird-dogs" got up from the two large, comfortable sofas, some snubbing out cigarettes, and headed for the door. Barnes took off his shoes, poured himself a drink and stretched out on one of the sofas.

He felt good. This was right up his alley. Just the fact that George Barnes, a man with an incredible record of success in the accident liability field, was representing some of the relatives of victims of the crash, was enough to intimidate the hell out of them. He'd received hundreds of millions of dollars in judgements or settlements for his clients in the 23 years he'd been in the business. A minimum of a third of that had been paid in the way of contingency fees to George Barnes. This one could be the biggest yet.

Nobody he represented ever begrudged him his fee. At the onset of a case, at least. They knew that Barnes was capable of extracting the maximum award for damages from tight-fisted insurance companies. Fees ranging from one third to as much as fifty percent of the award, depending on the circumstances, still brought a much higher net to the client than if some other lawyer was handling their case. As George liked to explain it; fifty percent of a million still beat one hundred percent of a quarter million.

Of course, once the actual award was gained, there were some expressions of dissatisfaction from a few of the greedier clients. Some clients thought that three or four million dollars in fees for what seemed like a few months of work was too much. They had suffered the loss, not Barnes. He would patiently explain once more the reasons the award had been so high. It was his skill and knowledge, he'd tell them. His experience. His reputation, which, many times, was enough in itself to gain a substantial settlement.

Fifty percent of a million was still better than one hundred percent of a quarter million.

And they would usually agree in the end.

He loved it.

He was large man, some of the muscle now turning to fat from the booze and the cigars and the lousy diet. He was in his early fifties, but looked more like a man of sixty. That was okay. Juries respected older men. They seemed wiser, somehow. His face was puffy and the eyes seemed too small for the face. The long, gray hair fell over his forehead in a losing effort to ward off the appearance of baldness. The heavy cheeks and jowls were streaked with red, as was the slightly large nose, the streaks caused by tiny blood vessels that had protested the regular intake of alcohol.

He took another drag from the cigar and pulled a notebook out of his shirt pocket. He grabbed the phone from the table and propped it on his chest, peering at the numbers through thick, metal-rimmed glasses. He punched some buttons and waited.

"Yes?"

"Mildred, this is George Barnes."

"Well . . . hello! Welcome to L.A."

"It's my pleasure. Which brings me to you."

"Yes indeed."

"You know what I like. As soon as possible. I need to unwind. It's been a long day."

"I'll take care of it. Are you staying at the Marriott, as usual?"

"Yup."

"I'll have someone there within a half—perhaps forty-five minutes. Your usual room?"

"Yup."

"Thanks for calling."

Barnes hung up the telephone and replaced it on the table. For a moment, he thought about taking a shower, then discarded the idea. He'd just have to take another one when the woman left.

In another room in the same hotel, a much smaller and more austere room, senior investigator William Powers of the Butler Casualty Insurance Company, was holding a meeting of his own. He'd managed to contact eleven private investigators who were now assembled in the cramped quarters, sitting on the bed, some even sitting on the floor, as Powers laid out the program.

Powers was a small man, with a thin face and a chin that came to a distinct point. The thin lips covered what seemed like too large teeth, something that the man was conscious of, for he rarely allowed the teeth to show. It gave one the impression that he had no teeth at all, the way he held his lips carefully in place as he talked.

The eyes were pinched by the skin around them, skin that had folded into a score of heavily etched wrinkles, as though pulled by some invisible force. All in all, the appearance was unattractive and when he spoke, in a high-pitched voice that seemed to fit the image, the result was less than impressive.

But the man's looks, like everything else about him, was a deception of sorts, in that the brain functioned well, within which a mind worked, one as devious as any who had tried to defraud the insurance company for which Powers worked.

He too had a reputation. Over the years, his ruthless pursuit of what he called the truth had resulted in the saving of millions of dollars for Butler Casualty. He believed that the company was required to pay reasonable damages to those injured by the actions of clients. And not one penny more.

The law was ubiquitous. And yet precise. The loss of an arm could mean relatively little if the arm belonged to an unemployed alcoholic. On the other hand, if the arm belonged to a professional pianist, it would be worth more. On the third hand, as Powers often liked to state it, if the pianist was a drug addict whose addiction was strong enough to cause an expected quick end to his career, the arm was worth much less.

There were 259 of them.

Two hundred fifty nine lives that had to examined carefully, each and every flaw discovered and verified. They all had them. They were human beings. And it was his job to dig up every bit of information that could have a bearing on the final award. A job he relished.

All his life he'd been looked upon with scorn for his appearance. The curse of genes. Few looked beneath the skin to see the true Williams Powers. Few cared. That he was hard-working, honest, virtuous . . . mattered not. He was judged by his appearance.

And when he'd discover that the handsome businessman in his thousand dollar suit was in fact a closet homosexual, and request a test to determine if the man carried the AIDS virus, they'd accuse him of being vile, when in fact it was simply a matter of justice. If the man was a candidate for a horrible death within five years, it was unfair that Butler Casualty be expected to pay an award as though the man had thirty useful years left. Simple justice applied to everyone, not just the so-called victim.

He'd earned the grudging respect of those in the room. They didn't like him, but they understood him. He stood there in front of them, his department store suit wrinkled and two years out of date, his feet planted apart in a stance that resembled a soldier standing at ease, and told them what he wanted.

"I've managed," he said, "to obtain a copy of the passenger list. As soon as it became apparent that the aircraft was in trouble, we used our computer to link up with PacRim's computer and make a print-out. Since we insure the airline for liability, we have the access codes.

"At the moment, it is unclear as to whether or not Butler Casualty is even liable in this case. However, a prudent course of action would dictate that we proceed as though we were, just in case. There is considerable confusion surrounding the circumstances that caused the problem and they may never be fully resolved. But you can be sure that there will be a number of attorneys foaming at the mouth to get in on this, and we need to cut them off at the pass.

"I have divided the names in the immediate Los Angeles area into eleven equal groups, according to location of residences, one group for each of you. I want you to work through the night, waking them up if you have to, and impress upon them that because the deaths were caused by a hostile act, the true facts of the case may not be known for years, if ever.

"In the interests of simple compassion, Butler Casualty will pay the next-of kin an amount of from one hundred thousand dollars to three hundred thousand dollars on the spot, provided they accept the payment as a full release of liability. Remember, the airline may not be at fault at all. Impress upon them the fact that it will be years before the courts decide who is at fault and apportion the degree of liability. Some court, ten years from now, may determine that Pacific Rim Airlines is actually blameless in this affair, and the money we offer does not prevent them from seeking damages from the guilty parties at some later date. The release applies only to the airline. So it is in their best interest to take the money now, while it's being offered in good faith."

There were snorts and laughs from his audience. One

of the investigators retorted, "Come on, Powers, save the bullshit for the peons. You know damn well you're in this up to your ass."

The insurance man's face reddened. "I'll hear no more of that! Anyone who desires to be involved in this will do it my way, or not at all. Is that clear?"

There were mumbles and then the group quieted down. There was money to be made here and Butler paid well for results.

Powers peered at them and resumed. "You'll have to make a quick judgment on the offer to present based on the surroundings you see. The size of the home, the furnishings, art objects, whatever. If you encounter a particularly expensive-looking place, get back to me. But we have to move quickly. The next-of-kin are being flown to Florida in the morning. I expect they'll be kept in Florida for some time. Any releases that are not signed before they depart will be much more difficult to obtain later, so I suggest you get at it. You have only hours to do your job."

He handed quantities of release forms to the investigators and they went on their way.

Powers took off his jacket and sat in the small chair near the window. He'd need to get to bed soon. This was going to be a long drawn out case, and he worked best when he got his sleep.

As he prepared for bed, he was struck by a strange thought. Almost a vision.

A Conestoga wagon traveling across the plains, suddenly attacked by hostile indians. The pioneers lying dead in the dust, their bodies riddled with arrows, their heads bereft of scalps. Months later, their next-of-kin launching suit against John Soule, as the man who had inspired them to make to perilous journey with the words, "Go west, young man."

American had become a nation where no one was responsible for their own actions. Whatever happened was someone else's fault. And the insurance companies were paying the price. When they raised the rates to compensate for the ridiculous judgments, they were pilloried in the press.

A smile came over his face.

The insurance companies were fighting back and it was having the desired effect. All across the country, doctors were being very careful, more than they'd ever been. They were demanding, and receiving, releases absolving them of any responsibility before they began dangerous medical procedures. General practitioners were acting as traffic cops, referring seriously ill patients to specialists in various fields, and confining their treatments to prescribing innocuous drugs.

Specialists were very careful in their recommendations, and in some cases, laying out the various alternatives and leaving the actual decision to the patient. And making sure that all releases were properly signed before performing operations.

And written reports issued to lawyers at the request of accident victims were now vague and muddied as to the extent of the injuries. Gone were words like "forever," or "definitely." In their place were phrases such as "undetermined period of time," or "possible, but not assured." Attorneys were having to rely on a stable of physicians who were referred to as "hired guns." Physicians who would examine a patient and be prepared to state in court that a certain injury was, indeed, permanent.

But these physicians were themselves under attack.

They were being branded in court as men who would testify to anything for a price. Men who were spending more time on pending litigation than the actual practice of medicine. The medical associations were putting pressure on them and so were the insurance companies. Pressures that were designed to eventually end the practice. Some subtle and some not so subtle. Malpractice insurance policies for "hit men" were becoming prohibitively expensive.

In addition, states were passing laws that refused to assess blame in accident cases. No-fault laws. Limits were being placed on amounts awarded in accident cases, no matter what the cause.

And insurance companies were refusing to insure certain risks whatsoever. In some cases, if the underwriter felt there was the remotest chance of a future claim, the insurance was denied.

The pendulum had swung back to the side of reason. The proof of the pudding was in the operating statement of Butler Casualty. After several years of mediocre earnings, the profits were becoming fat again.

He felt a shudder come over his body.

This case—the crashed airliner. If mishandled, it could seriously affect those profits. It was his job to make sure the case was not mishandled.

He would.

No matter what, he would.

Dan Wiseman sat in the Air Force van and tried to collect his thoughts. As was his custom, he made notes on a yellow legal pad as he tried to sort out in his own mind the route the investigation must take.

He was bone-tired. He'd been up for almost 24 hours and the horror of what he had seen had taken the sap out of him. The Army engineers were already hard at work, using divers and special nets to pull pieces of wreckage and parts of human remains from the watery crater.

One body was, miraculously, almost completely whole, and the two Atlanta doctors had done a quick, on-the-spot autopsy of sorts, determining that the bacteria, whatever it was, was dead, at least in this particular body. Tissue sections had been examined, then carefully packaged and rushed to Atlanta for further analysis. Water, soil, and air samples were being taken every fifteen minutes and so far, nothing seemed amiss. But the cautious doctors were wary of declaring the danger over. That would take days.

But it did look like the immediate danger of a possible killer epidemic was over . . . for the moment. The release of the tension that had gripped Wiseman since he'd entered the director's office hours ago seemed to drain him physically. He tried to fight it.

Bruce Evans had stated the case quite well. There were so many people in the world who had the knowledge and opportunity to create such a killer bacteria. But for what reason? Could it have been a terrorist act? So far, the CIA had no knowledge of any activity abroad that might connect, aside from what was already known about the Soviet experiments. The FBI had heard nothing domestically.

Of course, there were the American efforts in biological weaponry. The secret facility in Alabama. It would take some strong arm-twisting to get the Pentagon to allow the FBI to investigate those working in that building of horrors. If past history was any measure, the

Pentagon would demand to conduct their own secret inquiry.

And why Pacific Rim Airlines? Was it a random selection, or could it just as well have been another airline? Was someone on board the airliner the actual target, or was it the arrogant owner of the airline, Baxter Williams? A high-profile wheeler-dealer whose name was constantly mentioned in the press.

Was there a passenger responsible for the release of the bacteria on board, or had it been done remotely? On Dan's order, teams of agents were already hard at work on the west coast, investigating each and every person who had access to the airliner, not to mention the passengers themselves.

And then his thoughts turned back to the murder weapon itself. A microscopic thing that killed within hours. Something created in a test tube that might or might not be still active. Making thoughts of an investigation redundant if it was, in fact, still active.

It was almost more than he could handle.

It seemed a nightmare, divorced from reality. Impossible.

And yet . . .

He lay down on the hard floor of the van and closed his eyes. He almost begged for sleep, just an hour or two, something to take this feeling of malaise away. Give him some spark, get his mind to functioning properly, sweep away the fears, the negative thoughts that kept slipping into his consciousness.

Not thirty feet away from the van was a command center that had a comfortable cot he could use. But it also had radios and telephones and people. And the smell of fear. He'd wanted to be alone with his thoughts, so he'd chosen to crawl into the van instead.

Two hours later, he returned to the command center. he hadn't slept a wink.

# Chapter Seven

It was one in the morning in Washington when President Dalton finally went before the television cameras and talked to the American people. He did it from the press room, standing stiffly at the lectern, waiting for the red light atop the television camera to blink on.

As soon as it did, he began his remarks.

"My fellow Americans. I regret to inform you that a commercial airliner with two hundred fifty-nine people on board has crashed in Florida. I wish to express my deepest sympathies to the families of those who perished in this tragic accident.

"There has been considerable speculation in the press and on television regarding the cause of this accident. I would like you to be aware that at the present time, we don't really know what happened. We do know that the crew and passengers became very ill and died within hours. In fact, they died before the plane actually hit the ground. That has been confirmed without question, using some classified Air Force equipment that I am not at liberty to discuss. What we don't know is what caused the illnesses.

"Based on discussions between the crew of the stricken airliner and those on the ground, the Center for Disease Control in Atlanta has indicated that the most logical explanation would involve exposure to toxic chemicals of some kind. These chemicals could have been shipped as freight and their containers accidentally broken. It is possible that the release of these chemicals was a deliberate act by some sick, demented person or persons. We simply do not know at this time.

"I have ordered the FBI to thoroughly investigate the crash of this airliner and have directed that all local, state and federal law enforcement agencies provide assistance. At this very moment, elements of the Army and Air Force are offering assistance at the crash site.

"I am sure that we will have answers to the many questions we all have very soon. In the meantime, I urge all Americans to avoid making judgments until the facts are fully known.

"There are many things that could have caused this terrible accident. While it's entirely possible that the accident was caused by a criminal act, we have no evidence to support that theory at this time. And until we do, I would like to suggest that we all keep an open mind.

"As soon as we have some factual information, I will make sure that it is made available. In the meantime, I hope all of you will join with me in offering our prayers to the families of those who lost their lives.

"Good night and God bless you all."

He turned and left the press room without answering any questions. Within three minutes, the majority of media pundits were calling the speech an unmitigated disaster. The president, they screeched, was covering something up.

FBI director Edward Spencer sat at his own desk and

switched off the television set, using a small remote control device. He turned his attention back to the thick file in front of him. A file marked "Top Secret."

It was a transcript of the interrogation of one Boris Barakov, a Russian scientist who had defected to the United States three years ago.

He had been heavily involved in the Russian chemical and biological weapons development program and had been seized by feelings of deep remorse. After witnessing the aftermath of some field tests in the mountains of Afghanistan, he'd managed to escape to Pakistan with the help of some rebel tribesmen, and turned himself over to American CIA agents in Islamabad.

He knew much about the Russian program and when he reached the United States, he was turned over to the FBI for further interrogation, since it was the FBI who would have to eventually set up a new identity for this man.

The transcript was thick, running to one hundred and seventy pages.

And there, on pages 123 through 132, was a reference to a new bacterium that the Russians had developed. It was transmitted in water vapor and designed to attack the stomach and intestines of humans. Tests had shown that it disabled a subject within ten minutes of exposure and killed within one hour. The symptoms, as described by Barakov, were identical to those described by the pilot of Pacific Rim 234. Barakov knew how the bacterium had been produced, but that information was not included in this file. That information had gone to Huntsville.

The director closed the file and leaned back in his

chair.

Before being appointed to the post of director of the FBI by President Dalton, he'd been a judge. Right now he wished he was back behind the bench.

The Russians had created a monster germ. Obviously, Huntsville had duplicated the thing in an effort to develop ways to combat it.

Now, somebody had their hands on it and had used it to kill 259 people on board an airplane.

The director cursed as he picked up the telephone. Mickey Serson had said that the Pentagon would cooperate fully. This time, they damn well better.

President Robert Dalton was awakened from a sound sleep by the ringing of the telephone and told that Gen. Waldo Smith had arrived from Huntsville. Before retiring for the night, the president had left strict instructions that he was to be awakened immediately upon the general's arrival.

He replaced the telephone headset in its cradle and sat up. The pain in his head had receded slightly but still made its presence known.

He stood up and waited for the now-familiar dizzy spell to leave him. After a moment, it faded and he slipped on a blue, silk robe and his leather slippers and headed downstairs to the Oval Office.

The general and a very tired Mickey Serson were already seated, drinking coffee. They both stood up when the president entered the room. Dalton smiled and shook hands with the general. "It was good of you to come, General, on such short notice. I appreciate it very much. Please sit down."

"Thank you, sir."

The general sneered inwardly at the affected graciousness of the president. He'd been ordered to Washington immediately and forced to fly in weather that was below normal minimums. He still wondered how in hell that Air Force pilot had managed to land at Andrews in the middle of a raging snowstorm.

Dalton poured some coffee for himself and then took his seat behind the desk. He opened the cigar box, took out a cigar, thought better of it and put it back in the box.

"General Smith," he began, "As you are no doubt aware, there is considerable speculation as to the cause of the illnesses that created the problem with the airliner that crashed last night. I need to know two things.

"First, is there anything in our arsenal of biological weapons that could have caused the symptoms as they have been described to you?"

The general blinked and broke eye contact with the president. He stared at his coffee for a moment and then said, "That's difficult to say, sir. Upon receiving the phone call from Mr. Serson, I instructed our people to look into the matter tomorrow . . . today, rather . . . and get back to me as soon as possible."

President Dalton leaned forward. "You mean you don't know?"

General Smith seemed very uncomfortable. He shifted in his chair and said, "Well, we're talking about specific symptoms here and there are several weapons that cause similar symptoms—several. It's very hard to say whether or not one of them could create the exact symptoms. Besides, I understand that you've already determined that it was a toxic chemical of—"

President Dalton cut him off.

"General Smith. I'm not prepared to scare the living shit out of the American people until I know what the hell I'm talking about. You are the man in charge of our research project. You can't possibly expect me to sit here and accept the notion that you don't know what the hell is going on at your facility."

The general stiffened perceptibly. "Mr. President, the entire project is most secret. I can assure you in all candor that there is no way on earth that anything developed in the research center could possibly be connected with that airplane crash. If I seem to hesitate, it's only because of the absolute need to maintain security—"

Again, the president cut him off.

"Look, General, you're talking to the president of the United States. When I ask you a direct question, I expect a direct answer. Now, stow the bullshit and tell me what I want to know."

General Smith seemed to come to attention in a seated position. "Mr. President," he said, the voice beginning to boom a little, "with all due respect, I resent being addressed in this manner. I am a general officer in the United States Army with serious and immense responsibilities. Again, I state, unequivocally, that the Huntsville research center could not possibly be connected in any way with—"

"That's enough!"

The president was standing now, his eyes blazing, his hands formed into fists resting on the desk. He looked for all the world like he was about to leap over the desk and physically attack the man.

"You couldn't possibly make such blanket pronouncements. I am your commander-in-chief. You will answer my questions or face a summary court-martial post-haste! Do I make myself clear?"

The general locked eyes with the president for a brief moment and then looked away. In a voice filled with his own anger, he said, "Yes, sir. We do have a bacteria that produces symptoms similar to those described to me."

President Dalton resumed his seat. Once more, he opened the cigar box and withdrew a thick, brown stoogie. He went through his normal routine as he struggled to regain his composure. The cigar finally lit, he turned his attention back to the general.

"General, the FBI is in charge of the investigation. I want you to speak with Director Spencer personally in the morning. You are hereby ordered to reveal to him whatever is asked of you. I will sign an order to that effect.

"He will want to know the backgrounds and current status of each and every employee under your command. Probably going back five years. I would suggest that you get with it so that the information will be available to Mr. Spencer in the morning. Is your Huntsville computer tied in to the Pentagon?"

"Yes, sir."

"Good. Then you can spend the balance of the night putting that together."

The president took a deep drag on the cigar and leaned back in his chair. "If it gives you any comfort, General, I too am sure that there is no connection between what happened to that unfortunate airplane and the research center. But, I have pledged to the FBI my full cooperation and they shall have it.

"My second question now seems redundant. I was going to ask if there was any possible way that someone outside the research center could have gained access to the knowledge that such a bacteria existed. The answer is obvious. Of course there is.

"The FBI will have to explore each and every one of those possibilities and rule them out. Unless they cotton on to some lead that allows them to dismiss the research center altogether."

The general seemed almost in pain. "What," he asked, "makes the FBI think that we could be involved in the first place?"

The president sighed and said, "It's not that they think you are involved. It's simply the process of elimination. They don't know where to start, so they begin with the obvious. You make germs. Germs seem the most likely cause of the illnesses. A natural connection. Don't take it personally.

"Again, thank you for coming."

"Thank you, sir."

Mickey Serson stood up, nodded to the president and said to the general, "Right this way, General."

When he returned, Mickey shook his head. "Jesus Christ! I wonder how many more there are like him."

Robert Dalton glanced at Mickey and then stared at the cigar in his hand. "Don't knock it, Mick. We need guys like him."

Mickey grunted. "I'm not so sure. In any case, while you were sleeping, Spencer went through some old files on the Barakov defection. Remember him?"

"No. Who's Barakov?"

"He's a Russian scientist who defected three years ago. He was working with the Soviet biological weapons program. Anyway, the Soviets did develop a bacteria type that produces exactly the symptoms we're looking for. That information was given to Huntsville, so Smith knows damn well which bug did the job."

Dalton sucked on the cigar for a moment and said, "Well, he admitted that they have one that could do it. The question is really . . . who else has the damn thing now? And where did they get it? From us or the Russians?"

The two men looked at each other silently for a moment and then Dalton stubbed the cigar out in the large crystal ash tray on the desk.

His voice seemed uncertain as he asked, "Do you ever wonder, Mickey . . . if we're in over our heads?"

Al Disario found Donald James at the airport, still attending to the needs of some of the distraught relatives. He asked him to come outside and sit in the car.

"Mr. James," he said, "are you aware of any FAA inspection on Flight Two-three-four before it left for Hawaii?"

Donald James shook his head. "No, but that doesn't mean anything. It could have happened without the word getting back to me. The maintenance people would know about it and so would Baxter Williams. They'd be required to advise him of any snap inspection after the fact."

Disario grimaced. "Williams is at home. I wonder, would you phone him and ask him if he's aware of any inspection?"

"I'll be happy to," answered James.

Disario handed him the mobile telephone and James dialed the number. The phone was answered by Maria, the maid, on the second ring.

"Wheeliams residence."

"Marie, this is Donald James. Do you remember me?"

"*Sí* . . . Mr. James."

"Maria . . . I need to talk to Mr. Williams."

The maid lowered her voice. "Oh . . . *Señor.* Mr. Wheeliams, he in bed. Very seek."

James groaned. "You mean drunk."

"*Sí.*"

James turned to Disario and said, "He's drunk. You'd better go over there."

Disario rubbed a hand over his chin and said, "Maybe you should come with me and ask him. He might talk to you quicker than he'd talk to me. He hasn't been the most cooperative man in the world."

James grinned. "Sure, I'll be happy to talk to him. Let's go."

They drove to the affluent Bel Air section of Los Angeles and parked the car on the street. The gate was closed, barring access to the driveway. James got out of the car and pushed the button on the intercom.

"Yes?"

"Maria, I need to talk to you. This is Donald James."

"*Señor,* it is very late. Mr. Wheeliams is asleep."

"I know that. I want to talk to you. It's important. Open the gate."

There were other words of protest but finally, the lock buzzed and the gate slid open. While Al Disario waited in the car, Donald James ran up the driveway and rang the doorbell. Maria opened the door. She recognized him and from the look on her face, sensed trouble.

"Sorry, Marie," he said, "but I have to see him."

He swept past her protestations and made his way up

the stairs and opened the bedroom door.

Williams and his wife were both asleep.

James cleared his throat and a startled Mrs. Williams sat up quickly, drawing the bedspread up around her throat. Her eyes wide with fear at first, and then confusion as she recognized him.

"Mr. James? What on earth?"

He apologized. "I'm sorry, Mrs. Williams, but I must talk to your husband."

The fear was replaced by anger. "What right have you got to barge in here . . . my God!"

James ignored her and started to shake the seemingly comatose Williams.

"Wake up! Wake up!"

One eye opened. The odor of the man's breath was a heart-stopper.

"Wake up!".

A few light slaps on the cheek. Mrs. Williams reached for the telephone. "I'm calling the police," she said.

James ignored her.

"Baxter!"

Both eyes were now open.

"The FAA! Did they pull an inspection yesterday?"

He was still drunk. The words were mumbles. "Whaaa! Leave meee alooonn!"

Another slap. Harder this time.

"Answer me! Did you see anyone from the FAA yesterday?"

Confusion . . . a brain trying to function. The eyes trying to focus. And finally, "No. No FAA. Two weeks ago . . ."

James rose and smiled at a terrified Mrs. Williams. "Sorry for the intrusion, Mrs. Williams. Couldn't be helped. Have a nice day."

And then he left.

Back in the car with Disario, he couldn't help the feeling of excitement he felt. It was increased as he heard the sirens in the distance.

As Disario put the car in gear, James told him.

"He says the last inspection was two weeks ago. But, he's pretty loaded. He might be confused."

Disario gripped the wheel tightly and cursed. "I don't think so," he said. He pulled the car to the side of the road, parked and asked, "What's the number at your office?"

"My office?"

"Yes."

"It's seven-five-two-seven-eight-five-five."

Disario dialed the number on the mobile phone and asked for Agent Taylor.

Donald James could hear only one side of the conversation.

"Jim? Disario. Get a complete description from the lady of the FAA guy and then reinterview her contacts. Put as many people as you have to on it. I'll be back soon."

He pressed a button on the telephone and then dialed another.

"This is RAC Disario, Los Angeles. Patch me through to AD Wiseman at the crash scene."

While he waited, he turned to Donald James and said, "I appreciate your help. I want you to forget everything you've heard tonight."

James nodded. "No problem."

Disario smiled and said, "No offense, but I need you to step out of the car while I make this call."

Donald James felt his heart sink. For a moment, he'd felt like he was an integral part of the investigation. It felt good. Very good. Instead of the complicated mixture of anger and helplessness, empathy for the families, he was actually doing something. He stepped out of the car and drew the cool, night air into his lungs.

In Florida, Dan Wiseman took the call from Al Disario on the field telephone in the command center. Al sounded as tired as Dan felt. The Los Angeles resident agent in charge wanted to talk to Dan on a secure line. He had something important. The nearest secure line was Tampa, some fifteen miles away. It seemed on the surface to be a needless precaution, but it wasn't. Not only had the president indicated that the lid had to stay on regarding information relevant to this case, but Dan Wiseman was well aware of the growing concern being felt in all quarters regarding the actual import of what had happened.

If their worst fears were actually realized, a new, enterprising group of psychopathic killers was in possession of a deadly and potentially devastating weapon. Exactly who they were was unknown. What their plans were was also unknown. But Dan had the gnawing feeling in his gut that part of their plan would include extensive media coverage to bring home whatever the message was. If and when that happened, no one could accurately predict how the American people would react. They were liable to do anything.

He had one of the agents drive him to the Tampa office and Disario's call came in three minutes later.

The two men knew each other well. Al had been his

right hand when Dan had been in charge of the Los Angeles office. They'd always worked well together and at times, seemed to be able to read each other's minds. In spite of the circumstances, it was good to hear the man's voice.

"How're ya doing, Dan?"

"So far, so good, Al. We may have gotten lucky. Whatever it is doesn't seem to be contagious any more. What've you got?"

"Dan, we've got a solid lead. An FAA inspector was seen checkin' out the airplane a few hours before it took off. Except that he seems bogus. I've called the FAA, but it's the middle of the night and I can't get anyone to spring with information. I need your help."

Dan could feel his heartbeat quicken. "Have you got a good description of the guy?"

"Yes. I'll have an artist's sketch distributed to all law enforcement agencies within an hour. But some pictures from the FAA might help. Maybe the guy actually worked for them. He seemed to know what he was doin'."

Dan thought for a minute and then said, "I'll get to work immediately. Spencer will spring something loose. When you send out the bulletin, made sure you tag it with another label. It's a top priority, but we don't want anyone knowing it's tied in to the plane crash investigation."

"I'll take care of it. Anything new at your end?"

"Not yet. I'll have whatever I can get wired to your office. Keep me advised."

"I'll do it. You sound a little tired, Dan."

"Yeah. It isn't likely to get better either. I'll talk to you soon."

They said their goodbyes and then Dan called Washington. Edward Spencer wasn't sleeping either. Dan relayed the information and told the director what he wanted. Spencer told him it would be done. He also had some other news.

"Dan," he said. "I passed your other requests along to the president. He's brought up a Gen. Waldo Smith from Huntsville. Right now the general is over at the Pentagon putting together a brief for us. But he's pretty well confirmed that Huntsville does have a weapon capable of producing the symptoms experienced by the crew and passengers. That doesn't necessarily mean it's tied in, but you know as well as I do that it's a possible.

"I also reviewed the Barakov file. There's no question in my mind that the bacteria matches.

"I'm going to have the Huntsville office investigate the entire operation out there. I'll relay anything I get to you. The CIA is cooperating as well, but nothing's come back yet. That'll probably take a little time.

"What do the doctors have to say?"

Dan rubbed his eyes and told him. "They've looked at some slides and they're sure. A bacteria killed those people. They say every test they've done so far indicates that it's dead. The slides have been sent up to Atlanta so they can properly identify it, but the doctors say they've never seen anything like it.

"They've requested that every single body be transported Atlanta for a complete examination, so we're doing it. We've managed to get the cooperation of a Tampa ice-making plant and we're using that as a temporary morgue. The bodies are going from there to MacDill and then to Atlanta.

"The curious thing is this: You remember that the last

reports from the Air Force indicated that the heating system had failed. Well, according to the doctors, the bacteria died because of that failure. Things just got too damn cold. They say the bacteria uses the feces in the intestine as a source of food. They think the thing would still be alive if the heating system hadn't failed. Seems a strange coincidence, don't you think?"

The director's voice was tinged with fear. "Jesus!"

Dan continued. "I'm having the results from the CDC tests sent directly to you. But I'd be willing to bet money that this FAA guy screwed around with the heating system. I'll need a schematic of a ten-eleven. Better send one to Al Disario as well."

Spencer grunted. "No need. The NTSB boys are already in St. Pete. Have one of your people talk to a man named Lou Holt. He'll have plenty of copies. They're staying at the Ramada near the St. Pete airport. That's where the remains of the ten-eleven will be reassembled. I'll express one out to Disario."

Dan was scribbling furiously on his yellow pad. "Great. I'll be in touch soon."

He hung up the telephone and switched off the device that scrambled the conversation. Then he leaned back in the chair and tried to gather his strength.

There was so much to do.

## Chapter Eight

Police Officer Bill Turner parked the cruiser alongside the shoulder of winding Mulholland Drive, not far from downtown Los Angeles, and together with his partner, Zac Hamilton, grabbed his cap and nightstick and headed for the waiting hikers.

The two men had called in a report of a dead body and Turner and Hamilton had been sent to investigate.

One of the hikers seemed badly shaken. He was sitting on the ground. The other came forward to greet the two cops.

"Hi. My name's Tilson. I made the call. The body's over here."

The two cops followed the man to a spot that was less than twenty feet from the road and covered with brush. He stopped and pointed to a leg that was clearly visible. "There. You can see it from here. If you don't mind, I'd rather not have to look at it again."

Turner grunted and looked at his partner. It was his turn. Turner would look at the body while Hamilton took the hiker's statement.

He walked a few feet, being careful not to disturb anything, and looked at the body. He'd been on the force for four years and had seen more than a few bodies in his time. But this one almost made him lose his breakfast.

The body lay on its back, spread-eagled in the dirt. The face was gone, smashed beyond recognition, as though pulverized by some heavy object. The hands had suffered the same fate. Nearby, a rock the size of a football was covered with blood, obviously the instrument used.

The body was nude, and there were three small-caliber bullet holes in the chest, almost dead center, the grouping less than five inches. There might have been additional wounds to the head, but it was impossible to tell at this point. Whoever killed the man had either been consumed with hate, or was very sick indeed.

"Zac," Turner called to his partner. "Call it in. It's a body all right. A real mess. I'll take a look and see if I can find anything."

Less than an hour later, a report on the discovery of the body reached the desk of Capt. Wayne Peterson. He looked it over, remembered the bulletin from the FBI and made a call. Shortly after that, the captain and Special Agent Jim Taylor were seated in the assistant medical examiner's office, talking to the doctor who had examined the body at the scene and made a preliminary report. His name was Withers. Doctor Henry Withers.

"You want to have a look?" he asked the FBI man.

Taylor nodded and the men headed for the examining room. On the way, the doctor filled them in.

"He was a redhead all right. Shot three times in the chest and twice in the head. That's what killed him. The smashing of the face and hands was probably to prevent a quick I.D. He was killed somewhere else and the body dumped where the police found it. Kinda weird in a way. If they really wanted to hide the body, they picked a strange way to do it."

Taylor grunted. "Maybe not. You said he was killed before midnight last night."

The doctor nodded. "Right. The body was moved very soon after the killing. As you requested, we've done a rather quick autopsy and I can tell you that he's about mid-thirties, probably six, one, about two hundred pounds and . . .a very heavy coke user."

Taylor's eyebrows went up. "Really?"

"Really. I'd say about five hundred bucks a day. The heart was showing some damage already."

They stood by a table and the doctor pulled back a green sheet. Taylor looked at the body and shook his head.

"Will you still be able to make an I.D. with dental records?"

The doctor grinned. "It won't be easy, but I think we can do it."

Taylor wondered what it was that made anybody want to be a pathologist. "Doctor, I'd like to know everything you can tell me about this guy. Blood type, what he ate for dinner, the works. And I need it quickly. Can you help me?"

"No problem."

"How much time will it take?"

Doctor Withers pursed his lips for a moment and then asked, "Is this related to that plane thing?"

Taylor hesitated for a moment and then shook his head. "No. It has nothing to do with that. But it *is* important."

The doctor looked at him out of the corners of his eyes and smiled. "Hmmm," he mumbled. "Give me two hours. I should be able to have it done by then."

Taylor held out his hand. "Thanks. I'll have someone here to pick up the report."

The doctor shook the hand and headed back to the body. The two policeman left the morgue and headed for their respective cars. Taylor stuck out his hand. "Captain, I appreciate your help. This may be our guy or it may not. Anything you can come up with from your people on the street will be appreciated. If the guy had that strong a cocaine habit, somebody must know him. I'll see what I can find at my end. In the meantime, if you come across anything else, let me know."

Captain Peterson shook the hand and got in his car. Taylor got in his and headed for the federal building. There were some things to be done, but he didn't want to say anything on the radio.

Janet Talbot had stayed the night with Elizabeth Martin, finally persuading her to go to bed at close to three in the morning. Now, as she padded from the living room sofa to the kitchen to make some coffee, she noticed a man coming up the front walkway. It wasn't anyone she knew.

She rushed to the door so she could answer it before the doorbell woke up Liz, and poked her head out into the morning air. The man looked like he'd been up all night as well, with big pouches under his eyes and a suit that looked like it had been slept in.

He saw Janet and drew up short. "Mrs. Martin?"

The voiced sounded as though the man smoked to excess. The words seemed to come out after being rubbed against sandpaper.

Janet held up her hand. "No. Mrs. Martin is sleeping. Who are you and what do you want?"

The man reached in his pocket and pulled out a card which he handed to her. "My name is Frank Tercel. I'm an insurance investigator but I'm not here about that. I have some very good news for Mrs. Martin that I'd like to discuss with her."

Janet looked at him in awe. "Good news! What possible good news could you have. Her husband has been killed in a plane crash, for God's sake."

The man looked at his feet and put his hands in his pockets. "I'm aware of that, Mrs. . . .?"

"Talbot."

"Mrs. Talbot. I offer my condolences, but nothing can bring Mr. Martin back and that's a fact. However, a friend of mine, someone I'm sure you've heard of, George Barnes, has agreed to represent several of the families of the victims of the crash. I wanted Mrs. Martin to know that, should she wish, he would represent her interests as well.

"I'm sure you understand the importance of this. George Barnes is one of the nation's leading, if not *the* leading, trial lawyer who handles liability cases. Normally, he's simply not available to ordinary people. But since he's been retained by some prominent people, he agreed to make himself available to some of the families who might be affected, in the interests of fairness.

"Naturally, there's a limit to the number of people

he can represent, simple logistics being the main factor. I just wanted Mrs. Martin to be aware of the opportunity."

Janet shook her head. She'd never been involved in a law suit of any kind. Her husband had died of a heart attack three years ago. The lawyer for the company he had worked for had taken care of legal matters for her, at no charge.

But she had heard of George Barnes. Who hadn't? The man was famous for his courtroom antics and his penchant for women, and was a frequent guest on television talk shows. George Barnes meant money and lots of it.

Still, she hesitated. It had been a horrid night and Liz was working on her fifth hour of much-needed sleep. "Could you come back, Mr. Tercel? She's really just gotten to sleep. It was a terrible blow and . . ."

He was shaking his head. "I'd like to say yes, Mrs. Talbot, but I'm afraid that would be impossible. As I've explained, Mr. Barnes can handle only so many cases and in about two hours, his case load will be entirely closed."

They stood there looking at each other for a moment. Janet didn't really want to wake Liz, but . . . She opened the door and told the man to come in. "I'll talk to her. Please wait in the living room."

Tercel smiled, entered and took a seat.

Janet quietly entered the bedroom and carefully sat on the edge of the bed. Elizabeth was sound asleep, a look of tension on her face, the eyes underneath the lids moving rapidly, jerking back and forth. Her lips were opening and closing as though she were trying to say something, in the midst of a nightmare. A thin layer of perspiration clung to her upper lip and forehead.

"Liz?"

Janet kept her voice low but the eyes opened immediately. For a moment, there was a look of panic in the eyes and then she recognized her friend.

"Janet . . . God! I was having the most horrible nightmare. It was just awful!" She shuddered and put her hand to her eyes.

"Liz, there's a man here to talk to you. He's . . ."

Liz shook her head. "I can't see anyone just now."

Janet took a cold hand and rubbed it with her own. "Liz, I understand. But this man—well, I know how awful this is, but you really should talk to him. He—he's connected with George Barnes, you know, the lawyer. He says that he can get Barnes to represent you. I guess some wealthy people have hired Barnes to sue the airline or something. Anyway, he says he'll represent you too.

"I know it's a bad time, but there'll never be a good one. I think you should talk to him."

Elizabeth looked confused. "Sue? I don't want to sue anyone."

Janet gnawed on her lower lip for a moment and then said, "Liz, I know how you feel. But you've got to think of the future. When Bill died, I was devastated. I know how you feel. Really, I do. But Bill had a lousy ten thousand dollar life insurance policy that the funeral just about took care of. That and paying off some debts. I had to go to work right away.

"I don't want that for you. I don't know what Mark did regarding insurance, but I know what I read in the papers. Whenever there's a plane crash, people always sue. There was a man right here in Costa Mesa who was on that plane that went down in Chicago a few years ago. His family got quite a bit of money from what I understand.

"I know you aren't interested in money. But if Barnes will look after it for you, why not let him?"

Elizabeth sighed and closed her eyes. "Janet, I know you mean well, but I just can't . . . I just can't."

Janet didn't want to press it, but in her heart she knew that there was a possibility that Elizabeth Martin could end up with millions of dollars being represented by George Barnes. It was an opportunity, just like the man in the rumpled suit had said. She struggled to find the words that would convince Liz of the wisdom of her thinking. And then Liz made it easy for her.

"You talk to him," she said. "If you think it'll be all right, then you take care of it."

Janet let go of the hand, brushed back the hair from Liz's forehead and left the bedroom.

"Mr. Tercel," she said, as she sat down in the chair across from the man, "tell me what we need to do."

Tercel smiled as he drew the papers from his jacket pocket. This could be a good one. If the woman in the bedroom was the same age as this one, then the odds were that the man had been young. From the looks of the neighborhood, he was making a good living. It meant that he had many years of good income ahead of him. It meant that he was probably in good health. It meant that the suit could be for millions.

It was his second call of the morning. He'd signed

up the first family without trouble.

He could tell by the look in this woman's eyes that this one wouldn't be a problem either.

Dan Wiseman looked at Bruce Evans and then he read the report over again. Finally, he threw the report on the table in the command center and said, "This is all medical jargon. Tell me what we're dealing with here in words I can understand."

"Okay. The preliminary report from Atlanta indicates that the bacteria introduced on that airplane was a parasitic pathogen that uses human feces as food. It entered the respiratory system, gained access to the blood stream, found its way to the intestine and went to work. It was genetically altered and specifically designed for that job. The agitation produced by this upheaval caused the terrible distress initially and death was actually caused by damage done to the stomach and large intestine. The damage occurred very quickly."

The doctor looked away for a moment and then he said, "They all bled to death, Dan. The bleeding was so intense it sent them all into shock so they didn't suffer long. But that's what killed them . . . they bled to death."

"Jesus!"

"Finally, the report says that the bacteria may have had a reproductive capacity that's unheard of. They estimate that it could multiply itself every fifteen minutes as long as the food supply was available."

He stopped for a moment and then continued. "The only thing that saved us, and this is what's scary, is the fact that the heating system broke down on the aircraft. The bacteria was killed by the cold. If it hadn't been for that, everything around here would be contaminated beyond all possible hope. Atlanta is guessing that the bacteria survives in temperatures above fifty or so degrees Fahrenheit. Anything colder than that and it dies."

Dan let the breath he'd been holding escape. "So the crash site is safe?"

Evans shook his head. "Too soon to tell for sure. The bacteria taken from the bodies is dead, and all of the tests have been negative so far, but we can't be sure until everything has been tested . . . or . . ."

"Or what?"

"Or about three days. If the bacteria survived at all, it'll start to show up in three days minimum. But my gut instinct tells me that we're okay. This thing was designed for a particular purpose. I don't know what it is, but I'm sure those who developed it are aware of its lethal properties as well as its control mechanism, in other words, temperature. If I had to guess, I'd say that whoever placed this on board that airplane also made sure the heating system would fail. If only as a precaution."

"Why do you say that?" asked Dan.

"Because there was always the chance that the plane, when it crashed in the Pacific Ocean, would release the bacteria to the oceanic food chain. Maybe it works with them too. The whole oceanic population could have been infected. I don't think they wanted to take the chance."

Dan could feel the beginnings of a headache. He pulled a small package of aspirin from his pocket and took three of them, using cold coffee to wash them down.

"You said there was a lot of bleeding. According to the controllers in Los Angeles, the pilot talked about vomiting and cramps and diarrhea. He never mentioned blood."

"I know. There had to be a lot of blood in the vomit. I don't know why he didn't mention it."

The two men grew silent for a moment and then Bruce said, "Dan, this is a really serious situation. It'll take years to figure out how they designed this thing. More years to find a way to combat it. Whoever is responsible has us by the nuts. All of the nuclear weapons in the world won't help us if we don't find out who they are and stop them."

Dan picked up a copy of the report. "Did a copy of this go to the director?"

"Yes."

Dan slapped the doctor on the shoulder. "I'll let you in on a few things. It won't take long to figure out how they designed it. You were the one who tipped me to that. This *is* the thing that Barakov was talking about. And Huntsville *did* produce a twin, using the info supplied by Barakov. We know that much, thanks to that memory of yours. You saved us a lot of time, Bruce. You'd make a good cop, you know that?"

The doctor was starting to blush. "Oh well."

Dan picked up the newly-installed scrambler telephone and pushed some buttons. He told the person who answered that he wanted to talk to the director. Edward Spencer was on the phone in seconds.

"Dan?"

"Yes, sir."

"How's it going down there?"

"So far, so good. Bruce thinks we might be safe for the moment. Have you read the report from Atlanta?"

"Yes."

"And?"

"It looks more and more like this is tied to Huntsville. I haven't talked to General Smith yet, but the interrogations have already started in Huntsville. As soon as I have anything I'll let you know."

"Very good."

"I've been in touch with the FAA and photos of former and present employees have been wired to Disario."

"Good. I'm heading for Los Angeles. There's nothing more I can do here. I'll take Gil with me. Do you want him to hold another press conference before I leave?"

"Yes. The text is on its way now. It's all crap, but that's the way the president wants to play it at the moment. Frankly, I don't think it'll put out any fires."

Dan rubbed his forehead. "Anything else?"

"Just find them, Dan. The White House is practically coming apart."

"I can understand that. So am I."

He hung up the phone and leaned back in the chair. Through the window of the command center, he could see the work continuing. Parts of bodies, bits of metal, pieces of the aircraft interior; all being dredged up from a crater in the middle of a sports field.

Hundreds of men in protective clothing working

feverishly to recover each and every particle of the airplane and its contents.

And somewhere, he knew not where, the monster who had created a killer bacteria was planning his or her next move.

One of the NSTB men approached the desk. "Mr. Wiseman?"

Dan looked up at him wearily. "Yes?"

"Sir, they've just recovered the cockpit voice recorder."

"Good."

"They'll have to check it out in Washington."

"I know. Well, get with it."

The man turned and left.

In a moment, Gil Parker approached, a long sheet of paper in his hand.

"This just came down from Washington. The official statement. You want to see it before I go out there and face the animals?"

Dan shook his head. "As soon as you hold your press conference, we're heading to L.A."

"Right." Parker turned and headed out of the trailer.

Dan rubbed his tired eyes. It didn't matter what the official statement stated. It was pure fiction anyway. Nobody in their right mind was about to tell the American people what was actually happening. Or what might happen next.

Helen Porter was seated in her small office and interviewing one of the security people employed to screen passengers and visitors entering the terminal building.

At LAX, the security checks were done almost at the entrance to the airport itself, so people passing through the screening might be going to any number of flights. It was impossible to pinpoint a particular destination.

The woman Helen was interviewing had been asked to recall anything suspicious from the period of ten in the morning until one in the afternoon the day before.

Aside from the normal allotment of passengers carrying scissors or other sharp instruments in their hand-luggage, there had been nothing untoward.

Helen persisted. "Are you sure? Take your time. Usually, there are some weird images on that x-ray machine that get checked out. Hair dryers, toys for the kids, things that look like weapons.

The woman laughed. "Oh, yeah. We had all that stuff. But there was nuthin' really different. We get that every single day. You know that, Miss Porter."

"What about people? Anyone look nervous or excited?"

The security guard laughed again. "Sure . . . but that happens all the time too. White knucklers, old folks on their first airplane ride . . . I wish I could be more help. Jus' what is it you're lookin' for?"

Helen Porter shook her head. "I don't really know, Millie. I guess something that might tie in to that crash yesterday. I was hoping maybe one of you had noticed something . . . anything unusual."

The woman looked truly sad. "I wish I was more of a help . . . it's just that . . ." She hesitated and her black forehead wrinkled.

Helen leaned forward and asked, "What is it?"

Millie's eyes widened as the image came into focus. "The president said that this was a toxic chemical or somethin' didn't he?"

"Never mind that. What do you remember?"

"Well . . . there was this man . . . good lookin' too. He had a lot of glass tubes with different colored stuff in them. On the x-ray, we didn't know what it was so we made him open his briefcase up. He said it was chemicals. Samples, he said. He said they weren't dangerous and he had a letter from the FAA that said he was authorized to carry chemicals on an airplane. So we let it pass."

Helen's heart sank. It happened all the time. Nothing special. Besides, it wasn't a toxic chemical that had caused the problem, no matter what the president said. She was convinced of that.

Nevertheless, she asked some more questions and made notes. She still had two other security people to interview. Maybe they'd seen something important.

# Chapter Nine

Al Disario entered the coffee shop for the maintenance workers at LAX with a thick envelope tucked under his arm. The envelope held photos of FAA inspectors who were either still employed or had once worked for the agency.

Helen Porter had gathered together the five people who had seen the FAA inspector working on the ill-fated 1011 and the six of them sat around two tables that had been pushed together, drinking coffee.

Disario pulled up a chair and introduced himself. "Hi. I'm Al Disario, FBI. I've brought some pictures with me and I'd like you guys to take a look and see if any one of these people is the person you saw near that airplane."

He opened the envelope and placed the pictures on the table. Within a minute, one of the men exclaimed, "This is the guy!"

The others looked at the photo and agreed. It was definitely the one. Disario thanked the men and they went about their business.

He turned to Helen Porter. "Ms. Porter. You've been a big help. I can't thank you enough."

She grinned. "Forget the thanks. Who is this guy?"

Disario looked sad. "I can't tell you that. I'm sorry. I hope you understand."

"If you tell me, maybe I can be of further help. I know my way around this place pretty good."

Disario patted her hand. "My boss will be arriving soon. I'll see what I can do. Thanks again."

He turned and left her there, drinking coffee.

Dan Wiseman looked as tired as he felt.

He sat a desk in a small office in the Los Angeles bureau office and tried to sort out his thoughts. Al Disario sat silently and watched as his boss tried to put it all together.

Dan made notes on a yellow pad of the various components of the puzzle.

The photos of the FAA people had arrived. The mechanics had been shown the photos and had already made an identification of the supposed FAA man.

Once he'd been a real inspector. Until he'd been fired one year ago for substance abuse. After that he'd dropped out of sight, leaving his wife and children in suburban Detroit. The FBI office in Detroit had just wired that she claimed she hadn't seen or heard a word from him since the day he left.

Willard Young was his name. Thirty-six years old, an inspector with the FAA for seven years. The Los Angeles police department had searched their computer records and he'd never been arrested in their jurisdiction. The FBI had sent out a bulletin nationwide in an effort to trace the man's activities.

Throughout L.A., stoolies were being dragged in

and shown a photo of the man. A maximum effort was being made to identify any associates, suppliers or anyone connected in any way with Willard Young. So far, nothing, but it was early yet.

Their first lead, and the man was already dead.

The body discovered by the L.A. police hadn't been positively identified as Willard Young as yet, but Dan knew he would be soon. There were too many points of comparison that matched. The red hair. The general build. The blood type. The coke habit.

It would have to take them somewhere.

By its very nature, cocaine made people stupid. Subject to mistakes. They always left a trail that could be found. It was just a matter of time.

The men who had killed him knew that.

And on the surface, they'd been stupid too. Leaving the body out in the open when there were a hundred other ways to dispose of it.

On the surface, it seemed like stupidity, but beneath the surface Dan suspected something else.

The people who had conceived and executed the destruction of Flight 234 were clearly not stupid men. To be able to recruit someone capable of creating the bacteria and actually make it happen was an act that required considerable patience and careful manipulation over a long period of time. Bruce had told him some of what was involved and it wasn't something that could be done in a matter of months. More like years.

For what end?

They had killed Willard Young so he wouldn't talk. They had mangled his body so it would take longer to make the identification. But they could have taken steps to eliminate identification completely and they hadn't done that. Why not? Was it that they didn't care?

It puzzled him. It didn't make sense. There were elements of brilliance and elements of stupidity in this case, seemingly in parallel.

Terrorists. That was the first choice.

But not Arab terrorists.

Who?

Why?

The headache was turning into a migraine. He put his head down on the desk for a moment, but it only made the pain worse.

For a moment he thought he was going to be ill.

Disario kept his silence. It wasn't often that Dan Wiseman displayed such emotion. They both were quiet for a moment and then Dan lifted his head and asked, "What about the backgrounders on Williams and the others?"

Disario looked at his notes. "Well, there's a lot of people who don't like Williams, and there's been some real screwing around with the airline's stock, but we don't think there's any connection. As for the passengers, there were three heavy hitters from Japan who went down, one of them a guy named Osato, who runs a large electronics consortium in Japan. He's been accused of ripping off some American chip designs, but nothing's been proved as yet. State has been looking into it.

"The other two Japanese big-shots were with Mitsubishi. Way up there. They were here for some meetings with some auto guys, routine stuff. The rest of the Japanese were tourists.

"As for the Americans, most of them were tourists on vacation . . . a few business people, but nobody who would draw this kind of attention. There were some other nationals, but we haven't pinned them down as yet. If I had to guess, I'd say it was a terrorist act, rather than anything else. Probably random."

Dan ran a hand through his hair. "And what's the motive? We haven't received any messages, threats or demands. If it is terrorists, who the hell are they and what do they want?"

Disario shrugged. "I just don't know. Some of the guys are thinking it could be some Arabs who might have connections with the Russians. The Russians are heavy into biological weapons research. Maybe—"

Dan cut him off. "No way. The Russians wouldn't place anything this dangerous in the hands of some Arab terrorists. Not in a million years. And I don't think it's any Arabs. In the first place, they aren't this sophisticated. They like guns and bombs and stuff they can see. They like publicity. This is completely out of their league."

Disario changed the subject. He asked, "How're things in Florida."

Dan looked out the window as he gave the man the

answer. "We're not sure yet, but it looks like the bacteria was confined to the airplane. Everything was dead by the time it hit the ground. There's a possibility that the heating system was tampered with to make sure that the bacteria died. We won't know until all of the bits and pieces are brought up. That's gonna take some time."

He thought for a moment and then said, "The FAA guy. Very obvious move. They must know we'll track him down sooner or later. That means something."

"Like what?"

"Like we'll be hearing from these people, whoever they are. They didn't go to all this trouble for nothing."

Minutes later, they were seated around the conference table, where Dan was being briefed by several of the agents, when there was a knock on the door. A man entered and handed a document to Dan.

"It just came through, sir. The transcript of the cockpit voice recorder tape."

Dan grabbed the document from the man and started reading.

NTSB YT: 7844
FBI: FF24455

TRANSCRIPT OF COCKPIT VOICE RECORDER
PACIFIC RIM FLIGHT 234

CLASSIFIED: Release of this document to unauthorized personnel is a violation of sec .35(3664) subsection .388.33.

Symbol legend: C-Captain, FA-Flight Attendant, FE-Flight Engineer, CP-First Officer, LAX Cen-Los Angeles Center, CT-Controller, SP-Supervisor, (INT)-cockpit conversation, (RAD) radio transmission, (COM)-aircraft intercom conversation.

All Times Pacific Standard.
First reference related to accident. All non-accident text is contained on NTSB YT: 7843/FBI FF24454 See Footnotes.

1346:22 FA Julie Tremont (INT) Tom, we've got something weird going on back in coach.

1346:35 FE Tom Scales (INT) Like what?

1346:38 FA Julie Tremont (INT) Well, we have a lot of people complaining of airsickness. I mean, a lot! Maybe 20 or 30. And I'm not feeling that great myself.

1346:51 FE Tom Scales (INT) Christ Almighty! I thought it was just me! I've been really crappy for about five minutes. Captain. You feelin' okay?

1347:04 C Jack Walters (INT) No. My stomach's been a little queasy the last few minutes. Go on oxygen now!

1347:34 CP Bill Matter (INT) What the hell's going on? I feel like puking myself.

1347:44 C Jack Walters (INT) All right! Settle down. Something's wrong. We'll find out what it is. Julie, talk to the others. See if we have a doctor on board. I'll talk to the passengers. Get back to me right away.

1348:12 FA Julie Tremont (INT) Yes, Captain.

1348:16 C Jack Walters (INT) I've got cramps. What about you guys?

1348:24 CP Bill Matter (INT) Me too. I wanna puke, I need to crap. Jesus Christ!

1348:32 FE Tom Scales (INT) Same here. I'm really feelin' terrible, Jack.

1348:40 C Jack Walters (INT) Okay. No smoking seat belt sign on.

1348:51 CP Bill Matter (INT) On. Jack, I gotta go take a crap bad.

1349:05 C Jack Walters (INT) You'll have to do it in your pants. No choice.

1349:15 CP Bill Matter (INT) Jesus!

1349:19 C Jack Walters (COM) Ladies and gentlemen, this is Captain Walters speaking. I've turned on the no smoking sign. At this time, I want all passengers to return to their seats and fasten their seat belts. We've encountered a problem which is affecting some of the passengers and until we know what we're dealing with, I want everyone to stay in their seats. In a moment the oxygen masks will be released from their overhead compartments. Please release the mask by pulling the yellow cord, and place the mask over your nose and mouth. This is a precautionary measure. The flight attendants will assist you.

1349:51 FA Julie Tremont (INT) Captain, the whole place is sick. Everyone! The lavs are full and people are beginning to freak! Oh! There aren't any doctors.

1350:06 C Jack Walters (INT) Shit! Do the

best you can, Julie. I'm declaring. I can't help you much. (RAD) Los Angeles Center. PacRim 234.

1350:17 LAX Cen CT Brian Gibbs (RAD) PacRim 234, center. Go ahead.

1350:23 C Jack Walters (RAD) Center, PacRim 234. We are declaring an emergency and request and immediate vector back to Los Angeles.

1350:33 LAX Cen CT Brian Gibbs (RAD) PacRim 234, center. Turn right to a new heading of zero, seven, niner. Descend and maintain flight level three, three, zero. Advise the nature of your emergency.

1350:52 C Jack Walters (RAD) Center, PacRim 234. We have some sort of illness on board. Don't understand it. The crew, the passengers, everybody. Terrible cramps. Nausea. Diarrhea. It's crazy.

1351:22 LAX Cen SP Paul Graham (RAD) PacRim 234, Los Angeles Center. Have you polled your passengers to determine if there are any medical people on board?

1351:34 FE Tom Scales (INT) Jack! I can't straighten up! The cramps are . . . Jesus Christ!

1351:40 C Jack Walters (INT) Hang in there, Tom. (RAD) Center, 234. Affirmative. No doctors. Look. This all started less than fifteen minutes ago. The food hasn't even been served yet. My flight engineer is cramping so bad he can't sit up straight! The first officer is in terrible pain. Get a doctor on the radio! I don't know how long I can even talk to you.

1352:32 LAX Cen CT Brian Gibbs (RAD) 234, center. New heading of zero, niner, niner. Maintain flight level three, three, zero. We'll have a doctor on the line in a moment. Attention all aircraft on this frequency, contact Los Angeles Center on 127.2. PacRim 234 disregard. PacRim 234, you are cleared direct to El Toro Marine Station. Your heading is zero, niner, niner. There will be a new heading in about one minute. Acknowledge.

1353:53 C Jack Walters (INT) 234. Bill! Bill! Don't pass out on me, dammit!

1354:05 FE Tom Scales (INT) Jesus, Jack. We've had it. I'm losin' it. Dammit to hell.

1354:14 LAX Center CT Brian Gibbs (RAD) PacRim 234. Center. Acknowledge new heading of zero, niner, niner.

1355:12 C Jack Walters (RAD) Center, 234. Yes. Where's the damn doctor? We're about out of luck up here.

1355:45 LAX Cen SP Paul Graham (RAD) Pac 234. Center. I have the doctor now.

1356:17 LAX Cen Dr. Fred Pastori (RAD) Captain Walters. Can you describe for me your symptoms?

1356:43 C Jack Walters (RAD) Terrible cramps. I've never felt this sick. The cramps just double me over.

1357:14 LAX Cen Dr. Fred Pastori (RAD) Are you on oxygen?

1357:36 C Jack Walters (RAD) Yes. Ever since this started.

1357:43 LAX Cen Dr. Fred Pastori (RAD) Are there lots of cola drinks on board?

1358:11 C Jack Walters (RAD) Don't know. Couldn't reach them anyway. Can't move. Jesus!

1358:53 LAX Cen Dr. Fred Pastori (RAD) Captain Walters. Drink as much liquid as you can, as fast as you can. Cola might help with the nausea.

1359:32 LAX Cen Dr. Fred Pastori (RAD) Captain Walters!

1359:42 LAX Cen SP Paul Graham (RAD) PacRim 234, Los Angeles Center. Acknowledge.

1359:52 LAX Cen SP Paul Graham (RAD-)PacRim 234, Los Angeles Center. Acknowledge.

1400:12 C Jack Walters (INT) Oh, God! We're in trouble. There's blood in the vomit. I'm going into shock. I'm disabling the voice recorder. Tell my wife I love.

End of all transmissions.

Footnotes:

1. See File 3555 for explanation of symbols and description of sounds identified.
2. See File 3556 for analysis of speech patterns and actual time of words.
3. See File . . .

There was more, but it only confirmed Dan Wiseman's worst fears. The transcript wasn't going to tell them anything. Other than the fact that 259 people had suffered terribly during a few minutes of hell on earth.

And a very canny pilot had made a clever move, shutting the cockpit voice recorder off, as possibly his last act, in an effort to preserve what now seemed like a worthless testament.

He handed the document to Disario. "Well, this tells us that aside from the problem, nothing abnormal was taking place. There was no terrorist making threats either in the cabin or cockpit. There is no reference to any unusual behavior on the part of any passengers, no reference to any explosion, no reference to anything other than the illness.

"It all took place in minutes."

The room was silent. It was as though both men could hear and see the terror on board that flight.

The looks on their faces were undisguised. Few attempts were being made to hide feelings.

They were both afraid of what might come next.

There was a knock on the door and one of the agents popped his head in. "Sir?"

"Yes?"

"We think we've found the motel room where Young was killed. L.A. police have forensics there already and the night manager has identified the photo. We're trying to find out who visited the room. Nothing yet, but we're still interviewing."

Dan sat up straight and smiled. "Good. Keep me advised."

"Yessir."

He turned to Disario and said, "Why haven't we heard from these people, whoever they are?"

Disario shrugged. "I don't know."

What were they waiting for?

## Chapter Ten

The arrival of Elizabeth Martin's parents at her pleasant Costa Mesa home seemed like a tonic to the stricken woman. The crushing weight of grief lifted slightly and after some tearful hugs and a short explosion of uncontrolled sobbing, she actually smiled for the first time since she'd heard about the airplane.

An exhausted Janet Talbot, who'd stayed with her every minute, and who'd spent the last few hours since the passenger list had been made public warding off neighbors and friends wanting to offer their condolences, took it as her cue to go home and get some rest. The look of appreciation in Liz's eyes for her selfless friendship warmed Janet's heart.

Elizabeth's father was 63 and in the first year of early retirement from his former job as a middle manager in a large electronics company. He was a rather short man, with a full head of white hair and a manner of speaking that gave him a rather professorial appearance. Her mother, a petite woman of the same age, looked much younger, and slightly fragile, with thin bones and clear, white skin. The good looks that had drawn the initial interest of her husband of 40 years were still there.

In contrast, Elizabeth was a big-boned woman who

stood almost five, ten. Her dark hair and ruddy complexion, combined with soft, unstriking facial features made it difficult to understand how she was her mother's daughter. She looked neither like her mother nor her father in any way.

Her parents talked for a few moments about memories they had of Mark, for they had taken to him like the son they'd never had. Over the years, they'd wondered why Mark and Elizabeth had never had children, but had had the grace to keep it to themselves. Now, as they sat in the living room, sipping coffee, their compassionate pain was deepened by the ache for the grandchild that might never be.

Again, as it had all morning, the doorbell rang, and Roger Brackton said he'd look after it. He opened the door and looked up at the big man standing there, holding a business card in his hand.

"Good afternoon, sir. My name is Donald James. I'm the public relations director for Pacific Rim Airlines. I wonder if I might have a brief moment with Mrs. Martin?"

Brackton looked glum. "I don't think so. She's quite upset as you might well understand. Unless it's extremely important . . ."

James nodded. "I understand. My purpose is to inquire as to Mrs. Martin's intentions regarding the . . . identification and disposition of her husband. I appreciate how uncomfortable this subject will be, but, with all due respect, it needs to be addressed. I know how painful this is, believe me, and I wouldn't be here if it wasn't necessary. I'll try to keep it as . . .

I'm very sorry."

The look in the man's eyes was one of sincere concern.

Almost despite himself, Brackton felt a short pang of empathy for this man, forced to witness the grief of countless people torn apart by some terrible tragedy. He opened the door. "Please come in Mr. James. I'll introduce you to Mrs. Martin. I'd appreciate it if you would allow me to broach the reason for your presence here."

They went to the living room and Brackton introduced James to his wife and his daughter. "Mr. James is from the airline, sweetheart. I know this is . . ."

Elizabeth stood up and placed her hand on her forehead. "I know. They want me to go to Florida. Well, I can't! I just can't do it! I want Mark's body brought here. I want it taken to Harbor Lawn Mortuary. I'll make arrangements after that."

Donald James wished it was that easy. He had no knowledge of the condition of the body of Mark Martin. It was possible that the body was somewhat intact, that preliminary identification could be made at the crash site and the body shipped home for final identification. Possible. But it was also possible that such was not the case. That dental records would be necessary in order to make an identification. That the body had already been shipped to Atlanta for a complete analysis. It was also possible that the body was still submerged in the wreckage, not yet recovered.

None of this he mentioned to Mrs. Martin. Instead, he nodded and said, "That's fine, Mrs. Martin. I'll take care of everything personally. Don't you worry about a thing. On behalf of the airline and myself, I extend to you my deepest sympathies."

Brackton snorted. "Sympathies don't count for much right now, Mr. James. The way I hear it, the airline is going bankrupt. They said on the news this morning that this—whatever his name is—is broke. It strikes me that this action is a most irresponsible one in the light of what's happened."

James nodded. "It's true that the airline is bankrupt, Mr. Brackton. I think the papers are being filed as we speak. However, in actual fact, it's simply a technicality. A trustee will be appointed and the airline's affairs will not be wound up until all matters relating to this accident are settled."

Brackton wasn't to be mollified. "Please, Mr. James. I'm well acquainted with the modern business ethic. I used to work for one of the country's largest electronic firms until I was forced to take early retirement. The pension I worked for for thirty-two years suddenly shrank by half.

"We had assurances. We had agreements. And in the end, there wasn't a damn thing anybody could do about it. So now, too old to get another job, I'm forced to watch every penny. And all because I trusted the people I worked for. I suspect the decision to go into bankruptcy was taken simply to avoid paying off the hundreds of liability claims that are bound to arise over this."

"Actually," James said, "it has nothing to do with that. The airline has been in trouble for a few weeks. The accident was the final straw. As for liability claims, the airline was insured at the time of the accident and the insurance company is quite solvent. The bankruptcy will not be finalized until all claims are satisfied. It will have no bearing at all. You needn't worry."

"You soft-soaping me, Mr. James?"

"Not at all. I'd suggest that you consult with an attorney if you're concerned. I'm sure he'll put your mind at rest."

Brackton looked a bit taken aback. It wasn't the kind of response he'd expected. "You must be out a job then," he said.

James nodded. "In a sense, yes. However, I'll be working for the trustee until this is over, providing assistance and information to the relatives of passengers on our airline. The airline may not exist anymore in legal terms, but the people certainly do. Once I've done everything I can to be of assistance, I'll find another employment."

Brackton said, "So, you're saying that if my daughter decides to sue the airline, the fact that it's broke means nothing."

"Exactly, Mr. Brackton. That may seem illogical, but again I say, a consultation with your attorney should clear up any questions."

"I see. Well, for your information, I intend to advise my daughter to sue. How do you feel about that?" There was a hint of anger in his voice and in his eyes, as though he was looking for an argument from this representative of the airline that was, at least partially, responsible for the death of his son-in-law.

There was no argument. "I don't blame you," said James. As he said it, Elizabeth went over and picked up a paper from the fireplace mantel and handed it to her father. "It's already been done."

Brackton looked over the paper and his eyebrows rose into his forehead. "May I see that?" James asked.

Brackton looked puzzled for a moment but handed the paper to James. The big man looked at it and then smiled. He handed it back to Brackton. "Well," he said, "your interests will be well represented with Mr. Barnes, I can assure you."

At the mention of the name, Brackton looked at his daughter with some astonishment. "Barnes? George Barnes? Is that who you've hired?"

Elizabeth shrugged. "To be perfectly honest, I don't really know. A man was here this morning and Janet looked after it. All I did was sign the paper."

James said, "It's Barnes all right. The one and only. Perhaps this isn't the time, but I'd like to discuss the ramifications of this for a moment. If you'd rather, I could do it with your father."

"What ramifications?" asked Elizabeth.

James hesitated. "Are you sure you want to discuss this now? I'd be happy to brief your father and he . . ."

"No. I want to hear what you have to say."

They all sat down. And Donald James began to fill them in.

"Mrs. Martin," he began, "George Barnes is an expert in these matters. You couldn't be in better hands. However, there are certain people who will want to talk to you. Soon, you'll be visited by a representative of the company that carries the airline's insurance. He'll discuss with you other options."

"Like what?"

"He'll tell you some things about legal matters that you may or may not be aware of. For example, he might suggest that you dismiss George Barnes as your attorney and accept an immediate settlement from the insurance company. Or, he might suggest that you direct Mr. Barnes to accept the settlement. His arguments will be quite persuasive and you need to be aware of them.

"For example, he might tell you that this could take years to resolve. Because of the nature of the accident, the courts may have difficulty in determining fault and the various components of that fault. According to the FBI, the accident was the result of some sort of terrorist act, whereby a chemical was released inside the airplane which disabled the crew.

"The insurance company may insist that they should not be fully responsible for claims. They may propose that others, such as the airport, the security people, whomever, are really responsible. They may tell you that because of the complexity of the legal system, it might be years to resolve many of the issues surrounding the accident. And they might suggest that you accept an immediate settlement. It might seem the wise thing to do."

He stopped for a moment and then resumed. "No matter what happens, the airline insurance company will end up paying the bulk of the claims. Even if the airline is only one percent responsible. But there well might be a long delay. The insurance company will do whatever they feel necessary to reduce the amount of their loss.

"There are other factors. If, in fact, you decide to refuse the settlement offered by the insurance company, they may investigate your husband."

Brackton was incensed. "Investigate! What do you mean investigate?"

James ignored him and looked carefully at Mrs. Martin. It had been a mistake. She wasn't ready for this. Not at all.

They didn't know how it really worked. The whole stupid game that cared nothing for the emotions of the parties involved. "Perhaps I should . . ."

"No!" She also was livid. "Tell me! What investigation?"

There was no turning back. James had put his foot in it and he'd have to see it through. He kept his voice low and controlled, and placed his hands face down on the table.

"The amount of any judgment is determined by many factors," he said. "No matter what you read in the papers, it isn't automatic. Judgments are based not on the perceived dollar loss to you, but in actual terms. For example, if your husband was in good health and a young man and his salary over the next twenty years could be tracked with some degree of accuracy, that's one thing. If he was an older man, a smoker, or suffering from ill health, that's another thing. Once you are engaged in a law suit, the insurance company will conduct an investigation into every aspect of your husband's affairs, in an effort to keep the award to as low a figure as possible."

This time it was Mrs. Brackton who was outraged. "My God! How can they be so unfeeling? So heartless!"

James did his best to explain. "I know it appears that way and perhaps it is. Some insurance companies are worse than others. Unfortunately, the insurance company representing the airline is one of the worst. That's just my personal opinion, not the airline's. They will, I'm afraid, attempt to intimidate you in every way possible, in an effort to get you to force your attorney to accept a settlement. At the same time, you can expect a visit from one of Barnes's people, who will tell you much of what I've just said. That representative will urge you to hold out, saying that you'll be throwing away a chance at a very large amount of money."

Brackton asked, "Are you an attorney, Mr. James?"

James shook his head. "No. The only reason I'm aware of these matters is because I was once with another airline that was involved in a fatal accident. I was able to see at first hand the actual activities of all involved in the various law suits."

Brackton shot back, "So what are you really saying? That we should accept the airline offer, if and when it's presented? Is that your pitch? Is that the real reason you're here?"

They were all staring at him, the anger and the hurt clear in their eyes. For a moment he was angry too. He hadn't needed to pay this visit. He was simply trying to help. Prepare them for what was coming. Fend off some of the pain. Instead, they were heaping their frustration and anger upon his head.

And then his anger left him as quickly as it had arrived. They had a right to be angry. It was a terrible system. Innocent people caught up in the meat-grinder of the legal system, pawns in the fight for nothing but dollars. The attorneys for the victims fighting for the biggest buck possible, because their income was a percentage of that. And the attorneys for the insurance companies trying to make every victim look like a dead-beat, because that's what they got paid for.

It was a terrible system. And the saddest thing of all was that there was no other way. It was the way a democracy functioned.

James stood up and prepared to leave. "No, I'm not recommending anything. I just wanted you to be prepared for what is to come. I'm simply suggesting that you should consider what's best for you. Try to look at it as unemotionally as possible.

"I imagine that you were visited by a representative of Mr. Barnes. Just as you'll be visited by a representative of the airline's insurance company. They like to move fast. They like to get you when you aren't thinking clearly, while you're still being affected by the terrible pain you're feeling. Few attorneys and few insurance companies are this callous. It just happens that Mr. Barnes and Butler Casualty are among the worst in that regard. It's unfortunate.

"Having said that, let me reiterate that Barnes is a highly successful trial lawyer. If you decide to stick with him, you'll probably end up with more money than you would in any settlement offered by the insurance company. Even after his fees. But it could take a lot of time.

"As you mentioned, Mr. Brackton, I am just finishing out my job. I have no axe to grind. My personal responsibility is to be of assistance to you. That's all I'm trying to do. I am simply a man who is cognizant of the way these things go. Most people don't understand the manner in which these high-profile law suits are handled. I do. I've seen it first hand. I just want you to be aware of what's about to happen. Perhaps it will help you to make the decision that's best for you.

"Unfortunately, it's a battle between skillful attorneys with a vested interest and insurance companies with a lot of money to protect. I'm not saying it's wrong, I'm just telling you how it is."

He turned and faced Mrs. Martin. "Mrs. Martin, you've lost your husband and I realize it will take some time to heal that terrible wound. It's completely unfair that you should have to make decisions about other things at a time like this.

"But I just wanted you to know what's about to

happen. You'll be caught in the middle. It won't be pleasant. The decision is yours and yours alone."

Mrs. Brackton stood up and asked, "What would you do, Mr. James? If it had been your wife on board that airplane, what would you do?"

He shook his head. "Mrs. Brackton, I have no answer for that. I wouldn't want to influence you in any way. All I can say is this; Mrs. Martin should do what's best for her. And her alone. In the meantime, I'll arrange for Mr. Martin to be transported to Costa Mesa and I'll have Harbor Lawn contact you as soon as he arrives. You have my card. The telephones will still be working, so if you have any questions or if there's any way in which I can be helpful, please don't hesitate to call me."

He started to leave and Elizabeth called after him. "Mr. James?"

"Yes?"

"Have they . . . have they found my husband?"

Her eyes were filling with tears. He wished he could tell her something, but he couldn't.

"I don't know, Mrs. Martin. Would you like me to call you when I find out?"

Her voice was barely a whisper.

"Yes," she said.

They said their goodbyes and then James was sitting in his car, trying to force his mind to think of pleasant things. And then he saw another car pull up and park behind him and a man get out, clutching a briefcase. He recognized the man as one of Butler Casualty's investigators.

The tug-of-war was about to begin in earnest.

He got out of the car and ran to the man's side as he started up the walk.

"Carl?"

The man turned and smiled. "Oh, James. How's tricks? What you doin' here? I heard they shut you down this morning."

James ignored the question. "Listen," he said, "she's really shook up. Why don't you leave this for a few days?"

Carl Weese sneered at him. "They're all shook up, James. They'll be shook up for months. I can't help that. I hafta do my job, just like you . . . and that's to get as many of these put to bed as possible."

He was right of course.

They all had their jobs to do.

And there wasn't anything that Donald James could do about it.

In Palm Harbor, Florida, the tedious work of bringing up the bits and pieces continued. Now a full team of medical personnel assisted Doctor Bruce Evans and the two doctors from Atlanta as every particle was inspected and carefully examined for possible contamination.

Bodies and parts of bodies were placed in special rubber bags and taken to an ice-making plant in Tampa that had been commandeered and converted into a morgue. Isolation was total and the plant was surrounded by armed National Guardsmen.

The wreckage was also carefully examined for contamination, placed in crates that were then encased in heavy polyurethane sheeting and taken to a hangar at St. Petersburg airport. Once there, each piece was uncrated, checked again for contamination and then laid out on the hangar floor where National Transportation Safety Board inspectors, wearing protective clothing, tried to identify and correctly position it.

So far, the largest single item of wreckage was one of the three engines. It had been uncrated, declared safe and set on a dolly while two inspectors looked for serial numbers that would identify which engine it was.

Jim Cummings, one of the inspectors, located the serial number, checked his file folder and nodded to his co-worker.

"Okay, Al, this is number two. Have some guys wheel it over to the tail section."

His fellow inspector wasn't moving. Instead, he was staring at the engine, one rubber-encased hand brushing over a section of the turbine blade assembly, now horribly bent.

Cummings asked, "What's the matter?"

He could see the eyes of Al Fearing through the glass frontpiece of the protective suit. They were expressive eyes and right now, the expression was one of confusion.

"What is it?"

Fearing pointed to the turbine assembly. "Jim, look at this mother."

Cummings drew closer and looked at where the man was pointing.

They'd both been maintenance men in wartime. Cummings, the older of the two, had been an engine man in Korea, working on F-86s, while the younger Fearing had serviced F-4s in Viet Nam.

Both of them recognized the effects of cannon fire.

There was no question. Engine number two had been shot at and hit by cannon. There was no mistake, and they both knew it.

They looked at each other and then walked away from the engine and out of the hangar, into the hot Florida sun. Cummings took off his headgear, partially unzipped his suit and fished a cigarette out of his shirt pocket. He lit it, took a deep drag and then sat down on the hot concrete tarmac. His face was contorted in a look of consternation.

"They shot it down!" he said. "They shot the fuckin' thing down! Our own guys, for chrissakes."

Fearing shook his head and lit a cigarette of his own. "Jim, what the hell gives here?"

Cummings jumped up and started walking toward the motor home that served as a communications center between the command center and the hangar. "I haven't a clue," he said as he strode away, "but I sure as hell intend to find out."

Fearing was beside him in seconds and the two men walked purposefully toward the motor home, the anger rising with each step.

Their supervisor was filling out forms at the small desk as they barged in. He looked up at two scowling faces and knew immediately what the problem was. He'd been expecting it but had said nothing until the need arose. Now it had.

"Lou," snarled Cummings, "I've just looked at engine number two and the fuckin' thing is full of bullet holes. Cannon, actually. That airplane was shot down. Did you know that?"

The supervisor sighed and gestured to the sofa-bed. "Sit down, guys. Let me fill you in."

For the next five minutes he did just that, telling the two men the reasons for the action taken, reasons that seemed logical and sound.

The two men seemed to accept it and headed back to the hangar to resume their work. Lou Holt decided that he would have a talk with all of the investigators in the hangar. Right now. He cursed under his breath. They should have been told to begin with, he thought. It was stupid. These were experienced men, sure to see the signs of cannon fire. The man who'd made the decision to release the information to the investigators only if they discovered the evidence had been a fool.

What were they trying to hide?

He put on his protective suit and headed for the hangar. When he got there, the team of eleven men was hard at work. At least it seemed at first that there were eleven of them but on actual count there were only nine.

Jim Cummings and Al Fearing were not there.

And Lou Holt felt a burning sensation in the pit of his stomach.

At that moment, Jim Cummings and Al Fearing were seated at a small bar not far from the St. Petersburg airport. After the meeting with Lou Holt, Jim had asked Al to join him over a beer as he tried to make sense of what had just transpired. They'd removed their protective clothing, placed it in the trunk of their rental car and headed for the nearest bar. Now, both men sat looking into their glasses and talked.

"This really sucks," said Cummings, keeping his voice down. "They knew all along that the plane was shot down, but they put us through this bullshit anyway. Why? The plane crashed because it was shot down. That's all. Why make us go through the normal routine? Why not fake it? Just have some dummies go through the motions. Why us?"

Fearing put his hand on his friend's arm. "Because, like Lou said, they want this to look like the plane crashed on its own. It makes sense to me, Jim. Some terrorist plants a bacterial bomb on board that kills everybody. They need to find out what the hell it was and if the plane goes into the ocean, they may never find out. So they shoot it down to make sure they can recover the thing. I buy it. What else can they do?"

Cummings took a sip of his beer and shook his head. "I don't know . . . maybe I've been at this too long. Sixteen years of pokin' through wrecks . . . maybe it's too much. How the hell do we know that they were all dead? Maybe they were still alive. Maybe our Air Force shot down a plane full of live Americans."

Fearing tightened the grip on Jim's arm. "Jim, you don't believe that and you know it. They checked that sucker sixteen ways from sideways before they shot it down."

Cummings retort was filled with bitterness. "Says Lou!"

Fearing held his hand up as though fending off some invisible foe. "Okay, says Lou. But why would he lie? There's no reason for him to lie. There's no reason for the Air Force to lie! Jesus, Jim, what's gotten into you?"

The older man downed his beer and ran the back of his hand across his mouth. "I don't know. Maybe they should have told us before we started. Maybe they should have trusted us. Christ! Lettin' us discover the evidence and *then* tellin' us . . . that doesn't sit well with me at all. I don't like being used, dammit! And I feel used. Those assholes think that this is some easy job? Let them try it for a while. Pickin' bits and pieces of flesh off some hunk of aluminum and tryin' to figure out which of three million parts this sonofabitch is. Well, it isn't easy. It's damn tough. And I resent the hell out of bein' treated like some fuckin' asshole that can't be trusted to keep his mouth shut."

Fearing's concern for his friend's attitude was building rapidly. "Take it easy, Jim. You're letting this get out of hand."

Cummings turned to face him. "No I'm not. I'm tired of bein' treated like this. There's no need for an investigation at all! They know why the plane crashed. They shot the fucker down. They don't *need* us! They coulda used some other guys. They're puttin' us through a bunch of shit for no reason, damn it."

Cummings stood up and headed for the door. Fearing threw a couple of bills on the bar and followed him.

"Jim, where're you going? We need to get back!"

Cummings was striding down the sidewalk, away from the bar and the car. Fearing almost had to run to keep up.

"I don't know where I'm goin'. Just the fuck away from here, that's all."

The look in his eyes was one of anger. Fearing said, "I'll stay with you, pal."

Cummings stopped and whirled to face him. "No. You go back. Tell Lou to stick it up his ass. I'm goin' home. Home to Marie and the kids. Fuck this shit. I've had enough. Tell Lou I'll find my own way home. Not to worry. I'll be all right."

"Jim, I can't leave you like this. You're upset."

The anger left the eyes for a moment and Cummings put an arm on Fearing's shoulder. "It's okay. I'm okay. Don't worry about me. I'm just tired of it, Al. I'm burned out. I just need a rest. Let me be . . . it'll be fine. Okay?"

Fearing hesitated. "Can I drive you somewhere?"

Cummings shook his head. "No. I just wanna walk

for a while. Clear my head. Then I'll pick up my stuff at the motel and head for Tampa. Catch a flight back. No sweat. I'll talk to you later, okay?"

"You sure?"

"Yeah, I'm sure."

The grin was wide, the anger gone, the expression on the face one of peace. Al thought about it a moment and then shrugged. "Okay."

Cummings turned and resumed his brisk pace and Fearing headed back to the car. Lou would be upset, he thought. Jesus, he'd be really upset.

# Chapter Eleven

Edward Spencer sat in the tall leather chair, leaned back and listened as Gen. Waldo Smith, seemingly chagrined, verbally reported the details of the brief he had just presented after working through the night.

Even while Flight 234 was still in the air, the FBI director had considered a number of scenarios, and the one involving possible terrorist activity had been pegged as the most likely. Now, as he listened to the man from Huntsville, that scenario seemed chillingly real.

The general was almost beside himself. His voice was filled with doubt instead of the calm, confident tone he usually employed when discussing Army matters with civilians.

When he finished, Spencer exploded in rage. "It's absolutely beyond me. Beyond me! Dammit, we're supposed to be on the same side! If the FBI is a security risk, then this country is in one hell of a lot of trouble!

"You're telling me that a man heavily involved in that kind of research was fired a year ago, after testing positive on a drug test, which you performed after getting an anonymous phone call, and you just let it go? You didn't contact us? Didn't it ever occur to you that this guy might prove to be a problem at some future date?"

General Smith snapped, "Look, we were following normal procedure. What the hell are we supposed to do? Put a tail on every serviceman who's ever had access to secrets? Dammit! There are thousands of former government employees, both civilian and military, walking around with secrets in their heads. What are you doing about that? Nothing! Because you can't. Don't chew *my* ass out! I don't set policy. I just do my job."

Spencer was just getting started. "This scientist you dumped has secrets in his head that are probably more dangerous than nuclear secrets. Knowing the man has a drug problem would be reason enough to at least advise us. In case you didn't know it, it happens to be a felony to use cocaine in Alabama and you didn't even notify us! My God! What in the hell were you thinking of?" He banged his hand on the desk in frustration.

"Tell me about this Wilcox," he demanded.

The general wanted to defend his position further but instead, cleared his throat and nodded. "Roger Wilcox had been with us for six years. He's single, never married, aged thirty-seven. There's a photo in the file. He lived in a small, rented apartment in Huntsville, alone. At one point, we thought he might be a fag, but he wasn't. It didn't really matter, the guy did good work.

"Then we got a tip that he was using cocaine. He

tested positive, so we fired him. I'm sure he's not connected to this in any way."

Spencer sneered at him. "You're sure? How the hell can you make a statement like that? You can't be sure about anything! Just a minute."

The director pushed a button on the intercom and asked for Bill Torkis, one of the staff agents. He pulled the photo of Roger Wilcox out of the file and handed it to the young man as soon as he entered the room.

"I want this on the wire," he said sharply. "Full APB. Nationwide. Notify the Huntsville office that the man worked at the Huntsville Army research center until a year ago."

He hesitated for a moment and then thrust the entire file at the man. "Screw it. Run a copy of this entire file through to Huntsville and send another copy to Assistant Director Wiseman in Los Angeles. Top priority."

"Yes sir."

Once again, Spencer was alone with the general. The gaze from his eyes seemed to bore holes through the air as he said, "Tell me about this bacteria."

The general opened another file folder and started to read from it. "Our product is called BT thirty-three. According to your latest report from Atlanta, the bacteria used on the plane matches BT thirty-three exactly. It's created by altering the DNA in three existing bacterial types, then combining them into one specific-purpose entity. We got involved in this as a result of information provided by Barakov when he defected three years ago.

"According to Barakov, the Soviets have been trying for years to develop an antibiotic that will protect their own troops in the event that the stuff is ever used, and they've failed. At least, up until three years ago. We don't know what the status is at present.

"We've been trying to develop an antibiotic or preventative of our own for three years and we can't develop anything either. The Goddamn thing acts too fast. Before the body realizes it's been invaded, it's all over. The stuff is incredible."

Spencer shook his head, his face expressing incredulity. "Are you saying that we're defenseless against this thing?"

Smith grunted. "No, not exactly. Let me explain."

He paused, then resumed speaking, seeming to grope for the right words. "The bacteria has certain unique features. It reproduces rapidly, doubling its volume every ten minutes. It lives off the bacteria found in human intestines and feces, as well as stomach enzymes. Either will supply adequate sustenance. Its voraciousness destroys the intestine in minutes.

"The other unique thing about BT thirty-three is its ability to live on its own through cannibalization. It can survive for as long as an hour, in water, air or almost anything else, by feeding on itself.

"Control is achieved two ways. Through isolation and temperature. The bacteria cannot survive temperatures below fifty degrees F.

"As a weapon, it's encapsulated. You've probably seen those ads in magazines where you can scratch the page and smell the perfume or whatever they're selling. Well, that's actually encapsulation. Tiny little plastic bubbles are filled with perfume and when you run your nail across the surface, you break the little bubbles and release the perfume.

"When the BT thirty-three is encapsulated along with a food supply, it multiplies until it actually breaks the bubble on its own, which releases the bacteria into the air, or water or a larger container. If released into the air or water, it feeds on itself for up to an hour, depending, of course, on the quantity, unless it finds another host. Such as a human being. The size of the initial encapsulation determines the length of the danger period.

"The Russians developed it to use in the field. They could drop bombs of encapsulated bacteria on our positions and as long as they were far enough away, they'd be protected. But they're very nervous about it, and rightly so.

"The bastards who used it on the airplane knew what they were doing. A closed area with no escape. A small amount of encapsulated bacteria was probably placed in a thin container of some sort, with each encapsulated unit containing a specific quantity of food, so to speak, and the BT thirty-three started to multiply. Eventually, the BT thirty-three broke through the tiny capsules, fed off additional food supplies placed inside the container and continued to multiply until it filled the container to the bursting point. At that time it was released into normal air-flow inside the airplane.

"The air circulation system simply recycles the air and adds heat which is produced in the engines. In a one-oh-one-one, engine bypass valves take heat from the engines, then the temperature is controlled by small computers, one for each engine, located in the nose of the aircraft, just behind the radar antenna. So, just having the BT thirty-three in the air inside the cabin would ensure that it would be quickly distributed throughout the plane. The filters wouldn't be able to stop it at all.

"The timing was so precise as to be awesome."

Spencer slumped back into his chair and said, "Let me get this straight. You're saying that the bacteria can live without a host for almost an hour? But you're also saying that as long as there's some sort of food supply, such as you've described, it could live indefinitely?"

The general blinked twice and said, "I'm afraid that's so."

Spencer scratched his chin and leaned forward. "So, in actual fact, these people could place this shit in the water supplies of our major cities and kill us all."

The general thought for a minute and then said, "I know it sounds easy but it really isn't. Timing is the key. I think the most logical attack would come through use of the sewer systems of our major cities.

There you have a steady, continuing supply of fresh food. In that situation, if the sewer system was allowed to continue functioning, the bacteria would continue to multiply until it actually pushed itself through various traps and found air or water. Placed in a city's sewer system, it would be airborne inside homes within days."

"There'd be no stopping it?"

The general paused for a moment. "Yes, there is. Lower the temperature inside the sewer system to fifty degrees or lower and the bacteria dies. This could be done with cold water or chemicals. Compressed liquid oxygen or nitrogen in large enough quantities. There's a host of other compressed gases that would work, as long as it was done quickly enough.

"If the attack was wide-spread, covering many cities, the resulting epidemic would require strict isolation. I'm afraid the loss of life would be in the millions before you'd have a handle on it.

"Even though it's wintertime in the northern states, the sewer systems are still quite warm. Warm enough to sustain the bacteria."

Spencer ran a hand over his eyes. "So far, they've found nothing in Florida. All of the soil, air and water samples are negative. Is that because the temperature inside the plane was below fifty degrees before it crashed?"

"Exactly. The people who placed the BT thirty-three on board that airplane also must have blown out the heating system. The air inside the plane dropped below survivable limits, which killed the bacteria. As I say, they knew what they were doing. If the heating system hadn't been blown, you'd no doubt have an epidemic in Florida right now. That was no accidental failure."

Smith paused for a moment and then seemed to relax slightly, becoming less defensive and more interested in dealing with the problem at hand. "You must keep in mind," he said, "the fact that this was almost an experiment to these people. They weren't sure that things would go exactly as planned. The container had to be exactly the right size, or there was a possibility that the heating system would blow *before* the bacteria was released into the air. The plane would simply declare an emergency and land. There were all sorts of other possibilities.

"They didn't want to start an epidemic . . . at least that would be my guess. They wanted to prove a point. And they have. They've shown they can handle this weapon properly."

Spencer looked at the man with unconcealed disgust. It was almost as though the general had respect for these animals. "How difficult is it to manufacture this shit . . . this BT thirty-three?"

General Spencer was used to the revulsion people expressed regarding his line of work. Like some other career military men, he was of the opinion that civilians took the military for granted until their lives were in danger, at which time they couldn't do enough. He found that attitude patronizing, but being unable to change it, he'd learned to accept it. "The type of equipment required to produce the bacteria is widely used all over the world, except for the encapsulating equipment, which is American. In terms of difficulty, it simply isn't that tough. Not any more."

Edward Spencer continued to stare at the general. Intellectually, he knew the general was just doing a job for his country. But in his heart, Spencer thought of him as a man who represented the worst in humankind. As one of that peculiar breed of people who spent their time dreaming up new ways to kill. It really didn't matter whose side they were on.

He broke off his short reverie and hit the intercom button again. He'd need to talk to the president. And Dan Wiseman would have to be brought up to date.

They had a connection now.

Willard Young was an ex-FAA man who'd been fired for using drugs.

Roger Wilcox was an ex-Army scientist who'd been fired for using drugs.

They'd both been fired within a week of each other. And both had been required to take drug tests after an anonymous tip had been given to their employers. It was too much of a coincidence. The conspiracy was taking shape.

Cocaine was the connection.

His brow furrowed as another scenario began to take shape in his imagination.

They'd thought it was a terrorist group. A new group without ties to the familiar cells the FBI was used to chasing.

Maybe it was something even more sinister.

The illegal trafficking of cocaine was a major part of organized crime activities in the United States. Using a variety of new laws, the FBI had managed to put a record number of organized crime figures behind bars in the past few years.

Had organized crime stolen a page from the terrorist play book? Was the war against drugs being fully engaged by the enemy with no holds barred?

It was beginning to look like it.

That prospect was much more terrifying than anything he'd considered before. He could literally feel the blood draining from his hands.

President Robert Dalton, escorted by four Secret Service agents, entered the office of Dr. Herbert Tasker at Walter Reed Hospital. The agents checked the room and then three of them went back outside.

Doctor Tasker greeted the president warmly and smiled broadly. "Well, Robert, I've looked at the data and I'm happy to report that you've passed your physical with flying colors. You're as healthy as a horse."

Dalton grinned broadly and pulled a cigar from his pocket. As he did so, he noticed that his left hand was trembling slightly. "Good. That's great, Herb."

The doctor turned to the Secret Service agent and said, quietly, "I wonder if I could have a few minutes with the president. We're old friends and I'd like to discuss a personal matter."

The agent hesitated and glanced at President Dalton. Dalton nodded and said, "It's okay, Fred. We'll only be a moment."

The agent turned and left the room.

As he did so, the smiles left both the faces of the doctor and the president.

Tasker said, "Well, I've done as you asked but I don't mind telling you, I don't like it. Your health is *not* purely a personal matter, it's of concern to all of us. The whole country. There are a lot of dedicated technicians who have conspired, because I asked them to, to falsify medical information. You had no right to do that to me, dammit!"

President Dalton took a deep drag from the cigar and exhaled the smoke at the ceiling. "I'm sorry, Herb. I wouldn't have asked you to do such a thing if it wasn't for the fact that the next few days are vitally important. I just can't have Cecil Aubrey running the country right now." He paused and then asked, "So . . . how am I?"

The doctor sighed and ignored the pall of blue smoke stinking up his office. "I've just reviewed the Catscan printout. I won't bullshit you, Bob, never have. You have three brain tumors, one of which is inoperable. We'll need to operate on the other two immediately."

The trembling in the hand increased slightly, but other than that, there was little reaction from the president.

"What about the inoperable one?"

"I think we can treat it successfully with radiation and drug therapy, but again, we'll have to start immediately. I want you admitted today. You'll have to let Cecil do his thing. There's no other way."

Robert Dalton looked at the cigar and spoke softly. "You talked about bullshit, Herb. Tell me the truth. What is the success rate with the type of tumor I've got? The inoperable one."

The doctor sighed and said, "Statistics mean nothing. If only one in a million survive, that means that you can survive. But survival depends on moving quickly and adopting the proper attitude. If you want to get well, you'll get well, provided you devote all of your energies to that job."

"You didn't answer my question."

"I don't intend to."

"There are other doctors."

"Fine, see them. In the meantime, I'll hold a press conference."

"You're attempting to blackmail the president of the United States?"

They glared at each other for a moment and then the anger quickly disappeared. Doctor Tasker looked stricken. "Bob," he said, "For God's sake, we need to get moving. These tumors are fast-growing bastards. Besides, I'll never be able to keep the lid on this for very long.

"And another thing. Whether you start your treatment today or tomorrow, you're shortly going to exhibit personality changes. They'll be subtle at first and then more pronounced. Do you really think it fair to the American people?"

Robert Dalton sagged into the chair. "Can you give me ten days?"

"No. Damn it! You're a sick man. We must start treatment now!"

The president's eyes were pleading now. His arms were outstretched, the agony etched in his face. "Please, Herb. I'm begging you."

The doctor cursed under his breath and threw a pencil at the wall. After a moment, he said, "All right. Five days. You've got five days. If you aren't back here in five days, I'll blow this thing wide open. I'm trying to save your life, you idiot!"

Robert Dalton rose from the chair and embraced the startled doctor. In a voice choked with emotion, he said, "I know, Herb, I know."

Dan Wiseman sat in the small office he was using in Los Angeles and looked over the latest information that had just arrived from Washington. The director had relayed a full report on his meeting with General Smith and had indicated that the Washington staff would be checking on shipments of equipment that might have been used to manufacture BT33. That job was just another that would strain the resources of the bureau.

Already, with the cooperation of local law enforcement agencies, thousands of known cocaine traffickers were being dragged in for questioning and shown pictures of Roger Wilcox and Willard Young. So far, nothing had turned up.

There had to be a connection, Dan thought. There just had to be. The director's memo had concluded with his thoughts on the organized crime angle. While Dan agreed with the director in the broadest sense, he doubted that the established "families" would be involved in such a thing. They would know that such an act would create pure hatred in the hearts of Americans who previously winked at crime.

Most Americans never really considered placing a bet with a bookie as participating in organized crime. The odds on the numbers business in New York were better than the state lottery and that business continued to flourish. High-priced call girls, drugs, tax-free cigarettes . . . Americans had no idea how much and how often they enriched the coffers of the crime lords.

But if it became known that organized crime was involved in terrorist-style activities inside the United States, the people *would* know. Instead of winking at crime, an enraged public would demand action. And that would be bad for business.

The crime lords never like to do anything that is bad for business.

At least, the established ones didn't.

An idea began to form in the back of his brain.

He grabbed the yellow legal pad and made some notes.

There was a light rap on the door and Al Disario stuck his head in.

"Dan," he said, "I've got Helen Porter in my office. She's with LAX security. She may have something and I'd like you to hear it firsthand."

Dan nodded and followed Al into his own office.

Helen Porter was sitting on a chair in front of the desk, her hands folded over a stack of file folders in her lap.

When Disario had mentioned her name, it had run a small bell back in the caverns of Dan's memory, but when he saw her, he recognized her instantly.

It had been three years ago and while Dan had never met the woman, he remembered her case.

She'd been an L.A. cop. One night, she and her partner had been called to quell a domestic dispute in southside Los Angeles. When they'd arrived, the ramshackle house was dark and quiet. The neighbors insisted that there'd been a hell of a fight and someone inside was dead for sure.

Her partner had gone in the back and Helen had gone in the front of the unlocked house. She'd heard a sound in one of the front bedrooms and without waiting for her partner, had entered the room.

In the darkness, she'd made out the form of a man

sitting on the bed, the light from the streetlights casting a strong glow on his arm. The one that held the gun.

She'd fired instinctively.

But it wasn't a man. It was a fourteen year old boy, frightened at being alone and terrified by the fight between his mother and father who had both left the house.

The internal investigation had ruled that she had acted properly under the circumstances except for one small detail. She should have waited for her partner.

She'd left the force and become severely depressed. It had taken six months for her to get back to the basic rudiments of living and another year before she'd sought work. LAX had hired her on the basis of a glowing letter from her former captain. After the first terrible month, the press left her alone and she'd done a good job ever since.

Dan Wiseman had admired her then and he admired her now. The woman had a lot of guts.

Al Disario introduced the two of them.

"Dan, Helen has been a big help. She's the one who interviewed the mechanics who'd noticed Young messing with the airplane."

Dan shook her hand. It was warm and dry.

"Nice work, Ms. Porter. We certainly appreciate the help. Al says you may have something else."

She smiled and handed him one of the file folders. "I hope so," she said. "I talked to all of the people at the check-in screens and one of them noticed a man carrying tubes of chemicals on board. He had an authorization letter from the FAA so she didn't worry about it, but I asked the FAA to check their list of authorization letters with the names on the manifest of Flight two-three-four. They came up with a match. It might mean nothing, but I thought you should know."

Her voice had a certain musical ring to it. Dan Wiseman felt himself drawn to the intensity in her eyes. Certainly, she had a reason to be intense, but it seemed to be more than that.

"I'm glad you have that attitude."

"Thank you. I know the official word is that toxic chemicals were used, so I figured it might tie in. The man's name is Mark Martin and he works for a Newport Beach chemical firm called Burkhart Industries. I checked on them and they've been around a long time. Automotive chemicals. No problems with the police or with the EPA. They seem to be good corporate citizens."

Dan smiled at her. "Well. I'm impressed. You said he was carrying tubes of chemicals. What kind of tubes?"

"According to my witness, they were glass tubes. Like vials. Several different colors. The man said they were samples. She says he wasn't up-tight or anything. Seemed real straight."

Dan nodded. "Well, it's worth looking into. I can't tell you how much we appreciate your help." Then, he could hardly believe his ears as he said, "Look, I'm about to grab something to eat down in the cafeteria. Would you care to join me?"

She looked at her watch and then smiled at him. "Sure."

Dan turned to a smiling Al Disario. "Al, send some agents to talk to someone at Burkhart."

"Yes sir."

Dan Wiseman and Helen Porter took the elevator to the basement. They made small talk as they entered the cafeteria and went through the line. Once they were seated at a small table, the expression on Helen's face changed and she said, "Thanks for not mentioning it."

He looked at her in surprise. "What are you talking about?"

Her eyes were dark and deep. "I noticed that you recognized me the moment you came into the room. I get that a lot, usually from other cops. They usually bring it up right away. You didn't. Thanks."

Dan sighed. "It must be a bitch."

"No, I can't let it be. It happened. It got a lot of press but someday, it'll be old news. God, it's been three years."

He felt embarrassed. "I'm sorry I was so obvious. I usually manage to hide my thoughts better than that. Maybe I'm too tired. I can assure you that they were not critical thoughts. I did recognize you because I remember what you went through. You took an awful lot of abuse in the press and you handled it well.

Not without cost, I understand."

She blushed slightly. "Oh, there was cost all right. My husband left me and I had to undergo a lot of therapy. But I'm all right now. I really am. I enjoy what I'm doing."

"Are you divorced now?"

"Yes. He was a cop and he didn't think seeing a shrink was very macho. He couldn't understand why killing that kid bothered me in the first place. I was surprised at that. Most cops don't like to kill. He was an exception. Although, as far as I know, he's never killed anyone. Not yet, anyway. The strange thing is . . . I thought I knew him. But I didn't."

She said it without bitterness or rancor. Just a statement of fact.

"Well," he said, "I guess I'm in the same boat, in a way. I was married for sixteen years and one day my wife finally decided she didn't like being a cop's wife any more." He sipped at the soup and continued, "I guess it wasn't really one day. It happened over a period of time, but it certainly surprised me when she dropped the papers on me. Did you have any children?"

"No . . . thank God. You?"

"Yes. Two. The're here in California. I haven't even had the chance to talk to them on the phone. They're both at school, but I'll call tonight. As soon as this is over, I'll see them."

Helen coughed and said, "I wouldn't exactly call you a cop. You're an assistant director of the FBI.

That makes you a lot more than a cop."

He smiled and shook his head. "I'm still a cop. I may wear a suit and tie and have an office in Washington, but I'm still just a cop."

She played with her own soup for a moment and then asked him directly. "It is terrorists, isn't it?"

He hesitated for a moment and said, "I can't discuss it, Helen. I'm sorry. You understand."

Her gaze fell to the table. "I shouldn't have asked. I'm sorry."

"It's okay. Don't worry about it. You have a legitimate interest. I just wish I could tell you what I know. I can tell you this . . . you've been a very big help in the investigation and I'm not stroking you when I say that."

A small smile found its way to her full lips.

"Thank you," she said.

He stood up. "I've got to get back to work. Maybe, when this thing is over, we could talk some more."

The smile got larger. "I'd like that," she said.

As Dan stood in the elevator on the way back upstairs, he mused to himself about the sudden urge he'd had.

It had been a long time since he'd had a woman in his arms. A very long time. In throwing himself into work, he'd left little time for anything else. He hadn't taken a vow of celibacy—it had just turned out that way.

That was wrong. He had to do something about that.

He realized that he very much wanted to see Helen Porter again.

The blue car pulled into the visitor's parking area of Burkhart Industries and the two young agents got out. They walked the short distance to the entrance of the small building and went inside.

A pretty, young receptionist was seated behind a circular desk which held a computer terminal and a telephone switchboard. The two men showed her their credentials and asked to see the manager.

"Well, the company is managed by our president, Mr. Burkhart. Let me see if he's free."

The two agents waited while she used the telephone. When she hung up, she smiled and said, "Mr. Burkhart will see you now. His office is at the end of the hall."

The two agents walked down the hall while the young woman picked up the phone and dialed an outside line. When the line was answered, she spoke quickly and softly into the mouthpiece.

"Tell Cory the FBI is here. I don't know what it's about but I think it must be Mark."

Then she hung up the phone and tried to get her breathing to return to normal and her heart to stop pounding.

Her instinct told her to run for her life, but her brain told her to sit and wait it out. They didn't know anything. They *couldn't* know anything.

Only Mark Martin could tie her in and he was dead.

Damn!

All she wanted right now was a hit. But she couldn't.

Not with the FBI in the building.

She looked at her purse on the floor longingly. Inside the purse was the answer to her problem.

But she'd have to wait.

Her heart continued to pound as she waited.

Impatiently.

Alfredo Gravez sat on a small chair in the balcony of the Newport Beach condominium and watched the sailboats as they tooled slowly up and down the quiet waters of Newport Bay. He enjoyed these few hours each day, when he could sit out and watch the activity. Most of the time, he had to stay indoors, unless he wore a disguise, something he hated doing.

Four days ago, one of the sailboats had served as his entry into the United States. He could see it now, bobbing in the water, tied to its slip. An ocean-going 54 footer that had picked him up twenty-two miles from Newport Beach, away from the prying eyes of the Coast Guard.

He sipped on his beer and smacked his lips. He loved American beer and the large ice-box in his Bolivian mansion was kept fully stocked at all times.

A large man pulled back the sliding glass door

leading to the balcony and leaned over to speak to the old man.

"Sir, Cory just heard from that girl of his. The FBI are at Martin's company now."

Gravez jerked around in surprise. "The FBI? So soon? How could they know?"

The large man shrugged. "I have no idea. Cory says she sounded scared to death on the telephone."

Gravez cursed in Spanish. "Very well. I didn't want to move this soon, but we'll have to. We can't let them get too close. Tell Cory to take care of the girl immediately. And you and Predo find a motor home. As soon as you have one ready, get back to me."

"Yes, sir."

The large man went back into the condo and Gravez returned to watching the sailboats. But this time, the expression on his face was one of concern. Deep concern. It was impossible! There was no way the FBI could have found out about Mark Martin.

But they were there at Burkhart Industries.

It was very troubling.

## Chapter Twelve

Agents Jim Butler and Lionel Stokes took their seats across from the desk of Morris Burkhart and showed their credentials. The corpulent owner of the chemical company spread his chubby arms wide and asked, "How can I help you gentlemen?"

Butler opened his notepad and said, "Mr. Burkhart, we understand that one of your employees, a Mark Martin, was a passenger on Pacific Rim Flight two-three four. Is that correct?"

"Why, yes. We were all very shocked. Is that what this is about?"

"We're just conducting a routine investigation, sir. We're checking into the affairs of everyone on that airplane."

"I see."

The agent smiled and said, "We understand that Mr. Martin was carrying some glass vials with him and that he had a letter from the FAA authorizing him to do so. Can you explain that?"

Burkhart was eager to do so. "Certainly. We're in the chemical business. We manufacture—well we don't actually manufacture—what we do is buy large quantities of chemicals from a supplier and repackage them under our own label. Automotive chemicals . . . you know, engine cleaners, whitewall tire cleaners, mag wheel cleaners . . . stuff like that.

"Whenever we're about to introduce a new product, our sales managers travel to visit the various territories and take samples of our own product and those of our competitors. We're sticklers for accuracy, so we actually demonstrate to our salespeople why our product is superior, before we ask them to sell our customers.

"Mr. Martin was carrying samples of a new chrome cleaner that's better than anything we've ever had. Along with that, he had samples of eleven competitive products and he was going to use to prove just how good our new product is."

Agent Butler nodded, made some notes and asked, "Why glass vials? Why wouldn't he carry the samples in tins or cans?"

Burkhart grinned. "Well, we like to think we have some class here at Burkhart. Actually, that was my idea. When we're going through this procedure of introducing something new, we put the product in glass vials because it makes it look so much more important. Tins are so gross, you know?

"We have a special sample case that has a polyfoam interior specially designed to protect the vials. You could drop-kick the sucker twenty yards and never break a thing. I'll show you."

Burkhart got up and moved to a large wooden cabinet, opened it and drew out a briefcase. With a flourish, he opened the case and laid it on the desk. Inside the aluminum case was a thick foam cover, which when removed, revealed twelve empty glass vials, carefully cushioned in carved-out foam.

"You see?" he said. "We've been doing this for years."

Butler nodded. "Could we take a look at your operation?"

"Certainly."

For the next fifteen minutes, the man gave the two agents a guided tour of the plant, animatedly explaining each facet of the operation. When he was finished, he positively beamed. "Advertising and honesty . . . that's our secret. We spend thirty percent of our gross income on advertising and it works. And we never cheat the customer. Our products do exactly what we say they will, only better. I tell ya, it's the American dream."

The two agents asked a few more questions and left. It looked to them like the connection between Mark Martin's glass vials and the crash of Flight 234 was no connection at all.

Cory Farrow sat silently as Roberto Predo told him what he must do.

He didn't like it.

"Roberto," he protested, "killing Sondra doesn't make any sense at all. She called after the FBI left and told me that the only reason the FBI was there was because Martin was carrying some chemical samples, and the FBI found out about it. We had no way of knowing he was gonna do that. It had nothing to do with us. They never even talked to her. Besides, Mr. Gravez is gonna break the word soon, so what's the difference?"

Predo's face hardened. The thick eyebrows seemed to squeeze together as he said, "Look, we don't discuss this. When Mr. Gravez tells you to do something, you do it. He has his reasons and he doesn't have to tell you what they are. Understand?"

The young man put his head in his hands and groaned. "Jesus Christ! This is crazy!"

Predo reached forward and slapped him across the face. "Stop acting like a baby!" Then he handed the stricken man a small gun with a long barrel. "You grab a car and you take her down right after work. Put her in the trunk and park the car somewhere in Laguna. Ricardo will pick you up at the bus station on Pacific Coast Highway.

"Now you do this or it's your ass on the line."

Cory, his eyes burning with resentment, slowly nodded his head, took the gun and left the motel room.

At four-thirty in the afternoon, Cory Farrow parked the car he had stolen in the same slot the FBI agents had used when they'd visited Burkhart Industries. He got out of the car and waited near the front entrance for Sondra Olsen to leave her job as a receptionist.

She didn't keep him waiting.

Her face was flushed as she got into the car and

Cory backed out of the slot.

"God! What a day! Those FBI guys scared the hell out of me."

Cory said, "You said it was nothing."

"It wasn't. Like I told you, somehow they found out that Mark was carrying glass vials full of chemicals and that's what they wanted to know about. It had nothing to do with the package I gave him, thank God. Jesus! For a minute there, I thought I was gonna wet my pants. I'm sorry I got everybody excited. When they showed up, I just thought you should know."

Farrow gave her a hug. "I'm glad you called. You did right. But you shouldn't have been nervous. The package was just a present for someone, like I told you."

"Just a present! It was cocaine! You think I didn't know that?"

Farrow grinned. "It wasn't cocaine. It was just a present. A real present for a friend in Hawaii."

Sondra was astonished. "For real? I thought you were sending a small shipment of cocaine. Besides, I was worried that they might ask me questions and figure out that I was using. Those guys can spot a user a mile away. But they never talked to me at all. They just talked to Burkhart, the old fart. Cops make me nervous."

Farrow grinned at her. "Everything makes you nervous."

She made a face and looked out the window.

"Where are we going? And whose car is this? Where's yours?"

"Mine's in the shop. This is a loaner." Cory Farrow gave her another hug. "I have to make a delivery in Oceanside. Then we'll go out for dinner. Okay?"

"Sure."

Farrow lit a cigarette and asked, "Did you tell anyone about that present? The one you had Martin pick up?"

She looked hurt. "Of course not. You told me to keep it quiet, so I did. What's the matter, don't you trust me?"

The man with the beard laughed. "Of course I trust you. I was just askin'. Don't get nervous."

"I told you, cops make me nervous. I musta had three hits this afternoon. I'm about ready for another."

The car was now heading south on the San Diego freeway. Sondra reached for the large purse at her feet and as she did so, she heard a strange sound and felt a sharp pain in her side. She looked up at Cory, saw the gun in his hand and tried to speak. But she couldn't.

The pain was now excruciating. Her hand started to move toward her chest and then stopped as everything quickly faded into darkness.

In St. Peterburg, National Transportation Safety Board supervisor Lou Holt looked at the small black box one of his investigators had brought to him and whistled.

"You're right," he said. "You're as right as rain."

The twisted and partially crushed box measured twelve inches long, six inches wide and four inches deep. At either end of the box, the remains of a thick, gray cable hung lifelessly from the connector. The cables had been ripped apart from the force of the crash. But it wasn't the cables that had caused the investigator to bring the box to Holt's attention.

It was the fragment of silver duct tape still stuck to either end of the box and the three inch hole surrounded by a sticky gray substance.

The investigator grimaced. "Ain't it a bitch. It's gotta be C-four, and just enough to blow the box. Man, those assholes knew what they was about."

Holt looked at the serial number on the box. "Which one?"

"Number two. They haven't recovered the other two yet, but I'll bet they'll all be the same. That's why the temperature was so low. Shit, with all three heater controls out, the inside of that kite would be ten, twenty below zero."

Holt cursed and placed the device on his desk. "Good eye, Rick. Real good eye. Most guys would have missed it, figuring the damage was crash-related. Nice going."

The investigator smiled. "Thanks. But it weren't no big deal. You told us what to look for. C-four leaves its mark all over everything."

"I know, but it's still good work. I'll let the FBI know right away."

The investigator turned and headed back to the mass of wreckage accumulating in the hangar, while Lou Holt picked up the phone and dialed the command center.

# PART TWO

## Chapter Thirteen

Shirlee Simms sat at her desk smoking a cigarette, relaxing after the evening local newscast. It had been another good day.

The station was owned by United Broadcasting in New York and ever since the first bulletin that had gone out over the entire network, they had used Shirlee's updates on the national news broadcasts as well as the local broadcasts. That meant that her face was showing up on television screens all over the country. She was getting the exposure she'd been seeking for some time.

And she was feeling the effects of that exposure already. Kind words had been directed her way about the fact that her two and a half minute segments for the national news broadcast had been packed with new and interesting information about the mysterious circumstances surrounding the crash of Flight 234. It didn't matter that Bill Parkins had helped write the copy. Or that Shirlee was only one of three investigative reporters who were developing the story for the station and the network. It was Shirlee Simms, blonde, blue-eyed and looking like the typical girl next door, who was in front of the camera, telling viewers that there was much more to this plane crash story than the authorities were willing to admit.

When she'd first joined the station after working

for three years in the trenches up in Fresno, they'd pegged her as just another brainless bubble-head with big tits, screwing her way into a nice, cushy television job. In fact, she had slept with Bill Parkins, the news director, on a number of occasions, but that had been an act of compassion for a man who was saddled with an alcoholic wife incapable of fulfilling his needs. Besides, he was a handsome, gregarious man who respected her talent.

Then again, she had needs and her career goals ruled out any kind of relationship that might require a lot of time and attention. Bill took care of the physical needs, quite well in fact. The rest could wait.

His respect for her talent was now building quickly and Bill had just finished telling her that the station's ratings for the early evening news broadcast had risen two full points according to the "overnights." As she sat there, smoking and savoring her success, one of the gophers popped his head in the doorway and said, "Call for you on three six."

"Who is it?"

"Wouldn't say, but it's a man and he says he knows something about the crash."

Shirlee removed the earring from her left earlobe and picked up the telephone. "This is Shirlee Simms," she said.

The voice had an accent. A Spanish accent, just thick enough to be noticed, but the English was good, the voice well modulated, the tone easy and confident.

"Good evening, Miss Simms. My name is unimportant, but for the sake of discussion, call me Alfredo Predo."

She didn't have time for small talk. "Mr. Predo, they said you had some information about the crash."

"Yes. That is true. Information that will make you the most important person in the United States."

For a moment, she was ready to write this character off as just another crazy groupie, but there was something in the voice that held her fast. She decided to listen just a little longer.

"I'm listening, Mr. Predo. Go on."

As she said it, she threw a pencil at the glass partition that separated her office from that of Bill Parkins, who looked up and caught her pantomime motions asking him to pick up the phone. He did more than that. He activated a tape recorder as well.

The voice was relaxed, the man aware. "It's all right if you record this conversation but I won't be on long enough for you to trace the call, so don't waste your time.

"I want to meet with you. I know who placed the bacteria on the airplane and I know why. If you meet me, you'll know too."

She could feel her heartbeat quicken. He'd said bacteria. The FBI had insisted it was a chemical.

The voice continued, "Go to the telephone booths in front of the music center. I'll call you at eight. You may bring a cameraman with you. Just one. I'll give you the story of your life. If you follow my instructions and don't attempt to be clever, you'll never regret it. If you get carried away, you'll simply never hear from me again. Except on television. You'll see me telling some other reporter what I have on my mind."

Then he hung up.

Shirlee hung up the telephone and rushed into Bill's office. He was rewinding the tape and together they listened once more. After it was played back, Shirlee said, "I want to meet him. I think he knows something."

Parkins shook his head. "I don't. I think he's a loony tune, just looking for some attention."

Shirlee shook her head. "No. Not this time. He said we could bring a cameraman. That means he expects to be taped. He *knows* something. I'm sure of it."

Parkins said, "I think we should call the FBI."

*"No!"*

It was almost a scream.

Parkins looked worried. "Shirlee . . . this is L.A. The place is alive with crazies. Besides, the FBI has insisted that any and all information connected with this thing be relayed immediately. They've made it quite clear that this is a matter of national security and all of that. We're not protected by the First Amendment on this. We need to play ball or they won't be taking any prisoners. They're playing hardball, kiddo."

Shirlee grabbed a cigarette from the package on his desk and lit up. "Look," she said, "we'll tell the FBI everything as soon as we know what the hell it is we're talking about. Right now, we've got nothing. Besides, calling the FBI in will just queer it for us. The plane crash was caused by some terrorists with some sort of axe to grind. This guy has an accent—Spanish. There's just something about the voice and the manner that makes me think he's really connected. He hung up on us—groupies never do that. They want to talk your ear off. If we don't follow up, he'll just call another station and we'll be watching them get the biggest story they've ever had. We can't take the chance on missing out and you know it."

Parkins thought for a moment and then said, "Okay. Here's the drill. I'll send Billy with you. You take the call and talk to the man. But you call me right after you talk to him. Let me know where you're headed. Take a station car with a radio. If I don't hear from you, I'll call the FBI immediately, so you'd better call."

"No! We've got to play this straight. The man wants to tell us something. Let's not fool around. He's not going to hurt us or anything. He wants the story, whatever it is, on the air. We'll take the wagon. No radio."

Parkins exploded. "You do it my way or not at all!"

Shirlee refused to budge. "Bill, he asked for me by name. It wasn't a blind call. And he *knew* you were taping the conversation. This guy's no fool. If we don't do it his way, he'll just give it to someone else. I'll be all right."

They stood there and glared at each other for a moment, both of them knowing what would eventually happen. They couldn't take a chance on blowing the story, if there was one.

Finally, Parkins bowed his head and said. "Okay, but call me from the phone booth."

Shirlee nodded as she snubbed out the cigarette. "I'll call."

She rushed out of the office to keep the date. Parkins lit a cigarette of his own and chewed on his lower lip. He didn't like it. Not one bit.

Shirlee Simms waited for the telephone to ring. Exactly at eight, one of the three phones rang, and she jerked the receiver off the hook. She recognized the voice as being the same one she'd talked to before. Only this time, the tone was terse. Urgent. "Go to Union Station and park in front. Leave the back door of the wagon unlocked. I'll get in the back seat. You and the cameraman stay in front. Call no one and move now or the deal is off."

Then he hung up.

Union Station wasn't that far. For a moment, Shirlee considered making the call to Bill and then decided against it. The man had said wagon. He knew they were driving a station wagon which meant he could see them. He was probably in a car nearby using a mobile phone. She left the phone booth and headed back to the car. Billy was behind the wheel. She jumped in beside him and told him what was happening.

Almost as soon as the wagon came to a halt in front of the train station, the back door opened up and a voice, the same voice, said, "Don't turn around and don't look in the mirror. Drive away from here and go to Dodger Stadium."

They headed north toward the stadium in silence. At exactly that same moment, a very nervous Bill Parkins, back in the studio, picked up the telephone and called the FBI. He liked Shirlee a lot. But the FBI bulletin had been very specific. It was Parkins's responsibility. He wasn't about to ashcan his career for anyone. And that included Shirlee Simms.

Dan Wiseman sat at his desk and looked over the report from the agents investigating the death of Willard Young. The forensics report on the motel room wouldn't be completed for some time, but the preliminary indications were strong. There was little question that the man had been killed in the sleazy motel and moved.

The manager had identified the photo of Young and forensics had found a few red hairs on the carpet, traces of cocaine on the dresser and there was blood in several areas. It all fit.

So far, the police interrogation of the other guests had revealed nothing. Young had checked into the motel the night of the crash around six in the evening. Aside from the manager, no one had even seen him. And no one had seen anyone visit the room, nor had they heard any suspicious sounds.

The next morning, the maid had discovered the blood in the room and the police had been called. At the time, it seemed to be just another murder until someone in the police department put two and two together and notified the FBI.

Half of the guests who had been in the motel at the time of the killing had already checked out by the time the maid had entered the room. Most of the departed guests were tourists looking for a cheap place to spend the night. They'd left before any questions could be asked. They'd have to be tracked down, all of them.

Damn.

He looked over the reports from Huntsville. Still nothing on Roger Wilcox. He seemed to have vanished from the face of the earth. Several people known to be engaged in the cocaine business had been questioned, but they weren't talking. Not even the stoolies were talking.

Dan picked up another report and glanced through it. This one was from the crash site. There was now confirmation that the heating system had been blown.

Wiseman shuddered. Had it not been for that, an epidemic might now be raging unchecked throughout the country.

He wondered what kind of mind it took to murder 259 innocent people and yet take the care to ensure that they alone died.

So far, three terrorist organizations had claimed responsibility for the crash. While the FBI and the CIA discounted the claims, the press were having a field day.

He pondered the connections to organized crime once again. The idea that had been bubbling in the back of his brain was growing. He looked at the notes he'd made on the yellow pad.

Colombia. Cocaine.

Peru. Coca leaves.

Bolivia. Both.

Largest producer: Quartrall. Colombian.

Graves. Prison. Threats. Second largest producer.

Cocaine (again)

He threw the pad on the desk, stood up and stretched his tired body. Like a caged animal, he paced the floor of the small office while he tried to sort it out in his mind.

He'd discounted the possibility that organized crime was behind the terrorist attack on Flight 234, but . . . There was a new, more dangerous element making its presence felt in the country.

Colombian drug dealers had traditionally stuck to producing the cocaine and selling it to established distributions networks in the United States. Until recently.

There was evidence that the producers were setting up their own distribution networks, bypassing the normal channels, in an attempt to make even more profit. Both the Quartrall group, operating out of Colombia, and the Gravez group, operating out of Bolivia, had made inroads, much to the dismay of American crime lords.

Out on the streets, a small war was raging and the body count was rising on both sides.

The fact was that the established criminal organizations had many businesses to protect. The Colombians and the Bolivians, on the other hand, were engaged in drug production and distribution. Period.

Maybe . . .

He stopped pacing and picked up another report. Burkhart Industries had proved to be a busted lead. Everything that the owner had said seemed to check out. Bank records had been examined and discreet inquiries made. Nothing seemed to connect.

He rubbed his tired eyes. His stomach was telling him he was hungry. The cafeteria was normally closed at this time, but since so many agents were working around the clock, arrangements had been made to keep it open. Wiseman was just getting ready to head downstairs when the phone rang. It was one of the receptionists.

"Sir, I have a Helen Porter on the telephone. Will you take the call?"

Wiseman grinned and said, "Yes."

The musical lilt to her voice was a welcome sound. "Mr. Wiseman, I hope you won't misunderstand, but I appreciate your kindness earlier and I thought . . . well, I live six blocks from your office. I thought you might like a home-cooked meal for a change. It's all ready. I'll even pick you up. I know how busy you are."

Dan was pleased, but he hesitated. "Helen—call me Dan—that's very kind of you. But I don't have much time at all. It would be just eat and run. I hate to do that."

She seemed embarrassed. "I'm sorry. I know it was silly. I just do crazy things sometimes."

Dan scratched his chin and asked, "What is it?"

"Pardon me?"

"You said you'd already cooked dinner. What is it?"

"Spaghetti."

"Oh dear. Spaghetti?"

"Yes, with meatballs."

"Oh my . . . Can you guarantee to have me back here in forty minutes?"

"Absolutely."

He hesitated for a moment. It would be nice to get the hell out of this office, he thought. Get away from this investigation, if only for a few minutes.

"I'll be outside waiting," he said.

"Great. I'm on my way."

As Dan hung up the phone, he felt a blush rise to his cheeks. This was so incredibly stupid, he thought. The country is in terrible peril and he was on his way to have a spaghetti dinner.

He was too tired, he concluded. Much too tired. His brain was not functioning properly.

When Shirlee Simms and Billy Secord reached Dodger Stadium, they were told to park beside a motor home that was parked near the entrance. They did so and the man, now wearing a balaclava, got out of the rear seat and motioned for them to enter the darkened motor home.

"Bring your equipment," he said to Billy.

Billy lugged the minicam, some light and a battery pack out of the wagon and placed them inside the motor home. Then, he went back to the wagon and retrieved a small video tape recorder.

The man was tall and slim and his hands, the only flesh exposed, were dark-skinned and heavily wrinkled. There was a curtain that separated the main part of the motor home from the driver's section and it was impossible to tell whether or not they were alone. Shirlee sensed that they were not.

The man sat on the sofa-bed. "We'll start as soon as you are ready. I'll only say this once."

While Billy busied himself setting things up, Shirlee asked, "Why me? Why did you pick me?"

The man leaned back and crossed his legs. "Why not you? It has to be somebody."

Shirlee wondered whether or not this was some wild goose chase or something that would prove significant. It was now 8:30 and Parkins would be frantic. She watched as Billy attached two more cables, turned a switch and the small interior of the motor home was bathed in bright light. "Ready," Billy said.

As he did so, the man pulled out a piece of paper from his pocket, unfolded it and then looked at Shirlee. "Are you recording?"

Shirlee looked at Billy, who nodded and she answered, "Yes."

The man in the balaclava began to read from the paper in his hands.

"Names are not important here. However, I have a message for the American people. I represent a group of people who are responsible for the crash of the airliner in Florida.

"That crash was caused by a germ manufactured by the United States. A germ called BT thirty-three. The fact that we know this is proof enough that we are responsible.

"The airliner was attacked because we wanted to prove to America that we are in possession of this germ, and we have no hesitation to use it.

"The germ kills in minutes. We have very large quantities at our disposal and these have been placed throughout the country. Unless the demands that I am about to put forward are met, we will release the germs and tens of millions of Americans will die. The choice is yours. If you doubt our resolve, we suggest that you examine the remains of the airliner that crashed in Florida.

"Our demands are quite simple. One, Fernando Garcia Gravez, a man who has been kept in your prisons for three years, is to be released immediately and flown in a government airplane to La Paz.

"Two. The United States is to stop interfering in all Bolivian affairs of state.

"Three. The United States is to stop its illegal attacks on Bolivian farmers. And it is not to support any other government, including the Bolivian government, that seeks to destroy the farms.

"Four. There are to be no reprisals for the attack on the airliner."

The old man stopped and put the paper back in his pocket, then faced the camera again.

"What happens in Bolivia is none of your concern. When you attack our people in their native land and interfere in the lives of Bolivians, you tread on sensitive toes.

"The United States is rich and powerful. And a bully. Over the last few years, many innocent Bolivians have died at the hands of American bullies. The people who died on your airplane have paid the price for those acts. Unless you meet our demand, many more will die."

"These demands are not open for negotiation. You will not be contacted again. Any attempt at reprisals will result in terrible consequences for America. We have a weapon that we are unafraid to use. You have seen that.

"Release Gravez and leave us alone."

Shirlee Simms was stunned. The man had said it would be a big story. That was the understatement of the year. She had a few questions. "Do you really—"

The man rose from the sofa and held up his hand. "Turn off your equipment."

Billy switched off the lights and the camera. The

man in the balaclava opened the door to the motor home and stepped outside. He took a knife from his pocket and slashed two of the station wagon's tires. Then he turned to Shirlee and said, "That is all I have to say. You leave now. You have your story. I will expect to see it on your station by eleven o'clock at the latest. If I do not, I will simply contact another station."

He practically pushed them out of the motor home while Billy scrambled to save the equipment. Then, when they were both outside, the door closed and the motor home, its lights switched off, started up and rumbled off into the darkness.

Billy started putting gear inside the station wagon and Shirlee cursed the fact that the wagon had no means of communication. It was a quarter mile to the nearest telephone, a service station, and she started running toward it, her heart pounding with excitement.

What a story!

That's all she could think about.

The man had to be legit.

The name of Gravez rang a bell. Everyone knew who Fernando Gravez was. Until his capture in Colombia and extradition to the United States, he was one of the biggest cocaine honchos in South America. In fact, his prison location had been kept secret all these years because the feds were afraid of an all-out attack on the prison.

He was rumored to be worth billions of dollars. Billions! And now his friends, supposedly out of contact with him for three years, had boldly surfaced, killed 259 Americans in a completely ruthless act to set him free. And were threatening to kill more.

It was her story! Exclusive!

Jesus, she thought, panting as she neared the service station, this was it!

This would get her a network job for sure.

Dan Wiseman savored the spaghetti and smiled at Helen Porter. She seemed a bit anxious as she waited for his pronouncement on the state of the meal she'd prepared.

"It's delicious . . . really delicious," he said.

She beamed.

When she'd picked him up in front of the Federal Building, he hadn't failed to notice that she'd groomed her hair and applied some subdued makeup. She looked more like a model than a cop.

Her clothes were chosen to enhance her fine figure and it was clear to Dan that she was sending him a very strong signal.

Now, as he twirled the pasta on his fork, he felt flattered that this beautiful woman would find him attractive. It wasn't that he thought of himself as unattractive to women, it was just that he'd been "off the market" for so long and the steady devotion to his job the past two years had ruled out everything else.

For the first time in a long while, he was thinking of something other than the past and his work. He was thinking romantically and it felt so very strange.

She asked, "Did you get a chance to talk to your children?"

He nodded as he munched on the meatball. Finally swallowing, he said, "Yes. Both of them.

They're fine and we plan to get together as soon as this thing is settled."

As he said it, his eyes seemed to cloud over and his brow furrowed. Helen noticed immediately.

"I . . . I'm not really this forward normally. I don't want you to think I'm some man-hungry hysteric. I just couldn't think of a proper way to thank you for being so kind. I thought a break from the pressure might be worthwhile."

He waved his hand. "I know exactly why you did it. I'm glad you did. This spaghetti is wonderful. If I seem preoccupied, it's only because I feel guilty. I shouldn't really be here. This investigation is very important."

"Are you getting anywhere?" she asked.

"Well, yes. That lead you gave us didn't pan out, but you know how that goes. There are hundreds of leads that don't. But one will. That's why it's so important that people like you keep their eyes and ears open. You're a very aware lady, Helen."

"Thank you."

"We are making progress. I wish I could tell you what's happening, but . . ."

"I understand. I'm glad to hear it."

Wiseman's beeper signaled for his attention. Helen immediately pointed to the telephone on the kitchen wall. Dan got up and went to it. In a moment he was talking to Al Disario.

"Dan, we just got a call from Channel Three. Something's up. I think you should be there."

As soon as he heard the words, Dan could feel his pulse start to quicken. For some reason, he had a hunch that the shoe he'd been waiting to see drop, finally had. "Pick me up here. I'm at Helen Porter's. You have the address?"

"Yes."

"I'll wait for you outside."

Dan hung up the phone and reentered the dining room of the small apartment. Helen was already clearing the table. "I have to go," he said.

She smiled at him. "I know. I'm glad you were at least able to have your dinner."

"Me too. I can't thank you enough."

"You're very welcome."

He started to leave and then stopped. "Helen . . . this isn't the time, but . . . I'd like to see you sometime. You know, socially. I really would."

She almost beamed. "I'd like that very much."

When Shirlee Simms and Billy Secord finally made it back to the studio, Dan Wiseman, Al Disario and three additional agents were waiting. Dan had already listened to the tape recording of the initial telephone conversation and his hunch was growing stronger. As soon as he saw the look on the face of Shirlee Simms, he knew in his heart that it was no longer a hunch.

If looks could kill, news director Parkins would have been cold, stone dead. Shirlee knew instinctively that trouble was brewing. Secord, the cameraman, slowed his pace and started to turn away from what was to be a sure confrontation.

"Hold it!"

Wiseman's voice could be heard throughout the newsroom. He was in no mood for games. Disario and another agent relieved Secord of his equipment and Parkins suggested they all go to a conference room.

Inside, Dan glared at the reporter, his voice revealing an uncharacteristic lack of patience. "Okay, Miss Simms, let's have the story . . . all of it."

Her eyes were blazing with anger. "Nothing happened. Obviously, Mr. Parkins got a little excited for no reason. Nothing happened. The man never made the call."

Wiseman turned to Parkins. "I want to run the tape. Let's see what we've got. Al, you keep these two in the room until I get back."

Shirlee put her hands on her hips. She turned to Parkins. "FBI, right? You called the goddamn FBI?"

Parkins nodded. "I told you, Shirlee, they've already made it clear that this is a matter of national security. I didn't have any choice."

She hissed at him. "Asshole!"

Parkins took the video tape recorder from the agent and then he and Wiseman went into a small editing room. The recorder was plugged in and connected to a monitor, the tape rewound and then activated.

There were just the two of them watching the speech by the man in the balaclava. Wiseman could feel his heart pounding as BT33 was mentioned.

These *were* the people. His hunch had been right.

The problem was, the situation was much more serious than he could have imagined.

It all fit.

Too well.

And for the first time since he'd entered this case,

Dan Wiseman was well and truly frightened.

The tape came to an end. Wiseman turned to Parkins and asked, "Aside from you and the other two, who else knows about this?"

"No one," answered Parkins.

"Good. Bring Miss Simms in here, would you?"

Parkins went out to get her. When she entered the room, her eyes were still filled with hostility.

Dan said, "Miss Simms, tell me everything the man said besides what's on this tape."

She pouted and said, "He said he would be watching our station. If he didn't see the tape broadcast by eleven, he was going to call another reporter."

Dan groaned inwardly. He looked at his watch. He had one hour and twenty minutes. "That's it?" he asked.

"That's it."

There was no time. No time to get to a secure line and tell Spencer what was happening. No time. He'd have to use the phone here, run the tape and let Spencer at least hear the audio. Once the tape was broadcast, all hell would break loose.

And it was pointless to try and stop the broadcast. The man would just do as he had threatened. Call another reporter. In fact, he had probably already done so. The story might be going out over the air at this very minute. Dan's frustration was directed at the pouting blonde. "You know, Miss Simms, had you cooperated with us in the first place, as you were asked to do, we might have had the opportunity to interrogate the man you talked to.

"Clearly, he's one of those responsible for the deaths of hundreds of innocent people. In actual fact,

I could charge you with obstruction of justice.

"You were more interested in a story than you were in helping us find those responsible for this disaster. I would say that your attitude is one of the most selfish and self-serving I've ever witnessed. You may well hear from us later. In the meantime, I'd appreciate it if you'd get out of my sight."

As she left the room in a huff, Dan turned to Parkins. "I need a favor. I realize this has to go on the air. But will you give me as much time as possible? Say eleven o'clock?"

Parkins rubbed his chin. "I'd like to help, Mr. Wiseman, but if I hold this up and another station beats us to it, I'm unemployed."

Wiseman grunted. "Mr. Parkins, is it this industry or what? All you people seem concerned with nothing but your own careers! Don't you understand what's happening here? A group of terrorists is blackmailing the country by scaring the shit out of every living soul. They might very well kill us all. And you're worried about your job? Jesus!

"When that tape hits the air, there'll be some very frightened people out there. We need time to prepare an answer. I need every precious minute. If I have to, I can take the tape. Don't make me do that."

Parkins looked at the eyes of Dan Wiseman and slowly nodded his head, sheepishly looking at the floor. "Okay," he said, "I'll hold it until eleven."

"Can I trust you to do that?"

The color was rising to the man's cheeks. "Look, I may be a prick, but I'm not that big a prick. It was me who called you in the first place. Remember?"

Dan slapped him on the shoulder as a small smile

formed on his lips. "I remember," he said, "Tell me, will this be local or will it go national?"

Parkins's eyes opened wide. "Are you serious? This'll go national . . . lead item. I just hope we're first with it."

Dan grabbed the telephone. It was an open line, but it didn't matter much. In little over an hour, maybe less, the whole damn world would know what had happened.

The Gravez family was playing head games with the FBI. By releasing the information this way, they could frighten the hell out of the country, possibly forcing compliance with their demands.

Once the public knew the full details, they could come totally unglued. And there was no way to stop it from happening. Unless the president, a man who characteristically took forever to make up his mind, did something dramatic to diffuse the impact of the demands.

As he waited for them to connect him to Edward Spencer, there was a knock at the door and it opened. Dan whirled, the anger blazing in his eyes as he looked at a young, fresh-faced woman with a rueful look on her face.

"What is it?"

"Mr. FBI? I think you'd better take a look at the network feed."

"What?"

"There's a special bulletin coming through now. I thought you might find it interesting."

Parkins switched on the monitor and they watched in fascination as a man answered questions being posed by a woman with a microphone stuck in his face.

The caption underneath the picture said, "James L. Cummings, National Transportation Safety Board Investigator."

Wiseman couldn't believe his eyes or his ears. The man, seemingly in some sort of emotional distress, was saying, ". . . a bell. I mean, I've been in this racket for a long time and I'm tellin' you that plane was shot down. As for that crap about chemicals, that's bull too. It was a dangerous bacteria and they're still not sure what the hell it really is. That's why they shot the plane down, so's they could find out.

"Well, as far as I'm concerned, shootin' down one of our own planes on purpose is just—sinful. I mean, it isn't right and somebody ought to do something about it."

Spencer was on the phone. "Dan! What is it?"

As Wiseman began to relate the details, he could feel the migraine headache coming on like a runaway freight train. It was all beginning to explode in their faces.

And the fear became a living thing.

## Chapter Fourteen

President Robert Dalton sat in the high-backed leather chair, leaned back and went through his careful ritual of lighting a cigar as he listened to the report being presented by FBI director Edward Spencer. Two other men in the room also listened carefully. The president's senior advisor, Mickey Serson, and the Pentagon's man in charge of biological weapons, Gen. Waldo Smith.

Mickey Serson had been the president's friend and advisor since their college days back in California. Neither man had been much of an athlete, their interests running instead to intellectual pursuits. That didn't mean they weren't competitive by nature. They were. Both with women and grades. Mickey was the extrovert and Robert the introvert, his competitiveness refusing to allow Mickey to get the edge, which eventually conquered his natural shyness.

After college, Robert drifted into law school and eventually politics, while Mickey became a boy wonder in the development and marketing of various electronic gadgets. At the age of 35, Mickey, thoroughly bored with making money, decided to become Robert's campaign manager in his first attempt at national office. That success led to other successes and despite the constant battles over a twenty year span regarding Robert's "image," they remained the closest of friends.

It was Mickey who had turned the president's refusal to be "packaged" to an advantage during the presidential campaign, a feat of no small importance, since it was Mickey who had hired the image-makers in the first place. The "package" became the "real" Robert Dalton, something that hadn't happened in presidential politics in decades.

Although they were both the same age, Mickey looked much the younger, with a cherubic face, a full head of curly black hair and a seemingly permanent smile.

Right now, the smile was gone, replaced by a look of unaccustomed defeat. In fact, he looked almost ill.

As for the president, the look on his face was one of barely suppressed astonishment. Never in his wildest imagination had he expected the attack on the airplane to be other than a politically-oriented attack, involving some Middle-Eastern terrorist group. That was something the American public could understand, having been almost inured by the constant violent stream of seemingly mindless terrorist acts over the years.

But this! A terrorist act perpetrated by gangsters! Dope dealers! This was unthinkable.

His voice reflected the inner turmoil. "Ed, are you absolutely sure? This couldn't be a hoax, could it?"

Spencer looked at his notes and said, "The reference to BT thirty-three is the key. Very few people are aware of that code and Roger Wilcox was one of them. To me, it confirms my belief that Wilcox is the one who helped them on this."

Dalton slammed his hand on the desk. "Goddammit! We just can't keep a secret in this country. It's bad enough that our natural enemies probably know every time we take a shit and now . . . Gangsters! For Christ's sake! We're supposed to be the most powerful nation on earth and we're being blackmailed by a group of . . . Jesus H. Christ! This is intolerable!"

The president sucked on the cigar and asked, "How much time have we got?"

As he said it he looked at his watch and answered his own question. "Thirty-four minutes! What the hell am I suposed to do in thirty-four minutes? Can anybody tell me that?"

Edward Spencer ran a hand over his eyes. "We need time. As you know, there are some precautionary measures we can take, but they'll take weeks to set up. You need to stall these people, while at the same time making some statement that will prevent the country from going into a flat panic. I'd suggest that you make a statement on national television immediately following broadcast of that tape. I mean within seconds."

A solemn Mickey Serson said, "No way. It'll be two in the morning in the east. If the president of the United States goes on national television at that hour, the people will freak! We need to play this down, not play it up. It would be better if Tim went on and made some innocuous comment. Better yet, it's just another crazy claiming credit for the attack."

President Dalton looked at Mickey and then at Spencer. "What about the investigation?" he asked. "How close are you to nailing these people?"

Spencer sagged in his seat. "We're making progress, but there's so much to do . . ." His voice trailed off.

Mickey Serson was thinking out loud. "We've got to stall at first, and at the same time we've got to find a way to make them think we're going along. We can't let them release that bacteria."

President Dalton barked at Mickey. "I know, I know." He sucked on the cigar for a moment and then said, "Tim's asleep at home. Get him in here, but tell him to alert the networks before he gets out of bed. Fill him in as quickly as you can. He'll have to make a statement right after the tape is aired, while people are still watching the tube. At least most of the country will be asleep when this hits."

Mickey left the Oval Office to make the call.

Spencer said, "Don't forget, Gravez will be watching."

The president grimaced. "You're sure! You're sure it's him?"

"Dan Wiseman says he's sure that it was the father who made the demands. The general build fits and the enhanced video tape gave him a good look at the eyes. In the old days he didn't speak English and we don't have any voice tapes to compare, but I agree with Wiseman.

"The senior Gravez was the originator of the business in the first place and brought his son into it at an early age. We're showing his picture to every motor home renter in L.A., among others, but it might belong to one of the group members. The people from the television station say they never got a chance to get a license number. In the meantime, we've asked the DEA for an update, but they don't have that much. After that last fiasco, the Bolivians aren't too helpful."

They all remembered the fiasco. A coordinated raid on three Bolivian coca paste producing factories involving the Army, the Air Force, the DEA and the CIA had gone for naught because the dopers had been tipped. The source of the leak was still unresolved, but Bolivian government officials had been blamed and they weren't very happy about it. Right now, they weren't very happy about anything American and made no bones about it.

General Smith, who had remained silent to this point, spoke up. "I think I have something that might help."

Dalton smirked. "I'm all ears," he said.

The withering look in the president's eyes didn't go unnoticed by the general, but he let it pass. There was no time. "I'm sure," he said, "that they do not have BT thirty-three stashed all over the country. This material requires special handling. I think he's bluffing on that."

Dalton brightened for a moment. "You're the expert, General. Just how sure are you?"

Smith's eyes narrowed slightly and he bristled. "I'm very sure. If in fact he plans on using BT thirty-three as a weapon, he'll have to do it within twelve hours. The maintenance of BT thirty-three for periods longer than that requires special equipment. So, unless he's already placed the attack in motion, he's waiting. Which leads me to believe that the bacteria are all in one spot."

The president sucked on the cigar for a moment and then stubbed it out in the ashtray. His mouth tasted foul. To no one in particular, he said, "There's one thing we can be sure of. We're in one hell of a mess."

Mickey Serson reentered the room and took his seat. He said, "Tim's on his way. He's working on a statement that will cover the whacko from NTSB as well. We're looking into it, that's all. That's the theme."

The president turned to Edward Spencer, his face a mask of anger. "Okay, Ed, I want your people to take the gloves off. All of those people you've talked to—the ones who are keeping quiet. They have to talk. You can use whatever methods you have to, but we have to get to the bottom of this fast."

Spencer looked at him in surprise. "Sir, we can't do that. We just can't!"

Dalton's eyes were full of fire. "The hell you can't.

I know it's illegal but that's just too bad. I'll take full responsibility. I'll sign an order. They can nail my ass to the wall. But you've got to get serious. This country's very life is at stake. That bacteria has to be found and that's all there is to it. Whatever it takes."

Spencer looked horrified. "Mr. President, I cannot accept that kind of direction. You know that as well as I. It's not that—"

The president cut him off. His eyes looked as though he was pleading with the director of the FBI. "Ed, listen to me. I know all of the arguments. You're right. But this isn't the time to be right. We're talking about our survival here. You simply have to get to these people. I can't possibly give in to their demands. I'll try and stall, but I have no idea how long I can do that. Once they realize what we're up to, they'll start using that bacteria. They've already shown that they are capable of indiscriminate killing.

"The moment they realize that their plan has failed, and make no mistake, it has, they'll let it happen. We have to stop that. Torture, drugs . . . whatever. I just don't care. You've got to get them to talk. We must find out where the bacteria is and kill it. We're facing a major, major tragedy here. Can't you see that?

"There are times when the ends *do* justify the means. Are you going to stand on some high moral ground and watch while millions of innocent Americans die? You can't do that, Ed."

Spencer looked at the president in total shock. He

simply could not believe what he was hearing.

General Smith said softly, "Mr. Spencer, we've managed to produce something at Huntsville that's been thoroughly tested. We don't just make weapons, you know. It's a drug so superior to sodium pentothal you can't believe it. The subject is totally helpless and answers all questions put to him with complete honesty. It takes effect within five minutes.

"There are some unpleasant side-effects but that's to be expected. I can have quantities available within hours."

Spencer's head turned slowly and he looked at the general's eyes. They were shining.

President Dalton was smiling. "Now you're talking. Ed, you've got to move on this quickly. I understand how you feel, but we don't have a choice. Can I count on you, or do I have to waste time finding someone else?"

Edward Spencer looked at the president in awe. Here was a man renowned for taking forever to make up his mind on most issues. Now, he was issuing an illegal order to disregard the Constitution completely and use whatever tactics necessary to counter the actions of some insane criminals.

No matter what the outcome, the president's career, for all intents and purposes, would be at an end, the moment the order became public knowledge. Sooner or later, it would.

And the career of Edward Spencer would also be at an end. As would the career of every agent who had engaged in the illegal acts.

He thought about it for a moment and slowly, the true import of what was happening began to sink in to his consciousness. This wasn't a normal case. This was something extraordinary. The very life of the country was at risk. It was, truly, a case of survival.

California Highway Patrol officer Ben Cox parked his cruiser on hilly Trail Avenue in Laguna Beach, California and walked toward a three-year-old Chevy. The CHP had received a complaint from a woman who lived in the house in front of which the car was parked.

Officer Cox walked up the steps to the small house and the tiny, old woman was waiting for him. He took her report, went back to the cruiser and called in the license number of the Chevy. In a moment, the report came back.

The car had been reported stolen earlier in the evening. A wrecker would be dispatched to haul the car to the impound yard.

While he waited, officer Cox walked slowly around the car. As he neared the trunk, an odor assailed his nostrils. It was an odor he was, to his regret, quite familiar with.

He went back to the cruiser and removed a tire iron. With it, he managed to open the trunk and as the lid opened wide, he saw the body of a young woman.

Even though he'd seen dead bodies many times in his long career, it never ceased to sadden him. Slowly, he closed the lid of the trunk and returned to his cruiser.

Dan Wiseman was back in his office after making arrangements for the television studio to give him the original video tape, and use a duplicate for their broadcast. As he had three times previously, he reran the tape and watched carefully, trying to see if something—anything—could be noticed that had been missed.

The telephone rang and he picked it up. It was Edward Spencer.

"Dan, I've just left a meeting with the president and Serson. Here's the plan. They intend to stall for time by downplaying the entire thing. Tim Belcher is going to hold a press conference immediately after the Gravez tape runs. I want you to watch so you'll know how they're handling this."

"I will," Dan said.

"There's something else."

"Yes?"

"The Pentagon is flying a quantity of a new drug to every office involved in the investigation. It's a truth serum, Dan." He hesitated for a moment and then said, "We're going to have to break some rules, Dan. We simply have to find out everything we can. The rule book goes in the ash-can."

Dan sat up straight in the chair. "Whose idea is this?"

"The president's."

"Jesus Christ."

"Yeah. Look, as I said, he's going to try and stall for a while. He's hoping you can track these people down before they get the picture. Just in case, we're taking steps to protect as many people as we can. As you know, the bacteria dies at temperatures below fifty degrees and the most logical target is the sewer system. I want some of your people to locate all sources of liquefied gases in the Southern California area that can be used to reduce the temperature inside a sewer. Things like liquid nitrogen, oxygen. You tackle the commercial sources while the Pentagon goes after the defense contractors. We need to get our hands on every available bottle. Have the gases stored in warehouses or stadiums or whatever, but this all has to be done as secretly as possible. We don't want to tip off Gravez.

"They've made a judgment here that may or may not be correct. But we have to run with it. We're going to take every possible step to protect Los Angeles. The consensus of opinion is that the bacteria is stored somewhere in your area and that the first target will be the city of Los Angeles. They don't think the bacteria is in position anywhere else. Besides, it's not possible to protect the rest of the country.

"We have to pick a city and L.A. is it."

Dan was making furious notes. He said, "You're talking as though an attack was a certainty."

Spencer cursed. "I'd say the chances are very good. The president will have nothing whatsoever to do with the demands. They've been totally rejected out-of-hand. Once Gravez realizes that . . ."

He let the sentence trail off. Then he said, "While the gases are being collected, you're to interrogate every person who could possibly be connected with this and use the drug. General Smith assures us that they'll talk. I'll have the people in Huntsville do the same."

Dan Wiseman felt very cold. "Ed, if we do this we'll never get a single conviction. Not only that, but it could destroy the Bureau. We'll never be able to keep this quiet."

Spencer sighed. "I know that, Dan. But the thinking here is that it's redundant. We have to stop the bacteria from being released. If we don't, not much else matters."

Dan Wiseman listened as the director gave him some additional details and then signed off. He got up from his desk and turned off the video tape recorder, at the same time, switching the television dial from channel four to channel three. He looked at his watch.

In four minutes, the die would be cast.

He picked up the legal pad from his desk and looked at the notes he had made earlier. He underlined the word, "Gravez."

He'd been on the right track. Somehow, it didn't seem to matter much anymore.

He threw the pad to the floor and grabbed the phone. He had to talk to the kids again. Now! There was still time. They'd have to get out of town for a while, until this was over. They'd be confused, but they'd do it.

They had to.

At eleven o'clock in the west, two in the morning in the east, local news programs on the UBC network were interrupted by a bulletin from Los Angeles. The stations along the network had been previously alerted, and were ready as the scene switched to the Channel Three studios in Los Angeles.

Shirlee Simms, carefully coiffed and madeup, sat behind the desk and smiled at the camera.

"This is Shirlee Simms, UBC News, Los Angeles. UBC has a video tape of an exclusive interview with a man who claims to be a member of the terrorist group responsible for the crash of Pacific Rim Airlines Flight two-three-four." She paused to catch her breath.

"Earlier this evening, this reporter was contacted by the man who gave us the statement you are about to hear. While the FBI has refused official comment on the statement, informed sources here in Los Angeles have advised UBC that this man is indeed responsible for the deaths of two hundred fifty- nine innocent passengers and crew of the ill-fated airliner.

"Here now, is the statement given to me earlier."

The tape began to roll and the sinister looking man in the balaclava made his demands. When the tape was finished, Shirlee Simms started to resume her comments, but was interrupted by a voice heard through the small earpiece in her left ear.

"We understand that the White House had prepared a statement. We take you now to the press room in Washington."

By now, the other networks, previously alerted, had switched their own programming to take the feed from the White House. Tim Belcher, standing at the podium, was aware that the tape had run on UBC only. The other networks would be wondering what the hell it was all about.

He stood calmly at the podium, looking fresh, even though he'd been dragged out of bed less than an hour ago, and his face held a bemused smile.

"Good evening. As many of you probably missed it, I'll fill you in. UBC has just run a video tape of an interview with a man we believe is Alfredo Gravez, father of the notorious Fernando Gravez, now serving a life sentence in federal prison for drug trafficking.

"In the UBC interview, Gravez has claimed responsibility for the deaths of the passengers and crew on board Pacific Rim Flight two-three-four. He has claimed that the group he represents, which we believe to be the Gravez family, a group of Bolivian cocaine producers, has managed to procure some sort of deadly bacteria, which they say was responsible for the crash.

"He goes on to make several demands, such as the release of his son from prison, among others. He threatens to release the bacteria throughout the country if the demands aren't met."

He paused and sighed, as though the whole affair were boring.

"We've had the opportunity here, thanks to UBC news, to review the tape prior to its airing just a few minutes ago. As you know, whenever there's a tragedy of the magnitude of the one involving Flight two-three-four, any number of groups are most anxious to use the tragedy to further their own aims. Already, we've reported to you on a number of claims, all of which are being investigated, and all of which appear groundless.

"In this case, we haven't had time to check this claim out other than superficially. I can tell you that it will be investigated thoroughly, just like the others, and as soon as we have something, we'll get back to you. But at the moment, we have every reason to believe that this is just a clumsy attempt to secure the release of Fernando Gravez."

He shuffled some papers in his hands and resumed. "On another matter, involving the statement by a National Transportation Safety Board investigator that the plane was shot down by our own Air

Force, we've been in contact with the supervisor of the crash team and we've been assured that the allegation is completely wrong.

"The investigator who made the statement, James Cummings, has been a long-time employee who has a work record that is impeccable. However, like many people in high-stress jobs, he has come to an erroneous conclusion before fully investigating the facts, and decided to go public with it. While we sympathize with Mr. Cummings, we regret his error and the distress it has caused the families and friends of the victims of this incident.

"At a later date, the NTSB will release its findings, and those findings will be available to everyone. In the meantime, I can assure you that the plane was not shot down, but rather ran out of fuel as had previously been reported."

He leaned forward and said, "Now, I'm sure you'll have some questions. I'll stay here as long as it takes, so let's not get excited."

He pointed to one of the reporters. "Fred?"

"Yes. Fred Singer, AP. Where is the president right now?"

Tim smiled. "President Dalton is asleep. The White House staff has examined the tape and feels it unnecessary to wake him at this time. As I said, we've had several groups claim responsibility and this one is being treated no differently."

"A follow-up, Tim. I understand the tape referred to a bacteria called BT thirty-three, which they claimed is manufactured here. Is that part of our biological weapons arsenal and if so, how did these people get their hands on it?"

Belcher grinned. "In the first place, we are not engaged in the production of biological weapons, as you know. Where this guy got the name is anybody's guess. Frankly, we're a little surprised at such a blatant bluff."

On the balcony of the condominium on Newport Bay, Alfredo Gravez watched the small television set with growing anger, as the press conference continued.

They were treating him as though he were some crazy person. They were ignoring his demands. The president was asleep!

He picked up the telephone and dialed a number. When it was answered, he spoke in rapid-fire Spanish. Within five minutes, two burly men took their seats on the balcony.

Afredo Gravez gazed at the tied-up sailboats rocking gently in the on-shore ocean breeze. The moon was full and the air was cool. The air reminded him of his mansion in the mountains where the air at eleven thousand feet was always cool.

He turned away from the vista and stared at the two men waiting patiently for him to give them their instructions.

"Tomorrow night," he said, "there is a basketball

game at the Forum. I want the weapon released inside that stadium as soon as the game begins. Those watching on television will be able to see first hand what power we have. We'll see if they can brush off our demands after that."

One of the men seemed frightened. "But Senor Gravez. That could start an epidemic! It might never be stopped!"

The old man smiled. "Oh, you think I am an old fool?"

The large man looked at the floor of the balcony. "No *Señor.* You are no fool."

Gravez smiled. "You will assemble your entire group in the morning. I will tell you how it is to be done. There will be danger, but it will be worth the effort. Are you afraid?"

The man looked Gravez in the eye. "No, *Señor,* I am not afraid."

"Good. Come to this place at nine. The two of you. I will tell you then. Tomorrow night, the president of the United States will not sleep."

# Chapter Fifteen

William Powers sat in his hotel room and sipped a glass of milk. Ever since he'd watched the news on television, his stomach had bothered him. He'd slept fitfully, his rest interrupted by vivid nightmares of gigantic insects crawling all over his body. He'd awakened several times covered in cold sweat.

The White House was saying that this was just another crank, but Powers disagreed. He'd had a feeling about this case ever since he'd first become involved. Something didn't feel right and it bothered him.

He took another bite from the cold toast on the morning breakfast plate, and tried forcing his thoughts in another direction. In front of him were forty-two documents, releases signed by distraught relatives of victims of the airplane crash, signed, sealed and delivered.

The troops were still out there, beating the bushes, attempting to get as many releases signed as possible before a platoon of lawyers got to the relatives and convinced them that they'd be better off if they didn't sign releases.

Reports had shown that George Barnes had already reached twenty-one people who'd agreed to allow him to represent them. Knowing Barnes as he did, Powers expected a battle that could extend for years.

There were other lawyers involved besides Barnes, but he was the most formidable of the many they would have to deal with.

Forty-two releases. It wasn't nearly enough.

He looked over the other reports and tried to assess their chances. He'd given each report a grade, ranging from one to five, with a grade of one meaning the chances of getting a release were good. There were only seventeen of those. Not good enough by far.

The largest amount of any settlement was for $250,000. The settlement would be paid in about three weeks if normal patterns were followed. The adjusters in the field were rarely called to account for offering too much, but business was business and a few of the higher amounts would be carefully examined before the money was actually paid.

The telephone rang. He answered it.

"Bill?"

He recognized the voice of senior vice-president Taylor Madison. "Yes, Taylor. How're things back in Hartford?"

The voice seemed jovial. "Fine, Bill. Just fine. I have some news for you."

"News?"

"Haven't you been watching television?"

Powers answered, "Of course!"

"Well, there have been some recent developments

in this crash thing and Mr. Tupper is about to release a statement to the press. The statement goes out in about an hour. I thought you'd like to hear it."

Powers leaned back in the chair. "I certainly would," he said.

"The release reads as follows: 'Butler Casualty Insurance Corporation disclaims any and all liability for damages caused by the deaths of passengers on board the ill-fated Pacific Rim Airlines Flight Two-thirty-four.

" 'Butler Casualty Insurance Corporation takes the position that the crash of Flight Two-thirty-four was a direct result of actions taken by the United States Air Force and hence the government of the United States, in that the commercial aircraft was attacked by elements of the United States Air Force and shot down.

" 'In view of this action, Butler Casualty Insurance Corporation considers its client, Pacific Rim Airlines Incorporated, was in no way responsible for the deaths resulting from these actions.'

"That's it, Bill. Tupper's going to hold a press conference himself. As far as you're concerned, refer any inquiries here. In the meantime, carry on with what you're doing with one additional task."

Powers could hardly believe his ears. He asked, "Do you think this wise? The statement, I mean. It seems rather premature, don't you think? I mean, the government has flatly denied such a thing. Not only that, but the furor surrounding the attack on the plane has everyone upset. To announce this decision at this particular time seems rather cold and impersonal. I think it a poor public relations move at the very least."

"Premature? Not according to Tupper. He's sure that the plane was shot down and he's challenging the government to prove otherwise. He says no claims will be paid until the aircraft has been examined by our people. Tupper wants everybody to know right off that we're tired of paying off damages that aren't our fault. He's using this as a beacon and for my money, he couldn't pick a better situation. In the first place, LAX security never should have let whatever it was they put on that plane get aboard. And now, with these latest developments, he figures we're off the hook completely. So he's going for it. All the way. Let Barnes and the rest of those vultures go after the government." He chuckled as he said it. "That'll take centuries. Barnes will be dead and in his grave before he ever sees a nickel of contingency money. Serves the prick right."

Powers sighed and changed the subject. "What's the additional task?"

"We want a full investigation of LAX security people. The works. You know how that goes. Got to be a nigger in the woodpile there somewhere. Just as backup, you understand."

William Powers winced as he listened to his boss. The man was truly an uneducated and vulgar boor. How he'd ever retained the position he held in the company was a constant mystery. There was no secret in the getting there. The man had been a master salesman. But an executive he was not.

"Very well," Powers said, trying to keep the disdain out of his voice. "I'll get right on it."

William Powers hung up the telephone and turned on the television set. All of the stations were concerned with nothing but the flap over the Gravez tape and the White House reaction. There was a considerable amount of speculation concerning that reaction. The old expressions used during the Nixon and Reagan years were being dusted off and used again.

Words such as "stonewalling" and "coverup."

Powers snorted and switched off the set. Some things never changed. Only the players.

One thing was certain. It was going to be a muddled situation in terms of insurance claims. In a way, he felt sorry for the people who'd already agreed to a settlement. They'd been cooperative and reasonable, not trying to make a fortune out of a disaster. Now, they'd be forced to take other steps to seek redress for their damages. It would take a long time. A very long time.

Something like this had never happened before and when there was a case without a precedent, it could take decades to resolve. Now that the insurance company had disclaimed any responsibility, there'd be law suits galore. All of them complicated and prolonged. In the meantime, the families would receive nothing.

Not a dime.

It was sad.

He shook the thoughts out of his mind, picked up the phone and pushed the operator's button.

"Operator."

"Yes. Would you be so kind as to connect me with Mr. George Barnes?"

"One moment."

The phone rang twice and was answered by a woman.

"Mr. Barnes's suite."

Powers was grinning as he asked for George and identified himself. Barnes was on the line after a short delay.

"Powers! What the fuck are you doing calling me in the middle of the night?"

Powers laughed. "George, it's seven in the morning and if I know you, you've been up for hours already. Besides, I don't imagine you're doing much sleeping in the light of what's been going on."

"So what's that got to do with the price of cheese?"

Powers said, "I just thought I'd give you a little advance warning, George. Tupper is releasing a statement that disclaims any liability in the plane crash. The thing was either shot down or attacked by terrorists. Tupper's going with the Air Force shooting the thing down. He says you'll have to look to the government for your clients. I'm sure that'll be interesting."

There was a chuckle from the lawyer. "Really?" he

said, "Tupper's going public this soon? Hmmmm. Too bad. He'll look like the asshole he is."

Powers was a bit nonplussed by the lack of concern. "He's very sure of his facts, George."

The lawyer chuckled again. "I'm sure he is. Well, I certainly appreciate the information. Have a nice day."

With that, he hung up, leaving William Powers staring at the phone and wondering why George Barnes was so cool in the face of what should have been a disaster for him.

Donald James sipped coffee at his desk and took a break from the mountain of paperwork that confronted him.

Ever since the company had been placed into bankruptcy and the trustee appointed, he'd been forced to perform a hundred different tasks that were outside his normal purview. It was as though he were being punished in some way for having the temerity to ask that he be allowed to stay on until all contact with the families of victims was at an end. He'd explained his reasons, the fact that he'd been through it once before and felt his experience would be helpful in some small way to ease the terrible pain of those affected.

The trustee had openly sneered at that one, thinking instead that James simply needed the money. The small man with the accountant's bean-counting mind agreed on condition that James help in the collecting of other data unrelated to the accident, to be used in the final wind-up of the airline's affairs.

So James was burdened with lists of spare parts to recost and letters of notification to creditors to prepare along with the hundreds of letters and phone calls to families as new information arrived almost hourly from Florida.

He put the coffee down and picked up the latest report that had just arrived via computer link.

There were still thirty-seven bodies unaccounted for. Not bodies really, but parts of bodies. The grisly task of trying to match body parts had begun and they expected to have that completed within a few more days.

His eyes blinked at the name of Mark Martin.

They had found his body. Both legs had been severed and found. Tentative identification had been made by those on the scene from a billfold in the jacket pocket. The body of Mark Martin, like the others, had been taken first to the ice plant in Tampa, then shipped to Atlanta for autopsy, then back to the ice plant. Right now, the body of Mark Martin, the legs reattached after the autopsy, was back in Tampa and would remain there until formal identification was made. They'd been able to match the legs to the body by coordinating the cloth of the suit he'd been wearing with that found wrapped around the severed legs. A notation acknowledging James's request that the remains be shipped to Costa

Mesa for identification was listed and beside it was the legend, "request denied."

He wasn't surprised.

He'd told Mrs. Martin that he would arrange for shipment of the body, but in his heart, he knew that it was unlikely when he'd said it. At the time, he didn't want to cause any additional distress.

Now, he'd have to talk to her again. It wasn't something he felt like doing on the phone.

He got up from his desk and put on his jacket. Immediately, Thompson, one of the trustee's jackals, a man with the face of an owl and the manners of a goat, snapped, "Where do you think you're going?"

James shuddered as he thought of these ham-handed people dealing with distraught families. Insensitive assholes, the lot. And that's exactly who would be dealing with them if he hadn't asked to stay on. His desire to continue with it tempered his first reaction to the question which was to shove a chair down the man's throat.

In as calm a voice as he could muster, he said, "I've got to see one of the families in Costa Mesa. They've finally found one of the passengers who was missing and I've got to arrange for the family to go to Florida."

Thompson whined, "The families were supposed to be in Florida already. Just use the phone. There's no need to waste all that time driving out there."

James stiffened. "I'd rather see them personally. It's very difficult for them when you simply telephone."

The small man sneered, an expression that seemed practiced, as though to match the sneer of his boss. "You still think you're involved in public relations, James. You can't seem to get it through your head that the airline is out of business. There's no need to kiss ass anymore. Just use the fucking phone and forget about being Mr. Nice Guy. We can't afford the time."

There was a limit to the patience of Donald James. It had just been reached. He reached over and with one strong hand clutched the man's tie and shirt, drawing him upward from his seated position so that his nose was less than an inch from that of James.

"Look," he said, his eyes filled with fire, "I've already spent enough hours at that desk. I have things to do. Just leave me alone and let me do my job."

There was no response, other than a look of fear in the man's eyes. Reluctantly, James released his grip and the man slumped back into his chair.

The whine began anew, sounding like some distant air raid warning siren. "You can't speak to me like that, James. I am your superior. It was *you* who asked to stay on and Mr. Cooper allowed you to do so. However, you work for us now. If you can't control yourself, I'll have Mr. Cooper dismiss you on the spot. This job is difficult enough without the tension created by your presence. I won't stand for it."

James resisted another impulse and sighed. "I'll try to improve my attitude, Mr. Thompson. I'll be back in a couple of hours."

The sneer returned but the man remained silent, perhaps sensing that his well-being was in some danger.

James kept the window of the car down as he drove south on the San Diego Freeway toward Costa Mesa. It was another cool winter day and the air served to clear his head, sweeping some of the cobwebs away, and letting some of the unrelenting gloom dissipate.

The last 48 hours had been hell. The offices of Pacific Rim Airlines, already crowded with accountants involved in the bankruptcy, was also swarming with all manner of investigators, from insurance investigators to FBI. In fact, it seemed as though the entire airport was under siege by those involved in the continuing investigation surrounding the breach of security at LAX.

They knew what had happened. It was a breach that would have been almost impossible to prevent. There were thousands of people working at the airport and everyone knew that if some dedicated and skillful terrorist was bent on sabotage, there wasn't a hell of a lot anyone could do.

The fact was that LAX was a busy and vital airport. The type of security measures that would be needed to significantly reduce the odds of anything like this happening again were such that flights would be reduced by at least half. No one, not the airlines, the public or even the politicians, would stand for that. It was a problem that they constantly wrestled with and although security systems had been tightened over the years, there were still large holes that were impossible to fill.

But the investigation would proceed, because it was demanded. Precious hours would be spent considering thousands of recommendations and in the end, very few would be implemented. He had seen it happen before.

It was a thirty-five mile trip from the airport to Costa Mesa and at this hour the freeway was heavily traveled. It had been said that rush hour in the Los Angeles area ran from 3:01 in the morning until 2:59 the next morning. It wasn't that much of an exaggeration.

He took the Harbor Boulevard off-ramp and made a right at Gisler. In three minutes he was in front of the home of Mrs. Martin. Before he left the car, he mentally went over what he wanted to say to her, then, almost wishing he had called instead, got out and walked toward the front door.

The door was opened by Mr. Brackton and from the look on his face, he seemed blessed with ESP.

"Good morning, Mr. James. I imagine you're here about Mark. They've found the body."

It was a flat statement of fact.

James asked, "Has someone been in touch with you?"

"No," answered Brackton. "I could tell by the look on your face." He opened the door and said, "Won't you come in?"

James entered the comfortably furnished bungalow and said hello to Mrs. Brackton and Elizabeth Martin.

Elizabeth Martin seemed much better. Her eyes had lost that look of terrible pain and she appeared calm and controlled. "Have they found Mark?"

James sat down and nodded. "Yes. That's why I'm here. I'm afraid they've turned down my request that Mark be sent here for identification. They've asked that I arrange transport for you to come to Florida. I'm very sorry."

Mr. Brackton cleared his throat and asked, "Could I be the one? It doesn't have to be Elizabeth, does it?"

Elizabeth Martin held up her hand. "It's all right, Dad. I'll go. I can do it now. I'm fine."

James rubbed his chin. "All of you can go, should you wish. I can arrange for three seats anytime today or tomorrow. Just tell me what hour would be most convenient and I'll take care of it."

The look of pain returned to the eyes of Elizabeth Martin as she asked, "Was he . . . terribly . . ." and then she started to cry.

James shook his head. "Mrs. Martin, my information is that all of the passengers suffered for a very short period of time. That's all I know."

Brackton stiffened. "Could I talk to you outside for a moment, Mr. James?"

"Certainly."

The two men went out to the back patio as mother

and daughter comforted each other. Brackton didn't take long getting to the point.

"Just what the hell is going on? I've been watching television news and they're saying that the plane was shot down by our own Air Force, for God's sake! I've never heard of such a thing! Now the insurance company which, if I remember correctly you said was one of the worst, is saying that they don't intend to be responsible because of it. You just said that Mark didn't suffer long. Just what is the story, James? The real story."

The air was cool and still. The only movement was that of a cricket trying to extricate himself from a misplaced leap into the swimming pool. James thrust his hands into his pockets and scraped a shoe along the patio brickwork, "I don't know any more than you do, Mr. Brackton. The FBI is working hard to determine exactly what did happen, but I've listened to the rumors and the conjecture and if I had to make a guess, it would be this; somebody placed a chemical or gas or something on board our airplane for reasons I can't fathom. It killed everyone on board in minutes. It could be this Gravez family they talk about, and then again, it might not be.

"In any case, I think that somebody in our government made the decision that everybody on board was dead and that the plane should be shot down to ensure recovery of the bodies and to aid in the investigation. I listened to that National Transportation Safety Board inspector's remarks and I think he was telling the truth. I think the truth is what sent him over the edge mentally.

"There's much more than meets the eye on this and I'm sure that the powers that be are trying to keep a tight lid on it until they know what went on and why. I'm sure that, in time, everything will come out. Obviously, it's a very serious situation. This isn't the first time that an airplane has been used this way. In past cases, it's been an insurance scam. Somebody killing a lot of people to collect the insurance on one particular relative. But this appears to be something much more sinister.

"I feel confident that Mark was dead long before the plane was shot down. I'm sure his suffering was for a limited period of time. I can't tell you why I'm so sure, but that's how I feel. I do know that when the plane was in the air, we were asked to calculate a position where it might be expected to run out of fuel and that position was well past the east coast of Florida. That's between you and me.

"So, even then, someone was making a judgment about the possibility of shooting the plane down. I'm positive they would not have made the decision to do such a thing unless they were convinced beyond all doubt that the passengers were already dead. Of that, I'm very, very sure."

Brackton seemed unconvinced. "Well," he said, "one thing's for certain. Until all of the facts are known, my daughter is out in the cold as far as any law suit is concerned. I've been examining her financial situation and it isn't that good. Mark hadn't been with the company he worked for long enough to be included in their group insurance plan and he had no life insurance. I expect it will take years for Barnes to be able to sort through this labyrinth."

"I wouldn't be too concerned, Mr. Brackton," James said. "Our passengers were automatically covered by a liability policy that has a fifty thousand minimum payment for death, no matter what the cause, aside from war. By war they mean a declared war. So, despite what the insurance company says for public consumption, they'll have to pay that amount regardless of the outcome of any investigation. What the insurance company is disclaiming is their responsibility for amounts higher than the minimum coverage.

"You might check and see how the ticket was purchased. Certain credit card companies have additional coverages that would be in effect. I'm sure that the fifty thousand from Butler Casualty will be paid promptly and acceptance of that does not prejudice any future actions in any way. If you like, I can write you a letter to that effect, which you could use to borrow money at the bank, using the forthcoming payment as collateral. I'm sure you'd have little difficulty.

"Frankly, I'm a bit surprised that your attorney didn't tell you of this. He's very familiar with the situation."

Brackton snorted. "Our attorney, the eminent Mr.

Barnes, is more concerned with signing people up than he is with advising those already signed. I've tried to call him several times and all I get is, 'he'll get back to you.' As for the insurance company, they had a man out here to see us just after you left the first time you visited. He explained nothing once he found out that we'd engaged Mr. Barnes, other than to say that we'd been foolish.

"He said that people who hire lawyers in these matters end up with half of what they would if they'd simply let the insurance company handle it. He seemed quite arrogant."

James grunted. "Well, he's wrong. He's just trying to frighten you. In actual fact, people who settle with insurance companies in disaster situations without benefit of legal advice receive considerably less and the figures are there to support it. Unfortunately, you're becoming part of a battle between two forces. Try to be as patient as possible and not take it personally.

"As for Barnes, I wouldn't be too upset. I'm sure that George Barnes, no matter his notoriety, will represent your daughter's interests as well as they could possibly be represented by anyone. He may be a gruff, insensitive bastard in some respects, but he's without peer when it comes to getting results. In fact, if you do feel the need to borrow money, telling the bank that Barnes is representing you will almost be enough."

Brackton looked away. "I feel . . . iniquitous, talking about money and law suits at a time like this."

James patted the man on the shoulder. "Don't. It's part of the process. Anger. We all get angry and we want to get even somehow. It's normal. I'm sure all of the others feel the same way. There'll be plenty of time for grieving. Getting the anger out is good for you, I'm told."

They both grew silent for a moment and then Brackton said, "You know, fate is a strange thing. Elizabeth says that Mark almost missed the plane."

"Really?"

"Yes. He was running late that morning anyway and then he got a call from the office. The receptionist wanted him to take a present to a friend of hers in Hawaii. Mark told her he was late already, but she practically begged him, so he stopped by the office to pick it up. He was like that. Too bad she couldn't have held him back just a little longer."

Donald James felt a small tingle at the back of his neck. "Have you told anyone else about this?"

The man looked surprised. "No . . . we were just talking about it last night. Why?"

"No reason. I just wondered."

Brackton sighed and said, "I'll go with Elizabeth to Florida. I'll have Molly stay here and look after the place. Would sometime around noon be all right?"

James stared at the pool. The cricket was getting tired, the spasmodic jerking of the back legs becoming more infrequent. "That'll be fine. I'll have a car by to pick you up . . . say about ten-thirty. Would that be convenient?"

"Fine."

"Very well. I'm sorry I was unable to prevent the necessity of traveling to Florida."

"I appreciate the effort, Mr. James."

They walked back into the house where James said his goodbyes and then he was back in his car, driving through the quiet neighborhood and back on to the freeway. His mind's eye kept seeing the helpless cricket trying to extricate himself from the pool. Somehow, he felt a kinship with the black insect. Then, on an impulse, he took the first off-ramp and headed back to Costa Mesa. For reasons he couldn't understand, he felt the need to talk to the receptionist at Burkhart Industries.

George Barnes lay on his back and watched as the pretty young woman with the flawless skin worked feverishly to bring his limp penis to life. She'd been at it now for ten minutes and nothing was working. She'd licked it, fondled it, sucked it, kissed it and nothing was happening.

For a moment, when she'd first taken off her clothes and let her nipples brush against his face, there'd been a flicker of hope.

But even this woman, practiced in the art of mercenary love, couldn't arouse him today.

It hadn't happened often, but it had happened, and he wasn't surprised. Not with what lay before him. He was swimming in uncharted legal waters and he was getting too old for it. Too rich, too famous and too old. The fires were banking and it frightened him.

Whereas in the past he would storm forward, confronting and defeating the most formidable obstacles erected to prevent his clients from getting their just desserts, the case of Flight 234 seemed to be a mine field of problems. The critical bone of contention was whether or not the people on board the airplane were dead before the plane was shot down.

The government held the key to that information. If in fact the passengers were alive when the plane was shot down, then the government was the likely defendant in the legal action. A heavy stamp of "Classified" had been placed on the entire situation and George Barnes would have to fight like hell to get the information declassified.

If the passengers were dead when the plane was shot down, it would be an entirely different matter. The results of autopsies might be able to shed some light, but even they were classified. Death certificates were being issued that placed the cause of death as "traumatic insult." They served only to prove that the victim was dead and nothing else.

He spoke to the woman who was making all manner of sounds as she struggled with the task at hand. "Forget it sweetheart. We're flogging a dead horse here today."

He thought she looked relieved and worried at the

same time, if that was possible, "I'm sorry, lover . . . I just . . ."

He waved a fat hand at her. "Don't worry. You'll get paid. Tell Mildred everything went fine. I'll back you up."

The woman got up from the bed and started to get dressed. She was a stunner. At any other time he'd have had no problem with this thousand dollar a trick call girl.

He looked down at his limp penis. Maybe he was getting too old for sex as well. God! If that was the case, he might as well take a leap out the window.

He shook his head. He was just tired. This airplane crash couldn't have come at a worse time. It had been a lousy three days since he'd finished the Compton case. Nine months of relentless effort that had resulted in a pre-trial settlement of four and a half million dollars. And now he was plunging into this nest of snakes.

Terrorists! The Air Force. Jesus Christ! Was nothing simple anymore?

The hooker was dressed and bent over to kiss his cheek.

"Call me anytime, lover. I'd love another chance to make you come . . ."

"Yeah, yeah. I'll call. Now get lost."

She pouted briefly, turned and headed for the door.

He got up from the bed, put on a silk robe and then poured himself a drink as she let herself out. He sipped the drink for a moment and then punched some buttons on the telephone. When it was answered he almost barked into the mouthpiece. "Johnny! Get your ass up here. We need to talk."

"Yessir."

He hung up the telephone and sat back in the chair. This was going to be tricky. He had to get his hands on that information. Since it was a civil case and not a criminal case, the rules on admissibility were somewhat different. Nevertheless, he had to be careful. It had to look as though the information was given to him.

Besides, there were those in Washington who hated his guts. Just waiting for the opportunity to string him up by the balls. He was going to have to be careful.

Very careful.

On the other hand . . .

There were others in Washington. There were those who owed George Barnes a great deal. Some even owed their positions in government to him. There were skeletons hidden in many closets and George Barnes knew of several that were career-enders. As much as he despised the need, he felt the time was ripe.

It was time to call in some markers.

He didn't have time to play games. This case was going to be rough. He needed to shorten the odds and the time frame.

He started to grin as he lit a fat cigar but the grin

never made it all the way.

Damn!

He was finally getting an erection.

# Chapter Sixteen

FBI agent Paul Wiggins looked at the three men in the small holding cell within the Detroit offices. During the night, agents had picked up the men in separate parts of Detroit and brought them back to the office for further questioning. The interrogation had continued through the night. The men had said nothing other than to demand to see their lawyers. That demand had been ignored.

Wiggins looked at the package that had arrived fifteen minutes ago by special courier and for the second time, read the instructions that had been enclosed with the syringes.

There was no mistake.

They were to use the drug on anyone suspected of having had contact with Willard Young and they were to find out the truth. No Miranda, no lawyers . . . zip.

Wiggins shrugged his shoulders and sighed. Things had certainly changed in Washington.

As per instructions, he pulled out his lighter and burned the instructions. Once they used the supply of the new drug, they were to dispose of the syringes as well.

Wiggins turned on his heel and ordered one of the men to be brought into the interrogation room.

Two agents brought a swarthy, tired Latin into the room and handcuffed his arms behind the chair. He cursed at them in Spanish until he noticed the needle in the hands of Wiggins, at which time his eyes became as round as saucers.

One of the agents rolled up the man's sleeves and Wiggins, without hesitation, rammed the needle home.

The man screamed. And he cursed again . . . this time in English.

"You fuckin' assholes! You can't do that! I want my lawyer!"

They let him scream away while they waited. It didn't take long. Within three minutes, the man stopped screaming and his body slumped down in the chair. For a few moments, his head bobbed back and forth, while his eyelids dropped and partly covered his eyes, giving him a half-sleep expression.

Wiggins started the interrogation.

"What's your name?"

"Pedro Rodriguez."

"Where do you live?"

"Southfield. Two-five-five-seven-seven Magnolia."

"What do you do for a living?"

The man giggled. "I sell cocaine . . . want some?"

Wiggins ignored him. "Do you know a man named Willard Young?" he asked.

"Used to. He's gone."

"How did you know him?"

"He was a customer."

"That all?"

"No. He worked for the FAA. My boss told me to bring him to a meeting about a year ago."

"Who's your boss?"

"Pita Rima."

"Who's the big boss?"

"Big boss in jail."

"What's his name?"

"Fernando Gravez."

Wiggins smiled in satisfaction. "Tell me about the meeting with Willard Young."

"The boss wanted to meet him. After they met, Young got fired because he was a cocaine user and Pita ratted on him. Then Pita gave him a proposition. Young took the deal and moved to Bolivia."

"What was the proposition?"

"Just that he work for the Gravez family for a while. They were planning something."

"What?"

"I don't know."

"Where is Pita now?"

"Bolivia."

"Did Gravez have anything to do with the crash of that airplane?"

"I don't know."

"Do you know anything about the bacteria that he mentioned on television?"

"I don't know nothin' about that."

"Where is Alfredo Gravez now?"

"Bolivia, I guess."

Wiggins asked a few more questions and then they brought the next man in. After being given the drug, he confirmed the story of the first man. As did the third man interviewed.

Wiggins took his notes to the communications room and had them transferred to code and transmitted to Dan Wiseman in California. Copy to the director.

In Huntsville, Alabama, four men were given the drug by Special Agent Harry Tomkins. The first man knew very little. Same for the second. But with the third, they hit pay dirt.

His name was Paulo Gomez and he was Roger Wilcox's supplier.

Tomkins asked, "How did you meet Wilcox?"

"He was at a party that I was at. His girlfriend was a cocaine user and she suggested he try it. So he did."

"Did you know what he did for a living?"

"No. Not then. Later, his girlfriend told me. She dropped him because he was getting depressed all the time. So I told my boss about it, 'cause I knew he was trying to think of a way to get Fernando out of the slammer."

"Explain that."

"Well, they were talkin' about bustin' Fernando out of prison, 'cept they didn't know which prison he was in. You assholes were movin' him all the time. Anyway, Wilcox was braggin' about these bugs he was makin' and sayin' that a little of this and a little of that could get anybody outta anywhere. I jus' thought the boss should hear it."

"Who's your boss?"

"I work directly for Alfredo Gravez. I'm a district manager. I cover the entire Southeast."

The man said it with a certain amount of pride, like he was working for General Motors or something. Tomkins could feel his heart beating quickly. They had been seeking information on this drug ring for years and here it was, all in a matter of minutes, just by breaking a few rules and using some exotic drug. He thought how nice it would be if the technique became a regular feature of FBI work. It would take years to build enough prisons to hold them all.

"What did Gravez say when you told him about Wilcox?"

"Nothing then. But later he told me to tip off the research place that he was a user and then pick him up after he was fired. I did and flew him to Bolivia for a meeting with Alfredo Gravez."

"What happened then?"

"I don't know. But I never saw Wilcox after that."

"Where is Alfredo Gravez now?"

"Bolivia."

"Did he have anything to do with the airplane crash?"

"I don't know."

"Did you see him on television last night?"

"Yes."

"Do you know anything about the bacteria he's talking about?"

"No."

Tomkins also asked some more questions and then forwarded the text of the interview to Dan Wiseman. Copy to the director.

In code.

Dan Wiseman was doing some interrogating of his own. Two members of the Gravez family told him everything they knew about the killing of Willard Young, and said they worked for Fito Gravez, a second cousin to Alfredo. Fito, according to both, lived in Bolivia and entered the U.S. infrequently. Neither man knew anything about the bacteria.

According to the two men, Young had been hired by the Gravez family to do a job, but they didn't know what it was and they didn't know who killed him. But they were sure he'd been killed by the family.

He was asked to give complete details on how the drugs were brought into the country but he said he didn't know. All he knew was the address of a place in Los Angeles where he would pick up his supplies from Fito's people. Once a week.

Dan forwarded a coded copy of the transcript of the interviews to the director and then went back to his office and studied them, along with the reports from Detroit and Huntsville.

One thing stood out loud and clear.

These men were integral cogs in the Gravez organization and knew much about the distribution network. But not enough. Only what they needed to know. Gravez ran a tightly-controlled ship.

But they knew nothing about the bacteria.

In the tape, Gravez had said that he had men in place all over the country ready to release the bacteria if need be. The men that had been interrogated would be the logical people for that task. But they knew nothing.

It meant that the bacteria was being closely guarded and most likely in one location. Spencer's hunch was right. Los Angeles was the probable target, not the entire country.

Unless . . .

Unless the FBI had failed to grab the right people.

He leaned back in his chair and looked out the window.

So far, the White House tactics seemed to be working. Traffic was orderly and despite the screaming in the media, most people were going about their business with less concern than Dan would have expected.

His thoughts turned to something else that had transpired this morning. Last night, he'd reached the kids and told them as much as he could, begging them to get out of the city for a while and take their mother with them. At first, they'd argued, but after listening to him for a while, they'd finally accepted his concern as well-founded.

Half an hour ago, Danny had called to say that he and Dawn were on their way to San Diego, but that their mother had refused to go. A new boyfriend was taking her to the Lakers game this evening and she didn't want to miss it.

Well, the kids were the important thing.

Bernice could live her own life.

Al Disario knocked on the door and poked his head in. "Dan," he said, excitedly, "I've got something."

Dan followed the RAC into his own office where he was introduced to Donald James.

"Dan," Disario explained, "Mr. James is with Pacific Rim Airlines. He was talking to the Martin family earlier this morning and learned something that I think you'll find interesting." He turned to James and said, "Tell Assistant Director Wiseman what you told me, Mr. James."

James nodded and said, "Well, I was told that Mr. Martin almost missed the plane. He was called by a receptionist at his office and asked to pick up a present for a friend in Hawaii. I thought that was interesting so I went to his office to talk to the receptionist, but she wasn't there. I talked to her boss, a Mr. Burkhart, and he said she hadn't showed up for work.

"Well, he telephoned her home while I was there and her mother was very upset. It seems the girl hadn't been home all night and the mother had called the Costa Mesa police. They didn't have anything, so I thought I'd bring this all to you. I don't know if it means anything."

Dan shook the man's hand. "Mr. James," he said, "I don't either, but I can't tell you how much we appreciate your awareness, and your efforts. Really. We'll certainly check it out. I can't thank you enough."

He turned to Al and said, "Have you got Mr. James's address and phone number?"

"Yes."

"Good. Mr. James, if anything comes of this, I'll let you know. Again, my thanks. Ever think of becoming a law enforcement officer?"

Donald James grinned. "Not really. I don't think I have the stomach for it."

Dan shook his head. "Hmmmm. Too bad. You certainly have the instincts."

They shook hands again and James left. Disario immediately got on the phone and checked with the CHP to determine if they had any murder victims that were possibles.

They did.

Disario took down the information, then called Burkhart Industries. He asked for Mr. Burkhart and told him he wanted a description of the missing girl.

It matched.

Within a minute, the two men were on their way to Costa Mesa.

President Dalton and Mickey Serson were going over the latest information that had been forwarded to the White House by FBI Director Spencer. The FBI was getting closer, but time was running out and both men knew it.

President Dalton turned to his friend and advisor and with a voice filled with pain said, "Well Mickey, we've really got our hands full this time. Any suggestions?"

Mickey answered the president's question with a sarcastic smile on his lips. "I've been thinking about it, Bob."

"So fill me in."

Mickey ran a hand through his hair and said, "Well, number one, if I were you, I'd suddenly get very sick very fast and hand over the mantle of greatness temporarily to the vice-president. Or I'd declare war on Australia. That'll get you a few days of psychiatric examination."

The president looked at him strangely and said nothing.

Serson regretted his attempt at levity and tried to make light of it. "I speak only half in jest. This one's impossible. Absolutely impossible. You cannot win no matter what the hell you do.

"In the first place, releasing Gravez is no big deal. We've been moving him from prison to prison for security reasons and few people know where he is at any given time. The only person allowed to see him is his lawyer, who meets with him once a month. The last meeting was four days ago, so he won't know anything for another three weeks at least.

"These people have something that can kill us all, is easy to hide and hard to find. They've already shown that they're total psychos, making negotiations impossible. What'll they do next? Whatever the hell they want. And the press is bound to find out the whole story within a week. There are too many leaks already and too many people who know.

"When the great unwashed find out what's really going on, they'll go bananas. One of our own people creating some germ that's being used against us. Some doper we trained at taxpayers' expense, involved in a secret program that everybody finds repugnant. Jesus! The United States held hostage by dope merchants.

"This is a sure no-win deal. Even if you are able to capture these people and find the bacteria, the scandal will destroy you. We've said many times we aren't into this stuff."

Serson paused for a moment and then, in somber tones, said, "Actually it doesn't matter what you do, Bob. You've already ended your career. You did that the moment you allowed the FBI to operate like the CIA. I could scarcely believe my ears when you come out with that. No matter the justification, Congress will never stand for it. Not in a million years. You've committed political suicide and I would sure as hell like to know why."

The president continued to stare at his long-time friend for several moments. Then, in a voice barely under control, he said, "Because I'm dying, Mick."

Serson reacted as though slapped across the face. His voice was barely a squeak. "What?"

The president nodded. "You heard me. I'm dying. I have a inoperable brain tumor plus a couple of others they can dig out. The doctor has given me a few days to straighten this mess out and then he's going to blow the whistle on me. So, as far as my career is concerned, not to worry."

Mickey Serson could feel the tears welling up in his eyes. "You bastard! You bastard! Why the hell didn't you tell me, dammit!"

Robert Dalton smiled, stood up and came over to the couch where he embraced his old friend. "I didn't tell you," he said, softly, "because I knew you'd get all bent out of shape. And I was right."

Serson looked devastated.

The president released him from the embrace and said, "Look, Mickey, everybody dies sooner or later. It's no big deal. Now, come on, I need your help. We've got to solve this thing before Cecil gets his hands on this office. He'll screw it up good."

The president moved back to his desk and went through the cigar ritual while Mickey tried to pull himself together. After a few moments, Dalton said, "Mickey, I could care less about me right now. For Christ's sake, help me. Help me figure out what to do. My brain's a puddle."

Mickey Serson sighed deeply. With considerable effort, he focused his thoughts on the problem. "Okay," he said, "My first instinct is to work a deal with these people."

Dalton barked, "I thought you said negotiations were impossible!"

"I did," Serson answered. "I'm not talking negotiation. I'm talking deal."

"Go on."

"Okay. The only important thing is that bacteria. We need to find out where it is and destroy it. That's going to take some time and until we achieve that, they'll be squeezing our balls into little pellets. So we need time.

"We need to send someone to meet with these people. We tell them that we'll go along on certain conditions. The conditions being that they keep their mouths shut and turn over the bacteria to us. If they agree, we release Gravez and lay off the coca fields, the factories and everything. If they don't agree, we send out an all-out assault . . . total war . . . and burn the fields to the ground, blow up every paste factory, every coke factory, and kill every mother's son involved in the business."

He hesitated for a moment and then went on. "Maybe—maybe we can convince them that we might. We have to have something to make them deal."

President Dalton was looking at him carefully, not saying a word. He was about to say something, then stopped himself.

Serson continued. "I think they'll believe you'd do it and that's what counts. In South America, they think you've got a screw loose anyway. No offense, but you know that. That works to your advantage. These people are trying to preserve this empire of theirs that brings in billions of dollars every year.

"They want their boy back and they went to be left alone. So we hold out the carrot. But we tell them that if this deal becomes known, we'd suffer terribly politically. So, if you're going to go down in flames, you might as well take them with you. I think they might buy it."

"And if they don't?"

Serson ran a hand through his hair. "Then," he said, "we go to plan B. Whatever that is."

President Dalton rubbed his chin, removed his glasses and then replaced them. "Mickey, I can't make a deal with these people. They're the scum of the earth. You remember the problems Reagan had when he tried to work a deal for the hostages? It just doesn't work, Mick. You can't deal with them.

"You have to stamp them out, Mick."

Serson protested, "Stamp them out? Sure, I won't argue with that. But remember. They'll let that bacteria loose all over the country!"

Dalton stiffened. "Maybe . . . Perhaps we can prevent that from happening—perhaps not. But to make a deal with these people would be worse."

Serson said, "Worse? What could be worse than being dead!"

The moment he said it, he wanted to bite off his own tongue. Dalton stared at him for a moment and then smiled weakly. "Mickey. No one is to know. You must respect my wishes on that."

Serson nodded sheepishly. "I will, Bob."

Dalton remained silent for a moment and then suddenly slammed his hand on the desk and stood up. "These are dope dealers, for Christ's sake! If they use that bacteria again, they know it's all over. They've lost everything."

"But . . ." Serson just stared at the man.

The president started to say something and then stopped. He rubbed his jaw for a minute and then puffed on the big cigar. After a few moments of contemplation, he asked, "Do you think the Cabinet should consider this course of action?"

Serson stared at his boss. "You're kidding!"

Dalton stared at the wall for a moment and then, in a voice suddenly sad, said, "Mickey, we're in a real mess here. Not just me. The whole country."

He turned and faced his advisor. "There's no loyalty left. People are prepared to sell their country down the river for a few bucks or some dope or women . . . whatever. Everybody's out for what they can get and to hell with the rest of the country. We've all become self-serving, concerned with our own welfare and nobody else's. We've had Marines letting Soviet spies into our embassies, Navy guys selling secrets to Israel, Russia . . . anybody.

"If we don't screw up on purpose, we screw up by accident. Look at the Moscow embassy deal. Totally stupid! Christ! They bugged the place while we let them build it! Our security systems aren't working any more because nobody seems to give a damn.

"I've already broken my oath of office to try and get to the bottom of this mess. Are we going to have to resort to means that make a mockery of the Constitution? Is that the answer? Do we have to bug everybody who has access to secrets? Do we have to put a tail on everyone? And tail those who do the tailing? Are we ever going to be in a position where we can trust anyone again?

"Where the hell *are* we headed, Mick?"

Serson let his head drop and his hands fall to his knees. He'd never seen his friend so totally depressed. With good reason. "You ask some tough questions, Bob," he said. "They need to be addressed. But not now. Right now, we need to find a certain bacteria and kill it. We can deal with those other problems later."

The president allowed a rueful grin to reach his lips. "Not me, pal."

He sat like that for a few minutes and then pushed the intercom button on his desk.

"Ruth, contact as many Cabinet members as possible. I'd like a meeting in half an hour."

Serson remained silent as the blue smoke rose slowly toward the ceiling. He wondered when the nightmare would end.

And how it would end.

# Chapter Seventeen

Dan Wiseman and Al Disario parked their car in the Burkhart Industries parking lot and walked quickly inside the building. Mr. Burkhart was waiting for them. They showed their credentials and followed the man into his office.

The owner of the small chemical packaging firm was visibly upset. "I've just talked to Mrs. Olsen," he said. "She got a call from the Highway Patrol. They want her to identify a body they think is Sondra's. It's terrible. Just terrible!"

Wiseman asked, "I was told that Sondra talked to Mark Martin just before he left for Hawaii. Would you know anything about that?"

The man seemed confused. "Mark? Sondra? I have no idea."

Dan asked, "Did she have any friends here at the plant? Anyone she was close to. A boyfriend, maybe?"

Burkhart shook his head. "I wouldn't know. I'll get Mrs. Kelly in here. She's our foreman. She might know."

Dan waiting while Burkhart beckoned Mrs. Kelly on the intercom. In a moment she was in the office, looking upset herself.

"I just heard about Sondra. Is it true? Is she dead?"

Dan kept his voice low. "We don't know, Mrs. Kelly. It might not be Sondra.

"God . . . I certainly hope not."

Dan asked, "Does Sondra have any close friends here? A boyfriend perhaps?"

The woman shook her head. "No. She has a boyfriend, but he doesn't work here. Cory something. I don't know where he works. Real creep. I don't know what she sees in the guy."

"You've seen him?"

"Yes, several times. He usually picks her up after work."

"Would you recognize him if you saw him again?"

"Oh, sure."

"Would anyone else know anything?"

"I don't think so. But you can come out and ask them if you like. Sondra talked to me a few times, but she didn't have much truck with the girls. Truth to tell, she's a bit of a snob, you know?"

Dan smiled. "This Cory fellow. Think hard. Can you remember his last name?"

The woman thought for a moment and shook her head. "I don't think Sondra ever mentioned his last name." She stopped talking and picked a piece of fluff from her sweater, looking self-conscious for a moment. Dan spotted the change and waited patiently. Finally, he asked, "What is it, Mrs. Kelly?"

The woman twisted her hands together as she answered. "I'm not sure I should be talking like this, I don't know for sure . . . but I think Sondra was into drugs. I don't have any proof . . . just a feeling. Sometimes, she'd really act strange . . . aw . . . I don't really know. I'm being awful."

Dan stood up and patted her on the shoulder. "It's okay, Mrs. Kelly. Let's talk to the others."

They did and learned nothing more. Except for the make and model of the car Cory normally drove.

The two FBI men also talked to Patty Heran, Martin's secretary, but she hadn't talked to him that day at all and hadn't seen him stop by the office. As far as she knew, he'd worked at home that morning and gone from there directly to the airport.

Dan and Disario returned to their car and radioed the information back to the office for follow-up. Dan was told that a computer printout had arrived that listed all customers of the various companies marketing the kind of medical equipment required for genetic engineering. There were seventy-six companies in Southern California alone.

Dan groaned and spoke into the radio mike. "All right. Get telephone records of all long distance calls to and from Bolivia during the last five years. See if any of the calls originate or terminate with any of those companies. That might narrow it down."

"Yessir."

"What about Bolivia? How many customers are located there?"

"Nine. Eight in La Paz and one in Santa Cruz."

"Contact State and see if we can get a rundown on those companies . . . Ownership, the works."

"Yessir."

"How are we coming on the bottled stuff?"

"We've contacted several companies and arranged for Dodger Stadium to be the gathering place, but it'll be a couple of days before they start shipping."

"Not good enough," Dan barked. "We need that stuff now! Get back on it."

"Yessir."

Dan signed off and said to Disario, "Okay. Let's see Mrs. Olsen. Maybe she knows who this Cory is."

Disario put the car in gear and they raced out of the Burkhart parking lot. The window was open and the cold air was pouring in.

Dan said, "Christ! It feels like Washington. Close the window, will you."

Disario rolled up the window and said, "Yeah. They say there's even a chance of frost in the valley tonight."

Helen Porter waited in line at the bank drive-in teller and impatiently drummed her fingers on the steering wheel of her small compact car. She needed to get to the supermarket and then home. She was working the swing shift tonight and she had to be at work by four.

The car in front of her moved off and she pulled into position, putting her deposit slip and her paycheck into the plastic cannister. In a few moments, the cannister returned with her receipt and some cash. She was about to drive away when she heard a familiar voice in the speaker call her name. She looked up through the window and saw Bill Merton, the bank's manager. He was asking her to come inside.

She nodded, parked the car in the parking lot and entered the bank. Bill was waiting at the door and escorted her to his office. When they reached it, he closed the door.

His voice was low and filled with concern. "Helen, I shouldn't really be telling you this and I want your word you'll keep my confidence before I tell you."

She was confused. "What are you talking about?"

"Do I have your word?"

She hesitated for a moment and then said, "Yes."

He sighed and sat behind his desk. She remained standing, wondering what the devil he was so upset about. It didn't take long to find out.

"This morning," he began, "I was visited by a Ronald Nesbit, who's an insurance investigator with Butler Casualty. He wanted to know all about you. Bank accounts, financial worth, the works. Naturally, I refused to tell him a thing, but I think he'll be back. He mentioned something about a court order, but of course he can't get one unless you gave him a release. I thought you should know. Is there anything you want to tell me?"

The anger welled up inside her quickly. "Tell you? There's not much to tell. Butler carries the insurance on Pacific Rim. You probably heard that they are refusing to accept liability for the crash of that airliner in Florida because they say it was shot down."

"Yeah, I heard about that. Can they do that?"

Helen shrugged. "I have no idea. But I guess they're covering all the bases just in case. They must be checking backgrounds on each and every person connected with LAX security. Boy, they don't miss a trick. What did this guy look like?"

The bank manager scratched his head as he thought about it. "He was a tall man, and thin. About thirty five or so. Very well dressed. He had an eyesight problem I guess, he wore rather thick glasses. Talked in a bit of a drawl. Sounded like he was from Georgia or someplace like that. One of the southern states anyway. Reasonably good-looking. He was starting to lose his hair. Other than that . . ."

She paused and then said, "Bill, I really appreciate your interest and letting me know. I knew there was a reason I liked banking here."

He smiled, his concern eased now that he knew

what it was all about. Investigations of customers, even customers that owed the bank nothing, made him nervous. "No sweat, Helen. I just thought you should know. You're nice people."

She smiled back at him. "So are you, Bill."

She left the bank and headed for the supermarket. After picking up a few necessities, she headed home to the apartment building. Mr. Rodriguez, the superintendent, scurried up to meet her as she reached the elevator. He had a similar story. Two men had been there earlier asking all sorts of questions. The burly Mexican had threatened to throw them out.

"Can you describe them?" she asked.

"There were two of them. One tall and thin. He wore verrry theeeck glasses. The other man was tall also, but he was much bigger around. They look like cops. You in trouble with thee cops, eh?"

Helen shook her head. "No, I'm not. And they weren't cops. They were insurance investigators."

He seemed disappointed.

Helen asked, "How long did they talk to you?"

His face lit up. "I deedn't tell them notheeng. They kept asking questions but I told them to get out. When I told them I would throw them out, they finally left."

She asked again. "How long, Mr. Rodriguez? How long did all this take?"

The smile left his face for a moment. He thought he'd done well. Now, he wasn't so sure. "Ten, maybe fifteen minutes. What's wrong? Why are they bothering you?"

She smiled at him. "It's a bit complicated, Mr. Rodriguez. You did great. I appreciate it."

He lit up again, took one of the grocery bags and together they took the elevator up to the apartment. Once there, she took it back, thanked him again and went inside the apartment. She put the groceries on the kitchen table and looked over the place carefully.

They'd been careful, but she could still tell they'd been there.

She'd remembered how carefully she'd folded certain items as she put them in their places in the dresser. They were still folded, but she could tell they'd been moved, if ever so slightly. The desk drawer, stuffed with personal papers, was usually in disarray at the best of times. But there was a method to her madness. Now, it looked like a lot of papers had been disturbed. She bent down and sighted along the top of the desk, where disruptions to a thin layer of dust gave away the fact that papers had been placed on top, possibly photographed. Nothing seemed to be missing.

She went over and sat on the bed.

She felt violated.

This was her home. Her sanctum sanctorum. A place where she scraped away the dirt from the outside world and relaxed. And now some strangers had invaded her retreat and, like peeping toms, gone through her private things and violated her privacy. It was silly, but somehow, she felt she'd never feel the same about the place. It was as though . . .

Her heart started to beat wildly.

They were going to drag it all up again. If it ever got to court, they'd force her to be a witness. They'd stand there and relate ancient history all over again. Restoke the fires.

And she'd have to face it all over again.

The look on the boy's face as she pulled the trigger.

She put her head in her hands and started to weep.

Back in his office, Dan Wiseman sank wearily into his chair and drank some lukewarm coffee.

The desk was hardly visible, covered with file folders and computer printouts.

He looked out the window at the unusually gray skies. The clouds were low and thick, brought in by a low-pressure front that had brought cold air sweeping in from the north. Already, the temperature had dropped to 46 degrees and Los Angeles seemed more like San Francisco.

Reluctantly, he turned his attention back to the mass of paper on his desk. And then he noticed a pink note.

Edward Spencer was on his way to Los Angeles.

Wiseman groaned inwardly. That meant only one thing. The president wasn't satisfied with the progress they were making and had ordered the director to take personal charge of the investigation.

In a way, it was an insult.

But he understood it.

The president had no idea of what went into an investigation of this type and for that matter, neither did the director.

FBI directors were appointed. It was an administrative position and after the excesses of Hoover, police experience was not a criteria for appointment.

Spencer at least knew the law, being a former judge, but that didn't mean anything. They were breaking laws left and right themselves and after this was all over, they'd have to pay the price.

The only good thing was the fact that Spencer had clout. Maybe he could get some people in the private sector moving where Dan had failed. Perhaps that was why he was on his way.

He picked up another note. It was report on the Sondra Olsen killing. She'd died from two .22 caliber gunshots. One to the side, which had hit the heart, and another in the forehead, which had been redundant. The mother had made the formal I.D.

Mrs. Olsen had told Dan and Al Disario that she knew no Cory, nor did she know anything about drugs.

Al had asked to use the bathroom and had found

a small quantity of cocaine taped inside the toilet.

Cory was probably her supplier.

So far, the DMV records hadn't turned up a thing.

Wiseman could feel they were moving closer and closer but the progress seemed at a snail's pace when speed was of the essence. It was frustrating.

All day, the press had been speculating and the consensus of opinion was swinging sharply. There were now open claims of lying by the White House. Experts from many fields had been pulled in to television studios or interviewed by newspaper reporters and the bulk of opinion was that a real, dangerous threat existed.

According to the media, the whole country was at risk and the president was apparently sitting on his hands.

Dan knew that the strategy was to stall until the FBI could find the location, or locations, of the bacteria. They were pulling out all the stops to do just that, but in the meantime, Alfredo Gravez was soon going to be convinced that his demands were being ignored.

How would he react?

Where was he?

Some of his closest associates didn't know. The man had forged an organization that rivaled anything the government had in terms of secrecy.

Al Disario, once again, poked his head in the door. "Can I sit down?"

Dan waved a hand. "Sure."

Disario took a seat and sighed deeply. "UBC just put a bulletin on the air. A Naval task force has been diverted from a trip through the Panama Canal and is headed south. UBC says they're headed for Bolivia."

"Bolivia!" Dan exclaimed. "Bolivia is land-locked!"

Al nodded. "I know. But UBC claims the task force included three carriers and support ships that are loaded with napalm."

"Napalm?"

"Yeah. I think our president is planning to attack the coca fields."

Dan slapped his forehead.

Then he uttered a silent prayer. A prayer that Alfredo Gravez wasn't watching television. A prayer that he knew would never be heard.

George Barnes leaned back in the plush comfort of the rented limo and tried to relax as it made its way through Washington traffic toward Chevy Chase. The driver had said that busy Connecticut Avenue was the quickest way despite the traffic. Barnes was fast becoming convinced that the man was wrong when things seemed to ease a bit and the stretch Cadillac picked up speed.

He was anxious to talk to a man he'd telephoned from California just hours ago. A man who'd been reluctant to see him, but sensing a steeliness in the attorney's voice, finally assented to a thirty minute interview.

Thirty minutes! Barnes chuckled to himself. The man would talk to him for as long as it took and like it. They all liked to think they were in charge even when you had them by the shorts.

Barnes splashed some more scotch into the heavy glass tumbler and leaned forward. "How much longer?" he asked the driver.

The driver didn't turn his head but kept his eyes on the road, talking out of the side of his mouth. "We're almost there, sir. Ten minutes and I'll have you at the door."

"Good."

Barnes was on his way to see Senator Theodore Robert McGinnis, a revered and respected member of the Senate for over two decades and Chairman of the Senate Armed Services Committee.

McGinnis had good reason not to want to see the noted attorney from San Francisco. Ever since the investigator from the NTSB had blurted his thoughts to a waiting TV camera, the media had continued to speculate that a civilian airliner had been shot down over Florida by the Air Force, among other things. McGinnis had expected a call from George Barnes from the first moment.

Barnes was the country's most noted ambulance chaser and would obviously be involved in the legal affairs of some of the relatives of those killed in the crash. The complications of the case would be enormous unless the truth were known and the truth was being suppressed by a president who had slapped a classified stamp on every facet of the case. In McGinnis's opinion, Dalton had good reason to be concerned, but the man seemed hell-bent on lashing out quickly—much too quickly—for reasons nobody could understand.

But Barnes wouldn't care about that. He'd obviously made the assumption that McGinnis would be in a position to know the truth and he wanted that knowledge passed on to him. And there was scant concern about the methods used to get it.

George Barnes was the only man in the world who knew a terrible secret that could end the career of Ted McGinnis. It had happened a long time ago and George Barnes had saved what was then a fledgling career. He'd managed to buy off the parents of a little boy with McGinnis family money. A lot of McGinnis family money.

Barnes had explained that his client was drunk as hell when he abused the boy, that he felt bad about it and would never do it again. That by going to the police, they had started an investigation that would lead to his client, who would be punished. A good man would be ruined but it would mean nothing for them.

If, on the other hand, they encouraged the boy to recant his story and went to the police and withdrew their charges, they would receive a guaranteed income of $40,000 a year for life. That would ensure them a good life and a good education for the boy. They'd have to move half way across the country and start a new life but that wouldn't be too tough with the income they'd have. The boy would soon forget about the incident and everybody would benefit. And didn't that make a whole lot more sense?

It surely did.

For three years, McGinnis had lived under a heavy cloud until the day when news came of the family's demise in an auto accident. All three of them. He thought he'd been freed from the chains at that moment and acted as such. He began afresh a political career that had grown stagnant. And the treatment he'd been taking had helped him keep away from little boys.

It wasn't until twenty years later, when McGinnis's political star was rising rapidly, that George Barnes sat him down and told him that all of the evidence was in Barnes's possession. That Barnes had documented the entire incident and its aftermath.

Barnes had said he wasn't telling him this to blackmail him. He didn't want money. He didn't want information. Not now, at least. McGinnis's secret was safe, and would remain so. But someday down the road, Barnes would want something and McGinnis would be expected to deliver, without question.

That had been eleven years ago.

When he received the telephone call earlier this day, Ted McGinnis knew that the day had finally come.

The black limo pulled up in front of the fashionable Maryland home of Theodore McGinnis and stopped. As they had agreed on the telephone, Barnes would wait for McGinnis to join him in the limo. He did so now, impatiently tapping the index finger of his right hand on his drink glass.

He noticed a man in a heavy overcoat and fedora leave the garage entrance and head down the driveway. Barnes leaned forward and told the driver, "Okay Sam. Take a walk. Don't come back here for twenty minutes."

"Yessir."

The driver put on his cap, got out of the car and walked down the street.

In a moment, McGinnis was seated beside Barnes and removing the fedora.

Barnes was grinning. "Well, Teddy my boy. Care for a drink?"

McGinnis was scowling. "No. Look George, I know what you want and I can't do a thing. The White House is in a full flap and the lid is on tight. Something very big is up but we're not being told a thing."

Barnes smiled. "Really?" he said. "Tell me more."

McGinnis cursed. "Damn it, there's nothing to tell. Not yet, anyway. We're all shooting in the dark here. I don't know if the plane was shot down or not. That's what you're after, right?"

"You have a discerning mind, Senator."

McGinnis sneered at him. "Not really. I just understand how yours works."

He paused and then said, "In any case, we're calling for a special investigative hearing in the Senate tomorrow, but the White House is calling this a national security issue and they're really giving us trouble. I left a very important meeting to keep this appointment with you and I have to get back as soon as possible.

"Besides, all you're worried about is your case. I don't know what the hell your hurry is. You've got years before you have to bring action and this thing is about to blow sky high in a matter of days! Why the pressure now? What's your blessed hurry?"

Barnes blushed slightly. "I have a score to settle with a certain insurance company president. The sooner I know the real facts, the sooner I can stick it up his ass. The sonofabitch had the nerve to disclaim any and all responsibility for liability. I want to shove those cocky words right back down his throat and I want to do it immediately!

"The case will be won regardless. I'm not worried about that. I represent fifty-four families and they'll get their damages whether it be from the government of the United States or Butler Casualty. But I want it to be Butler. I want it to be Butler so bad I can taste it!"

The last sentence was said with such vehemence

that some of the drink spilled to the carpet. "My instincts tell me that the plane was shot down all right. But there had to be good reason for it and there had to be proof of some kind that the people were dead first. The government holds that evidence and I want it. I want it soon. You can get it for me."

McGinnis sighed in exasperation. "Well, I'm in the dark on this."

Barnes growled like a wounded bear. "Bullshit! Who the hell do you think you're talking to! Some wet behind the ears candy-ass? You know everything that goes on in this town! Now you tell me what the hell I want to know or you'll find yourself on the outside looking in! I told you I want that information and I want it now!"

The senator's face reddened and he started to get out of the car. Then, he stopped in mid-movement and sagged back into his seat. "It really doesn't matter," he said, a heavy note of resignation in his voice.

"How so?"

"Like I said, the White House is in a total flap. There are things going on that defy credibility. It's all going to blow up. They'll never keep a lid on this. It's much too big. I might as well tell you . . . everyone will know within a few hours."

Barnes was getting angry. "You keep saying that! Exactly what the fuck are you talking about?"

McGinnis sighed again and said. "Well, as near

as I can tell we're about to launch an unprovoked attack on Bolivia. God! A complete task force. Navy bombers, Airborne, Marines . . . the works . . . Jesus! We're planning on going in there and burn the place to the ground. Enough napalm is being moved offshore to burn up half the world. It's nuts!"

Barnes exploded. "The hell it is! It's about time the president made a move on those assholes! You should be dancing in the streets!"

McGinnis shook his head and reached for the scotch decanter. "You have no idea, George. You have no idea at all."

"What do you mean?"

McGinnis looked away, his gaze focusing on his home. "This Gravez character has the bacteria he says he has. As soon as he realizes that the president won't even discuss his demands, he'll use it. A lot of people are going to die."

Barnes looked surprised. "Jesus! Is the press on to it yet?"

McGinnis poured himself a drink. "Of course."

"And this is strictly a Dalton thing?"

"Absolutely."

"But it isn't his style! The man hardly takes a crap without getting the opinions of fourteen people!"

"I know that! We all know that. But he's different somehow. I've never seen him so angry and upset. He's refused to consider any negotiations with this

Gravez character. Flatly refused. It's like a game of chicken, except that we're bound to lose. It doesn't matter what the hell happens to Bolivia if that bacteria is let loose here. Gravez is telling the truth and we're all in serious trouble."

Barnes sipped his drink for a moment and lit a fresh cigar. The back seat of the limo began to fill up with smoke. The motor was still running and McGinnis pushed the electric window button to open the window a crack. Finally, Barnes said, "It's true then. This guy has his hands on that bacteria. He wasn't bluffing?"

McGinnis sighed. "No, he wasn't bluffing. He's got it all right. And he'll damn well use it. The man's a psycho."

Barnes thought about it for a moment and then asked, "The plane—was it shot down or not?"

McGinnis looked disgusted. "In the light of all this, what difference does it make?"

Barnes grabbed the man's arm and squeezed it hard. "It matters to me!"

The senator snorted and said, "Yes, it was shot down. But all of the people were dead before that happened. This will all come out at the Congressional hearing."

The senator put his hat on, opened the door and got out of the car. Before closing the door, he leaned forward and said, "If I were you, George, I'd head right back to L.A. The word is that the target is Washington. From what I understand, that's where this guy has stashed the germs."

Barnes tipped his glass. "Thanks, Teddy. I appreciate the tip. I think I'll take your advice."

# Chapter Eighteen

At three in the afternoon, Los Angeles time, the White House announced that the president would make a major address to the nation that night. The address would be made at the unusual hour of eleven o'clock Eastern time, eight Pacific time, and the speculation was that the timing was coincidental with the progress of the task force making its way south.

Dan heard the news as he waited for the arrival of Edward Spencer at the charter air terminal at LAX. He hoped Spencer would know what the speech would contain.

He did.

As soon as the Lear pulled to a stop, Spencer practically leaped from the plane, shook Dan's hand and quickly moved to the car.

"Dan," the director said, "the president has run out of patience. He's going to tell the people the truth about this whole thing and make some demands of his own to Gravez. He plans to attack the coca fields in Bolivia and destroy everything remotely connected with cocaine."

Wiseman was stunned. "He's going to do this on television?"

"Yes."

"Christ! That will practically guarantee that Gravez releases the bacteria!"

"I know. Dalton says that we'll just have to find a way to stop that from happening. The Pentagon has arranged for about sixty tankers of gas to be assembled in Los Angeles and there'll be more tomorrow. How're you coming with the private sector?"

Dan winced. "It's been slow. I haven't been able to tell them what it's about and they're all concerned with getting paid. They say they want official purchase orders. Otherwise, they say, they have trouble getting paid."

The director cursed. "Well, I'll work on that. We need all of that stuff we can get our hands on. I agree with your latest analysis. I think Gravez will strike in Los Angeles and I think it will be the sewer system. That way, the bacteria will be difficult to kill."

Dan nodded. "We have a break there. There's been a cold front moving in and the temperature is cold enough to kill the bacteria. But the sewer system will still be warm. At least any bacteria that gets in the air will die. Of course, Gravez might wait until it warms up."

Spencer thought about that. "He might. He just might. There's also the chance that he might actually be intimidated by the president's reaction. Gravez has a fortune invested in those fields of his, not to mention the paste factories and the coke plants. Maybe—maybe he'll think twice. He's got a lot to lose. Taking on the United States is a formidable undertaking."

He cursed under his breath and then said, "Just in case, I've ordered the biological weapons decontamination team to come here and be ready for anything. They're on their way."

Dan sighed. "Good move. I wouldn't count on Gravez being intimidated. He must have known what he was getting into before he decided to destroy that airplane. I doubt that this guy is intimidated by anything. He thinks *he's* the one with the power. That's a classic symptom of a person using cocaine. Do you think that after all these years, the man has gotten stupid and starting using the stuff himself?"

Spencer asked, "I don't know. Anything's possible. What about this Cory thing? Any luck there?"

"Not yet," Dan answered. "We've had a woman looking at mug shots all day, but so far, nothing. Maybe this guy doesn't have a record. We've distributed an artist's sketch to all law enforcement agencies but we haven't got a read on him yet.

"We're programming the computers to run a cross check on phone calls to Bolivia with the medical firms on the list. It's taking forever to put the lists into the computer. We expect to run that sometime during the night.

"The DMV lists have come up dry. I guess Cory uses another name on his driver's license."

Wiseman looked out the window as Disario wheeled the black car through the heavy traffic. "Time," he said. "We need more time. Isn't there any way we can get the president to delay this speech?"

Spencer groaned. "No. We've tried, but to no avail. He has his mind made up."

At 7:43 in the evening, the Los Angeles Lakers and the Boston Celtics tipped off to begin their basketball game. A crowd of 14,460 had arrived to witness another exciting game between these two long-time rivals.

The announcers had expressed surprise at the size of the crowd in view of the fact that the president of the United States was going to make a major speech to the nation at eight o'clock, not to mention the fact that it was bitterly cold outside the heated Forum. Southern Californians were not used to 40 degree weather.

By five minutes before eight o'clock, most of the late arrivals were seated, and the parking lot surrounding the Forum became devoid of ticket scalpers and most of the security people, the latter seeking shelter from the cold, bitter wind by stepping inside the building.

Twelve men in dark clothes left two vans and walked slowly and carefully toward the building. They checked their watches and then circled the building. Each man was equipped with a small walkie talkie. Each man had been assigned a separate entrance. When he reached it, he was to wait until the final word was given.

The word would come from Alfredo Gravez himself, who was parked in another van equipped with a television set. Before committing himself, he wanted to see for himself what the president of the United States had to say.

# Chapter Nineteen

"And now, the president of the United States."

With those familiar words, President Dalton was introduced to a waiting television audience. He was seated behind his desk in the Oval Office, wearing his glasses and holding his speech in his hands.

He looked calm and composed, unaffected by the controversy that was, even at this moment, swirling like a tornado around him. His hands were still, the expression on his face one of serenity, as though all was right with the world.

Obviously, all was *not* right with the world, but the president wanted to project an image of a man in control. And indeed, he *was* in control.

At this moment in time, he was in complete control, to the consternation of his Cabinet, his party, his friends and the Congress. Even before the speech was begun, there were looks of concern on the faces of many in Washington, some even using the word, "impeachment," in their conversations with others. While only a very few were privy to the actions being planned by the president, the fact that he was going public had removed the veil of secrecy from those "in the know" and they were all chattering like magpies.

The president nodded once at the camera and began his remarks. "My fellow Americans. I speak to you tonight on a matter of grave urgency. What I have to tell you is the truth, the whole truth and nothing but the truth, so help me God. Much has been said in recent days about a lack of candor on my part and I assure you that tonight, you shall hear the truth.

"For many reasons, I have remained silent over the past few hours concerning the investigation into the crash of a civilian airliner. Tonight, the reasons for my silence will become clear. Tonight, you will know everything I know. Nothing will be kept from you.

"You will learn things that will cause you some discomfort. I am going to tell you about matters that have been held secret for many years. I will explain to you the reasons for the secrecy and I will ask for your understanding.

"Americans are unique among the peoples of the earth in some respects. By that I do not mean to imply that Americans are better than any other people, just that they are different. When the very life of this country is at risk, Americans are unique in that they stop being the most critical people on earth, and start becoming the most supportive of their leaders. It's a tradition that has warmed the hearts of presidents before me and a tradition that I am sure will prevail.

"I seek your support tonight because this country is in danger. And we must work together to put an end to this danger. Working together, we can meet the challenge that confronts us. None of us can turn our backs on this."

He stopped for a moment and took a deep breath. Then, smiling ever so slightly, he carried on.

"Three years ago, a notorious gangster named Fernando Garcia Gravez was captured, tried and convicted of twenty-three felonies relating to drug-trafficking. He was sentenced to life in prison. He is still there, serving out his sentence.

"One year ago, a group of his supporters put into action a plan for his release. It was a very complicated and expensive plan that found its culmination in the crash of Pacific Rim Flight Two-three-four. I feel it important that you understand some of the elements of this plan because they point out the extreme dangers that exist in this country having to do with the use of illegal drugs in general and cocaine in particular.

"We are all aware that the country has a drug problem. Not only are many Americans using illegal drugs, but there exists another problem, that being the improper use of prescription drugs.

"We have seen the damage that drug addiction can do. We've all been heartbroken by the specter of our heroes falling victim to the disease of drug addiction. Heroes in sports, the arts, the military and in business.

"We've been witness to religious leaders drawn into the vortex of drug addiction. Political leaders. The problem cuts across all lines, affecting rich and poor, black and white, men and women.

"Fortunately, our children are beginning to benefit from the tremendous effort being made by concerned Americans and for the first time in years, the number of high school students involved in illegal drug use has decreased. That is a happy sign and a welcome sign. But the problem is still a large one. Tonight, I speak about a serious situation that is totally rooted in the business of drugs and the victims who fall prey to drugs."

He stopped again and shuffled the papers while he gathered his thoughts. Then he began anew.

"To digress for a moment, let me explain to you that the United States has for years been involved in the research and development of both chemical and biological, or germ, weaponry. This has been necessitated by the fact that we know the Soviet Union is heavily involved in similar research. In order to develop defensive measures to counter this Soviet threat, we have been forced to conduct research of our own. To put it plainly, our research has been conducted to find ways to protect Americans against possible use of these chemical and biological weapons by the Soviets.

"If we were to fail to conduct research of our own, we would be defenseless in the event the Russians decided to attack us with these weapons. There would be no vaccines available, no antibiotics, no protection whatsoever. That would be intolerable.

"The production and use of weapons of this kind is contrary to several treaties that remain in force and is counter to everything humanity should stand for. They are vile, loathsome weapons.

"So, while we have implored the Soviet Union, without success, to cease and desist in their research, for the benefit of all mankind, we have been forced to do research of our own in order to develop some sort of protection for all Americans. To do less would be a dereliction of our responsibilities.

"One of the people involved in this research became addicted to cocaine. His name was Roger Wilcox. His supplier was a man who worked directly for Alfredo Gravez, a Bolivian national, the father of Fernando Gravez.

"The Gravez family is responsible for much of the cocaine that finds its way to America. The family lives in Bolivia, in the mountains near La Paz. It consists of the father of Fernando Garcia Gravez, three of his sons, several cousins and hundreds of armed and dangerous employees. Many of these employees are scattered throughout the United States, engaged in the cocaine business. In Bolivia, the family is engaged in the growing of coca leaves on farms large and small, spread out over the mountain ranges that traverse the country. They also run factories that convert the coca leaves to coca paste and eventually cocaine, most of which ends up in the United States.

"It is estimated that the Gravez family earns two billion dollars a year from their illegal enterprises. That's two *billion* dollars in a single year. Of and by itself, that is an intolerable situation.

"Roger Wilcox, a man involved in our biological weapons research, his judgment clouded by his use of cocaine, revealed to Alfredo Gravez the nature of his work with biological research and he was kidnapped one year ago by the Gravez family and taken to Bolivia. He was a key element in their plan to free Fernando Garcia Gravez. They transported Mr. Wilcox to Bolivia where they built, with his help, a research lab capable of producing a deadly bacteria that had first been developed in the Soviet Union, and then here, in the United States.

"We don't know at this point whether or not this man willingly assisted in the effort or not, but it really doesn't matter. He would never have been contacted had he not allowed himself to become dependent on drugs.

"The bacteria that was developed by Roger Wilcox in Bolivia is similar to the bacteria he was developing in this country, in an effort to find ways to counter the effects of the Soviet bacteria. This bacteria is so deadly that no drug has yet been produced that will stop it. It kills in minutes."

The president paused and held up his hand. "I know how frightening this sounds, but I want to assure you that there are protective measures that can be taken. While a very real danger exists, there *are* ways that we can protect ourselves and I will refer to these later in my remarks."

The president paused again and picked up the papers containing his speech. His hands were still steady, his demeanor calm. He looked into the camera and the expression on his face became more serious.

"As I have stated, Roger Wilcox spent a year in Bolivia creating a bacteria that is extremely dangerous. Once it was ready, it was placed on board Pacific Rim Flight Two-three-four. The plane was on a flight to Hawaii when the bacteria was released inside the airplane. All of the crew and passengers succumbed within minutes.

"At the time of the death of the passengers and crew on board, the plane had turned around and was heading back toward Los Angeles. It was on automatic pilot and heading in a direction that would take it across America right to the Atlantic Ocean. Estimates were made and investigations begun. I quickly realized that these investigations would be severely hampered if the plane fell into the ocean.

"I ordered specially-equipped Air Force planes to determine if all on board were dead and the tests that were conducted confirmed that they were. I then ordered that the airplane be shot down over land, to ensure that a proper investigation could be conducted. My orders were carried out.

"At the time I made that fateful decision, I was assured by our biological weapons research team that there was little likelihood of contamination on the ground, and this has been proven out. The area of the crash has been carefully tested for a number of days, and there is no contamination whatsoever.

"There was, however, one horrible misjudgment for which I accept full responsibility. Our calculations led us to believe that the plane could successfully be shot down in an area where there were no people. That was a mistake. Due to some unforeseen circumstances, the plane crashed in a heavily-populated urban area. The fact that no one on the ground was killed is due to a miracle of chance. There is nothing else I can say on that.

"Let me say again, that there is absolutely no question regarding the condition of the passengers and crew at the time the plane was shot down. They were all dead. Evidence gathered by the Air Force while the plane was still in the air confirmed that fact and this evidence will be released to the media tonight.

"Shortly after the airliner crashed, Shirlee Simms, a television reporter in Los Angeles, was contacted by a man we now know was Alfredo Gravez, the father of Fernando Gravez. She was allowed to make a videotape record of her interview with him, in which he revealed that the Gravez family was responsible for the crash, and the reasons it was done.

"Pure and simple, it was done to frighten the United States and set the stage for a unbelievably arrogant demand made by the Gravez family. By the commission of a terrorist act against innocent people, they hoped to frighten us into complying with the demands made on the videotape. I wanted to assess the situation fully before releasing the information to you, the American people."

The president paused and took a drink of water.

"Alfredo Gravez has demanded that the United States release his son, Fernando Gravez, and stop all efforts to prevent the illegal operations of the Gravez family. Operations designed to enrich the family and enslave Americans in a vicious and deadly habit. The cocaine habit.

"Should we not abide by these demands, the Gravez family has threatened to release additional bacteria in their possession, killing other innocent Americans."

"It is a bold and arrogant blackmail attempt by a rich and powerful group of criminals. A family so drunk with their own power that they think they can force an entire country to its knees. I want you . . . and I want the Gravez family to know tonight. That cannot . . . must not . . . will not happen."

He hesitated to allow the words to register and then resumed.

"The United States will not be blackmailed by a group of drug dealers. I will simply not allow this to happen.

"Instead, I hereby send the following message to the Gravez family and to the people of Bolivia.

"I, as president of the United States, do hereby declare that the action taken in the crash of Pacific Rim Airlines Flight Two-three-four was, in fact, an act of war against the United States. Not by a nation, but by a small family of greedy criminals.

"This action cannot be allowed to go unpunished. And the Gravez family will be punished. As well, we have some demands of our own. The amount of punishment that will be inflicted upon the Gravez family will be determined in great part by how precisely they adhere to *my* demands, which are as follows:

"One. The bacteria is to be turned over to the United States Embassy in La Paz within twenty-four hours. All of it.

"Two. The Gravez family is to cease and desist in the importation of cocaine in any of its forms into the United States.

"Three. The Gravez family is to compensate the families of the victims of this plane crash within seven days. The compensation is to be in form of cash, American funds, which is to be delivered to the American Embassy in La Paz. An amount of two million dollars is to be paid to each family.

"Four. The Gravez family is to dismantle their biological weapons research unit immediately.

"Five. Roger Wilcox is to be delivered to the American embassy within twenty-four hours.

"Six. The Gravez family is to turn over to the United States the people responsible for the planning and execution of the attack on our airliner."

He paused and allowed the last few sentences to register. Even through the heavy make-up, it was clear to see that President Dalton was red-faced and angry. His eyes were flashing with fire that seemed almost out of control. He placed his hands in front of him and locked them together. The knuckles quickly turned white from the force of the pressure he was exerting.

"If each and every one of these demands is not met," he continued, "I will order a military attack against the Gravez family wherever they might be. The attack will ensure that coca leaves will never again be grown in Bolivia. Ever. The coca fields will be burned to the ground. The earth will be made infertile for a hundred years. Every Gravez family member and employee will be hunted down and captured and brought before an American court to face justice for the death of the passengers and crew of Flight Two-three-four.

"This *will* be done. I want it clearly understood that this attack is against a group of people, not against the country of Bolivia. Unfortunately, innocent Bolivians may be affected and this is something I sincerely regret. However, the Bolivian government is well aware of our constant efforts to discourage the growing of coca leaves, and has been less than enthusiastic in their support. Perhaps other countries will heed the ancient warnings that making a deal with the devil can never be painless.

"The Bolivian government has twenty-four hours to assist their citizens to remove themselves from the danger zone. Naturally, we expect the members of the Gravez family to leave the area before the attack. No matter. They will not escape the punishment they deserve.

"It is possible that the Gravez family may release the bacteria into the air or the water supplies of our cities and towns. For that reason, I urge each and every American to boil all water for three minutes before they use it from this moment forward. That will kill any bacteria present in the water.

"I want you to understand that we have no reason to believe that the water has been affected. This is simply a precaution.

"As a further precaution, I urge all Americans to stay away from sewer systems, even to the point of refraining from using toilets connected to a city sewer system. I realize the inconvenience but unfortunately, this is very necessary. The bacteria feeds on the material found in sewer systems.

"As well, I am declaring the United States of America to be in a state of martial law at this time. All commercial activities are to cease until further notice. All Americans are to remain in their homes until advised that it is safe to leave. All businesses are to close until further advised. All transportation systems are to shut down. All interstate highways are to close. In short, this country, is to shut down entirely.

"The bacteria cannot survive in air temperatures of fifty degrees and below. Therefore, those of you in the northern parts of the country have little to fear. As well, the bacteria has a very short life span. Less than an hour. If all Americans in the warmer areas of the country stay away from physical contact with others, a massive release of bacteria into the air will have little effect.

"We don't know how many Gravez family members are in possession of the bacteria or where they are located. But we will find them. Every last one of them. The bacteria will be recovered and destroyed.

"Naturally, the entire strength of our Armed Forces will be alerted and every effort will be made to prevent any such release of bacteria. They will be assisted by national and local law enforcement agencies. But you can all help by staying in your homes until we have isolated and eliminated this threat to our health.

"I feel confident that we will put an end to this threat in short order. Your cooperation and support will ensure our success.

"The actions I am taking tonight will cause some short-term economic problems for all of us. They will bring disappointment to many. Sports and other events will have to be rescheduled. There will be many inconveniences.

"But this country must never surrender its national purpose to a group of thugs whose only mission in life is to create misery for millions. Whose only connection with humanity is the fact that they breathe the air we do.

"These vermin cannot be allowed to dictate to the United States of America. And they will not escape just punishment for the actions they have taken.

"Tomorrow, I will address the Congress of the

United States and seek their support for the actions I have taken tonight. I am sure that the support will be forthcoming. In the meantime, my actions are covered by Executive Order.

"To the Gravez family I say this: Consider carefully your position. Do not attempt to try the patience of the American people further. We have tolerated your illegal acts for too long a time. Time is up. It stops tonight.

"To my fellow Americans I say this: We face danger tonight. We face it together. Together, we will conquer this evil threat. Together, we will take steps to ensure that such a thing can never happen again. This is the first of many steps that will be taken to stamp out the curse of drug addiction for all time. The first of many steps to bring America back to the greatness that is its destiny.

"Good night and God bless you all."

The president was still smiling as the screen faded to black.

And in Los Angeles, an enraged Alfredo Gravez barked into his walkie-talkie and twelve men moved inside the Los Angeles Forum, presented their tickets and walked toward their assigned seats.

# Chapter Twenty

Many of the fans who had come to the basketball game had brought radios or small television sets with them. During much of the first and second quarters, they had watched or listened to the president's speech, and a steady buzz of conversation could be heard throughout the Forum as the game progressed. Many were wondering whether or not they were actually in danger, or just how they would comply with the president's wishes once they got home.

In front of them, the game continued, even though it was obvious that the players knew what had happened and seemed to be playing the game with less than their normal enthusiasm.

The two announcers calling the game for the television-radio simulcast were having difficulty concentrating on the game as well. They kept making constant references to the speech and various aspects of what had been contained within the speech.

Tom Sifton was the long-time Lakers announcer and Larry Taft was his "color" man. Sifton, a man with a rapid-fire delivery and deep knowledge of the game, seemed more subdued than anyone could remember.

Sifton was speaking into his headset microphone as one of the Laker players pushed a long, arcing shot through the hoop.

". . . and another three-point shot from Brown. He's had three of those tonight and we're only in the second quarter!"

"Right you are Tom. Actually, Brownie is keeping the Lakers in the game tonight. If there is a game. I guess we'll hear about that shortly."

In twelve separate sections of the arena, twelve men sat quietly and watched the basketball game, furtively checking their watches from time to time. They didn't act like normal fans, but they escaped notice because many people were upset and confused by what had happened in Washington. Several people were just sitting in their seats, seemingly unresponsive to the game, lost in thought.

At precisely 8:30, like a well-rehearsed drill team, each of the men carefully removed a small plastic pouch from his pocket and placed it on the concrete floor beneath the seat. Then, as each man withdrew his hand from the pouch, he slit it with a razor blade secreted in the palm of his hand. Each of the men was able to make the move without being observed.

A light blue liquid spilled from each pouch and made a small puddle on the concrete beneath each seat, mixing with the litter of beer cups, popcorn boxes and hot dog wrappers.

Slowly, the twelve men got up and headed for the exits. One of them was stopped by a security guard who said, "If you're going out, make sure you have your ticket stub or you won't be able to get back in."

The man stared at the security guard, his mind racing. He didn't understand a word of English and had no idea what was being said to him. For a moment, he thought of reaching for the small caliber semi-automatic in his jacket pocket, then cool reason prevailed. He made the correct assumption that what the guard was saying was not threatening, judging by the look on the man's face. So the terrorist smiled, nodded, and continued on his way. To the guard, he was just another Mexican, probably an illegal alien.

Once outside, the twelve men headed for the two vans, got in and drove slowly away from the Forum.

Five miles away, in a shopping center not far from the San Diego Freeway, Alfredo Gravez sat in another van and continued to watch the small television set.

He had switched channels. Instead of the national network channel that had carried the president's speech and was now broadcasting a roundtable discussion concerning the incredible ramifications of the dramatic address, Gravez was watching the broadcast of an independent station that was carrying the basketball game locally.

He checked his watch. If everything went as planned, the bacteria would eat their way through the microscopic capsules in another two minutes. Five minutes from then, the first signs of a quick and deadly illness would be evidenced.

There were nine minutes to go in the second quarter of the game. More than enough time, what with time-outs and the normal flow of the game. Gravez had done his research well and knew that nine minutes on the game clock equalled about twice that in real time.

He watched and listened as the announcers continued to cover the game under the shadow of the larger news that had thrown a cloud over everything.

Sifton said, "Well Larry, this is certainly a most unusual situation. It's the first time I've ever called a basketball game where there's a possibility the game may be suspended at half-time due to the actions taken by the president of the United States."

Larry Taft seemed in a fog. His voice was low, missing that frantic tone that most sports announcers employ. "That's what it looks like, Tom. As I understand it, a call has gone out to the commissioner. Nobody seems to know what to do, really. Actually, under the circumstances, I'm not sure it wouldn't be the best idea. The players seem upset, the fans are certainly upset and I think it should be called."

Sifton agreed. "I have to support you on that one, Larry. I guess there were a lot of radios out there and there's been a constant hum of conversation running through the place ever since the speech.

"If you joined us late, we're in the second quarter of what surely must go down as one of the most unusual games in the history of professional basketball. Or any kind of basketball for that matter. We have less than eight minutes to play in the first half of a game that is being played at the same time as the president of the United States has announced that the country is under martial law.

"In case you missed it, the president has ordered all Americans to remain in their homes and all sports events cancelled.

"So far, much to my surprise frankly, very few fans have left this place and if I had to make a guess, I'd say that it's because they're stunned. Simply stunned, as are we all.

"As for the game, the score is tied at forty-six in what has been a heck of a ball game. Right now, during this time out, there seems to be a lot of discussion at both benches and I think . . . yes . . . the players are actually requesting that this game be stopped at half-time. I can hear some of the conversations just to the right of me and I can tell you that most of the players just want to go home.

"Right at this moment, basketball seems to be the furthest thing from everyone's mind. And we'll be back right after this word from Karl's Light, the beer that tastes like a fine ale."

In the van five miles away, Alfredo Gravez tensed. Perhaps he had waited too long. The game might be called off right now and if that happened there would be too many people who would escape the fate Gravez had planned for them. A plan designed to impress upon a recalcitrant president that he, Alberto Gravez, held great power in his hands and was not afraid.

This president, the circumspect Robert Dalton, would no more attack Bolivia than fly to the moon. Unfortunately, that same part of his character would make it difficult for Gravez to persuade him that he must submit to the demands made of him. If the demonstration at the Forum didn't do the trick, there would be others, until the pressure exerted by the people would literally drive the man to accede to the demands.

There was an edge to the Bolivian's voice as he hissed at the television set. "You must stay!" he said. "You must all stay!"

Inside the Forum, the two announcers resumed their patter after the commercial was over.

"Okay, this is Tom Sifton, speaking to you from the fabulous Forum in Los Angeles. The score is tied at forty-six and play has not yet resumed. An official time out has been taken by the referee who is on the phone right now to the commissioner of basketball. In a moment, we should know whether or not this game will continue. It's possible, Larry, that they may not even want to go right to the half. They might stop it right here."

At that moment, the first effects of the bacteria were already being felt in the areas closest to where the pouches had been dropped. People were getting up and moving toward the washrooms, some of them doubled over in pain. There seemed to be a flurry of movement in twelve distinct areas of the arena. A movement that did not escape the attention of Larry Taft, whose eyes had been scanning the arena for the past few minutes.

The movement toward the washrooms became almost herdlike and the heightened level of activity began spreading quickly throughout the stands.

"Well Larry, it seems the people are starting to move out of here in droves now. Which is kind of strange in a way. They sat there for some time after the speech by the president and then, all of a sudden, they've started to head for the exists. As I said . . ."

Larry Taft interrupted Sifton. "Tom . . . Those people aren't . . . Tom, they're sick . . . Andy! Get a close-up of some of those people. Something's wrong!"

The camera zoomed in to one group of people that were in motion. In seconds, everyone watching could see the pain and fear etched on their faces. Quickly, the director switched cameras to another one that was focused on the benches where the players were still gathered around their respective coaches. A look of confusion was on all faces.

The referee was off the telephone and telling the coaches that the game would be suspended at half time.

Suddenly, the attention of the players and everyone else was drawn by the sounds of screams in the seats. First one, then another and very quickly, hundreds of people were screaming at the top of their lungs.

The voice of announcer Tom Sifton rose a few notes as he finally became aware of what was actually happening.

"We've just had word that the game . . . my God! I'm sorry, ladies and gentlemen, but there are people all over this place who are very ill. If the health authorities are watching, I'd suggest that ambulances be sent out here right away. Something is terribly wrong . . ."

Dan Wiseman was at his desk when Al Disario, his face ashen, ran into the office, his chest heaving and said, "Dan . . . Gravez! He's hit the Forum. Right now! It's happening right now!"

Disario quickly turned the television set on as Dan grabbed the walkie-talkie on his desk and barked into it. "Attention all units! This is Omega. We have a strike. The Forum in Inglewood is the target. All units acknowledge."

As the acknowledgements came in, Dan stared at the scene being played out on the television screen.

It was a full-blown panic. People in terrible pain were struggling to climb over other people already immobilized by their own pain; all of them striving to get away from a danger they could neither see or hear. They just knew it was there.

And Tom Sifton, his brain wrestling with the

images he was seeing not only in his television monitor, but in the rows of seats behind him, uttered the words that would stick in everyone's mind. "Oh, my God! It's the bacteria! Someone has used the bacteria in the fabulous Forum . . . We're all dead!"

As though some signal had been given, the floor of the arena became a mass of writhing humanity, with men, women and children trapped in an impossible grid-lock, knocking hapless players from both teams to the floor as they fought to get to their dressing rooms or away from the arena all together.

The cacophony of screams was enough to make anyone's blood run cold.

Finally, mercifully, the screen went blank. And then the face of a man at a news desk appeared.

"This is Frank Hill, Channel Thirty-two News. As you can see, something very awful has happened at the Forum. We don't know what it is, but in the interests of common decency, we feel obliged to take it off the air. As soon as we can, we'll . . ."

Dan Wiseman didn't hear the rest. He and Al Disario were in a car, headed for Inglewood.

And a smiling Alfredo Gravez ordered the van back in motion, back to Newport Beach. In a voice that seemed filled with glee, he said, "I don't think President Dalton will be sleeping tonight. In fact, I don't think he'll be sleeping for some time."

* * *

President Robert Dalton was seated behind his desk in the Oval Office, trying to get a reading from Mickey Serson and Tim Belcher as to the impact of the speech. Belcher had the floor.

"I just finished talking to some of the TV guys and the reactions are mixed, at best. But you know those guys, they're always negative until they find out which way the wind's blowing. We should get some reactions soon from the ones who really count. I'll get on the phone in about five minutes and talk to Chicago, Denver, Dallas, you know, the usual sources."

Mickey Serson was more sanguine. "I thought it went very well. You laid it out just like it was. I don't think that many Americans are going to want you to make deals with drug pushers. I think they'd rather take their chances."

Dalton looked at an unlit cigar and sighed. "I hope you're right, Mickey. You know as well as I do, that martial law is impossible. I've ordered it, but we couldn't enforce it in a million years. I guess what's really important is what Gravez feels. If we've succeeded in putting the fear of God into him, then everything else is worthwhile.

"Surely he must realize that his days are numbered if he doesn't agree to my demands."

The telephone on the desk rang. Tim Belcher picked it up and told the operator to put Edward Spencer through.

"Yes, Mr. Director. This is Tim Belcher."

He listened for a moment and then cupped a

hand over the mouthpiece. "It's Spencer. He wants to talk to you. Do you want to take it?"

Dalton nodded and took the telephone.

"Yes, Ed. What is it?"

As he listened, his face became white and his breathing shallow. His hand began to tremble and tears welled up in his eyes.

Very slowly, his head started to descend toward the desk until it was resting on the leather cover. The telephone was still at his ear, and his face was twisted into an expression of pure agony.

Mickey Serson's jaw dropped and he gently reached for the telephone. As he did so, the door to the Oval Office swung open and two men entered. They both looked shocked. One of them yelled, "Gravez has just used the bacteria in L.A.! There are thousands of people dying right now! Thousands!"

Robert Dalton's face was pressed against the desk and he was beating a fist against the top. He kept repeating the same thing over and over.

"I was wrong. I was wrong. I was wrong. God help me! God help me!"

And Mickey Serson felt his entire body go numb.

The scene outside the Forum was surrealistic, like something conjured up in the mind of a demented painter.

People lay all over the parking lot. Some of them were still alive, their bodies jerking convulsively, while others lay still, in the last moments of life. Fire trucks, ambulances and police vehicles were everywhere but very few people were being attended to, due to the shortage of protective clothing. Only the firemen were so equipped and they knew that in reality, there was nothing they could do to help. The main concern was to stop the illness from spreading.

It was a full forty minutes before the Army Biological Weapons Decontamination Team arrived and swung into action. Along with the team were three tankers filled with liquid nitrogen.

The team started to attach the metal tubes that would direct the chemical to the entrances of the Forum, entrances that had been blocked solid with masses of people, trampled in the mad attempt to escape.

Smaller cannisters of liquid nitrogen were being used to spray the people in the parking lot. People who were now unconscious or dead. They had managed to escape from the Forum, but it was to no avail.

BT33 had been designed to be transmitted from person to person by a single breath. It had succeeded.

Several medical vans arrived and samples of dirt and air were taken, along with saliva from some of the victims.

People in bright orange coveralls, with full helmets and scuba tanks on their backs, were everywhere, trying to determine if the feared epidemic was now becoming a reality.

Dan Wiseman, clothed in similar garb, assessed the situation and tried to coordinate the multitude of rescue personnel.

Rescue . . . there would be no rescue.

There was only one question. Had the bacteria been confined or had it not?

As he moved around, barking into his walkie-talkie, his mind kept focusing on the fact that the temperature outside was a crisp 42 degrees. Just as Gravez had with the airplane, the man had attacked under circumstances that would lessen the chances of a full-blown epidemic. It seemed incongruous that the man would have the brains to take such a precaution and yet be so utterly stupid as to not realize the impact of what he had done.

Thousands, perhaps tens of thousands of people were dead. It was impossible to accept the idea that those deaths would go unavenged. Surely, Wiseman thought, Gravez must know that.

His beeper chirped.

Wiseman went back to the car and grabbed the radio.

"Omega!" he barked.

"Omega . . . this is Alpha. We just ran the computer program. I need you back here. We have a major breakthrough!"

The director's voice was filled with excitement. An excitement that Dan did not share. He acknowledged the call and numbly went looking for Al Disario. As he did so, he grabbed one of the medical people coming out of the van with slides in her hands. "Anything?" he asked.

The woman shook her head. "Looks like it was confined to the inside. Some of the bodies are still contagious but we're isolating them. I think we'll be okay."

"How many?" Dan asked. "How many bodies?"

The woman's eyes misted. "At least fourteen thousand. Everyone inside is dead and the ones that did get out never made it to their cars."

Dan turned away and looked at one of the crews pumping liquid nitrogen through one of the entrances to the arena. Great white clouds of gas obscured whatever might be seen inside. It wasn't enough. Dan's mind could still envision the scene he'd witnessed on the television screen at the office. It was a scene he'd never forget as long as he lived.

He felt terribly cold. It wasn't from the weather, but rather a numbing coldness that seemed to come from inside his body. He felt as though he'd been given a powerful drug that had dulled his senses. His mind flashed to some old newsreels he'd once seen of the Hitler death camps and his body started to quiver uncontrollably.

And then, for the first time, it hit him.

Bernice!

Danny had said that Bernice was going to the basketball game with a new boyfriend.

Bernice.

Slowly, Wiseman lowered himself to the ground, sat cross-legged and buried his head in his hands.

They'd been married for sixteen years and had hardly spoken since the divorce. Now, they would never speak again.

The old arguments flashed through his mind. It had been so strange. The marriage had worked so well for so long and then it had disintegrated for reasons Dan Wiseman would never understand. Bernice had said he worked too hard, spent too much time on the job.

He'd told her he had a job to do and a career to follow. For most of their marriage, it hadn't been a problem, and he couldn't understand why it was such a big one now.

When he wasn't at work, he was at home. He was attentive to her needs, supportive of her own career. The kids were in private school at the time, her time was her own . . . what was the problem?

Him, she'd said.

She'd bitched about everything.

She hated Washington.

She hated police work.

She was beginning to hate him.

When she finally asked for a divorce, it was almost a relief. He couldn't make her happy any more. Didn't know where to start, really. He'd suggested counseling and she'd told him that he was the one that needed counseling. Just him. He was the one who didn't seem to realize that there were more important things in life than a job.

How were they supposed to eat, he'd ask.

Now she was dead.

Since the divorce, they'd hardly uttered a word to each other. She'd continued to live in the Palos Verde home they'd once shared and Dan had moved into a small apartment, then to Washington.

He'd seen the kids on a regular basis and to her credit, she'd never tried to tear him down in their eyes. But he could see in those same eyes the terrible confusion and disappointment in parents unable to keep a terrific marriage working.

They hadn't taken sides, bless them.

The kids!

Jesus!

They were in San Diego with their Aunt Claire. They'd be watching this on television! They'd know!

Oh God!

Wiseman rushed to his car and grabbed the mobile phone. As he did so, he had another thought. Maybe she hadn't gone to the game. Maybe they'd decided to watch the president's speech instead. He punched the familiar numbers on the headset and was met with the cruelest of ironies.

It was Bernice's voice on the phone.

On the answering machine.

"Hi! This is Bernice Wiseman. There's no one here to take your call at this time, but if you'll leave your name and the time you called when you hear the beep, either Dawn or I will get back to you."

Dan hit the hook button on the telephone savagely and then punched another series of numbers. "This is Wiseman! Patch me through to the San Diego operator!"

"Yessir."

The operator came on and he gave her the number. Claire answered the telephone, her voice thin and fragile.

"Yes?"

"Claire, this is Dan Wiseman. I'm . . . are the kids there?"

She started to sob. "Oh, Dan, is it true? Is Bernie dead?"

Wiseman didn't know exactly what to say. "I . . . I don't really know. Let me talk to Danny."

In a moment, the voice of his son was on the phone.

"Dad? What about Mom? They say that everybody died in there. That nobody got out alive. Is that right, Dad?"

Wiseman could feel the pain in the boy-man's voice.

"Danny," he said. "I just phoned home and there's no answer. But they might not have gone to the game. They might have changed their minds."

There was a pause and then Danny said, "No. She knew where we were. She'd have called, Dad. Jesus!"

Wiseman found the next words difficult to say. "Danny, I want you and your sister to stay there until you hear from me. It's still too dangerous and there's nothing you can do here. Will you do that?"

Danny said, "If only she'd listened. If only she'd come with us. Jesus Christ, Dad."

Wiseman tried to make his voice reflect the empathy he felt. "Danny, I'd be there with you if I could. You know that. I have to get this guy, son. You understand?"

There was a pause and then a very quiet, "I understand."

Wiseman said, "I love you. I'll be with you as soon as I can. I'm really sorry, son. Let me talk to Dawn."

For a few moments he talked to his daughter. She was in mild shock and talked haltingly. He told her he loved her and would see them soon. Then he hung up.

The horror of what surrounded him had closed down Dan Wiseman's ability to feel any more pain. He knew that Bernice was dead but at that moment, he could feel nothing, other than to note the fact. The children would miss her, he thought.

He said a silent prayer and continued his search for Disario, all the while hoping that this wasn't really happening. None of it. It was more than his mind could accept.

# Chapter Twenty-One

Dan Wiseman raced back toward the office at some 90 miles an hour, with a shaken Al Disario at his side. They were both listening to the car radio and the debate was in full song.

As they listened, Dan was aware of an unusual occurrence. The streets of Los Angeles, just like the streets of other major cities throughout the country, were almost empty.

Empty!

It was eerie.

According to the news station they were listening to, from all reports, the people of the United States were fully behind the president. There had been no panic, no rioting in the streets, just a massive outpouring of support, expressed through telegrams and telephone calls to newspapers, radio and television stations and the White House itself.

When the news of the tragedy in Los Angeles had hit the airwaves, people were understandably shocked. But so far, nothing had changed. Not yet, at least.

The death toll was estimated at over fifteen thousand, which included all members of both basketball teams, concession stand workers and others.

Throughout America, people were staying at home, hunkered down in front of their television sets, settling in on this strange night for a what seemed like a vigil. Dan knew it wouldn't last. They were in shock. Within hours, they would start to understand the danger they were in and blame it on the president's proposed actions. They would start to think things over and the response would change. There would be screams of outrage.

If nothing else, the media would get them thinking. Already, scores of pundits were being interviewed and the opinions being expressed ran the gamut. Had the president done the right thing in threatening Gravez? Some were highly critical of that threat, saying it was directly responsible for the deaths of the people in Los Angeles. Others were more supportive, expressing the view that Gravez was insane and would have done it anyway.

If the proposed attack on Bolivian soil was carried out, some felt, there was no question that the bacteria would be released throughout the nation, and millions would die. Others were of the opinion that it would be better to die in a war of principle than to submit to the demands of a criminal.

Some urged the president to negotiate with the Gravez family immediately. It was the only way, they said. Others called for the president to carry out his threat and bomb Bolivia back to the stone age.

Where had he heard those words before, Dan wondered, sarcastically.

Dan Wiseman had his own thoughts.

In a few hours, people would become fully aware of the dangers that confronted them. They would start to wonder about their food supply, their water supply, the air they breathed. And they would start to panic.

And the whole country would come unhinged.

This was the calm before the storm. And unless they recovered the bacteria very soon, the storm would be unleashed with full fury.

When they finally made it back to the office, they hurried to the main conference room where an excited Edward Spencer explained the reasons for his radio call.

The director's tired and puffy eyes almost sparkled. It seemed incongruous in light of the disaster that had just occurred, but he could see the light at the end of the tunnel and an end to this nightmare.

"Dan," he said, breathlessly, "The computer program has been run, and they've hit the jackpot!"

"We checked the phone records between the U.S. and Bolivia and cross-matched those telephone numbers with those of the various medical companies who have purchased stuff that might be used in the production of BT thirty three."

He paused for a second and then said, "Baldwin

Medsearch! We got a match on Baldwin Medsearch. They're a medical research outfit in Newport Beach owned by an off-shore company that'll take weeks to trace . . . but I'd bet money that Gravez is involved.

"We ran another program, one that gave us the list of employees under the federal employment number assigned to Medsearch. It provided the name of Corwin Farrow. Sounds like the Cory you're looking for."

Dan was listening carefully. "How come DMV didn't have his name?"

Spencer smiled. "Because his license had been suspended for two years and he doesn't own a car. The computer didn't have it in the active file and we simply forgot to go further. But Medsearch owns several cars and one of them matches the description of the car Farrow used."

"Holy shit!"

"Right!"

"Dan," the director continued, "Medsearch has exactly the kind of equipment needed to produce BT thirty three, including encapsulation equipment. It all goes together. In fact, of all of the companies, it's the only one where everything matches. It has to be the lab!"

Slowly, the images of the death and horror in Inglewood started to recede, to be replaced by images that had yet to occur. Images of a raid on Medsearch and the end of this agony.

Spencer was still ebullient. "Not only that, but we're really starting to close down his entire organization inside the country."

As Spencer explained it, the entire Gravez network was being laid bare and the organizational skills that were being revealed surprised everyone. These were people who could have been successful running a Fortune 500 company, as was so very often the case. In fact, they *were* running a number of legitimate corporations, but the brilliance displayed in the setting up of their drug distribution organization was almost frightening.

They had developed a network of legitimate businesses such as shipping lines, trucking companies, communications companies and a score of wholesale food distributors. Through these legitimate channels, they funneled tons of cocaine on a daily basis in parallel with the normal techniques used by other cocaine traffickers.

It was set up in such a way that the authorities' full attention was given to the prevention of the illegitimate smuggling with not a hint that 90% of the Gravez family's cocaine traffic was coming through the other way. In a sense, the smuggling was a cover for the other channels.

Dan watched his team still hard at work. Air Force reconnaissance photos of Bolivian buildings were being examined by DEA agents who'd recently spent time in Bolivia.

Sales records of companies manufacturing equipment that could have been used to produce the bacteria were being examined by teams who were double-checking the results that had been given earlier. No one wanted any more mistakes.

Telephone records of calls between the United States and Bolivia were being examined and locations pinpointed. Passenger lists of flights between the two countries were being examined and names checked against master lists. Then those names were being cross-checked with telephone records.

A picture had finally appeared, like some giant jigsaw puzzle being worked by a score of busy hands. No matter how clever the system, it was unable to prevent being penetrated by knowledge, some of which had been been gained through the use of illegal interrogation methods. As much as Dan despised the method, he had to admit that the results were impressive.

But—and it was a very big but—the main information garnered, the information that had led them to Medsearch, had been gaining using established police techniques. The other stuff had helped locate the bad guys, but there was little they could do with it. Not really.

In fact, Dan ruminated, they could have left the drug at home.

Except now they might really need it.

There were a lot more questions that needed to be answered and very little time for formalities.

Was the bacteria in Newport Beach or Bolivia?

Or both?

The bacteria had to be found and destroyed.

And it had to be found quickly.

And every man in that room knew it.

Dan sighed and looked over the printout one more time. Then he nodded to Al Disario and Edward Spencer. "Give me two hours to set this up and then I'll be ready. If I were you, I'd say nothing to Washington yet, just in case."

Spencer shook his head. "Can't do that, Dan. Besides, those poor bastards need a lift. They're really down. They're worried that the entire country may lose control at any time. The news that you are closing in might help a lot."

Dan groaned. "For God's sake, don't let them leak it!"

Spencer looked hurt. "I won't," he said, softly. Then he asked, "What about the sewers? Should we start getting ready?"

Dan thought for a moment and then said, "I think we had better be ready for anything, but my gut tells me that Gravaz will be contacting the president before he does anything else. My God. He's just killed fifteen thousand people."

Elizabeth Martin and her father, Roger Brackton, sat in their Florida hotel room and held hands. It was almost dawn and neither one had slept a wink during the night.

Elizabeth had viewed the body of her husband and identified him. Then she had come completely apart.

Perhaps, in some corner of her mind, she had imagined that it was all a mistake. A nightmare that would end when the sun came up and the darkness receded. That somehow, her husband would come bounding in the door, his face beaming with a salesman's enthusiasm, ready to tell her about his latest triumph over a reluctant purchasing agent.

But the sight of him lying there in that strange factory converted to a morgue, the gray walls covered with some makeshift drapery, the coldness permeating every cell in her body, was shattering.

His face seemed so much older, as though the last moments of his life had aged him unmercifully. At first, she wasn't sure it was even Mark, and her heart skipped a beat. And then the recognition had hit her like a hammer blow.

The room had begun to spin like a top and the concrete floor came rushing up to meet her. And then she was screaming, beating her fists against the chest of her father who was holding her in his arms, the tears streaming down his face at the sight of her agony.

And then they'd come back to the hotel and watched on television as the president made his speech.

And the thoughts had whirled around in her head

like bees around the flowers in her backyard garden. The images, the memories, forming and fading, refusing to leave her alone.

Her father had wanted to take her to a hospital and have her given a sedative, but she'd refused. She wanted to confront the pain, deal with it, not suppress it. She'd have to face it sometime. It might as well be now.

She looked at her father now, exhausted, sitting there holding her hand, trying in some way to make her pain his, to relieve her of it.

"Daddy," she said. "I'm sorry. I'll be all right. I really will."

He leaned forward and kissed her on the forehead. "I know, sweetheart, I know."

George Barnes was back in his hotel room in Los Angeles, still fuming over the events of the day.

He'd watched the president's speech and had seen the bulletins regarding the attack on the Forum.

His mind went back to his conversation with Senator McGinnis. The bastard had set him up! McGinnis must have known that the suspected target of the next attack would be Los Angeles, not Washington, and he'd lied, hoping that Barnes would somehow be killed in the attack.

The sonofabitch had tried to kill him!

It was the middle of the night in Washington, but to hell with it. Nobody would be sleeping anyway.

Not on this insane night.

Barnes reached for the telephone and punched some buttons. He still had a lot of friends in Washington. They'd be more than happy to settle McGinnis's hash.

William Powers pushed the room service dinner table away from his chair, picked up the thick file folder from the desk and began reading again.

The investigators had done their work well. It gave Powers a certain sense of satisfaction. He'd fought many battles with the head office over his penchant for hiring more expensive investigators than the company would have preferred. But time and again, the extra money had been well spent, saving the company many times the actual cost. But each time there was an investigation, he had to refight the same foolish fight. Frank Tupper was indeed a stupid man, as was his vice-president, Taylor Madison.

It was galling.

William Powers was a senior investigator for Butler Casualty, charged with the responsibility for making sure the company never paid more than was necessary in the hundreds of cases that had to be carefully examined every year. Powers's skill consistently saved the company millions of dollars in any given year. More in a bad one.

And yet his salary was a meager one hundred

thousand dollars a year with a bonus arrangement that netted him another ten thousand at most. And his investigation budget was paltry by any standard.

He'd given his life to this company and they didn't appreciate it. Every meeting with Tupper seemed to turn into an argument over the money that Powers was spending. The money he was *saving* the company was never allowed into the discussion. He was, after all, simply doing his job. That's what he'd been hired to do.

He snorted out loud and drained the last of the red dinner wine from the glass.

He looked at one of the reports in the file. It was a good example of the difference between proper investigatory efforts and sloppy work. The difference between hiring a qualified investigator and saving perhaps fifty dollars a day on a lesser person.

The victim was a man named Mark Martin.

He'd been knocking around as a salesman for most of his thirty-six years. The most money he'd ever made was right now, as a sales manager for Burkhart Industries. The company he'd worked for prior to that had gone broke. Martin had worked for them for two years. And the company before that three years.

He'd gotten himself solidly in debt. He had three bank credit cards and all of them were at the limit. That smacked of irresponsibility. A man who lived beyond his means.

He had no children and his wife didn't work.

But that didn't tell the whole story. The investigator working the case had interviewed former employers of Mark Martin. One of them was prepared to state that Mark Martin was hot-tempered.

Another said the man had a habit of partying when on the road. Letters from women had arrived at the office addressed to Martin and they'd been opened by mistake. They revealed a man who spent a lot of time with women other than his wife.

All in all, the report on Mark Martin marked him as a man with anything but an assured future. The family was being represented by George Barnes.

Barnes was a show-boater, but he was also a hard-nosed lawyer. When they dumped the file on Mark Martin in his lap, he'd be eager to make a settlement. Two . . . maybe three hundred thousand. Tops. He'd be forced to discuss a settlement with his client. She sure as hell wouldn't want the embarassment of sitting in a courtroom and listening to a lot of testimony from women all over the country about her husband's sexual appetite.

So she'd force Barnes to accept what was offered. Case closed.

A sloppy investigator might not have turned these things up. Just this one case represented a saving to Butler casualty of at least two hundred thousand dollars. And the investigation expense was under a thousand.

And still, Tupper would be screaming about that.

Powers picked up another report.

This one was not about a family, but rather one of the LAX security people. A woman named Helen Porter. She was an ex-cop who'd had a nervous breakdown and left the force after accidently killing a young boy. She'd undergone therapy for six months, had been pronounced sound and been hired by LAX sometime later.

A tragic story with a happy ending.

Maybe.

It wouldn't be hard to tear this woman apart if the need arose. It wouldn't be difficult to make it seem like she was incompetent and that the phony FAA inspector might have been stopped by a more aware security policeman. It might not be the truth, but it didn't matter. Juries tended to view people with mental problems as incurable. Once a nut, always a nut.

So the back-up strategy was coming into place. They already had one security person who was dead meat. There'd be more. Everybody had hang-ups these days and good investigators would find out about them. There were no secrets anymore. Once information was keyed into a computer somewhere, it was always there, ready to be recalled when the need arose.

Powers threw the file folder on the desk and stood up. He looked out the window of the hotel room and marveled at the quietness of the streets.

Martial law!

The president of the United States had flipped out!

What was next? Would he really attack Bolivia?

He'd called the attack on the airplane an act of war.

The president's exact words!

In legal terms, an act of war voided any liability whatsoever. The president had said this was an act of war by a group of criminals, not by a nation, but he was about to attack a nation.

The courts would have a picnic with this one.

As stupid as Tupper was, he had used his head in one sense. He wasn't about to pay a single claim until the courts decided several issues. And that could take years.

Powers made a note on the yellow pad to drop half of the investigators. There was no hurry now. No need to spend what precious few dollars he had in his budget. The rest of the investigation could be conducted at a more leisurely pace.

Nothing was going to happen for a long, long time.

He walked over to the bed and lay down.

He was still thinking about those reports. For perhaps the first time in his long career, he felt a pang of sympathy for those people.

He grunted and tried to shake the thought from his mind. This was no time to be getting soft. It was a tough world. Those who couldn't take it should get out of the way. The strong would survive and the weak would wither.

It had always been that way and it always would. He was just doing his job.

He made a mental note to have it out with Tupper the next time they met.

One hundred thousand dollars a year wasn't enough. Not nearly enough. Tupper would have to give him more money or he'd walk. There were other insurance companies who'd be glad to have him at twice the salary.

He'd stayed with Tupper because he'd always believed that a man should be loyal to the company he worked for.

But there was no need to be silly about it.

President Robert Dalton sat as his desk and rubbed his forehead. The headache was a dandy. He'd taken two of the pain killers the doctor had prescribed, but they hadn't done much good.

The doctor had told him that the headaches would get worse. He'd also told him that there were drugs that could knock the headache out, but they'd also knock the president out.

That wasn't what Dalton wanted. Not now.

He had to deal with these criminals first. He had to smash their organization and destroy the source of their income; the coca leaf fields in Bolivia. Then, he could step aside and let the vice-president take over. Maybe that action would force the governments of Peru and Colombia to be more cooperative. Maybe they would get serious, fearing an attack on their own soil.

Unless Cecil Aubrey decided to undo everything that Robert Dalton had started.

Aubrey was an opportunist and a dyed-in-the-wool bureaucrat. His interests were primarily centered around himself. He'd make a lousy president and everyone knew it. During the campaign, he'd been needed to balance the ticket. As usual, nobody concerned themselves with the chances of the man actually becoming president. Not then. After all, Dalton was a healthy, young man.

Sometimes, the presidency changed a man and he grew into the job. They'd said that about Harry Truman. Dalton doubted that Cecil Aubrey and Harry Truman were remotely similar in character. The thought of Aubrey taking over was almost as frightening as the thought of not stopping Alfredo Gravez. But there was nothing they could do. He would become the president.

But not now.

Right now, Robert Dalton still had the power and intended to use it. For years, the United States had played footsie with the Bolivian government, trying to reach some agreement to shut the coca leaf farms down. But the cooperation had been limp at best, and in some cases, it was obvious that the two countries were working at cross purposes.

Well, that would soon end.

He rubbed his head again.

Damn, it hurt!

He closed his eyes and leaned back in the chair.

Fifteen thousand people!

The Oval Office was quiet. The television sets had been turned off and the telephone had stopped ringing. Out there, people were thinking all manner of things, many of them blaming Robert Dalton for those deaths.

They were saying that he should have negotiated with Gravez, that he shouldn't have made it appear that the man was just another crackpot. He should have been taken seriously, they said.

Some historians had cited examples of the government actually working in tandem with criminals. There was the case of Frank Costello who had been helpful during World War Two. A known criminal helping in the invasion of Sicily.

And they cited the case of organized crime figures being employed to assassinate Fidel Castro. That plan hadn't worked too well, but it had served to point out the fact that sometimes, deals could be made with criminals.

Others had cited the fact that the established crime families were already at war with the Gravez family. They had suggested that organized crime should have been given whatever information the FBI could gather and use it to eliminate the competition.

The bulk of opinion was swinging toward the

blaming of the president for the deaths of those unfortunates in Los Angeles. Demands were being made that he open up negotiations now, before any others were killed. Perhaps millions.

They didn't understand. None of them.

It was impossible to make a deal with Gravez. As long as the man possessed the bacteria, he would actually be in control of the country. Didn't they understand that?

No. He had to be stopped.

And the call from Ed Spencer was the only good news he'd had in days.

According to Spencer, they were sure they had pin-pointed the location of the lab, the bacteria. Before the sun was up, they would attack and maybe . . . just maybe, this thing would be over.

Except for Bolivia.

Those bastards would pay dearly, no matter what the outcome of the raid.

The Bolivian ambassador was waiting to see him. He'd been sitting in the waiting room for four hours, begging for an audience with the president.

Well, screw him.

President Dalton had nothing to say to him.

Helen Porter sat on the bed and stared at the pistol in her hand.

Once before she'd considered suicide. In fact, she'd come very close to eating her gun, as the cops liked to put it, three years ago.

Very close.

Now, she was seriously considering it again.

The deaths of fifteen thousand people in the Forum was tied to the deaths of the people on board that airplane. The investigation would be the most intense in the nation's history.

If anyone lived to carry it out.

She knew that the insurance company had searched the apartment and knew about her troubles. Troubles that had seemed in the past.

She knew that soon, everyone would know.

As in any disaster, there had to be scapegoats. Someone had to be held responsible. Only then could the event be put in the past.

Helen Porter was sure that she would be one of those scapegoats, a minor one to be sure, but one drawn into the investigation simply because of her past.

Once, she'd made a mistake. Worse than that, she'd exhibited signs of emotional instability.

That was the sin.

They would crucify her for that more than anything.

There was only one way out.

She started to put the gun in her mouth and stopped. In a corner of her mind, a small thought was nibbling away at her consciousness, pecking at her depression, trying to make itself known.

There was another way.

Remote, but a possibility.

It was worth a shot. She could always kill herself. Anytime she wanted.

## Chapter Twenty-two

Dan Wiseman stood in front of the room, a pointer in his hands, and faced one hundred tired and anxious FBI agents.

A diagram of the interior layout of the Baldwin Medsearch building had been drawn on a large blackboard and Dan touched the pointer to one of the rooms depicted. "This," he said, "is where we think the bacteria is produced and stored. According to the information we've received from the Pentagon, the bacteria has to be constantly monitored. When the supply reaches a certain density, it is processed and about ninety-five percent of it is killed. The remainder is allowed to develop until the supply reaches that density again, and the process is repeated. So at least three or four technicians must be there at all times.

"This area is sealed off from the other research rooms and it's possible that the other employees aren't even aware of what's going on. Nevertheless, we can't take any chances.

"We'll be making the attack at four in the morning. As near as we can tell, there should be fewer than fifteen people inside the building itself. However, you must be ready for anything. Take nothing for granted.

"We'll go in through six different entrances. You've been given your team assignments and your entrance location. We'll blow all doors at exactly the same moment. The demolition boys will take care of the doors. Remember, as soon as the front gate and the shipping and receiving gates are blown, the alarms will sound, even though the power will be off. The alarms have battery-powdered backup.

"When you enter the building, you'll be wearing your potective clothing. Each suit has a large 'FBI' logo on the front and back. We'll use bullhorns to announce who you are to the security guards, but if they resist, you'll have to shoot. You'll use your liquid nitrogen on anything and everything. The gas will freeze whatever it comes in contact with almost instantly. There'll be a lot of different bottles and vials in the main research room and you'll have to make sure that everything in there has been frozen.

"Each of you will be carrying two cannisters of liquid nitrogen. As soon as we enter, there'll be additional cannisters brought in. When you run dry, grab another cannister and keep at it. We want everything in that building frozen solid.

"Keep your protective suits on until advised otherwise. And let's try to take some of these people alive. We need some answers and we need them fast. Gravez's people may already be in position somewhere. We need to know.

"As for Gravez, if he's there, it's absolutely vital that he be taken alive. Vital. If you're forced to shoot, aim for the legs. We need this man badly."

"Any questions?"

There were a few and Dan answered them. He looked at his watch. "Okay," he said, "we're coming up on two-eleven. Mark."

The men set their watches.

"All right, let's get moving."

The agents left the building in downtown Los Angeles and headed for a variety of vehicles waiting in the rear of the building. The protective clothing would be put on once they reached Newport Beach.

The Baldwin Medsearch building was located in a small industrial park in Newport Beach, less than an hour way. It was a square, almost windowless one-story tip-up surrounded by a chain-link fence. The room thought most likely to contain the bacteria was almost in the center of the building and according to the contractor's building plans, had its own concrete walls and steel doors.

The men were to assemble in a park about three blocks from the building, check their equipment and then make the assault. First, electrical power to the building would be disconnected and the fence would be breached at the two gate entrances. Then, the six doors leading into the building would be blown and the men, wearing protective clothing that included miner's lights on their helmets, would converge on the internal concrete-walled room, the research area. Once again, explosives would be employed to blow the single steel door.

Of the one hundred agents, twelve were demolitions experts.

The Newport Beach police would be advised immediately prior to the raid but would not participate.

Director Spencer walked with Dan as they walked to the parking lot. He had some last minute updates. He seemed tense and nervous, as were the rest of the group.

"I've just talked to Washington and they've heard nothing from Gravez. President Dalton is still sitting in the Oval Office where he's been all night. I guess he's pretty shook up."

Dan grunted. "Can't say that I blame him."

Spencer looked at Wiseman for a moment, but did not respond. As they prepared for the raid on Baldwin Medsearch, Spencer and Wiseman counted one blessing. The hundreds of people interrogated and detained were still in the hands of the FBI. There was no way Gravez could know the FBI was aware of the Medsearch connection. Not yet. It was conceivable he might be in the building which was, even at this moment, being monitored from the air and the ground.

Spencer clapped a hand on Dan's shoulder and said, "I don't have to tell you how important this is. We'll be waiting by the radio. The moment you have anything, we'll be ready to go. Good luck, Dan."

Dan nodded and got into a waiting car and the convoy headed south toward Newport Beach.

It was 5:30 in the morning in Washington. Senator Ted McGinnis was chairing a discussion with four senior and influential senators, three congressman, Mickey Serson and Vice President Cecil Aubrey.

When Mickey Serson had received the telephone call from Cecil Aubrey, his first response had been anger. Aubrey was not involved in the problem that surrounded the White House and here he was sticking his nose into things that didn't concern him. Not yet.

And then the vice president told Mickey that he knew.

He knew that Dalton was dying.

There were things that had to be discussed.

Mickey Serson, feeling like a man entering an enemy camp, joined the others and listened as McGinnis laid it out.

"The thing of it is, Mickey, that this Bolivian thing is a bad move. A very bad move. I've been talking to some of my people back home and I don't mind telling you that they don't look kindly on this at all."

Serson snorted. "Sure. You've talked to some bankers who are worried about their Bolivian loans."

McGinnis retorted, "You may sneer if you like, Mr. Serson, but those loans were made at the behest of the administration."

"Not *this* administration!"

McGinnis smiled weakly. "That remark is totally redundant, Mr. Serson. Let's be realistic. There's more to this than just the loans. American foreign policy will be in a shambles. If the attack is allowed to proceed before Congress has a chance to stop it, irreparable harm will be done to American interests throughout Latin America.

"We'll be in serious trouble with the entire damn world! And what if this Gravez character drops this bacteria in the sewer systems of our cites? He's already shown that he'll stop at nothing! For God's sake man, fifteen thousand dead people are lying in warehouses throughout Southern California! Doesn't Dalton realize the dangers?"

Cecil Aubrey answered the question. "Of course he doesn't. The man has a brain tumor that is clouding his judgment. He doesn't know what he's doing."

Serson, the tiredness pulling at him like a heavy weight, fought on. "Really?" he said. "And just where did you get that information?"

"You deny it?"

"I asked you a question. I'd like an answer."

Aubrey smiled. "You won't get one. But you know damn well I speak the truth."

"That'll be a first."

McGinnis held up his hands. "Look, this isn't getting us anywhere. Section four of the Twenty-fifth Amendment to the Constitution is quite specific. The vice president may assume the presidency as acting president if he and a majority of the principle members of the administration go to the president pro tempore of the Senate and the speaker of the house and declare the president unfit to carry out his job. If necessary, that will be done."

Serson smiled for the first time. "Fine. But that will require a deposition from Doctor Tasker and collaboration from a team of respected doctors who have seen the evidence. But in the meantime, the president can send his own declaration stating that he's fine, resume the presidency and then the whole matter will be dumped in the lap of Congress.

"There's no way the president can be prevented from launching the attack."

Aubrey drummed his fingers on the table and said, "Unless he is convinced that he must resign."

Serson stared at the man. "And you expect me to sell him on that?"

"Yes."

"Well, you can forget it. I won't do it."

McGinnis leaned forward. "Listen to me, Mickey. The president is a dying man. He really has no idea what he's doing. We'll take the necessary steps and he'll be removed from office, but it will be in disgrace. He'll be revealed as a man who took actions while he knew he was seriously ill, imperiling the entire country.

"If Gravez releases that bacteria, millions could die. The country will be thrown into a state of pure anarchy. The president talks about martial law, but you know full well that we can't enforce that. There are too many independent people out there. Too many guns. We'll have a Goddamn blood-bath!

"Listen to me! Our people are spoiled! We've never been under attack. Not in World War One, or Two or Korea or Nam! We don't know what it's like! The people will come apart.

"The only way to deal with this is to negotiate with Gravez. Let him have his precious son back. Leave Bolivia alone. Shit! We haven't made a dent in the operations anyway. Why risk the total breakdown of the country for nothing?"

He paused to catch his breath and then said, "Besides, there are those in the Pentagon who will listen. Once we present our evidence, clearly showing the president's condition, they will be very hesitant to follow the orders of a man who is about to be replaced. Don't forget, these people have careers to worry about.

"This raid cannot be allowed to take place. In fact, it will not take place. I can guarantee it. So, save everyone a lot of needless embarrassment and make Dalton back off."

Serson looked at the senator in disgust. "You've already talked to the Pentagon?"

McGinnis nodded.

Serson sighed. "Senator, that almost amounts to treason. There's never been a time in this country when the military refused to carry out the orders of the commander-in-chief and I doubt very much that they'll start now. I don't know who you talked to but talk is cheap.

"You know, it's very interesting, Senator. Earlier this evening, I received a telephone call from a highly respected member of the legal profession. He had some rather unpleasant things to say about you. He also said he had the evidence to back him up.

"I dismissed his suggestion that I make it public, because I didn't think it was true. I may have been wrong on that. In any case, I'm sure the man won't stop with me. He seems upset. If I were you, I'd probably spend a little time covering my own ass."

McGinnis gulped once and shrank back into his chair like a man looking for a place to hide.

Cecil Aubrey barked, "What the hell are you talking about? Ted? What's this about?"

McGinnis just shook his head.

Then Serson turned to Cecil Aubrey. "Mr. Vice President," he said, "you can do what you want. History will have to make the final judgment on Robert Dalton's actions. As for me, I support him wholeheartedly. If we are ever to conquer the drug problem that exists in this country, it will be through education. Only when the demand is killed, will the problem be killed. I know that and so do you.

"But that will take some time. A long time. It'll take a lot of money and a strong desire on the part of the American people to spend that money instead of using it for other purposes. I don't have to spell out the issues at stake here. You know them as well as I do. But if burning the fields in Bolivia cuts the cocaine supply in half, it will force some people to seek medical treatment. While the odds on kicking the habit are long, there are still thousands of success stories.

"As well, it will make other countries realize that we really are sincere about stopping this constant flow of poison into this country. Maybe that will do some good. Only time will tell.

"But, I do know this: if the world suspects that we've made some sort of deal with the Gravez family, no matter *what* the pressures, what little respect left for this country will die altogether. The United States blackmailed into submission by drug pushers? Absolutely unacceptable!

"Robert Dalton decided to stay on as president for a few days because he knew what an opportunistic, gutless bastard you really were. He was right about that.

"You do what you have to do, and I'll do what I have to do."

With that, he rose and walked out of the room.

Williams Powers was awakened by the light that bathed the hotel room. For a moment, he thought he'd fallen asleep with the bedside lamp on but he remembered distinctly turning it off. He rolled over in bed and it was then he saw the woman sitting in a chair, the gun in her hand pointed directly at his head.

His heart stopped beating for a moment.

He knew this woman. Frantically, his tried to get his brain to function. Tried to recall where he'd seen the face. The face of a woman sitting silently, pointing a gun at William Powers's head.

And then he had it.

LAX security.

The woman's name was Helen Porter. It had only been hours since he'd reviewed the file. Photos of her had been stapled to the folder.

He tried to speak. At first, the words wouldn't come out. Then, slowly, agonizingly, they came in spurts, just like the breath in his lungs.

"What . . . are . . . you . . . doing . . . here?"

The look in the woman's eyes was one of pure unadulterated hatred. Savage. Almost insane. Powers felt very close to death.

Helen Porter asked, "Are you fully awake?"

Powers croaked an answer. "Yes."

"Good. Now I want you to listen carefully. Very carefully. Understand?"

Another croak. "Yes."

Porter crossed her legs and kept the gun pointed at the insurance man's head. The hand was still, the knuckles white. The voice was calm and controlled in contrast to the eyes.

"I understand how you people operate," she began. "You don't care much who you destroy just as long as you save some money. Well, I've been through hell once and I imagine that the federal investigation will put me through it again.

"I have to take that shit, but I don't have to put up with your shit. You broke into my apartment, you bastard."

Powers cringed. "No, not me. They did that without my authorization."

Helen Porter raised the gun in her hand. "Sure they did."

Powers's back was against the headboard. He kept moving his legs as though he could somehow push himself through the wall, away from the danger, away from this insane woman, but the headboard held him fast.

"Allright. I'm sorry. Look, I'll destroy your file. I'll tear it up. I'll make sure you aren't involved."

The woman smiled. "Yes . . . yes, you will. And you'll also tear up the information you've collected on everyone else, you asshole. The families of the victims. The ones you'll brand as queers and perverts and thieves and whatever else you can manufacture."

Powers looked ill. "Miss Porter, that won't do any good. If I don't do my job, they'll just send someone else. I can't prevent that information from being used."

She rose and pressed the gun against his forehead.

"Think of something," she said. "Because if you don't, I'll personally blow your fucking head off. Not just yours, but anyone who's ever cared a thing in the world about you. Your wife, your kids . . . whatever.

"I have nothing to lose, buster. Nothing. Maybe I can help some other poor slob who has to put up with your shit. Just thinking about it will give me a reason to live. Right now, I need that. Do you understand?"

Powers was feeling faint. "I . . . I think so."

Slowly, she removed the gun from his head and moved back from the bed. "I hope so, asshole. I really do."

Then she turned and left the room.

William Powers remained in the bed and listened to the pounding of his heart.

She was insane! Totally insane! Her file had stated that she'd spent time in therapy after the incident with the child. Obviously, something had slipped past the doctors.

He knew in his heart that the woman would do as she threatened. She'd kill him. She surely would.

He reached for the phone to call the police. As he started to punch the buttons, he thought about it some more and replaced the headset. What could they do? What would they do? They had other things on their minds.

Jesus Christ!

The whole world was going crazy.

And Williams Powers started to weep.

At exactly ten seconds before four in the morning, the power to the Baldwin Medsearch building was shut off and telephone lines cut. Ten seconds later, the attack began. The front gate to the compound was attended by an astonished security guard who blanched at the sight of a horde of men in what appeared to be orange space suits with 'FBI' stenciled on their chests.

He simply stared in awe as he was told what was about to take place and opened the gate. The rear gate was unattended during the night. A loud noise signaled the news that it had been blown open.

Seconds later, amid the sound of clanging bells, all six entrances to the building itself were blown and Dan Wiseman, a bullhorn on his hands, announced the raid to those inside.

"This is the FBI. Everyone inside the building is to remain standing with their hands on their heads. No one moves."

Even as he spoke, the agents were disarming confused security guards and moving toward the inner concrete-walled main research room.

As the demolitions team began to set the charge around the perimeter of the steel door leading to the room, it opened slowly and a very frightened man in a white coat came forward, his hands in the air, his eyes squinting from the light being cast by the helmeted agents.

His voice was squeaky with fear. "Please," he said, "Don't shoot."

The agents quickly entered the room and found three more men, similarly attired, standing in the center of the room, their hands also in the air.

Wiseman used his walkie-talkie to tell the electricians to turn the power back on.

The room was flooded with light. Immediately, the agents turned the valves on their cannisters of liquid nitrogen and began spraying the gas on everything in the room.

The room measured 30 feet by 25 feet. In the center, a long stainless steel table was covered in a clear glass housing. Every two feet, holes had been carved in the glass and long rubber gloves reaching inside had been inserted, allowing the men to work with the equipment in some sort of safety.

Along the inner walls of the room, steel shelves ran from the floor to the ceiling, shelves filled with a variety of glass containers, themselves filled with liquids running the full color spectrum.

While the army of agents went about the task of applying liquid nitrogen to the research room, Wiseman herded the four workers outside the room and ordered them to sit down on the floor against the wall. Hypodermic needles appeared and the sleeves of the four white-coated men were rolled up. One of them, the man who had opened the door, protested. "Wait," he said. "There's no need for that. I'll tell you whatever you want to know."

Dan looked at him in disgust. "Can't take the chance," he said, and motioned for the shots to be administered.

Three minutes later, the four men were separated and the interrogation begun. Wiseman stayed with the only man who'd uttered a word so far, while the other three were to be interrogated by other agents.

The man was in never-never land. He was having difficulty focusing his eyes and his head bobbed up and down like a ping-pong ball.

Wiseman asked, "Is all of the bacteria in this building?"

The man, now slack-jawed, looked up at him and said, "Yes."

"Are you sure?"

"Yes."

Wiseman wanted to cheer. He wanted to scream at the top of his lungs.

They had done it!

He waited a moment to allow his emotions to cool and then pressed on with the questioning.

"Where is Gravez?"

"At his home."

"In Bolivia?"

"No. Here. He owns a condo. Newport Towers. Fourteen thirty-four. He stays there when he's in town."

"Has anyone contacted him since we arrived?"

"No . . . No time."

"Does he live there alone?"

"No. He has six bodyguards at all times."

"What kind of weapons do they have?"

"Uzis. They all have Uzis."

"Where is Roger Wilcox?"

"Dead. Gravez had him killed three weeks ago."

"Why was Wilcox killed?"

"Gravez didn't need him anymore."

"Why not?"

"Two of the men here are microbiologists who now know how to produce the bacteria."

"The people with you tonight?"

"Yes."

"What were you doing here tonight?"

"Gravez wanted me to keep an eye on the doctors. They have to be watched all the time."

"Why?"

"They don't like what they're doing."

Dan grimaced. They'd done it just the same.

He asked, "Why did Wilcox do it, do you know?"

"Sure. He needed the money. He was a cokehead and he also owed money to some loan sharks. He was afraid they'd bust his head."

Al Disario tapped Dan on the shoulder. "Dan, none of these guys speaks English. Where's Gomez?" Gomez was the FBI interpreter.

Dan handed Al the bullhorn. "Here, use this. That'll get his attention."

Al took the bullhorn and asked, "How're you making out?"

Dan smiled through his faceguard. "Great, just great. The bacteria is all here, according to this one. Make sure that room is frozen solid and have the techs take some slides before anyone takes off their gear. Let's not get careless now."

Disario took the bullhorn, nodded and started calling for Gomez. Besides being an interpreter, the Latin was also a demolitions expert. Wiseman went back to his man.

"What's your name?"

"Corwin Farrow."

"Really?"

"Yes. That's my name."

"Well, well. Tell me, why did you kill Sondra Olsen?"

"Because Gravez told me to."

"And why did he do that?"

"Because she knew I'd given Mark Martin the bacteria to take on the plane."

"How'd you do that?"

"I gave her a package for him to take to Hawaii. It looked like a bottle of perfume underneath the wrapping. But it was encapsulated bacteria. I told her it was a present for a friend of mine."

"Did Martin know anything about the bacteria?"

"No."

Wiseman asked, "How could the bacteria get out of the bottle?"

"The cap was made from a special material that cracked as soon as the pressure inside the airplane was equal to four thousand feet. The wrapper was made from a sugar-paper loaded with bacteria that was kinda like food."

Dan felt like smashing the man in the mouth. "Why, Cory? Why did you involve yourself in this? How could you let thousands of people die like that?"

The man looked at him blankly. In the words of a true psychopath, he said, "I didn't think about it. I needed the money. People die every day."

For a moment, Dan just stared at the man, unable to speak, wanting so very badly to kill him where he sat. How do we create such people, he wondered. How? It was something he'd never been able to understand, nor would he ever understand. He fought the emotions that roiled within him, then stood up and walked over to where the other men were being interrogated by agent Gomez. The same story was being heard all around.

Dan tapped Disario on the shoulder. "Al, put someone in charge here and tell them to make sure the Newport cops keep the press away from here. Then pick twenty guys and we'll pay Gravez a little visit."

Disario lit up like a light bulb. "You know where he is?"

"Yup."

"Great!" Disario moved toward one of the entrances and Dan returned to the inner research room.

It was clouded in mist and getting very cold. Several people were taking samples of materials and placing them under a microscope. As Dan approached each one, they gave him the thumbs up signal.

The BT33 was dead.

Dan went outside and removed his helmet. Then he grabbed the walkie-talkie and tried to contact Los Angeles, but the range was too far. He headed to his car and grabbed the mobile phone, punching the buttons with fingers that were shaking again.

"Central, this is Omega. Let me talk to Alpha

One."

"Stand by."

In a moment, he heard the voice of the director. "Go ahead, Omega."

"Alpha. This is Omega. The genie is back in the bottle. I'm on my way to see the stranger."

There was silence for a moment and then the director came back on. He seemed to be sobbing. "Are you sure, Omega?"

Dan couldn't blame him for getting emotional. "Yes," he said. "I'm sure."

"I'll tell the boss. He'll be very, very pleased."

"Yeah. Omega will talk to you again after I've seen the stranger."

One of the Newport Beach cops approached Dan and stuck out his hand. "FBI? Captain Walters, Newport Beach Police. Could you fill me in on what's going down here?"

Dan shook the hand and said, "I'm sorry, Captain. There'll be no comment at this time. Not for some time actually. I'd like you to keep it that way. When the press show up, tell 'em zip. We still have people to round up."

The captain nodded. "Will do. This got anything to do with that Bolivian thing?"

Wiseman shook his head. "Nope. Just a little problem with some theft. Large-scale theft. Because the place was a medical research place, we weren't sure what we might run into, so we wore protective clothing just in case."

The captain looked over Dan's shoulder. "You

sure as hell brought enough people with you."

Dan grunted. "Yeah. Well, you never know what you're gonna run into some times."

The cop looked at Dan suspiciously and then slowly moved away. Dan called after him. "Captain!"

The man turned around and stared at Wiseman, who was chewing his lower lip as he considered the next step.

They had to get to the top of the building that housed Alfredo Gravez. They needed a diversion. They also needed to ensure that no more innocent people were hurt. They needed the help of the Newport Beach police to do that.

"Captain," Dan said, "I wasn't really straight with you. This does have something to do with the Bolivia thing. I need your help."

The captain's face broke into a smile. "If there's anything we can do . . ."

Dan filled him in and five minutes later, Disario and the rest of the smaller team gathered around, while the Newport beach cop took off to get things started.

Dan looked at the men and said, "Okay, we'll take four cars. I'll drive the first one. Gravez has at least six bodyguards and they're equipped with Uzis, so be careful."

He told them about the plan and then gave them some final words.

"Bring some cannisters, just in case and . . . whatever you do don't kill Gravez. We want that bastard alive. Oh, anyone got some hypos?"

One of the men called out. "I have two."
Dan grinned. "Okay. Let's hit it."
The men piled into the cars.

# Chapter Twenty-three

In Washington, an exhausted Robert Dalton sat at the same desk where he'd spent the night chastising himself for a decision he now believed had been wrong.

Fifteen thousand people had died in Los Angeles. They had died moments after the president had demanded that Gravez bow to the power of the United States. A power the president thought was strong enough to make even this madman give in.

But it hadn't.

Instead, it had goaded him into inflicting another disaster upon the American people.

It was clear to the president that the timing of the attack on the Forum had coincided with the speech he had made to the nation. Had he done as some had suggested; given the appearance that some arrangement, however distasteful, could be made, it might have prevented the attack. Of that he was convinced.

And how he bore the pain of knowing that he, Robert Dalton, should have heeded that advice. By not doing so, he had caused the deaths of fifteen thousand people.

It wasn't that he needed to make a deal with Gravez. All he had needed to do was make it appear that way. But he had acted imprudently, hastily, needlessly. Instead of preventing a disaster, he had practically guaranteed one. He knew that now.

All night, he had wallowed in agony. In a way, he looked forward to the final release that would soon be upon him.

Throughout the long, horrible night, friends had tried to make him understand that it was Gravez who had done the killing, not Robert Dalton. Tried to make him see that he had done the only thing he could do; that making deals with terrorists of whatever stripe, be they political or criminal, would only serve to inspire others. Their entreaties fell on deaf ears.

And then there were those who came by to inform him that meetings were being held all night by those less interested in the concerns of Robert Dalton. The word had spread rapidly throughout the Hill that the president was dying. Plans were being made to force him to resign. It would only be a matter of hours before the press would know of his illness and then everything would collapse.

Mickey Serson had told him of the efforts of the vice president to garner support for his desire to become president within hours so that he could stop the raid on Bolivia to protect American interests in that country.

And then, at 7:33, came the call from Edward

Spencer in Los Angeles.

The bacteria had been found and destroyed. The FBI were on their way to capture Alfredo Gravez.

It was wonderful news.

And yet, it also served to plunge the knife of guilt even deeper into the soul of Robert Dalton.

The bacteria had been destroyed! Only hours after the speech and the attack on the Forum.

It was even more obvious that had he not acted so precipitously, stalling instead for time, the FBI might well have destroyed the bacteria before anyone had suffered.

At that moment, Robert Dalton tried to will himself to die. And then, he felt ashamed. Deeply ashamed.

He lit a cigar and put in a call to the chairman of the joint chiefs. He wanted the general to come to the Oval Office.

Quickly.

Dan Wiseman and his team parked their vehicles a block away from the Newport Towers and regrouped. The men quietly assembled, put their protective helmets back on and checked their equipment.

Gravez occupied one of the four condos on the top floor of the luxury building, nesting comfortably at the edge of Newport Bay.

The entire west wall of the building, the one

facing the bay, was glass, a series of sliding glass windows. The east wall was also glass, with fixed windows that looked over the peninsula. The south and north walls were almost windowless.

Wiseman looked at his watch. In three minutes, they should hear the first sirens, then swarms of Newport Beach fireman would appear and start to evacuate the building.

They had to be ready by then.

Dan barked into his walkie-talkie. "Go!"

The team moved quickly into the building and up the stairwells to the fourteenth floor. They waited, catching their breath and carefully opened one of the doors leading to the hallway. They pin-pointed Gravez's unit and waited some more. In the distance, they could hear the wail of sirens.

Five fire trucks pulled up and stopped in front of the building, escorted by several Newport Beach police units. Dan could hear a man using a bullhorn telling the occupants to evacuate the building because of a gas leak.

Three of Dan's men left the stairway and started knocking on doors. Dan and four additional men stopped in front of the unit marked, "1434."

It was at that moment that Wiseman realized he'd forgotten one vital thing. One terrible oversight.

The protective clothing they wore still bore the legend 'FBI' stenciled on the front and the back. It was like they were wearing neon signs. In the frantic efforts to kill the bacteria, they had completely forgotten about it.

He stepped away from the door.

The evacuation of the floors below them was already underway. The people in the units adjoining Gravez were being hustled down the stairwell. There was no time to change the plan.

Dan, in a loud whisper, said, "I screwed up. I forgot about the FBI logo on the suits. We'll have to shoot our way in. Damn! Turn off your helmet lights."

The men all reached up and switched off the lights on their helmets. At that moment, the door to Gravez's suite opened a crack and quickly slammed shut.

No time.

Dan yelled for the back-up team as he pointed his own Uzi at the door and pulled the trigger.

The door sprang open and three bottles of tear gas were thrown through the door. The men stayed away from the doorway as the bottles exploded and started to spread the gas. Other FBI agents burst through the doors of the unit beside Gravez's, in a move designed to prevent him from getting to the next balcony.

Then, staying close to the ground, Wiseman, Disario and two others crawled into the Gravez unit.

The place was pitch dark. They could hear the sounds of heavy coughing in the next room and two voices arguing in Spanish.

Then the room was filled with the sound of automatic weapons fire. It was a fire-fight inside a darkened room. Hundreds of bullets were flying through the air every second. It was over in less than five seconds but it seemed like an eternity.

Then silence, except for the sound of coughing and a man moaning.

Wiseman crawled back toward the doorway and reached upward along the wall until his gloved hand located a light switch. He shoved another clip in the Uzi and flicked the switch on.

Two men were immediately visible through the clouds of gas, their weapons at the ready. Before they could fire, they were literally blown apart by Al Disario.

Slowly, the men moved toward the balcony.

He was standing there, his hands raised in the air, a smirk on his face.

In perfect English, Alfredo Gravez said, "I want to see my lawyer."

Wiseman leveled the Uzi at the old man and said nothing.

At last, he was face to face with the man who had caused so much terror, had killed so many innocent people.

The numbness that had plagued the FBI man all night was replaced by an anger unlike any he'd ever felt in his life. The rage within him begged to be fed, fired every nerve in his body with an electric charge, consumed his soul with a blood-lust that almost screamed for satisfaction.

He let the emotions run rampant for a few moments. Let his heartbeat quicken and his breath come in short spurts. He felt the hate leeching from every pore like water through a fine wire mesh.

And then he lowered the Uzi and handcuffed Gravez to the balcony.

Quickly, he took stock. They had one man badly wounded and another with a superficial injury. Three of the bodyguards were dead and two more were wounded. The sixth was standing in the corner of the kitchen with his hands in the air.

Disario was on the walkie-talkie and within minutes the room was filled with FBI men, paramedics, and firemen.

Dan watched dispassionately as the firemen put out a small fire that had been started by the tear gas bottles, and the paramedics worked on the wounded. After a few moments, they took away the dead and wounded and set up large fans to blow away the tear gas. Once the suite was habitable, Wiseman removed his protective suit.

The team had gone over the place with a fine-tooth comb and aside from a large quantity of cash and about a half kilo of cocaine, there was nothing. The living room walls were riddled with bullet holes and most of the furniture was in splinters.

Dan finally ordered everyone except himself and Disario out of the suite and then the two returned to the balcony where a now shivering Alfredo

Gravez remained handcuffed to the balcony.

The cool on-shore breeze was biting. During the night, the temperature had dropped to 37 degrees and the coatless Gravez was shaking like a leaf. His teeth were beginning to chatter and the frustration on his face was evident. Here was a man who did not like to show the slightest indication of fear and he was concerned that the FBI men would mistake his involuntary quivering for just that.

"I want my lawyer," he said.

Wiseman turned to Disario. "Call Spencer. Tell him what's happened. Tell him we're about to interrogate Alfredo Gravez."

Disario checked the telephone. Miraculously, it still worked.

Wiseman pulled a hypodermic needle kit from his pocket, removed the protective cover and held it up to the light. Gravez's eyes seemed to widen.

"You can't do that!" he said. "I told you, I want to see my lawyer. I have my rights!"

Wiseman looked at him without speaking. They were all the same, he thought. People capable of the most unspeakable crimes suddenly confronted with their captors, and the first thing they screamed for was their rights. It was almost automatic.

Wiseman grabbed an arm and rolled up the sleeve. Without a word, he rammed the needle into the upper arm and pressed the plunger.

"You can't do this!"

Wiseman spoke to him for the first time.

"I just did," he said.

Robert Dalton sat and faced a deeply disturbed Gen. James T. Briscoe, chairman of the joint chiefs.

The general's face was red with rage.

"Mr. President," he said, "I don't know where you got that information, but I can assure you it's completely false. I'm a soldier, as are we all. I do not engage in partisan politics and I'd very much like to interface with the person who told you this.

"The joint chiefs serve at the pleasure of the president of the United States and until I am officially notified to the contrary, you are that man. I've talked to the others and I can assure you that no one has discussed with any of us, in the remotest sense, the possibility of us not carrying out your orders.

"The task force is completing final preparations as we speak. By sixteen hundred hours it will be in position. F-one eleven's will be in the air at twelve hundred hours and will be refueled on their way there and back. This attack will be the largest ever made since the Korean War. In terms of firepower, it'll be the largest non-nuclear attack ever made, period. We await your final orders."

Dalton leaned back in the chair and rubbed his forehead. "Thank you, General. I was sure that was the case, but I had to ask you directly, in view of the circumstances."

The redness left the general's face. "I understand, Mr. President. May I speak freely?"

"Please do."

"Is it true, sir? Do you have a tumor?"

Dalton nodded slowly. "I have more than one, General. The doctors say that there is a very remote chance, but I know better.

"The problem I have is this: Do you have any concerns that the attack I have ordered is irrational? It's possible, you know, that some of what is being said about me is true. Maybe I am nuts. I've heard it said that truly insane people don't understand when they are behaving badly. Is this a concern to you, Jim?"

The general blinked twice and said, "Not in the least. I think your actions are long overdue. I also think that you're taking this action now because you believe in it, but . . ."

The general's voice trailed off.

"But?"

"Well, sir. You think you're dying. Maybe you are. I certainly hope not. But if you are, if you think you are, it means that you've set yourself up to take the blame for whatever happens.

"There'll be a lot of shit flying around about this. But that doesn't mean you aren't doing the right thing. We've sat back and had our asses handed to us too many times. This crap has got to stop! It's bad enough that the Palestinians and the commies and every other screwed-up organization is taking pot-shots at us . . . kidnapping our people all over the world, but this; some Goddamn asshole drug dealer's killing innocent people . . .

"Goddammit! We've got to take a stand! We've got to deal out some punishment!

"You made that clear. You've given the Bolivians ample warning. You've told them to get the hell away from the field. That's a lot more than I would have done.

"Someday, we simply have to let the world know that we've had enough. Today is as good a day as any."

Mickey Serson knocked once and entered the room. Dalton looked up. Serson was smiling.

"They've got Gravez! Alive. They're interrogating him right now. They're using the drug and he's talking his head off. He's giving us the names and addresses of every drug dealer in his outfit.

"All of the bacteria was at the one location. It's over, Bob! It's over!

Robert Dalton sighed and said, "Part of it is over, Mickey. Fortunately. Tell Tim I want to make an address within an hour. National."

"Right."

"And tell Spencer that I want him back here immediately. I want to pin a medal on his chest before I'm kicked out of this office."

"Will do."

"Oh, Mickey, I want presidential pardons prepared for all of the people involved. I don't want some short-ass going after them now. Spencer gets one and every man who performed illegal acts during the investigation. If I've got the power, I may as damn well use it. They can only crucify me once."

"I'll take care of it."

Mickey left the room to do just that. General Briscoe looked at the president rather quizzically and asked, "That drug Mickey mentioned. What drug is that?"

The president rubbed his tired eyes and said, "Something that Huntsville came up with. Works like a truth serum."

"How many people have they used it on?"

"I don't know. Why do you ask?"

"Did General Smith tell you about the side effects?"

Dalton looked at the general with puzzlement. "He mentioned something about some unpleasant side effects, yes, but he didn't spell them out. Why? Why are you getting at?"

"Just this," the general said. "That drug was tested and abandoned. Three weeks after first use, the subject goes blind. Two weeks after that, he goes deaf and then about two weeks later, he dies. That drug is a killer."

President Dalton just stared at the general.

Briscoe said, "While you're making out those presidential pardons, you'd better make one out for General Smith."

After a few more minutes, the general left and

Robert Dalton was alone with Mickey Serson once again. In less than half an hour, he would speak to the nation again, only this time, he would use no script. He would speak from the heart.

For the last time.

Strangely, he felt relieved, as though someone had opened the door to a darkened room and allowed the light to enter. His voice was strong and filled with glee. "We gave it a hell of a run, didn't we, Mickey? A couple of guys from the sticks. Jesus Christ! So much for pollsters! Ha! They had us counted out every time and we beat them. Just like old Harry Truman.

"They always think that the people are stupid, sitting in front of the tube all damn day, their minds turning into mush. But they're wrong. They don't know shit about the people. They've got minds of their own and every once in a while they use 'em. Thank God for that."

Serson nodded.

Robert Dalton stood up. "Mickey, you've been a true friend all these years. I hope you'll stay on and help Aubrey. Christ! The man will need someone like you. I wish I was going to be around to see what Cecil Aubrey is made of. Christ! The first thing he's gonna do is crap right here in the Oval Office. That'll be his first official act as president. Crapping his pants."

Now both men had tears in their eyes. An exhausted Mickey Serson pulled himself upright and threw his arms around the president of the United States, who stroked his head as a mother might stroke her child.

"Mickey," he said, "pull yourself together. We've got things to do. I want you to get Aubrey in here. Will you do that for me?"

Serson released his grip and wiped his eyes. "Yes. I'm sorry."

"It's okay, my friend. Later, when this is over, we'll both sit down and get really stupid. Just you and me."

Serson tried to smile but couldn't.

Dan Wiseman sat on the chair and stared at Alfredo Gravez, who was still speaking into a tape recorder, giving them whatever information was stored in his head.

Gravez had told them much.

How he had planned it all from the first time he'd heard about Roger Wilcox.

That's where it had all started.

Roger Wilcox had bragged to someone that he knew how to make a germ that could kill millions. The word had filtered through to Gravez and he had seized upon the idea of blackmailing the United States of America.

One stupid drug addict had shot his mouth about things he was supposed to keep secret and it had resulted in thousands of deaths.

A single man, obsessed with the idea of freeing his son from captivity, equipped with enormous amounts of money and a total lack of conscience, had held an entire nation captive for days.

One man.

There were those in Washington who worried about nuclear devices getting into the wrong hands.

Now they had something else to worry about.

As for Gravez, he showed no remorse. Only surprise.

Never for a moment had he considered that the president would not eventually yield. Over the years, hundreds of men had given in to the demands of Alfredo Gravez. Even those in the Bolivian government. He'd given them a choice. They could be rich or they could die. Very few of them had chosen death.

Gravez had told them that he never considered that President Dalton would allow his country to be put at such risk. He was positive that a steady increase in pressure, a rise in the body count, would achieve his goal.

Wiseman was rubbing his hand along a tired forehead. It had been a long night.

And now he was faced with more unpleasantness. Someone would have to identify the body of Bernice Wiseman. He wouldn't force the kids to do that. He'd have to do it himself. He'd have to arrange for the funeral and make sure everything was properly attended to.

He'd spend some time with the kids and help them get over the loss of their mother. Later, they could decide whether they wanted to stay in California, perhaps with their aunt, or if they'd rather come and be with their father. Danny, he guessed, would probably want to stay. Dawn, on the other hand . . .

Maybe it was the tiredness. Maybe it was the release of all of the tension. But for some reason, at that moment, Dan Wiseman, for the first time, realized that his marriage was truly over.

He felt very alone.

# Chapter Twenty-four

The president's address to the nation was scheduled to begin in fifteen minutes. Already, the media had announced the capture of Alfredo Gravez and the destruction of the bacteria. Throughout the country, an almost audible sigh of relief could be heard.

Cecil Aubrey was alone in the Oval Office with Robert Dalton. Already, the vice president's demeanor had changed from that of a glad-handing politico to that of a man full in the knowledge he was soon to inherit incredible power.

Aubrey sat on the sofa, sipping coffee, one arm slung along the back of the sofa, totally relaxed, a look of satisfaction on his face.

He was a large man with an imposing presence. His round face was crinkled from the almost constant smile he wore whenever he was "on." A smile that usually turned into a frown when he was alone or at home with his bewildered wife, Florence.

Although she loved him, she'd always felt that her husband was a man of limited ability and the bewilderment came from knowing that some day, this man, her husband, could become president of the United States. It never ceased to amaze her. No matter how hard she tried, she simply could not envision herself as a "First Lady."

Aubrey's gray hair lay flat and lifeless on the top of his head and then clustered around his ears where it curled up and became tousled, an affectation that Aubrey believed made him appear more "human." The dull, gray eyes were slightly hooded by folds of flesh that were scheduled to be removed before the next campaign.

His large hands contained heavy calluses from the almost never-ending series of handshakes he made in an average day.

Cecil Aubrey was the quintessential politician who seemed to have a million friends. His major flaw was that nobody seemed to trust him. It wasn't that he had overtly broken agreements made, or done more than his share of back-stabbing. It was his look! The smile of a snake-oil salesman.

Just as Gerald Ford had been branded as a man who couldn't chew gum and walk at the same time, a charge that bore no basis in fact, Cecil Aubrey was considered a man who bore careful watching. Somewhere, somehow, he had developed an unearned reputation that he fought valiantly to overcome. It was a tag that he resented bitterly but found impossible to fight with words. He'd been in public life long enough to know that any man who went around telling people he could be trusted was asking not to be.

And now, in the Oval Office, Robert Dalton was attempting to persuade the man to his bidding. When there was nothing whatsoever in it for Cecil Aubrey.

At that moment, in stark contrast to the cheerfulness of Cecil Aubrey, Robert Dalton looked exactly like what he, in fact, was. A man who was dying and knew it; a man who hadn't slept in over forty hours. A man close to dropping from sheer exhaustion caused by the mental anguish of the heavy loss of life, and then the buffered joy of knowing that the immediate danger had passed. He still deeply mourned the deaths of over fifteen thousand innocent people. And he still felt responsible.

"Cecil," the president said, his voice reflecting the inner tiredness, "I know what's been going on and I can't really fault you for that. It would have been nice, however, if you'd deigned to speak to me first. On the other hand, I guess turnabout is fair play. Like most vice presidents, you probably think you've been treated like a mushroom."

Aubrey said nothing.

The president said, "I want to make a deal."

"A deal?"

"Yes."

A look of curiosity covered the vice president's

face. "What kind of a deal?"

Dalton pulled a cigar from the box and went about the business of getting it ready. "You know as well as I that I can hang on to this job until the Bolivian raid is a *fait accompli* . . . and if I have to, I will. But for several reasons, I feel it would be better if I resigned at noon, and let you direct the raid."

Aubrey's jaw dropped. "What? Me! No way. That's your baby. I'll have nothing to do with that can of worms."

Dalton continued to fuss with the cigar. "Hear me out, Cecil."

The president removed his glasses and turned to face Cecil Aubrey. "There are many reasons this raid must take place. I don't have the time to relate all of them to you, but the most obvious ones are important enough that they could be totally negated by the fact of my illness."

Aubrey asked, "Meaning?"

"Just this," the president answered. "You aren't in favor of this action for reasons that are partly selfish and partly sincere. I'm well aware of your ties to the banks. You and McGinnis. No big deal."

"So?"

"Just this. You are about to become the president of the United States. Like every man before you, you can't possibly be aware of the real weight dropped on your shoulders until it actually hits you.

I wasn't. Nobody is.

"If you take the position, after I'm gone, that the raid was a mistake, and simply dismiss it as an action taken by a president whose judgement was skewed by a brain being eaten away by ravenous cancer cells, the coca fields will still be laid waste, but the political impact will be lessened considerably. Much of the good that can come from this will be thrown away.

"You will have succeeded in making me look like a fool, but you will have negated the impact on the very people I'm trying to impress."

Aubrey snorted. "Just who *are* you trying to impress?"

Dalton put the cigar to his mouth and lit it. After a moment he said, "The people who produce the stuff and the people who use it. In the first instance, we let the producers know that they'll never be safe. That we're really and truly going to attack them wherever they may be. That this country is committed to wiping out the suppliers of illegal drugs, be it cocaine, heroin, grass or whatever.

"In the second instance, I'm trying to impress the people of this country. By demonstrating that we're sincere in our efforts to stop drug addiction."

He waved the cigar through the air and said, "Sure, I know that there are those who scoff at such naivete . . . the ones who say that trying to stop people from taking drugs is like prohibition. It won't work. Compulsives are compulsives."

Then he leaned forward, his elbows on the desk. "But I don't accept that. Just because it's difficult is no reason to quit. And the experience we've just been through ought to drive the point home that we must fight it with everything we've got."

He picked up a piece of paper from the desk, glanced at it and let it drop from his fingers. "According to the FBI, Alfredo Gravez has been in the cocaine business for over forty years. Three years ago, he started using the stuff for the first time, when his son was arrested and imprisoned. That's a cardinal sin to these people. Most of them never use the stuff, seeing first hand how it wrecks the minds of their customers.

"But, he did it. He started using his own stuff. And look what happened! We have over fifteen thousand people dead as a result of actions taken by Alfredo Gravez. I don't know if his cocaine addiction was responsible or not . . . maybe it had nothing to do with it, but the fact remains that a cocaine addict, with tremendous amounts of cash at his disposal, almost brought this country to its knees.

"Doesn't that impress you?"

Aubrey didn't answer. Instead he reached for the coffee and sipped it noisily.

Dalton continued. "I've listened to all of the arguments 'til I'm blue in the face. It's too costly! The people aren't supportive! All that other bullshit. The fact is that the stuff ruins lives and we must, if we have any sense of responsibility at all, do whatever we can to slow it down.

"If you support this raid, and if you, as president, fight like hell to get more funds for education, treatment and the rest, maybe, just maybe, we can start to reverse the flow. Maybe we can begin the process of teaching our people how to cope with life without reaching for some powdery penacea."

President Dalton sighed and leaned back in his chair. "I want this raid to take place very much. But I know damn well that it isn't right for me to be the one to do it. That's a cop-out. Everybody knows I'm a goner. Whatever I do now can be considered the mindless act of an idiot.

"But I'll do it, if I have to. Just to slow things down a little. Burning those fields will be a fitting epitaph and I'll be happy to accept that. But it still isn't right, Cecil. I'm a sick man and I don't have the right to make this kind of decision. I know that. It's wrong. Not the decision, but me making it. This decision should be made by a man who will stand there and take the flak when the screams of protest start.

"It should be made by the man who'll occupy this office for some time, not by some fart who's about to kick off. If you do it, it'll mean something."

Aubrey put the coffee down and leaned forward. "What in the world is the matter with you? I realize you're suffering from a brain tumor and I'm sorry about that. Truly. But my sympathy has nothing to do with my convictions. And they haven't changed. This action is wrong! It will just make our relationships throughout Latin American tougher. These people aren't going to stand for this! You'll bring the Russians pouring into South America. Can't you see that?"

Dalton sighed and shook his head. "You're a tough nut to crack, Cecil."

Aubrey bristled. "I'm not without my own opinions on foreign affairs."

Dalton held up his hand. "I'm aware of that." Then he said, "Look, try and see it this way. The raid is going to take place. The damage, whatever it is, will be there for you to deal with. Don't you understand that by dealing from strength, your control is much greater? By being the man who ordered the strike, you're the man they have to deal with. By being a man who stepped in after the strike, an apologist, you look weaker in their eyes.

"These people don't think like we do. They're used to having things done differently. They change governments by having coups, not elections. It's a completely different culture. They understand power, and the people who use it. Actually, if you're the one who orders the strike, you'll be a big man in their eyes. In your first official act as president, you'll seem to be a man who acts decisively, firmly. You'll scare the crap out of the Russians. That's the kind of guy they really understand. Frankly, I think it'll be a big plus all the way around."

Aubrey shook his head. "I think you're so very wrong. This raid of yours will simply antagonize not only the people of Latin America, but most of the free world as well. We'll be looked upon as a bunch of crazed animals seeking revenge for Gravez's killings in Los Angeles and that airplane crash.

"And another thing . . . you talk about a war against drugs . . . education, treatment and the like. Where the hell is the money for that going to come from? Congress would never approve expenditures of that kind. Their attitude is no big secret. If some idiot wants to kill himself with drugs, that's his or her problem. And even if Congress was of a mind to be cooperative, there's no money. We're still running a terrible deficit and the last tax increase went over like a concrete cloud.

"I don't think you've thought this out, Robert. I think your judgement is being bedeviled by your personal emotions. I think you should step aside now, get the treatment you need, and let me take over. You *are* acting like a fool, if you want to know the truth."

Dalton looked crushed. "Is there no way I can

convince you?"

Aubrey shook his head. "Not that I can see. As I told you, I think it's wrong."

Dalton sighed and said, "Then, there's no other choice for me but to stay here in this office and order the raid myself. You'll be faced with the task of telling the world what a fool I was, and watching the dwindling respect for this country grow even smaller. Not an auspicious start for your presidency, Cecil."

"You won't resign now?"

"No way. You can try and use the Twenty-fourth Amendment if you like, but there's not time enough for that. That raid is going to take place come hell or high water."

Cecil Aubrey looked uncomfortable now. He sat there and thought things over. Then he asked, "If I were to agree to this . . . agree to allow the raid to go forward, would you resign today?"

"Absolutely," Dalton answered.

The room was silent for a moment and then Robert Dalton grinned. "If you agree to do it, I'm not worried about you changing your mind once you're the president."

Aubrey looked up in surprise. "You're not?"

Dalton shook his head. "Not a bit. I've never really liked you, Cecil. You know that. But, unlike others in Washington, I do think you're a man of honor. I trust you, Cecil. I really do.

"I've never told you this, but I wanted you as my vice president. You weren't forced upon me as the popular story would have everyone believe. I see qualities in you that seem to escape the attention of some others. I think you'll make a fine president.

"Besides, there's another reason you must support the raid."

Aubrey looked at the president and asked, "What's that?"

Dalton smiled and put the rimless glasses back on. "I'm a dying man, and this is my last wish. You can't refuse a dying man his last wish, can you?"

Aubrey started to say something and stopped. He sat there for a moment and considered the situation. Then he said, "Let me think about this for a while. I'll get back to you."

Dalton shook his head. "No time, Cecil. You better get used to that. Things have a way of moving fast in this job. Sometimes you don't have the luxury of taking time to consider all of the issues. Sometimes you have to act instinctively. That leads to mistakes being made, but that's the way it is. That's what presidents are made of . . . Mr. President."

At nine in the morning, Washington time, Robert Dalton stepped in front of the podium in the White

House press room and faced a group of journalists who were almost beside themselves in anticipation.

To say that the last forty-eight hours had been heavy with news would be a gross understatement. most of the reporters were as red-eyed as the president, having been up all night followed a story that seemed without end.

Shock had been stacked upon shock, until it seemed like there could be nothing else.

The president smiled weakly and gripped the podium with both hands.

"Ladies and gentlemen, my fellow Americans. I have a short statement I'd like to make and then I'm going to get some rest. I'm sure most of you are as tired as I am. It's been a long night."

Nobody was about to argue with that statement.

"I'm pleased to report some news that all of you are familiar with by now, but I'd still like to make it official. The FBI, under the direction of Edward Spencer, and with the cooperation of local law enforcement agencies throughout the country as well as the Armed Services of the United States, has successfully captured Alfredo Gravez and destroyed the bacteria that threatened the lives of all of us."

Even though most of those in the room were well aware of the details, a lusty cheer went up. President Dalton waited for things to quiet down and then continued.

"The pleasure I feel in making that announcement is tempered by the almost overwhelming sense of sadness I feel at the loss of so many Americans at the hands of this criminal terrorist.

"Over fifteen thousand people have died because of the actions of a man who shall forever stand as an example of the worst that humanity can produce.

"If there is a purpose to this holocaust, I sense it must be in the fact that it alerts us to several dangers that we, as Americans, face.

"We live in a country of incredible opportunity and freedom. All of us have a tendency to take these wonderful things for granted. The vast majority of the five billion people in this world live under conditions that Americans would find unacceptable. And yet, it we are not careful, the future will see us living much less well than we do now.

"We must guard against complacency in many areas of our daily lives. There are those who would see us destroyed. Enemies of the United States who view democracy as a threat to their existence.

"And there are those among us, loyal Americans all, who accept the failings of the human spirit as simply the way it is. Who feel that nothing can be done and we should spend our money and effort on more important things.

"There is nothing more important than the quality of life in all its aspects. And in this country, we have a very large problem. A problem that requires the attention of all of us.

"I speak of the problem we have with drugs. Illegal drugs and legal drugs, such as alcohol and nicotine.

"We have just seen fifteen thousand Americans murdered by a man consumed by the very drugs he distributed to others throughout the world. We find that abhorrent and so we should. It's shocking and revolting and my heart is sick with the grief I feel for the families of those unfortunate people.

"And yet, in the next fifteen months, we will see another fifteen thousand Americans murdered, either by drug overdoses or drunken drivers. Because it happens gradually, a daily occurrence, we are less shocked. We accept it as just another part of our society. But the deaths are no less real than the deaths of the people who died at the hands of Alfredo Gravez.

"Where is the outrage?

"How long will we allow this to continue?

"Do we really care?"

Dalton stopped speaking and stared angrily at the television camera.

"Somehow, we must stop accepting this as normal human behavior. Somehow, we must find a way to stop our own self-destructiveness. We are blessed with the ability to think and yet so many of us reach for substances that will destroy that ability.

"We have a choice. We can ignore the reality of

drug abuse, or we can work to put an end to it. It is my view that the future of this country will be determined in large part by the choice we make."

He stopped again and allowed a small smile to reach his lips.

"I really didn't come here to pontificate and that seems to be what I'm doing. I guess that's what happens when a president chooses to speak without benefit of speechwriter."

There was some nervous titters of laughter.

"In any case, martial law is hereby rescinded."

At that remark, another cheer went up. President Dalton nodded and then said, "On some other matters of lesser importance, I have the duty to inform you that I have contracted an illness that will require extensive and prolonged treatment. I realize that the rumors have been flying and I'd like to set the record straight.

"I found out about this a few days ago. I have three small tumors in the brain, one of which is inoperable. My doctors informed me that the prescribed treatment has been successful in other cases and I intend to enter the hospital to begin that treatment this afternoon. Tim Belcher is preparing a press kit that will give you complete details on the illness and the therapy.

"At noon today, I will resign as president of the United States. Vice Preisdent Cecil Aubrey will take the oath of office at five minutes past noon."

That came as a surprise to everyone.

"Many of you may wonder why I didn't resign immediately. Perhaps I should have, but I guess I reacted like many others who have experienced something like this. I denied the reality of it.

"But, it is real. Inescapable.

"However, that was then and this is now. Now I have accepted the reality of my illness. I understand what I have and I understand what has to be done. I intend to get to it. It is my earnest hope that all Americans will take a hard look at the other realities I have just mentioned.

"As you know, preparations are being finalized for an attack on the Bolivian coca fields controlled and operated by the Gravez family. Vice President Aubrey has been briefed on those plans and will, as president of the United States, make the final decision on that action. Whatever action he takes will be his own.

"I have one other announcement to make and I do this with some sadness.

"The crash of Pacific Rim Airlines Flight Two-three-four was seen immediately for what it was. A terrorist attack of such viciousness that I was certain other attacks would soon follow. When Alfredo Gravez made his demands, I was faced with the prospect of the deaths of millions of Americans, so I ordered the FBI to use whatever means necessary to put an end to this terrible threat. Including the denial of Constitutional rights to individuals suspected of being involved.

"That order was illegal and FBI Director Edward Spencer brought that fact to my immediate attention.

"Nevertheless, at my insistence and urging, some Constitutional rights were ignored during the investigation. That was wrong. Very wrong. I see that now. Clearly.

"I accept full responsibility for the instructions that were given by me. And, as president, I have issued presidential pardons to Edward Spencer and those members of the FBI who engaged in these illegal acts. In fact, as my last act, I intended to bestow upon Edward Spencer the highest civilian honor this country can bestow on any citizen.

"He has refused to accept it. In fact, he has tendered his resignation, taking upon himself the punishment for actions to which he was opposed. As for myself, I will make myself available, if possible, to answer for my own actions.

"To Edward Spencer and the others, I offer my apology. To my fellow Americans, I offer my apology.

"There was no excuse for my lack of good judgment.

He paused again and then, with a voice that seemed to be faltering, said, "To my fellow Americans I say this: you have honored me as few men have ever been honored . . . by allowing me to serve as your president. I thank you for that. To all of those who helped me along the way . . . I give my thanks. To all of the people over the years who served in so many ways so that we Americans could enjoy the opportunities that stand before us, I offer you my tribute.

"I love this country. I love the people in it. I've loved almost every second I've served as your president. In truth, I wish I could stay on forever.

"But I can't.

"My fellow Americans, from the bottom of my heart, I wish you the best of everything.

"Goodbye and God bless you all."

With a little wave, he turned and went back into the hallway, and not a single reporter called after him to ask a question.

That was not the case in Los Angeles as reporters swarmed around the Federal Building looking for a chance to talk to some of the major figures in this incredible story.

Shirlee Simms was one of them. Somehow, she and Billy Secord had managed to place themselves inside the parking garage and as Dan Wiseman left the offices, heading for his car and some sleep, she pounced.

Dan's tired eyes were blinded by the brightness of

the light atop the minicam and Shirlee Simms thrust a microphone in his face.

"Mr. Wiseman!"

He could hardly recognize her in the light.

"Mr. Wiseman, President Dalton has said that you used illegal methods to capture Alfredo Gravez. Do you have a comment on that?"

Dan blinked, and said, "No. I have no comment."

She persisted. "Isn't it true that you are one of the men who are to receive a presidential pardon?"

"No comment."

"Edward Spencer has resigned over this. Don't you think you should resign as well?"

Maybe it was the tiredness. Maybe it was the anger. Maybe it was the insolence of the woman. Whatever the reason, Dan Wiseman could hold his tongue no longer. He glared at her, his temper barely under control and said, "Yes. I think I should resign. I think we should all resign. I think there should be total anarchy in this country for about a month. Maybe then, you people would appreciate us, instead of spending most of your time making us look like idiots.

"In the Gravez case, we were facing a madman who had the power to kill millions of Americans. We broke a few rules to get our hands on him and stop a disaster from ever happening. If we'd moved a little earlier, we might have stopped him earlier. I don't really know.

"But you're right. I broke the rules, so I should resign. I probably will. And I want to thank you for making the suggestion. Now, if you don't mind, I'd like to see my kids, bury an old friend and get a little sleep. Would that be okay with you, or would you rather have me shot where I stand?"

Even while he was getting into his car, the camera light was still burning brightly and the questions were still being hurled at him.

She'd go far, Dan thought, as he sped out of the garage.

# Chapter Twenty-five

At five minutes after twelve o'clock, Cecil Aubrey took the oath of office in the White House press room, in front of a national television audience. The normally effusive Aubrey seemed subdued and nervous.

After the swearing-in ceremony, he stepped to the podium used just hours ago by Robert Dalton and pulled some papers from his jacket pocket.

"My fellow Americans," he began, "I know you will join with me in offering prayers for the speedy recovery of President Dalton. America has been served well by Robert Dalton and I hope that I will serve this country half as well.

"Within the hour, I will meet with leaders of Congress to discuss several matters of extreme importance, not the least of which is the pending attack on the Bolivian coca leaf farms."

Even as he was speaking, ancient B-52s, loaded with leaflets, and B-1 bombers and F-111s, both crammed with napalm, were taking to the air from bases all over the United States. Off the shore of Peru, a U.S. Naval task force, equipped with three aircraft carriers and a variety of support vessels, was making final preparations for the part they would play in the attack.

President Aubrey continued his brief remarks.

"Whether or not the United States presses forward with this action will depend in great part on the support of the Congress. I believe that support is vital in that I have just this moment taken office as your president.

"I want you to know that I will do my very best to serve you well."

He shuffled his papers and leaned forward.

"I would like to offer my deepest sympathies to the families of those who suffered at the hands of Alfredo Gravez. And I would also like to extend to Edward Spencer and the many law enforcement officers under his direction, my heartfelt congratulations on a job very well done.

"While it is true that many lives were lost in this unprecedented terrorist attack on the United States, many more lives were saved because of the swiftness and diligence of the Bureau. We are all in their debt. I sincerely hope that Director Spencer will reconsider his decision to resign. We need him.

"That is all I have at this time. I will report to you as soon as I have met with the leaders of Congress and the Cabinet and a decision has been made. Thank you."

At one o'clock, Robert Dalton, alone except for Mickey Serson and six Secret Service personnel, was admitted to Walter Reed Hospital. He had left the White House without being seen by anyone.

At four o'clock, President Aubrey reappeared in the press room and made a short statement.

"After consultation with leaders from the Senate and the House, and with others in the administration, I have decided that the attack on the coca plant farms in Bolivia shall proceed as planned, with one major change. The farms in Peru will be additional targets."

The press room practically exploded with noise. A visibly angry President Aubrey glared at the reporters rushing to telephones or hurling questions at him.

Quickly, quiet was restored and Aubrey continued.

"I have sent the following message to the governments of Bolivia and Peru:

" 'The United States of America will, in two hours, begin destrying coca leaf plants being grown in your country. This action is being taken for the following reasons. One, the continued and increasing use of cocaine throughout the world poses an extreme danger to both the health and economic strength of most of the nations of the world.

" 'Since most of the world's cocaine is derived

from leaves grown in Peru and Bolivia, it is clear that the destruction of these leaves will be an effective step in the reduction of the production of cocaine throughout the world.

" 'Two. For many years, the United States has sought cooperation from Peru and Bolivia in cutting the production of coca leaves in those two countries. Cooperation has been limited despite the extensive amounts of money that have been advanced to both countries for that purpose.

" 'This cannot be allowed to continue.

" 'While we stand firm in our resolve to put an end to this threat to the health and welfare of all of the citizens of the world, the United States reaffirms its commitment to assist our neighbors in South America toward the reestablishment of economic reforms, and pledges its support to the people of both countries.

" 'The actions being taken today do not reflect a decrease in our concern and affection for the people of Peru and Bolivia, but rather our dedication to stamping out the sickness that is drug addiction.' "

President Aubrey never smiled once. In fact, he hadn't cracked a smile since he'd become president of the United States. He left the room, again, without answering any questions.

Two hours later, waves of F-111 bombers, augmented by two hundred naval aircraft, attacked the coca fields of Bolivia and Peru. The initial attack lasted four hours.

The next morning, the planes returned and attacked for another four hours.

Hundreds upon hundreds of square miles of Bolivian and Peruvian coca leaf farms were ablaze. The thick, black clouds of smoke from the burning fields were strong enough to blot out the sun in many parts of South America and could be clearly seen in satellite weather photos.

In the afternoon, the planes returned for a third time, only this time they carried chemicals designed to make the land infertile.

Throughout the series of raids, B-52s criss-crossed Peru and Bolivia dumping millions of hastily-prepared leaflets warning the people on the ground of the dangers of getting near the fields. Those who could read were urged in the leaflet to warn those who could not read.

During the series of attacks, President Cecil Aubrey went on national television twice more, to report on the progress of the raids and to explain in more detail the reasons for them taking place. He referred to the attacks as the beginning of a new war being fought against illegal drugs.

The United Nations Security Council was called into emergency session by the Soviet Union, who promptly demanded that the United States be condemned for its actions.

Cecil Aubrey addressed the United Nations personally and stated his position. The war against illegal drugs had just begun, he said. The world should be on notice that attacks against drug peddlers would be pressed no matter where they lived, be it inside or outside the United States.

At the same moment Cecil Aubrey was speaking to the United Nations, Dan Wiseman went to a high school gymnasium in Watts and formally identified Bernice Wiseman as his former wife. The children waited in the car outside at his request.

The cold weather that had gripped Los Angeles for the past two days had given way to a new front that brought heavy rain with its warmth.

Dan Wiseman sat at Bernice's gravesite, Danny on his right and Dawn on his left, and listened as the words being said were almost drowned out by the sound of the heavy droplets hitting the canvas canopy above his head.

The cemetery was a busy place. Thirty funerals were being held at this very moment and the grounds were covered with people wandering around in the wet, trying to move cars that were blocked by other cars. It gave the place an almost comic atmosphere, shattering the solemnity of the proceedings.

It had been two days since Dan's team had captured Alfredo Gravez, who now awaited trial in a federal prison. A trial that would never take place.

The drug they had administered would kill him first.

During those two days, Dan had spent his time exclusively with the kids, except for two periods where he slept for long hours. He felt like he'd never catch up on the sleep, but he certainly had covered a lot of ground with the kids.

Kids.

They weren't kids anymore.

Danny was now a grown man, and had been for some time, although Dan hadn't seemed to take notice until now. He looked like his father, dressed as he was in a black suit and tie. Dawn, almost; no, not almost . . . truly a woman, a beautiful young woman, bravely fighting back the tears as she said her final goodbyes to her mother.

Now, as they stood at the graveside, listening to the minister talk about Bernice, Dan's mind drifted away and he thought about other things.

Bernice's will had been found and the executor, the same lawyer who had handled her divorce, had requested a meeting with Danny and Dawn after the funeral. Dan was invited to attend, although the lawyer made a point of mentioning that Dan was not mentioned in the will.

Dan had briefly discussed the future with the children. They were confused and unsure. They'd both shared the big house in Palos Verdes with their mother and now she was gone. They assumed Dan would soon return to Washington and as much as they wanted to be with him, they hated the idea of leaving California.

He'd suggested they put it on hold for a while, because Dan wasn't sure that he would be returning to Washington at all.

The news had leaked about the drugs the FBI had used on Gravez and the others. Somehow, the knowledge that the drugs had fatal side effects had been made public as well. While there was little sympathy for Alfredo Gravez, there was a great amount of disgust being expressed by the media at this horrifying news.

That numbing feeling of shock had returned to haunt Dan Wiseman. He'd been responsible for administering a drug that would blind, deafen and eventually kill. While he hadn't known of the side effects at the time, he had known that what he was doing was illegal. His feelings of guilt were strong.

During a long career with the bureau, Dan Wiseman had bent the rules from time to time, like every other cop. But they'd been minor things, easy to rationalize and quickly forgotten. This was something else again. Especially, since the finding of Baldwin Medsearch and the destruction of the bacteria had been realized as a result of plain, old-fashioned police work.

Former President Dalton had given presidential pardons to a number of people, but Gen. Waldo

Smith had not been one of them. The general was facing a possible court martial and the entire subject of biological weapons was scheduled for a full-scale Congressional hearing.

Even though Dan Wiseman was in possession of his own presidential pardon, he was of the opinion that his usefulness as an FBI assistant director was at an end.

While that might have bothered him deeply as recently as a few weeks ago, on this day it didn't really seem to matter. He was forty-two years old, the kids were almost all grown up and once they went on with their lives, he'd be completely alone. The fires within that had driven him to devote his energies to his work had banked, and he thought a leave of absence might be called for.

The emotional batteries needed some recharging.

He would leave it to the kids as to what they wanted to do with the house. They could sell it, or live in it. They could afford a housekeeper, but that seemed a bit silly. Two teen-agers living in a house, alone, except for a housekeeper seemed a bit much even for California. Perhaps, if he decided to stay in California, they'd allow him to rent a room. Then, a housekeeper would make sense.

That thought brought a smile to his lips.

As for his own plans; aside from taking a long vacation, he didn't have any.

The funeral service was almost over.

The casket containing the body of Bernice was lowered into the ground and the final words were said.

Dan stood by the hole in the ground, said a few words and turned away. The children followed.

They were surrounded by old friends who hadn't seen Dan since the divorce. They were all very gracious, inviting him and the children for dinner, or conversation until they finally sought refuge from the rain and drifted away.

One man continued to stand by the graveside, alone, staring at the casket with hard eyes. Dan didn't know the man and the kids didn't either. He might have been a friend of Bernice's, or a lover. It didn't matter.

They started to walk toward the car and it was then that Dan noticed the woman, holding an umbrella in her hands but looking wet just the same, standing by one of the large oaks that dotted the cemetery.

Helen Porter smiled softly as they approached and said, "Hello. I just wanted to say goodbye to you before you left for Washington. They told me you'd be here. I'm so sorry."

Dan introduced Helen to the children.

"I was nice of you to come, Helen. Very nice."

She seemed embarrassed. "Well, you were very kind to me and I just wanted to say goodbye."

Dan turned to the kids and said, "Will you wait

for me in the car? I'll only be a moment."

They nodded and moved off. Dan turned to Helen and said, "I remember a promise I made to you. I said that when things got back to normal, I'd like to talk to you again. I'd like to keep that promise. How about dinner tomorrow night? Are you free?"

"Yes," she lied. She was supposed to work but she'd arrange for someone to cover for her. "About seven?"

"Seven it is," Dan said.

Dan continued on to the car and had almost reached it when the man with the hard eyes stepped in front of him. The trenchcoat he wore was soaked through and the rain had plastered his hair to his skull.

He opened up a leather wallet that contained his credentials. "Mr. Wiseman? Fred Barnett, Treasury."

Dan nodded. "What can I do for you, Mr. Barnett?"

The man grinned. "Not a thing, sir. I was asked by the Secretary to speak to you personally as soon as possible. I've been told the Secretary wants to thank you himself as soon as he can, but he thought you should know right away."

Dan smiled himself. "The numbers were good?"

"They sure as hell were. We just got the report about an hour ago. The Swiss bank accounts held 1.56 billion. That's billion, not million.

"The Panamanian accounts were worth another four hundred and fifty-seven million and the Bahamian accounts were worth three hundred forty-five million. President Aubrey turned the information on the Bolivian accounts over to the government there.

"We've recovered over two billion dollars, sir. Thanks to you. To tell you the truth, I don't know if I'd have done what you did, turning over that information on the secret bank accounts. That's a hell of a lot of money."

Dan grinned again. "What makes you think I gave you all of the numbers? Do I look that honest?"

The treasury man stared at him.

"Just kidding," Dan said. "Just kidding."

That same day, on the other side of the country, George Barnes sat at a small conference table talking with a man he hated with extreme intensity. Frank Tupper had requested this meeting and Barnes had been curious enough to come to Hartford to learn what the man wanted to talk about. He didn't have long to wait.

After some pleasantries and a drink of twenty year old scotch, Tupper got to the point.

"George," he said, his face expressing genuine concern, "You and I have been adversaries for a long time. Frankly, I think we're both getting too old for this shit.

"The events surrounding the crash of Pacific Rim's airplane raise some very complicated issues. You and I both know that. I'm no lawyer so I won't insult your intelligence by attempting to discuss the law, but I do have a feeling that his could turn into a protracted legal sinkhole. I understand that there's to be a Congressional Committee looking into all aspects of this terrorist thing, including the crash of the plane. What with everything involved, this situation could get out of hand.

"I'd like to avoid that if I could. This is a real nest of snakes, George. To get to the point, I'd like to avoid a legal battle. I really would. I'd like to suggest that we work together and try and arrange some settlements that are reasonable and fair, and that we do it without getting the courts involved at all."

Barnes lit a cigar and said, "Well, Frank, we all want to avoid unnecessary court battles. My job, as you well know, is to make sure my clients are properly compensated for their loss. That's always been the problem with us. I have a figure in mind that you think is too much and we end up having the courts decide. In this particular case, I haven't even done enough research to have the foggiest notion of what's involved. Christ! It's only been a few days."

Tupper held up his hands. "I know that."

Barnes asked, "Then what's the hurry? It'll be months before I even have a chance to figure out what demands would be proper."

Tupper refilled his glass and said, "I know that too. I'm not suggesting that you rush with your research. I'm simply suggesting that you do your research with a view to coming back here, sitting down with me personally, and ironing these things out."

Barnes broke into laughter. "Come on Frank! What the hell is your problem? This isn't the Frank Tupper I've gotten to know and love. You've got a bug up your ass about something. What is it?"

Tupper was beginning to perspire. "I'm not gonna bullshit you George. You'll find out sooner or later, so what the hell. I'm just gonna come clean and tell you what's on my mind."

Barnes sat back and waited.

Tupper said, "I lost my senior investigator. The man had worked for us for twenty years and he up and quit. No explanation, no nothing. The man looked frightened out of his mind.

"He wouldn't discuss it and worse than that, he junked all of the data he's accumulated. We have to start all over again. I can't figure it out, but I don't mind telling you, it gives me the creeps."

Barnes looked at Tupper in surprise and asked, "Are you talking about William Powers?"

Tupper nodded. "None other. I'll tell you something else. I think the man has either had a religious experience or he's headed for a rubber room. He threatened me, George."

"Threatened you?"

"Yes. He said he's got a diary that covers every move he's made for us during the last ten years. It covers every case he's been involved in and every trick he's ever pulled to save the company money.

"Now you know damn well that we all have our ways, George. Hell, we understand the system, we know how it works. But Powers is threatening to make the diary public and I just can't have that happen. The press will twist that sucker around until it looks like we're the worst bunch of bastards to ever walk the face of the earth. Shit, some of stuff he did was illegal. Not that I ever condoned illegal acts by our investigators, but you know nobody'll listen to a word I say."

Barnes smiled, "You're right about that, Frank."

It warmed George Barnes's heart to see Frank Tupper in so much pain. "What exactly does Powers want?" he asked.

Tupper sipped some of the scotch and then said, "He says he wants all of the cases relating to Flight Two-three-four settled out of court. He says the moment one of them hits the courts, the diary becomes public.

"Like I said, I'm not gonna bullshit you, George. We're in a lot of trouble here."

Barnes was beaming. "Correction. *You're* in a lot of trouble. I'm in fine shape."

Tupper grimaced. "George, this is tough enough as it is. Don't rub it in."

Barnes said, "So what are you proposing, exactly?"

Tupper sighed. "I guess what I'm trying to say is this: let's work together this time. You take your time and keep your demands reasonable. We'll look at each case with a view to being fair and reasonable. You know as well as I do that some of these people would be quite satisfied with less than millions of dollars. Let's work together and see if we can't settle these cases without beating our brains out. We'll save a fortune in legal costs and we'll pass those savings along in the form of additions to the settlements."

"That's it?"

Tupper looked like a man with a mouthful of spiders. "No, of course not. If you agree to be reasonable, and these cases are successfully settled out of court, we'll make a cash payment to an offshore bank of ten million dollars. In your name. That's ten million dollars, George."

Barnes sucked on the cigar and smiled again. If William Powers had been in the room, he would have kissed the sonofabitch. He had no idea what had triggered this sudden attack of conscience, but he wasn't about to fight it. In his entire career, he'd never been in a better position.

To the troubled president of Butler Liability he said, "Frank, I think we can do business. To be candid, I was looking forward to another battle with you, particularly one that might go down in history as a memorable one. My last hurrah, so to speak.

"I stand to make about forty million or so, if I handle this right, and I think I can. But I'm not getting any younger and in the interests of my clients, I'll give your proposal serious consideration. With one minor modification."

"What modification?" Tupper asked, with a look that indicated the spiders were getting larger.

Barnes stood up. "As soon as I have confirmation that the ten million has been deposited to an account bearing my name, I'll get to work. I'm confident that we can reasonably settle each and every case without too much difficulty. In fact, I'm sure of it.

"However, I'm only one lawyer involved in this case. At last word, I think there were sixteen others. Are you planning on paying them all ten million?"

Tupper was beginning to look ill. "No. We'll make some arrangement that'll be satisfactory to all concerned. You're the one who always gives us the most trouble, George. I don't want any more trouble."

Barnes stuck out his hand. "As you wish. I'll wait

to hear from you then. But if you want some advice from an old hand, There are nine or ten of those lawyers you'd better never mention this idea to. They'll have your ass in a sling so fast, you'd never believe it."

"Which ones, George? And what do I do with them?"

Barnes stuck a cigar in his mouth and said, "I'll draw you up a list. When the demands from these guys come in, you get in touch with me. I'll tell you how to handle it. I won't even charge you, Frank."

"How come?"

"Because I don't want to see you land in jail. I don't want to see your company go broke. I stand to get very rich from your company, Frank. Unfortunately, there are a lot of honest lawyers in this business. We're doin' our best to weed 'em out, but you know how it is. These things take time."

Barnes was grinning from ear to ear.

Tupper shook the hand limply. "We have a deal?"

Barnes nodded. "We have a deal."

The next night, Dan Wiseman, a small bouquet of flowers in his hand, knocked on the door of Helen Porter's apartment.

He felt very strange this night, his emotions still a tangled mess.

Yesterday, the will had been read and everything had been left to the children. The house that had been transferred to Bernice in the divorce settlement was covered by mortgage insurance and her death had meant it was now owned by Danny and Dawn free and clear.

This morning, they had begged him to stay in California when they learned of his ambivalence toward a possible return to Washington. This afternoon, Acting Director Franklin had called and told him that the bureau was counting on his return.

The flak had abated somewhat, probably mitigated by the fact that the tempest over the attack on Peru and Bolivia had settled down as well. The Soviet attempt to make much of it in the United Nations had proven to be a bust, particularly when the government of Bolivia released an official statement that refused to condemn the U.S. action.

It appeared as though the Bolivians were as happy as everyone else to have Gravez out of their hair. The move by Cecil Aubrey to increase foreign aid to both countries to help in the reemployment of the coca-leaf farmers hadn't hurt either. No one outside of government knew that the money being spent was money that had been seized from accounts previously owned by one Alfredo Gravez.

The Bolivian government had made no mention of the money they had seized themselves. Dan could only guess where that money had gone.

Ah, well, he thought.

Three Special Congressional Committees had been formed. The first was charged with the responsibility of investigating all aspects of the crash of the airplane, the attack on the Forum and ways in which future terrorist attacks could be prevented. Dan Wiseman expected to be called as a witness at that one.

The second committee was to investigate the entire matter of biological weapons.

The third committee was to determine possible abuses of presidential power and to consider possible amendments to the Constitution. Dan had the feeling he'd be called as a witness at that hearing as well.

Washington was going to be a busy place for years.

Edward Spencer was in Europe, taking a vacation. Dan expected the next time they'd meet would be at one of the hearings. So far, he hadn't changed his mind about the resignation. Dan didn't expect he ever would.

But at this moment, Wiseman was standing at the door of a woman's apartment, with flowers in his hands, something he hadn't done in two decades. He felt like an idiot as he rapped on the door.

Helen Porter answered the door wearing a flowing red caftan that highlighted the darkness of her face and hid the curves of her body.

"Hi," she said, cheerily.

He stood there like a statue staring at her, the arm holding the flowers thrust forward.

She giggled and took them from his hand. "Won't you come in?"

He entered the apartment and his nostrils were immediately greeted by the smell of something outstanding cooking in the kitchen.

"I thought I was going to take you out to eat," he said.

She took him by the hand and motioned to the sofa. "Sit down and relax. I thought that after what you'd been through, you might appreciate a home-cooked meal. I expect you don't get too many of those."

"No, I don't," he said. "It smells incredible. What is it?"

"I'm not going to tell you," she said. "It's a surprise. I'm a good cook among other things. Can I fix you a drink?"

Dan smiled at her. She was teasing him. Outrageously. The look in her eye was bold, unabashedly expressing her interest in this man.

In Dan Wiseman, feelings that had been suppressed for so very long started to make themselves felt. It was pleasant.

"I'll have a little white wine, if you have it."

"I have it," she said.

She brought the wine and sat beside him,

smoothing the dress with her hand. She started to say something just as the telephone rang.

Quickly, she picked it up. "Yes?"

For a moment she just listened and then, wordlessly, she hung up the telephone.

She turned to face Dan with eyes that were filling with tears. "Would you hold me please?"

Dan put an arm around her and held her close. "What is it? Can you tell me?"

She pressed her head against his chest. "It was a friend of mine. She was watching television and they just announced that Robert Dalton has died on the operating table."

# Epilogue

Two years after the attack on Bolivia and Peru, 67% of the coca leaf farms are still incapable of growing anything. Scientists who have examined the soil say it will be incapable of supporting any kind of agricultural product growth for at least ten years.

The remaining 33% of the fields, untouched in the attack, are still producing coca leaves. For a time, the price of cocaine skyrocketed and then a new type of synthetic cocaine began to flood the market. It is estimated that the overall usage of cocaine in the United States had dropped less than 1% in the last year.

The idea to expand the war on drugs died quickly, as funds were hard to come by. For a while, the money seized from Gravez not earmarked for foreign aid programs was used to increase educational and treatment efforts. But eventually, the well ran dry and the new programs were quietly abandoned. Most of the money available today is still being used for regular law enforcement.

The legitimate businesses run by the Graves family were taken over by other members of the family. Because much of the information leading to their discovery was obtained illegally, efforts to seize the businesses failed. However, a steady barrage of attacks by the IRS and the Immigration Department, forced almost all of the family members to flee the United States. Many of the businesses went bankrupt.

Aside from those efforts, American organized crime lords suddenly found themselves in possession of lists of names and addresses of Gravez family members and employees. Suddenly, it became very dangerous for South American nationals engaged in the drug business to be residents of the United States. All of their deals are now made outside the country.

The Select Congressional Committee investigating the crash of Pacific Rim Airlines Flight 234 made a number of recommendations, most of which have yet to be acted upon. Dan Wiseman and Edward Spencer both testified as to the parts they played in the investigation, including the use of truth serum type drugs. The committee officially censured the FBI and the individuals who took part in the use of the serum. Because of the presidential pardons, no other action was taken.

Helen Porter was never questioned about her role as a security guard and her background was never brought up.

As for the other two committees; the one looking into biological weapons determined that all such weapons should be banned worldwide and meetings were set up to discuss treaties that would achieve that aim. So far, nothing has happened.

The Huntsville research facility was closed and a new, secret facility was built in Virginia. BT33 is still a stock item. Efforts at developing a vaccine have yet to yield results.

Gen. Waldo Smith resigned from the Army and was indicted for multiple counts of manslaughter. His trial is still pending. He is being defended by George Barnes. Barnes had threatened to reveal certain confidential matters as part of the defense and the smart money is betting that the charges will eventually be dropped.

The other committee worked on a draft of an amendment to the Constitution for some time; an amendment that would limit the powers of a president. After considerable discussion, the proposed amendment was dropped.

All of the lawsuits surrounding the crash of the airliner were settled out of court. Elizabeth Martin accepted an offer of $300,000 for the death of her husband. She never learned of his various affairs.

Shirlee Simms is now the Sunday night anchor on the UBC Evening News.

Donald James works for another airline.

Mickey Serson finished writing a biography on the life of Robert Dalton and is now a consultant in Washington.

Senator McGinnis retired from public life.

William Powers is retired and lives in a small home in the Colorado mountains. He still sleeps with a pistol under his pillow.

Baxter Williams, the one-time owner of Pacific Rim Airlines, is in a treatment center for alcoholics. It's his third attempt at kicking booze.

Danny and Dawn Wiseman are both students at UCLA. They live in a small condo they bought as an investment after they sold the house in Palos Verdes. Danny plans to go to law school. Dawn has yet to make up her mind on a career.

Dan Wiseman is now the president of his own security services company in Hawaii. The small company is growing rapidly and Helen, his wife of four months, is pregnant with their first child.